THE NICKUM

THE NICKUM

DORIS DAVIDSON

ISIS
LARGE PRINT
Oxford

First published in Great Britain 2008
by
Birlinn Limited

Published in Large Print 2009 by ISIS Publishing Ltd.,
7 Centremead, Osney Mead, Oxford OX2 0ES
by arrangement with
Birlinn Limited

British Library Cataloguing in Publication Data
Davidson, Doris, 1922–
    The nickum. – Large print ed.
    1. Boys – Scotland – Aberdeenshire – Fiction
    2. Young men – Scotland – Aberdeenshire – Fiction
    3. World War, 1939–1945 – Social aspects
    – Scotland – Fiction
    4. Scotland – Social conditions – 20th century
    – Fiction
    5. Large type books
    I. Title
    823.9'14 [F]

ISBN 978–0–7531–8196–6 (hb)
ISBN 978–0–7531–8197–3 (pb)

Printed and bound in Great Britain by
T. J. International Ltd., Padstow, Cornwall

Acknowledgements

First, I wish to express my sincere thanks to the staff of the Gordon Highlanders' Museum in Aberdeen for the trouble they took to find answers to my queries. They do a wonderful job.

I come now to my reason for writing *The Nickum*. In the 1930s, I read a book called *Wee McGreegor*, by J.J. Bell, describing the antics of a little Glasgow boy. I was absolutely enthralled by the Glaswegian dialogue, and vowed to write a book some day about a little Aberdeenshire boy. I read and re-read it, and eventually read it to the children I taught, until, alas, it fell to pieces — beyond repair.

My son delighted me about a year or so ago by finding a copy in a charity shop, and my old vow was rekindled. I started to write about a mischievous little boy in Aberdeenshire. I swear I did not copy any part of *Wee McGreegor*, but most of Willie's pranks were taken from real life, carried out by different boys of my acquaintance.

I know that the Doric dialect is difficult for people outside Aberdeen to understand, but I hope that all who read *The Nickum* will be able to follow it — and enjoy it.

Part One

Part One

Introduction

1930

Emily Fowlie heaved a long sigh as she stuck her hand in the next sock, much smaller than the last one she had darned. I should have known, she mused. We should all have known, but we thought nothing of it at the time — it was so normal.

Looking back, of course, she could see their mistake. Such an event never happens on the day it's expected. That was the crafty thing about it. And to happen between dinnertime and teatime, so nobody was inconvenienced much — that was probably contrived to save folk suspecting the devil incarnate himself was entering our lives.

She brought her wandering mind to a sharp stop. No, no, she must be exaggerating . . . mustn't she?

Just because the brain had been up to some kind of mischief or other ever since he was able to crawl didn't make him a devil incarnate — not even an ordinary devil. He was just a "wee nickum", like Jake's mother said he was. Yes, that was all, just a wee monkey. Her mother-in-law was a good judge of character — usually.

In spite of convincing herself that this was so, various images crept into Emily's mind; images of the outrageous things her son had done already in his short time on earth — he would only be nine on his birthday next week.

CHAPTER
ONE

21 September 1921

Emily Fowlie had been feeling quite uncomfortable since not long after they had come to their box bed in the kitchen, but not bad enough to rouse Jake. After all, he had an early start in the morning, and it wasn't her first child. Connie was ten past August and Becky had turned seven at the beginning of this month, and she'd had no trouble bringing either of them into the world, going by what she'd been told by other women. Of course, Beenie Middleton — the neighbour who acted as midwife for most of the births on the farm town of Wester Burnton — had said she'd got off lucky both times, yet there was no reason to think this one would be any different.

By the time the parish church bell struck midnight, however, the discomfort had become pain, an ever-increasing pain, but it could be hours yet before the infant was born. It crossed her mind then that it was a good thing the bell could be heard for miles on a still night, for without its help she'd have no idea how long the labour was taking.

Half past, one o'clock, half past, two o'clock . . .

It was beginning to be unbearable, but she'd just have to grit her teeth and bear it. Jake couldn't have it for her — nobody could — and if she didn't let nature take its own course in its own time, she'd be in real trouble. Maybe it would burst out of her stomach — through her belly button? When she was a bairn, she'd often wondered what that particular bit of her was there for — she had to be extra careful in keeping it clean, or else it collected bits of fluff off the vests her mother knitted for her. She'd thought maybe that was why people had a belly button; in case they couldn't give birth the normal way. But men had belly buttons as well, and they never gave birth whatever way you looked at it. She wasn't a bairn now, anyway. She should know better than to think stupid things like this.

Emily lay as still as she could. If she started wriggling around, Jake would waken, and he'd get all worried about her. Mind you, it would be good to have him worrying about her. Sometimes she felt he took her for granted. That wasn't fair on him, though. He wasn't like some of the other farm workers — bairning their wives every year, often in less than a year. She and Jake had been wed for almost two years before she realised she was in the family way, and it was another three before another one came. Then the war had come, and he'd been away for nearly five years fighting the Huns, but he hadn't "knocked her up" like most of the men when they came home. He'd always been gentle with her, loving, respectful. If she said she didn't feel like it, he didn't force her. Some of her neighbours said their men went at them like an animal, they were that starved of a woman. Oh, that was half past striking. Half past what, though? She'd lost count.

It was just after four when Emily was forced to shake her husband. "Jake, it's time."

"You want me to run for Beenie?"

"Aye, it's real bad."

"Ach, you should have woke me afore this, ma lovie."

Jumping up, he struck a match from the box on the end of the mantelpiece and held it to the candle in the china candlestick next to it. Then she watched him hopping about trying to put on his trousers. It always made her laugh, since it would have been easier to put them on if he sat down, but tonight she couldn't even summon a faint smile.

"You'd best hurry, Jake," she whispered.

"Is't affa' bad, ma lovie?"

"Aye, Jake, awful bad."

Emily was clutching at the blankets in desperation when, only minutes later, Jake ushered Beenie in, her huge rubber apron almost engulfing her round little body, her bright eyes full of concern but her voice as professional as any fully qualified midwife; in fact, having done the job for over twenty years in whatever farms her man was fee'd at, she was probably more experienced than most. "How long between the pains?" Her normal mode of speech in the broad vernacular was dropped when she was carrying out her "professional" duties.

"There's hardly any time . . ."

The other woman nodded briskly and turned to Jake. "Right! Get the rubber sheet out of my bag and we'll get it under her, then you'll have to go out. I never let my fathers bide to watch, as you should ken."

His smile was forced, but as soon as his wife was made ready for the delivery, he grabbed the rest of his clothes with some relief. "I'll mak' some breakfast for the bairns and see them aff to school afore I feed the beasts. I'll come back at dinnertime to see if it's a laddie or a lassie."

His curiosity was destined not to be answered until the following day; his poor wife's labour continuing for almost a day and a half. Jake and the two girls had been given their supper by Beenie's seventeen-year-old daughter, and had also slept in makeshift beds in the Middletons' house.

Remembering, Emily felt pain shooting through her body, only imaginary thank goodness, but it proved that, whatever anybody said, you did not forget the pain of childbirth when it had been far worse than normal.

Ever since those thirty-five hours of excruciating agony, Willie's behaviour had gone steadily downhill. Jake, of course, was absolutely delighted to have a son at last — a man wasn't a man until he had a son. As he'd heard people saying, "It's easy to make a daughter when the pattern's lying under you." So he excused his son by saying, "He's a normal boy, Emmie. They're aye up to some mischief or other. I was the same mysel'."

Emily wasn't quite so happy when the new infant continued to be fractious. Her two girls had been no trouble as babies, sleeping and feeding being the way their days — and nights — were spent but this one yelled night and day, newly fed or not. It was hard going to be allowed to sleep for only half an hour now and then, for that was the most this one ever slept.

When he was three months old, and she confided to Beenie Middleton how little rest she was getting, that good woman shrieked with laughter. "It's well seen you havena had a laddie afore. They're hell on earth wi' the colic at three month or so. It'll wear awa'. Jist gi'e him anither twa or three weeks."

It hadn't worn away, of course. He was still screaming his head off at six months, even at ten months, but her body had seemed better able to cope by then.

Emily had been looking forward to this day for months. It wasn't very often that she got the chance to be away from her own home, and Aberdeen was like going to a place of exotic sights and thrills. She wasn't jealous of her younger sister, although Vi's husband-to-be was a real catch — only son of a wealthy jeweller — and they were to be living in London after their month-long honeymoon in Paris.

No, she decided. She wouldn't like the stir of either of the capital cities. She loved the tranquillity of her own part of Aberdeenshire, and was blissfully happy with her own husband, thank you very much. But one day out was different; whatever happened, enjoying herself in Aberdeen or not, there would always be the comforting thought that she'd be home at the end of the day. She was glad that only she and Jake had been invited — Gramma Fowlie had volunteered to look

9

after her three bairns — but she knew she would miss them, even for such a short time.

"I hope nothing goes wrong when we're away," she had whispered to Jake as they were dressing.

Struggling with his front stud, Jake had shaken his head. "What could go wrong? Ma's used to . . ."

"I know that, but Willie's only fourteen months and he's into everything since he started crawling."

"Ma'll watch him, dinna fret. She kens the mischief bairns can get up to. She's brocht up twa o' her ain, me an' oor Davey." His eyes clouded for a moment, as he remembered his curly-headed brother who had been killed in the war.

"Aye, but . . ."

"Nae buts, Emmy. Forget aboot everything else except enjoying your sister's wedding. You micht never get another chance to see the inside o' the Caledonian Hotel."

"No," she nodded. "You're right there."

As soon as her son and daughter-in-law had left (driven away by the farmer's son in a big Austin) Williamina Fowlie lifted the *People's Friend* she had taken with her to pass the time. The two girls would keep an eye on wee Willie, for she was dying to read the last instalment of the serial by Annie S. Swan. Connie at twelve years old was already really dependable and would try to make Becky, still a bit of a flippertigibbet at nine, behave herself. In fact, it looked more than likely that the younger girl would always be a feckless cratur, so it

10

would be a good thing if she found a steady-going husband when the time came.

Having reached the heart-warming conclusion of the story in about twenty-five minutes, Mina nodded off, and was going over the plot with herself as the heroine when she felt somebody or something pulling at her sleeve. Rubbing the sleep from her eyes, she looked round and let out a scream at the sight of the black-faced dwarf by her side.

Two pairs of feet came running through from the other room. "What's the matter, Gramma?" Connie was asking when Becky let out a great skirl of laughter.

"Look at the bairn!" she spluttered. "He's covered himsel' wi' blake."

Indeed, this was exactly what had happened, as was proved when Mina ran through to the back porch, where every available inch that the toddler had been able to reach — and some that he'd climbed on a chair to reach — was streaked with the black shoe polish, the tin still sitting open on the floor.

"Oh my God!" Mina exclaimed. "Your Da must've forgot to put the lid back on. What a bloody mess!"

Connie frowned her disapproval of the word. "You shouldn't say that, Gramma. What if Willie picks it up and says it. Mam wouldn't be pleased, I can tell you."

"No, my lambie," Mina said, ruefully. "I'm sorry I said it, but this is an affa mess. We'll ha'e to hurry an' clean up afore your Ma gets hame."

It was easier said than done. The makers of Cherry Blossom Boot and Shoe Polish had made quite sure that their product would stay on for as long as possible, waterproof, sunproof, snowproof and any other things that needed to be made proof from. Becky got the job of scrubbing her little brother in the big zinc bath that was generally used only on Friday nights, but no matter how hard she wielded the scrubbing brush the blackness seemed to spread further instead of disappearing. Connie had been told to clean the stone floor, which also proved impossible, while Mina took herself in hand to get the child's clothes clean, another futile task.

An hour later, and making it all so much more difficult, little Sambo Willie was slithering about naked doing his best to help but getting in everybody's way, while Becky was sitting beside the bath yelling her head off with frustration, and, possibly, fear of what her mother would say when she came home. It would have been no comfort to her to know that her grandmother and sister were feeling exactly the same.

A little after two o'clock, Mina decided that enough was enough. Her back was killing her and the scrubbing board had practically left her knuckles red raw. All the hairpins had worked loose from the knot at the nape of her neck, her white hair was doing its best to keep her from seeing. Added to which, young Willie was girning because he was hungry, and the two girls were definitely the worse for wear — blonde wavy hair striped with black, the neat print dresses their mother had made for them now so distressed they looked more like rag dolls than nice little girls.

The pot of tattie soup Emily had left for them was soon heated up, and the four exhausted beings sat down to sup it, bolstered by the oatcakes they always crumbled through any soups they were given. This was followed by a cup of milk each for the children and a nice strong cup of tea for Gramma Fowlie to which she had added a good slosh of the whisky Jake always kept, just in case.

Their hunger assuaged, they looked at each other and saw the funny side of things at last. Willie wasn't the only one to look like a darkie, or at least, a white actor made up to look like a darkie, bits of pink skin showing through. The only difference from actors was, of course, that their own clothes were also unevenly covered with the shoe polish. Becky was the first one to laugh, but Connie soon joined in, followed, wryly, by their grandmother, and wee Willie chuckled merrily, not understanding, as the old woman did, that this period was exactly like the French revolution, with the aristocracy pretending not to be afraid before they were to be beheaded.

Strangely, Emily did not lose her temper when she came in. While she had enjoyed her day out, and was glad that she'd experienced the cuisine of the Caledonian — the best hotel in Aberdeen — she was glad to be home, and the sight of the little group of semi-niggers made her love them all the more.

The novelty wore off, naturally, when she had to spend a large part of every day trying to reduce the size of the blackened areas. Willie's skin needed less effort, as the colour was gradually replaced by his usual covering of dirt and grime, but the floor and the other areas that had been affected stayed stubbornly blackened, fading to a dirty grey only after a good few weeks. This episode made Emily determine never again, ever, to leave her family in someone else's hands — not even the usually dependable Gramma Fowlie's.

CHAPTER
TWO

1924

Willie kept everyone on their toes. Nobody knew what he would do next to upset the household, and Emily learned that not only could she not trust anyone else to keep track of him, she couldn't even trust herself. There were lines across her brow, her waist had thickened a little, her fair hair had several strands of silver through it and she was forced to admit that bringing up Willie was fast putting years on her. Jake didn't have any of the worry; he never seemed to notice anything and his sandy hair, always brushed straight back, was still the same colour as when they had married.

Brought up in Balmedie, only a few miles from Aberdeen, she had privately felt herself slightly better than her cottared neighbours. It was a comforting thought for her, but, no matter how hard she had tried to made Jake stop using the Doric — something her mother had always told her was common — he carried on in his own way. Connie nearly always remembered to speak properly, but Becky sometimes forgot and Willie, being Willie, was speaking fluent Burnton. It was a hard life for a woman trying to better her family.

In May, Emily seemed to have caught a really bad summer cold and was feeling quite unwell one afternoon. Two and a half years old, Willie was playing outside and when she looked out of the window, he was engrossed in trying to kick a ball into a toy fishing net that Jake had found in a rubbish dump some weeks before, but his son had lost interest in fishing after standing for some time at the edge of the Bandy Burn without even catching one bandy. So his father had jammed it up against the wall of the coalshed, and Willie spent a lot of time counting how many times he could kick his ball into it. Since his aim was not particularly good, nor his ability to count, it was sheer rugged determination that kept him going at it, so his mother knew it would occupy him for some time. For long enough at least for her to have a wee sit down before making the supper. How was she to know that the boy's luck had changed and that he'd had a run of what he felt were twenty consecutive goals?

Having reached his target at long last, Willie kicked the ball around the backyard for a few minutes until he spotted the hens foraging around at the far end and wondered how many he could hit if he aimed for them. Still not three, it didn't occur to him that he might hurt the poor creatures, so he set about this new game with gusto. The hens, naturally enough, took exception to their space being invaded by a young hooligan, and ran hither and thither, flapping their wings as they squawked their heads off. This reaction made Willie whoop with delight, and fortunately his control of the ball had reverted to practically nil, so none of the fowls were harmed.

He must have been at it for almost half an hour before the noise penetrated his mother's senses and she came running out to see what was what. "Willie!" she yelled. "Stop that this minute. You'll put them off laying." Her forecast later proved to be true.

His wide blue eyes regarding her curiously, he said, "Mam, why does hens lay eggs?"

"Because they do," his distracted mother replied, trying to fob him off.

He did not accept this as a proper answer. "The eggs come out of their backsides, I ken that."

Emily ignored him in the hope that he would give up and go out to play again, but his next question made her recognise the direction his brain was taking, and she prayed that he wouldn't, but he did.

"Mam, have we got a hole in our backsides like the hens?"

What could she say? "Yyyes."

"So fit wye can we nae lay eggs and all?"

She decided it might be a good thing to correct his speech and make him forget the question. "It's not 'fit wye', Willie, it's 'what way'. Or better still 'why'. 'Why can we not', that's what you should have said."

"Well, why can we not lay eggs like the hens?"

Thoroughly exasperated now, having driven herself into this corner, she snapped, "For goodness sake, go and play at something else and leave the hens alone."

As usual, she left her husband to dish out the boy's punishment, but when Jake heard what had been happening, he could do nothing for laughing.

"It's not funny!" his wife said, sharply. "You let him off with everything. He's needing to be held in about."

"Ach, Emmy, he's only a bairn — nae enough sense to ken what's richt and what's wrang."

"Well, it's time you learned him the difference. He'll never ken if you never tell him."

"I will, Emmy, lass. I will, when he's a wee bit aulder. Afore he starts the school."

"That's years yet, Jake, and he'll need to know how to behave before that."

The subject of their argument was listening with a smile. "Am I gettin' a real schoolbag when I start the school, Dad?"

"Aye, my loon."

"A real leather ane, Dad?"

"A real leather ane."

Emily decided that this just wasn't good enough. "I'll tell you this, my lad. If you don't behave yourself, you'll not get to go to the school. They don't want ruffians there, you see." She turned to frown at her husband as he opened his mouth, presumably to point out that the law said every child had to go to school when they were five years old.

Emily appealed to her mother-in-law the next time she came visiting. "Jake was never as bad as Willie? He couldn't have been."

"Oh, aye was he. You've nae idea the tricks he got up till, Emmy."

"Tricks maybe, but it's not just harmless tricks with Willie. He could've killed some of the poor hens."

"He could've, but he didna."

CHAPTER
THREE

1925

This episode with the fowls, much as it upset and irritated his mother, did not seem to affect young Willie, who continued to kick his ball into the net, or as near it as he could, without a thought to the hens, who soon learned to stay out of his way. He was growing rapidly now, and was taller even than five-year-old Poopie Grant who lived at the other end of the row of six houses and had had his nickname bestowed on him for obvious reasons. He had taken to coming inside the Fowlies' backyard to play with Willie after he came home from school, but Emmy wasn't too happy about it. The holidays were coming up, and she had no wish to be saddled with Poopie for days on end. For one thing, he was still prone to accidents, and Willie often came running in to tell her, "Poopie's shit his breeks again, Mam."

She wasn't sure how to deal with these emergencies, and generally just told the boy to, "Run away home now, Willie's supper's ready and then it'll be time for his bed." She felt quite sorry for the boy when she watched him making his way homeward on legs splayed open in the manner he'd obviously perfected to save them from being absolutely "clarted".

At times, Willie went home with Poopie to play at his house, and it was Tibby Grant who attended to running noses, scraped knees and torn breeks.

"It's a good job you twa are nae twins," she sighed, one afternoon. "I'd never get naething daen for sortin' the pair o' you oot."

The summer of 1925 was a good one — long hot days with a gentle breeze now and then to make them bearable, and cool evenings, light until after ten o'clock, when Jake and his wife sat at their front door and enjoyed the peace; Willie in bed and the girls allowed to go to the "moorie" to play with their chums.

Of course, there was no peace for Emily during the days. Her son seemed to be hell-bent on proving that he was a "nickum", and she had to be on her toes from dawn to dusk. However much she disliked having Poopie Grant seeking Willie's company, she did realise that he was better to have a companion of some kind. Being too much on his own could make him introverted, as Gramma Fowlie often pointed out to her.

In any case, Poopie seemed to have more or less learnt to control his bowels, and stopped Willie from doing many of the wild things he proposed doing, which was a great boon to her. There were, however, the occasional hiccups, as if her son was making sure she didn't get too complacent.

For instance, there were the two days that Poopie was sick from eating green apples — whether at Willie's behest or not was never established — and Willie was on his own. Emily carried out all her chores with one eye on him, but there came the time when she had to get supper ready for her family of three, the girls being with their Gramma McKay in her new house in Aberdeen for a week. Willie had not been invited, but in any case his mother wouldn't have felt happy if he had been. Her own mother was not accustomed to boys of any kind, particularly not of Willie's kind. Maybe when he was a little older and had settled down.

She prepared all the vegetables, having got her son to help her get carrots, turnips and onions, glancing out of the kitchen window every now and then to make sure he wasn't doing anything stupid, and seeing him sitting on the edge of the drying green making a daisy chain, she was lulled into a false sense of security. She had just put the vegetables into the pan where the beef was already simmering nicely, when the back door burst open and a strange, horrifying apparition stumbled in.

"Willie!" she screamed, after making sure that was who it was. "What in God's name have you been doing?"

No answer was forthcoming, but she didn't really need one. The rotten cabbage leaves, putrefying tea leaves, scraps of all kinds of food, plus the unmistakable splotches of human waste that Jake emptied into the midden from their dry lavatory every night revealed the sad truth. Her stomach lurched at the thought of having to clean him, but there was no one else there to take over the sickening task.

The simplest way would be to strip and scrub him, so first covering the stone floor with an old newspaper, she set about it. Filling the zinc bath with water — hot from the kettle on the hob on the range plus some cold from the pail in the porch at the back door — she then laid out an old scrubbing brush and a bar of carbolic soap. Thankfully, after she got him into the tub the boy stood perfectly still, his big brown eyes fixed on her mournfully, his nose wrinkling as the varied stinks assaulted it . . . and hers.

She didn't give in to his tiny whimpers when she scrubbed a little too forcefully, for it was the only way she could get him clean. Her son's skin was shining red by the time she was finished, from the roots of his curly brown hair to the soles of his feet, but she felt no sympathy towards him while she rubbed him vigorously with an old towel. She was taking no chances that any dirt would be transferred from him to anything else.

"Get up to your bed!" she ordered, giving him the slap on his bare bottom that he so thoroughly deserved. "And it's no supper for you this night."

Still silent, for he did know he had pushed his mother too far this time, Willie scrambled up the rickety ladder to his attic room, stark naked and looking like a skinned rabbit. With all the mess left behind to clean up, Emily's anger kept festering away, and by the time that Jake came in for his supper, she turned to him furiously, forgetting her "proper English". "You aye manage to bide out o' the road till all the work's done!" she screamed, then burst out crying, through sheer frustration and exhaustion.

"Oh, Emmy, lass, what's got you so upset?" he asked, for it wasn't often that she was driven to tears. "Was it

22

something Willie did?" That was usually why she was angry.

His wife did not get the support and consolation she was expecting. When Jake heard the story — and his wife had quite a graphic way of describing their son's misdemeanours — he couldn't stop laughing. "Oh, Em, he's just doin' what boys do. I fell in oor midden at hame when I was his age, mair than once, and Ma gied me a hot backside and sluiced me doon oot in the yard wi' a' the neighbours getting their kill. Aye, an' when I was aulder as weel."

"But I'm not like your Ma, Jake. She'd two sons, don't forget, and I've never had nothing to do with boys till we had Willie. And surely all boys canna be as bad as him?"

He slid an arm round her waist and pulled her towards him. "No, I suppose yer richt there, Em, but a lot o' them are. D'you nae think he's better like that than bein' a cissie? You'll never ha'e to worry aboot that."

She gave a watery smile. "You'd better tell him to come doon for his supper. Oh, Godamichty!"

Alarmed by her stricken expression, her husband said, "What is it, lass?"

"I havena had time to think aboot makin' the supper."

"Sit doon, Em, for ony sake. You're dead beat an' nae wonner. See, I'll mak' some scrambled eggs an' a puckle slices o' toast, that'll fill oor bellies."

When Jake shouted up to give Willie the good news he waited in the tiny lobby for him to come down, almost giving in to the temptation to clap the boy on the back in a proud fatherly manner. That would be like saying he had done no wrong, when he had disobeyed all the tellings his mother had ever given him about the midden. Jake heaved a sigh as he went back to the kitchen. If only he could get a job with a more up-to-date house — a house with an inside lavvy — so there wouldn't be a midden for Willie to fall into. But he supposed he was lucky to have a job at all; there were hundreds who hadn't. Hundreds who still had a dry privy in their backyard.

CHAPTER
FOUR

August 1926

Things in the little end-of-the-row cottage had changed considerably. There was great excitement because Willie was starting school, although he wouldn't be five until the 21st of September. On the great day, Willie was ready and waiting for Poopie Grant to call in to take him there, as he had promised ages ago. He ran to open the door as soon as the knock came, ushering his friend in to prove he didn't need his mother to go with him.

Emily had always been embarrassed to call the child Poopie, so she said, "What's your right name, er . . ."

"Grant," came the instant reply.

"Um . . . no, I mean your right first name."

"Oh, aye, I was gan to tell Willie nae to cry me Poopie at the school. I hinna pooped masel' for a lang time noo, so it's better . . ."

"What is it, then?" Emily was a little bit frazzled anyway, having had to make her own son ready, much against his will, in an uncomfortable pair of new trousers and a shirt with a collar that she had starched to make sure it would sit properly.

"Ma sez it's efter her granda," Poopie hedged, clearly unhappy about it.

"Aye," Emily encouraged, while Connie and Becky could barely keep back the giggles surging up.

"Cecil," he murmured. "It's a affa Jessie-Annie name, in't it?"

The two girls rose hastily from the table and rushed out, and Emily herself found it difficult to keep a straight face. "Um . . . no, it's a real nice name for a . . . laddie. A lot o the rich folk name their sons Cecil."

"Is that right?" Poopie's back straightened, his eyes brightened.

"Cecil Grant," the woman said reflectively. "That sounds real good. It does, really."

But Willie was impatient to be off. "Come on, Poopie, or we'll be late, and I dinna want to be late on ma first day."

"It's Cecil," his friend said sadly. "Try an' mind that, Willie."

"I'll try." But being a naturally honest child, Willie added, "But I winna promise."

His mother picked up his satchel. "Well, don't forget this, for your dinner's in here — a flask of soup, a hunk of loaf and an apple. That should be enough. Now, off you go, and don't caper about and spoil your new clothes. Just walk nicely, the pair of you."

She stood at the door and watched them as they walked sedately down the path and along the cart track, knowing full well that the minute they were round the bend out of her sight, they would be their usual rowdy selves. At least Willie would, though Poopie — Cecil — was a good bit quieter. At that moment, her two daughters appeared from the side of the house.

26

"So that's Willie an' Cecil away," Connie grinned. "I nearly burst trying not to laugh. I can't think about Poopie as a Cecil."

"You'll just have to get used to it, but what a name to give the laddie."

Emily found the day unusually long. It was the first time for many years that she had been on her own, and it was heaven. She got through her usual housework in doublequick time and, taking an early dinner, she went out to collect the eggs. Her hens were in the habit of roaming around the place quite a bit, and she never quite knew where to look, for they weren't all that particular where they laid. They had fully recovered now from what Willie did to them some time ago, and they were good layers. After searching all the known places, she had found nearly six dozen of the still-warm eggs and decided to call a halt. She could sell the whole lot of them since there were still over a dozen in her pantry left from the week before. At least she didn't have to walk to the village for a buyer; the grocer was usually delighted to take them off her when he called. "They tell me they're really good," he had told her once. "Fine an' big, wi' decent-sized yolks. Some o' my customers winna tak' ony ither anes."

After arranging them neatly in the big basket she kept for the purpose, she went out to weed her little kitchen garden. Jake kept her supplied with tatties, carrots and turnips — they were kept in pits in the sheltered corner of the yard, but she grew her own leeks, shallots, cress, parsley and the herbs she liked to use in her cooking. Some of the other cottared wives believed that she thought herself better than them because she put "fancy stuff" in her soups and stews, plus the fact that she'd been born in the town. But her parents' house had been a few miles from the last houses in Aberdeen, though so many new houses had been built since she left that Balmedie looked as if it would be part of the city before too long.

She went inside when she felt the need of a cup of tea. Half past three. She had time to chop some kindling before she started making the supper. While she had a seat and enjoyed her "cuppie", she wondered what life would have been like without Willie. He was the cause of most of her work, and definitely the most worry. Neither of her girls had been any trouble, just a few coughs and sneezes, and they'd both caught the measles when it had spread through the school a few years ago. Hopefully, though, Willie wouldn't succumb to any childhood illnesses. He was tougher than his sisters.

When Willie came running in at just after five she was busy preparing the supper, so she let him ramble on about what had happened during his day.

"An' d'ye ken this, Mam, the teacher's a little wee toot, nae muckle bigger nor me, an' her name's Miss Cow, an' she gied me a row for sayin' 'Moo', an' she said it was cheeky, an' bad manners to mak' fun' o' fowk. An' she said it's nae spelt the same as a moo-cow, there's a extra e at the end. I didna ken what she meant wi' that, though."

Stopping to take a decent breath, Willie also took a piece of carrot to crunch. "An' d'ye ken this, Mam?

We're getting a readin' book next week, a primer, she cried it, an' we've to learn some words every nicht. I'll be able to read afore I ken faur I am." Chomp, chomp! "I dinna ken if I like her or no', for she was aye telling me aff for fidgeting, but she surely doesna expect me to sit still a whole day without movin', but she said I'd jist ha'e to learn. An' some of the other bairns had their soup in flagons, like Dad gets oor milk in, and they set them along the range first thing when we went in so they'd keep het. She said twelve o'clock was dinnertime, an' when I said I couldna tell the time, she glowered and said I would ha'e to learn that as weel."

Chomp, chomp! "I'm nae gan to like the school, Mam. There'll be ower muckle stuff to learn. But she did tell us a story afore we come hame. It was aboot a wee black boy cried Pammy something."

"Epaminondas?" Emily supplied, for the name had conjured up a memory of her own early days at school.

Willie related the story, ending each little episode with, "An' his Mammy said, 'Oh, Pami thingummy, you ain't got the sense you was born with.' He was ayeways daen something wrang."

"Like you," his mother said wryly. The pot of stew now simmering gently, Emily straigtened her back. "So you liked the story, then?"

"Aye, Mam, it was real good, an' real funny. We was a' laughin'." Emily could just imagine — especially her son. "An' Miss Cow says she'll tell us mair stories if we're good. But I wisna happy to get a slate to write on, wi slate pencils, she cried them, but they mak' a affa noise when you write. Scraichin' like a stuck pig."

29

His mother was outraged. "What d'you ken aboot stuck pigs?"

"Nae much, but Poopie . . ."

"Cecil."

"Aye, Poopie-Cecil tell't me he'd seen it once, an' he made the noise, an' it was just the same as the slate pencil mak's. But Miss Cow wrote up some numbers on the blackboard, an' we'd tae copy them on oor slates, an' we've to practise them at hame. Mair stuff to learn. My brain winna be big enough to keep a' that in it."

"You've got to keep on working at it, Willie, that's how you learn."

For two days all went reasonably well, with the boy sitting down to do his "home lessons" as soon as he came home in the afternoon, and Emily was wondering if she had misjudged her youngest child. He wasn't too bad when he was doing everything his teacher told him. That was Progress with a capital P, and he'd soon get into the habit of learning.

It was on the second Monday that things started to go awry. Willie was almost half an hour late in coming home, and she had begun to wonder what had happened. Maybe the teacher had kept him in as a punishment for something? Maybe he'd been climbing a tree on his way home, or a wall, and had fallen down and hurt himself? Maybe he was lying somewhere unconscious with nobody to see to him?

But Poopie Grant would have been with him surely? He'd farther to go than Willie, so they'd be together all the way. She wasn't really worried, not really, but it was a bit upsetting just the same.

It was almost six, just before Jake was due in for his supper, when the two little boys trailed in together, Poopie-Cecil's lip was bleeding and Willie had a scrape on his cheek. "Have you two been fighting?" she demanded to know, anger welling up inside her at the thought.

"No, Mam." Willie turned accusing eyes on her.

"He was defendin' me," Poopie whispered.

"What . . .?" Emily couldn't understand.

"It was twa loons in the control class," the older boy explained, his cut lip clearly giving him some pain.

"They was playin' fitba' wi' his schoolbag," added Willie, "but I got it back for him."

"Good lad!" Jake was standing in the doorway, having heard his son's last statement. "I'm richt prood o' you, standin' up to bullies."

"No! He shouldn't be fighting like that. You shouldna encourage him."

Jake ignored her. "You got the bag back, I hope?"

"Aye," he nodded, "I punched the biggest lad in the face, and they baith ran awa'. Big fearties!"

Jake turned a stern eye on his wife. "Get Poo . . . Cecil's face cleaned up first an' I'll see him hame."

His voice showed that he would brook no refusal, and Emily hurriedly filled a bowl with hot water and sponged the cut lip gently.

"Now, then, Cecil my loon," smiled Jake, "come on. I'll let your Ma ken it wasna your fault."

Not even waiting for them to go, Emily tended to her son's injured cheek, and then said, her voice just a fraction more sympathetic than it had been, "It's all right for the men to praise the fighting, but it's us women that have to do the cleaning up and seeing to the injured. Now, sit down and learn your letters and numbers, and when your Dad gets back we'll get our supper."

About to point out that he was hungry now, Willie thought better of it. He'd got off lightly, considering. He'd expected his mother to smack him and his father to wallop his backside, so it was better to leave things as they were.

By the following August, Willie being what he was, and Poopie-Cecil being what he was, it had become accepted that it was always the younger who defended the older, and, as he assured himself, his mother would just have to get used to "seeing to the injured". Coming to the end of the summer holidays, he didn't want to go back to school. Why should he waste the lovely weather doing reading and practising his letters and numbers? It tired him out much more than when he was running all over the place playing tick and tack or hide and seek with his pal. And he would have to go to school till he was fourteen. He'd asked Connie how long that was and she'd said, "About eight years yet, but it'll soon pass. It's two years since I left and it just feels like two weeks."

This helped to put some cheer in the boy's soul, but he was even happier when he discovered that

32

schoolchildren would get a week off in October — the "tattie" holidays, when farmers expected local children to help with harvesting the potato crops. Willie offered his friend and himself to his father for the job but Jake had to turn them down. "I'm sorry, son. I can manage mysel' wi' my wee tattie patch an' besides, I canna afford to pay you. See, the fairmers'll pay you for workin' for them."

Reasoning that the bigger the farm, the more money they would get, Willie suggested the Mains first, then Ricky Muirhead at Easter Burnton, but his father just laughed. "I'll see if McIntyre'll tak' you. He's nae a bad boss, an' he'll nae cheat you."

Johnny McIntyre of Wester Burnton, a roly-poly of a man with a big wart on his cheek, said, "Ach weel, Jake, they're a bit young yet, but if they're prepared to work hard, I'll gi'e them a try. My horse an' cart goes round the cottar hooses at six every mornin'. So tell your laddie to get himsel' to the Grants on Monday, he'll get lifted wi' the rest o' the bairns."

There was great excitement on the big day before Willie was ready in his oldest clothes, a pair of wellies on his feet and an old peaked bonnet of his father's on his well-brushed hair. Emily had been at her wits' end making him stand at peace until she made sure all his buttons were fastened, that he had a handkerchief in his pocket, that he remembered to take his dinner with him, but at long last he skipped out, leaving her to collapse on a chair and pour herself a cup of tea. Jake had already gone, taking Becky with him to help him

33

with his "crop". Connie had already left for her work at the Mains.

Willie ran as fast as his podgy legs would carry him and was knocking on the Grants' door before any of his fellow tattie-pickers were assembled.

"You're in plenty time ony road," laughed Mrs Grant, "but my Poopie'll nae be lang. I made him gan to the privy to be sure . . ."

Guessing why, Willie couldn't help a little smile, but he didn't have long to wait for his aptly nicknamed chum, who said sharply, "Come on, then, Willie, or we'll be late an' Da says they'll nae wait."

By the time they reached the end of the dirt track that led to Johnny McIntyre's clutch of houses for his workers, there were a good dozen boys of all ages already there, a motley crew in their varied modes of dress, hand-me-downs from fathers or older brothers, which were mostly of the over-large size, or old clothes of their own, which were too small and too tight.

Most of the younger boys were there for the first time, showing their nervousness by shuffling their feet (whether in Wellingtons or tackety boots) and giggling quite a lot. The older boys wore an air of boredom to prove that they had been doing this job for years and knew they were good at it. For once, Willie thought it better not to ask questions, but was somewhat disappointed to find that their transport, when it arrived, was an old cart, drawn by an equally old looking Clydesdale, not the splendid modern bus, as he had imagined.

34

Still, what did it matter? It did the same job and their journey wouldn't be very long. It was farther than he had thought, however, as they were taken to one of McIntyre's more distant fields, a huge expanse of green vegetation among the evenly distanced furrows. The drills were marked out with branches of broom for the pickers: one length for the older boys and the few retired men who had turned up, half lengths for the younger boys and the few handicapped men. McIntyre himself came over to the two youngest. "I'll let you tak' half a dreel atween the two o' you," he stated firmly. "You should manage that, and if you canna manage that, you needna come back anither day. Is that understood?"

Willie Fowlie did not join the chorus of "Aye, Maister McIntyre." His eyes and his total attention were taken up by the big wart on the man's face. "I've seen some big warts afore," he muttered to Poopie-Cecil as they looked for their designated area, "but yon's like a . . . a . . ." He searched for an appropriate description and finally came up with, ". . . like a bloody aipple."

Flabbergasted at the swear-word, for he'd never heard Willie swearing before, Cecil made no reply. He didn't want them to lose the job before they'd even picked up one tattie.

It was a back-breaking task going behind the tractor (Clydesdale pulled, not motorised) and picking up the potatoes, large and small, and putting them in the wooden container they had been given for the purpose. The day grew warmer, then hot, then almost suffocating, and within a couple of hours, most of the younger "howkers" were stripped to the waist. Only the older, wiser from past experience, kept on their semmits for protection and wore a handkerchief knotted at the corners to protect their bald heads.

The farmer's wife and daughter came round at half past nine with some tea and a biscuit, and by noon both Willie and Cecil, and probably several other youngsters, were feeling that they couldn't go on much longer. Half an hour was allowed for eating their dinners, sitting round the grass verges at the edges of the field, and then it was back to the grindstone again. The sustenance had given them all a good boost, so they set to with almost as much vigour as they had had first thing in the morning. It didn't take long to fade, however, as Cecil observed, "My backbone's broke, I think. I can hardly bend."

Wiping the sweat from his face and out of his eyes, Willie warned, "Dinna let onybody see you're tired. We'll nae get back again."

"Yokin' time, lads," came a voice from somewhere on their right. "The grieve'll be roon' to collect your boxes an' you'll get your wages ower yonder."

Both boys swivelled round to see where the money was to be given out, and were pleased to see the farmer himself standing at a wooden trestle table set up just inside the field gate. The reward for all the excruciatingly hard labour would be coming, very very soon.

They watched as the horse went up each drill, stopping for Frankie Wilson, the grieve or farm foreman, to pick up the boxes and write in his little book which box belonged to which worker. Several other collections had been made during the day from those able to work at a good speed, each one being marked with the number of the collector, and they would be added together when the final tally for the day was made.

"Weel, then, lads," came the greeting in a few minutes, "let's see how much you've got." Frankie swung their box on to the cart. "Nae bad, nae bad. You've daen better than I thocht. Ower you go, then, an' wait in the line. It'll nae tak' lang, jist the weighin' o' this last lot."

It didn't take long, for which the boys were extremely glad. Having to stand in the sun, even at seven at night, was hard on poor exhausted bones, but at last it was their turn. Their day's work was weighed, Mr McIntyre stating, "You're two grand wee workers, I'll say that for you. Are you thinkin' on comin' back the morra, or can you nae face it again?"

It was Willie who said boastfully, "Oh we'll be back, we're nae that tired."

Poor Poopie-Cecil, scarcely able to make a move, just nodded, but both faces lit up when they were handed a half-crown each.

Willie had been watching what the co-workers in front of them had received; most of the other boys got a good few coins, some of the older youths even pocketing a paper note of some kind. Ten shillings, maybe, or, like the men, a pound note. As they left the field and stood waiting for the cart to take them home,

Willie whispered, "Will you manage the morrow, Poo . . . eh . . . Cecil? You'll get another half-croon."

His chum heaved a telling sigh, but murmured, "I'll be fine if I get a good night's sleep."

When he reached home, struggling to keep upright for the last hundred yards or so, Willie handed his half-crown to Emily. "See that, Mam? If I gan evey day this week I'll ha'e . . . what's seven times half a croon, Becky?"

"Not seven," warned their mother. "You'll not be tattie-pickin' on the Sabbath, even though Johnny McIntyre's heathen enough to expect it."

"Eight half-croons mak' a pound," announced thirteen-year-old Becky, looking smug, "so four would be ten shillings, an' two would be five, so six would be fifteen shillings."

She looked hopefully at her father, who said, "Na, na, lass, I canna afford to gi'e you as muckle as that."

The following morning, however, told a different story. Becky wasn't wanting to gather potatoes with her back aching in every bone, and Willie felt every bit as sore. Furthermore, his bright red skin was burning up under the old shirt, but he didn't want to admit to such a weakness. Emily could tell by his gait, however, that he was not as fit as he was making out, and felt a touch sorry for him. She waited until the boy went out to the privy, then said to her husband, "He's only five, Jake. He's not fit to be picking tatties."

"He's fine. He'll need to learn to put up wi' a lot harder work than that if he wants to be cottared."

"He mebbe doesna want to be a farm servant," she snapped.

"He's ower young to ken what he wants to be, and you havena aye been so worried for him."

Their son's return stopped their bickering before it became a full-blown quarrel, but Emily was hurt that her husband would argue with her like that. Where was the old gentle Jake, the man who had come back from the war quieter even than when he left, and had never been able to speak about his experiences, not even after all this time, and not even to her?

That week was the longest week Willie had ever lived through, or, as he said to Poopie-Cecil, "I'm sure this tattie howkin'll tak' a year aff'n my life."

"Mair like a year aff for every day," nodded his friend.

CHAPTER
FIVE

The trouble had begun long before this, of course, but had developed as time went on. He'd never had anything to do with girls before, and it seemed to him that they were fair game for tormenting. He would pick his victim, find a decent place of concealment, then jump out on her with a "lion's roar". The resulting flood of tears pleased him, but he discovered that it also led to a reprimand from Miss Cowe, and that several reprimands led to a smack over the fingers. This didn't hurt so much as the ignominy of being punished in front of the whole class. The other boys, however, didn't laugh at him as he had feared, but treated him with some respect, thus prompting him to find various other ways of annoying the poor little girls.

The next few terms followed much the same pattern as Willie's first — gradually including fights with the bigger boys who targeted Cecil as a prime recipient for all their bullying, but learning fairly soon that he had a protector who could give as good as, if not better than he got. Eventually, they gave up altogether and Willie turned his energy in other directions. Most of the girls wore their hair long, some being fortunate enough to sport lovely dark curls, or fair tresses, and one even had lustrous auburn hair. Each female head was also adorned with a ribbon, tied with various sizes of bows which were like red rags to Willie's bullish humour. In the playground at playtimes, he would manoeuvre himself into such positions that he could, with one little quick tug, undo the bows and send the owner's hair cascading down around her shoulders and sometimes, hopefully, over her eyes.

He always ran off laughing, which encouraged the other small boys to point their finger at the victim and laugh their heads off. This carried on for some weeks, with Miss Cowe threatening to report him to the dominie, but never carrying out her threat. Willie was becoming a bit of a hero to the boys in his class, a composite of five, six and seven-year-olds, but a wicked being to be avoided by the poor girls.

Willie himself took pride in fuelling his reputation as fearless, and relished watching the apprehension in the girls' eyes when he went near them. It wasn't until he caught Lizzie Cordiner breaking her heart in a corner of the bike shed that he gave any thought to the consequences of his pranks. Lizzie, a tiny five-year-old with big blue eyes and hair as straight as the yardstick they used for measuring the length of things like their classroom or the corridor, wasn't quite as pretty as some of the other little girls, but she looked so miserable that Willie felt a rush of shame at what he had done to her. "I'm sorry, Lizzie," he said, quietly, but she wept all the harder.

"You ... thought ... it was funny," she sniffed accusingly, "and my Ma says you're a heartless little brat, and if she gets her hands on you ... "

There was no bravado left in her tormentor now. "What did she say she'd do?" he asked, for Lizzie's Ma was a giant of a woman, strong enough to break him in two if she felt like it, or tear him limb from limb if she so desired.

"She . . . said . . . she'd . . . um . . . skin you alive."

They looked at each other silently, each picturing how the woman would go about such a task, then Willie muttered, "I'll nae dae it again. It was just a bit o' fun."

"It wasna funny for us. The big loons took the ribbons and put them in the lavvy, or cut them up . . . an oor Mas said they couldna afford to keep buying new ribbons. My Ma even says she's gan to cut my hair aff so's I can see."

"Oh, I'm real sorry to hear that. I didna ken. Look, I'll get money oot'n my bankie and you can buy a new ribbon."

"Ma would still be angry wi' you," Lizzie murmured, sadly. "She thinks your Da should skelp your . . ." She stopped, unwilling to use the exact word her mother had used.

For the rest of the afternoon, Willie thought about what had been said, and made up his mind to do something to repair the damage he had done, and because his mind was not on what was going on in the classroom, he got several raps over the knuckles from Miss Cowe for not paying attention.

At three o'clock, when the janitor wielded the school bell, Willie walked behind Lizzie and her little chums, but with no intention of playing any tricks on them. He did, out of sheer habit, put his hand in his jacket pocket at one point and took out the matchbox he kept a dead spider in. This was another of the twisted pleasures he got, by telling a girl he had something in the matchbox she would like to see and then holding his sides with laughter when she screamed in terror. It worked every time . . . but it wasn't funny, he realised now, and threw it into the ditch at the side of the road.

When they reached the first small group of Wester Burnton cottar houses, the girls dispersed to their various homes, and Willie hung back, watching which door Lizzie went through. Allowing a few minutes for Mrs Cordiner to ask Lizzie what had happened at school today, Willie girded his loins bravely and marched forward. His courage, however, had failed somewhat after the first few steps, so that his knock on the door was rather hesitant.

"You!" burst out the woman who answered. "I dinna ken how you've the cheek tae . . ."

"I've come to say I'm . . ." Willie swallowed and carried on, "I'm sorry for makin' Lizzie lose her ribbons. I didna mean that to happen. It was just meant to be a bit o' fun."

"A bit o' fun, eh? Weel, my lad, it micht've been fun to you, but poor Lizzie here comes hame every day greetin' her een oot."

"I'm richt sorry, Mrs Cordiner, that's a' I can say, but I'll gi'e you money oot'n my bankie so you can buy some mair, honest I will."

Taken quite aback by this, the woman's ferocious expression changed and Willie's spirits rose. She wasn't going to skin him alive, thank the Good Lord, as

Gramma Fowlie sometimes said . . . though it might have been interesting to see how she went about it.

"Lizzie's Da says you're just ill-trickit, nae coorse, so maybe he's richt. You needna brak' into your bankie, though, but I hope you've learnt your lesson. It's nae funny to torment ither fowks."

"I hiv, Mrs Cordiner. I hiv learnt my lesson an' I'll never dae it again."

"Weel, weel, then, let that be an end till it."

He said not a word to his own mother, and for some days he was afraid that Mrs Cordiner would tell her, but that good lady was not as bad as he had feared, and the episode was soon forgotten.

CHAPTER
SIX

"Mam, I'm fed up. Whit wye can I nae get oot to play?"

"Stop saying 'Whit wye'. I keep telling you. It's 'What way' or 'Why'."

"Well then, why can I nae get oot to play?"

"It's owner cauld." Emily found it difficult to maintain her proper mode of speech when no one in her family took any notice of her constant criticism of theirs, but, remembering, she hastily corrected herself. "It's far too cold, that's why, and I don't want you catching your death."

"I'll never die fae catchin' a cauld, Mam. I'm . . . whit is it Gramma Fowlie says? She kens a lot o' big words."

"Indestructable. It means nothing can destroy whatever she's speaking about. If you'd concentrate on learning your reading, you'd be able to use big words, and all."

"Mam, did Gramma Fowlie learn her reading when she was little?"

"I don't know that, but she must've done."

"But she's cleverer nor me."

"She's not cleverer nor you, she's . . ."

"She is cleverer . . ."

"That's not what I meant. It should be, 'She's more clever than me'."

"That's whit I said. She's cleverer nor me, so it was easy for her."

His mother heaved an exhausted sigh and gave up. "Put on your wellies and your coat and muffler. And don't stay out till you're frozen to the marrow."

"Whit's a marrow, Mam?"

"It's what I use to eke out the last of the berries when I'm making jam."

But the boy had already run to the back porch to get the clothes he needed. If it meant getting away from his mother for a while, he'd willingly have gone out in his semmit and drawers. He wouldn't have caught cold. Not him. He was disgustable! His Gramma said so!

There had been a good fall of snow a few days ago, which had been repeated several times since, but most of it had disappeared now, just deep heaps of dirty slush here and there, the stuff you wouldn't chance making into snowballs or anything else. Willie wondered what he could do to amuse himself. Poopie Grant was in bed with the flu, and he'd nobody to play with, so he'd have to think up something. He let his eyes scour round the back yard. Not one single thing moved, so he was absolutely on his own. Why were the two dogs not running around? They usually bounded out when they heard him coming. It was all right for them being shut up in the shed — there were two of them, so they both had a companion and they had old blankets laid out for them for they weren't allowed inside the house. In spite of that, they were luckier than he was, because Mam was always chasing him out from "under her feet", as she kept saying, though he couldn't understand that, for he kept well clear of her feet. But where else could he come but here?

Folk would think his sisters would play games with him — ludo or tiddly winks or something like that — but Connie and Becky said they were too old to play childish games. At eighteen and fifteen maybe they were, but it would be more fun for them than sitting reading the magazines they got from Mrs Burns at the Mains, sniggering and whispering to each other and shooing him away if he as much as put his head round their bedroom door. They weren't here just now, anyway. They'd got a few days off for Christmas and had gone to Gramma McKay's till Sunday. He'd been asked, as well, but there was nothing for him to do there, either. He was just told to sit still and not touch anything.

His roving eyes caught a movement on his left, not much of a movement but still a movement that meant something or somebody was out here with him. Three silent sideways steps took him to the spot, and he stood motionless, waiting to see what came from under the upturned pail. Nothing happened for a minute or so, and then his ears picked up a faint mewing sound. Willie screwed up his nose in puzzlement. It wasn't loud enough to be one of the four cats that belonged to the farm but divided their attentions between all the cottar houses and crofts related to it. It could be a hedgehog; he'd seen a few of them but never in his own backyard. It could be a mole, but they usually burrowed underneath the ground and came up somewhere that was easier to get through than this hard-packed patch. It could be anything, really, and there was only one way to find out. Bending down, he lifted one side of the pail off the ground to find a tiny kitten, eyes beseeching him to lift it up. One of the cats must have had babies somewhere near here.

Cradling the sopping wet little animal against his chest, he wondered how it had got into such a state, and the only answer he came up with was that it had jumped up on the edge of the bucket and tipped it over on top of itself. There had likely been a lot of melted snow inside so it had got soaked.

"Poor little kitty, kitty," he crooned, stroking the wet fur. "Poor kitty, kitty, but Willie'll soon have you dry."

This was easier said than done, however. He couldn't take the wee creature inside the house or Mam would go off her head at the water dripping all over her clean floor — it always seemed to be newly washed. She didn't like cats much any road, so it was best to steer clear of her . . . and trouble. It was cold outside but the sun had come out. A soft wind was blowing and some clothes pegs had been left on the washing line. Just perfect, he decided. Just perfect. Mam always gave the rope a wipe over before hanging clothes out in case they got marked, but no dirt would show on this wee black bundle. It had a white patch on top of each of its tiny paws but they wouldn't need to touch the washing line.

Being as gentle as he could so as not to hurt his patient, he put the dainty tail over the rope and eased the peg over it. He couldn't understand why the animal was making so much noise — he couldn't be hurting it — and carried on in an attempt to peg up the ears next. He was astonished at the din issuing from the little mouth. For all its size, it could make a proper racket . . . and he was only trying to help it.

Suddenly, with no warning whatsoever, his mother's open hand caught him round his ear. "Willie! What on earth d'you think you're doing to that poor wee kitten?"

"I was only . . ." His head was snapped back by another wallop before he could say any more.

"If I hadn't heard it yowling you'd have killed it. You're a wicked, wicked laddie, Willie Fowlie! Get inside this minute and right up to your bed. It's no dinner for you, my lad, and your dad'll have something to say to you when he comes in for his supper."

Knowing from past experience that it did no good to argue with his mother, the boy did as he was told and spent the rest of the forenoon feeling sorry for himself for having such a cruel parent. Why would she never listen to him? She laid into him without waiting for any explanation. Always. Whatever he did, or whatever she thought he was doing, wowf! Her hand connected with his lug, his shoulder or his back, or sometimes his backside, if she took him inside first. Backside was kept for what she said were the worst bad things he did.

His stomach rumbled loudly in an hour or so, making him realise that it was dinnertime, so Mam hadn't been joking, and with Connie being away he wouldn't even get anything smuggled up to him. Maybe he should have gone with them, but he wasn't like the girls. He didn't fancy sitting poring over old photos or helping the old woman to dust the hundred and one fancy ornaments she had sitting about, especially in her parlour; little crystal dishes, flower dishes, china shepherd and shepherdess, even fancy cherubs or sturdy Clydesdales. The worst things were the artificial flowers sheltering under their domes of glass. If he tried to take them out and dust them, it was sure he'd let them drop. That kind of thing wasn't a job for a boy. He didn't think she even liked boys. She wasn't like his other Gramma.

He could hear Mam moving about downstairs. She wasn't one to sit doing nothing, like some of the other mothers at Burnton. Paulie Johnstone's Mam aye had a fag hanging out of the corner of her mouth and her fingers were nearly as brown as the bars of chocolate Gramma Fowlie brought with her when she came to visit. That was why he was determined not to start smoking when he was older. He'd even seen some of the bigger lads, twelve or thirteen maybe, standing in the bike shelter at the school puffing their heads off. What would their insides be like by the time they were as old as Paulie's Mam?

He rubbed his stomach as it gave another gurgle, but he knew better than to sneak down and try to pinch something from the pantry. Mam had ears that picked up "a flech farting" as Dad sometimes laughed, and she could see what you were doing even if she'd her back to you, which proved she'd eyes in the back of her head like she said she had.

50

It was an awful long time from breakfast time to suppertime without one single thing to eat. A person could die without even a drink of water. It wasn't fair! It just wasn't fair when he hadn't done anything wrong. He was being punished for trying to do something good, something to help another living being. That was the unfairest thing of all. A little teardrop edged out now, and he dashed it away with a finger. What was the good of being so sorry for himself? He'd just have to make up his mind to go through life getting blamed for things he hadn't done, and taking his punishment like a man.

He sat up suddenly. Yes, if that was how it was going to be, that was how it would have to be. He would get used to it. People would say how brave he was, how well he could stand up to . . . what was that word the dominie used one day in his morning talk? Advertisement! That was it. He would stand up to advertisement. No, that didn't sound right, but whatever the word was, he would stand up to it and people would think he was a hero.

Some hero! His mother slapped him for nothing and starved him of food and drink, and he did nothing about it. People wouldn't think much of a hero who couldn't stand up to his own mother.

He shut his eyes and pictured some of the daring deeds he would do when he was older, deeds like killing dragons and giants, rescuing damsels in distress, saving somebody from drowning. There were hundreds — thousands — millions of brave deeds he could do when he was out of Mam's clutches. He sometimes thought about running away, but he realised he was still too young for that. He'd just have to put up with "the slings and arrows of out-something fortune" as Mr Bremner, the dominie, sometimes said, and he always added, "That is a quote from William Shakespeare, boys and girls, whose writings will be studied by those of you going on to higher education." Willie shook his head. He wasn't going on to higher education. He'd had enough already, though he knew the law would make him stay on at school until he was fourteen.

Six years yet. That was an awful long time to be still learning stuff. He'd had Miss Bell for about six months now — Old Belly, they called her behind her back — and she kept saying he was useless, but there wasn't room to stuff everything into his brain. Any road, he wanted to be doing things, not sitting on his backside in a stuffy room all day. He hated writing fusty compositions like she wanted — A Day in the Life of a Penny, or Describe the Common Spider and Its Habits. What kind of habits could a spider have? Sneaking up on poor little flies after they'd got caught in her webs. All spiders must be girls. Boy spiders wouldn't be so underhand. He wanted to be so famous other people would write about him. And he still had six more years to go before he could leave school and start being a hero.

He was playing a guessing game with himself, going through the alphabet thinking of animals beginning with each letter, and had just reached M for Monkey when he heard the old ladder creaking. He didn't hold even the teeniest hope that his mother was bringing him something to eat, so it was an extra-special surprise when she carried in a bowl of soup and a thick chunk of her home-made bread.

"Willie, I couldn't bear to think of you up here in the cold, so here's something to keep you warm." She handed him the bowl and went out before he could bring himself to thank her. The soup did heat him, although he hadn't really been cold, snuggled under three woollen blankets, a crocheted bedcover and a flock-filled quilt.

Five hours later, having carried out some other exercises with the alphabet — flowers, boys' names, girls' names and having the odd five-minute naps in between, he heard his father come home, having a short low conversation and then the ladder groaning again, the heavy feet telling him it was his father coming up.

"What's this your Mam's been tellin' me? You surely werena bad-usin' a wee kittlin'?" Jake's expression was stern as the boy began his explanation but, by the time he came to the end, the man was having difficulty in keeping a straight face.

"I was trying to help the poor wee thing," Willie gulped. "I didna mean to hurt it."

"No, I understand," Jake said, carefully keeping his amusement hidden. "But you were hurting it, just the same. You wouldna like if somebody pegged your tail . . ."

"I havena got a tail, Dad, but I can see what you mean and I'm sorry."

"Weel, weel, then, we'll let it be now, so come doonstairs and get your supper."

His wife made no reference to the incident until their son was in bed. "Did you skelp his bottom, Jake?"

"Oh, Emmy, the poor laddie didna ken he was . . ."

"So you didn't?"

"No, I didna, but I made him see he mustna dae things like that, and I'm sure he understands now and we'll say nae mair aboot it."

Emily felt a sense of relief. However badly the bairn behaved, she did not like to see his father chastising him. Jake had a really heavy hand — though it was necessary sometimes. Still, if Willie had learned something from this caper that was enough for her — for now, any road.

CHAPTER
SEVEN

February 1930

Of course, it wasn't the end of Willie's troubles. He couldn't help himself doing the things he shouldn't be doing, but as he often reassured himself, he didn't know he was doing wrong until he was told what he was doing was wrong. So how could that be bad?

He had never got on well with Miss Cowe, who confided to Emily when she met her in the village post office one day, "You know, Mrs Fowlie, your William is not a dunce, although I sometimes used to think so. He has quite a good brain, but only when he wants to use it. I had him for — three years? Yes, he moved to the next class when he was almost seven, and he is over eight now, is he not? I would really have liked to see him making more progress while he was with me, and Miss Bell, who will take him through Primaries Four and Five, says the same. Perhaps, however, he will blossom out when he goes into the headmaster's class. It is often the case that one teacher can make more of a pupil than another. A clash of personalities, in some cases. At least I can congratulate myself that his behaviour has toned down considerably, so no doubt his learning powers will increase with age. I do hope so."

Emily had been quite heartened by this brief conversation, telling her mother-in-law on her weekly visit, "At least she said he was behaving better at school, but why can't he behave better at home?"

Gramma Fowlie shrugged. "I canna gi'e you an answer to that, lass, but what's he been up to that's so bad?"

"Oh, nothing that bad for a while. It's just the little things that annoy me. He ayeways needs more than one telling to do what he's told."

Mina smiled knowingly. "And what laddie ever does what he's tell't the first time he's tell't? You're expectin' ower muckle fae him, Emmy. In fact, you're makin' mountains oot'n molehills. If you'd some laddies for a son, you'd ken a gey difference."

Emily bridled at the criticism and pretended not to understand the true meaning of her mother-in-law's words. "Yes, of course some boys are like angles, never answering back and obeying whatever their parents ask them to do."

Luckily, Mina was not one to take offence easily. "No, lass, I meant that Willie's just an ordinary loon, playin' tricks, nae likin' to be disciplined, aye lookin' for something exciting to dae. He wouldna be a right laddie if he sat on his backside fae morn till nicht like you want but there's dizzens o' laddies worse nor him."

"Aye, I suppose you're right. It's just — well, it's wearing, that's what."

"An' it'll wear by. In nae time, you'll be wonderin' where your wee laddie's gone, an' wishin' you had him back. He'll be gettin' in trouble for other kinds o' things."

"What other kinds of things?" Emily asked, already fretting.

"Oh, lass, you're an affa ane for worryin'. Enjoy your bairns when they're young, for they'll tak' their ain roads when they grow up."

Although Connie was the older, it was Becky who took the first step into the adult world some months later. She had grown into a real beauty, rounded figure, lovely fair silky hair that waved round her elfin face in a very becoming fashion now that she had started to wear it up. Her cheeks were deep pink, her startling blue eyes were always dancing mischievously and her lips always turned up in a smile. She drew boys to her like a flame draws moths, and she made the most of it, playing one off against another. At first, she showed no preference for any one of the half dozen who hung around her and her friends at the kirk soirees and dances, but gradually it became noticeable to the others that she was very much attracted to Jackie Burns, the only son of Thomas Burns of the Mains of Burnton, where both girls were employed. The other girls teased her — or rather, accused her — of picking him because he came from a well-to-do family, but Becky denied this. She pointed out that, although her father was only a farm servant and they had little money, her life had always been a happy one, and that wealth didn't always bring contentment.

"I love Jackie for himself, not for what his father is," she declared.

She could see that the other girls did not believe her, but what did it matter? Resentment, jealousy, hatred — love conquered everything, and so she went on meeting Jackie Burns as often as he asked her, this increasing from once a week to almost every night. His ardour also increased as the weeks went past. For the first few nights, he had contented himself with taking her hand shyly when they were walking out, which did disappoint her a little, but then, after sitting down one night in a clearing in Calder's Wood and talking for a while, he put his arm round her and drew her against his chest.

"Oh, Becky," he breathed, "I like you an awful lot."

Her heart had speeded up, but she said nothing. She wanted more than this from him, much more. He had held his arm at her waist all the way home, and she went to bed feeling quite frustrated. "He's awful slow," she complained to her sister.

Connie studied her closely. There was no sign that anything untoward had happened, yet she knew that Becky loved the boy.

A few more weeks passed, with Jackie progressing to a goodnight kiss at her door, which endearment grew steadily more fervent as the weeks went past, until the time came that Becky had been waiting for. Jackie let his hand stray to her breast, and after a very slight resistance, she let him carry on, fully understanding that he was stimulating himself as much as he was stimulating her. But she did not intend to let him go all the way. Her mother had warned her against that.

"Once you let a boy have his way with you," she had said, "he'll lose interest. Don't think because he's making love to you that he really loves you. Many a lassie has been left in the family way after letting a boy do what he wanted. Boys — and men — are usually after one thing, and when they get it, they move on to another girl. Keep your hand on your ha'penny till he's put the wedding band on your finger."

Becky had believed her, and even though she loved Jackie with all her heart, she had come to acknowledge that marrying a boy with prospects would be much better than marrying a farm worker, and she didn't want to jeopardise her chances of marrying into the Burns family.

"How're you and Jackie getting on?" Connie asked one night, after Becky had stayed out until well after ten.

"Great. He's on the boil, pleading with me to let him . . . you know, and I just say no."

"You're playing with fire."

"I know, and I'll make sure the fire doesn't go out." Becky threw her underclothes over a chair and grinned. "Don't you think I've got a lovely body? Jackie says I have, and that's what he wants. My body, Connie. And I want him to have it, but not unless he weds me."

Connie's eyebrows had shot up. She could only agree that Becky had a lovely body, for she was quite jealous of it. Her own body wasn't curvy. Her breasts were quite small, her hips weren't voluptuous, her waist wasn't so slim. Everything about Becky shouted, "Come and get me. I'm waiting for it." And the Burns laddie wouldn't wait for ever. If Becky didn't give in to him, he would soon get some other girl who would.

Although Emily had been preparing herself for her elder daughter, who would be twenty in August, to meet a lad and eventually want to be wed, she was utterly devastated when Rebecca, just sixteen past September, asked at breakfast time one morning, "Mam, can I ask Jackie Burns to come for his tea some night this week?"

It was Jake who said, jokingly, "Is this a lad you've gotten?"

"We've been keepin' company for a good few month, an' he wants to ask you something, Dad."

The girl was blushing now, letting Emily know exactly what was in the wind, but her husband was grinning. "Aye, tell him to come the morra if he wants. I'll be glad to answer ony question he likes."

The girl jumped up to hug him. "Oh, thanks, Dad. That's great. I'll tell Jackie the night it'll be OK."

She took her father's arm and they both went out together, leaving Emily gazing helplessly at her other daughter. "Did you know about this, Connie?"

Guiltily red-faced, the girl said, "Becky and Jackie Burns, you mean?"

"Of course I mean about Becky and Jackie Burns."

At this point, Willie, who had been drinking everything in, decided to put in a word or two of his own to lighten the atmosphere. "It's a shame his name's nae Robbie, in't it?"

Glad of the interruption, Connie gave him the answer he was obviously waiting for. "Why is't a shame his name's nae Robbie?"

"He'd need to watch and nae go ower near the fire."

"Ower near the fire? I dinna see what . . ." Connie's nose was wrinkled in puzzlement.

"In case his robbie burns," Willie laughed.

"What's Robbie Burns got to dae wi' this? He's Scotland's greatest poet, Mr Bremner used to say."

"He's being very rude!" Emily's mouth was drawn in. "And stupid! Not many men call it their robbie, it's usually called their willie, so he needn't laugh at other folk." Her scowl deepened. "You haven't answered my question yet, Connie."

Having just got the joke, the girl had to straighten her face before saying, "I didn't think you were serious."

"You knew she was seeing him, though?"

"Aye, Mam."

"And what were you doing the time she was with Jackie Burns? Have you a lad, and all?"

"Not a steady lad."

"You go out with lads, though?"

Stung into defence, Connie blustered, "What if I do? I'll be twenty-one next year and I'll not need your permission to have as many lads as I want."

Taken rather aback by this, Emily was less abrupt. "Aye, you're right, Con, and I'm sorry, but Becky's still just sixteen, and she hasn't seen much of life. She doesn't know how many evil men there are in the world that prey on young lassies."

His eyes as wide open as they could possibly be, Willie said, "How could they pray on young lassies,

Mam? Do they mak' them sit doon an' jump on their backs to pray?"

Angry at passing the remark in front of the boy, Emily shook her head. "No, it's not that kind of praying, it's . . ." She halted, stuck for another explanation.

"Willie," Connie said quietly, "you ken when a cat catches a mouse and plays wi' it afore he kills it, well, the mouse is the cat's prey, spelt P-R-E-Y. And there's men that catch young lassies and torture them. They mebbe dinna kill them, but they hurt them as much as they can. That's what Mam was meaning."

The matter sorted out to everyone's satisfaction, Emily rose to clear the table, Connie went to take her coat off the peg in the porch before setting off on her bicycle to Home Farm, where she was employed as dairy-maid and Becky as kitchen-maid. They were the only two servants in the house, as the farmer's wife liked to do most things herself.

Willie got his satchel from the porch, stuffed in his dinner box, his mind concentrating on one thing — what was Jackie Burns going to ask Dad tomorrow night?

Naturally, his first question to his little chum on their way to school was, "Hiv you ever heard o' men jumpin' on lassies' backs to pray?"

Shaking his head vigorously, his eyes alight with naked curiosity, Poopie said, "I never kent men did that. I've never seen ony man jumpin' . . ."

"Neither hiv I, but that's what my Mam tell't Connie. Mind you, Mam often tells us things that's nae true, jist to mak' us dae something, or nae dae something."

More confused than ever, the other boy blinked several times before saying, "I canna understand what you mean."

"Ach, you dinna listen richt, that's your trouble. She said men jump on . . ."

"Aye, I got that bit, but it's this dae something or nae dae . . ."

Willie gave up. "Never mind. Come on, we'll be late if we dinna hurry." But he couldn't help wondering about the picture his mother's words had conjured up. What could any man be praying for if he was sitting on a lassie's back? Letting his mind puzzle over various things a man might want, it slowly dawned on him what he would want most if he was a man. A horse! That was it! He fancied sittin' on horseback fighting off his enemies. But why had his mother made such a secret of it?

Having solved the problem, he buckled down to concentrating on what Miss Bell was saying, then realising that the rest of the class already had their heads down doing whatever they had been told to do, he had to nudge his neighbour to find out which page of his sum book he should turn to.

It had been a long hard fight — Emily had been dead set against her daughter marrying so young — and week after week had gone by with constant arguments between Becky and her parents, until Jake was won round by his daughter's tears, and claimed his right as head of the house to give his permission. Once this had been given, Jackie dropped a bombshell by telling them that his mother wanted the wedding to be at the Mains, upsetting Emily, who had visualised being in charge of all the arrangements in her own house. This contretemps also took some days to settle, but finally everyone was agreed that it should be the bride's choice. Greatly relieved that the battle was over, Jackie had arranged a date with the minister, who had agreed to perform the ceremony in the bride's home on the first Saturday in June, which didn't give much time for other arrangements to be made.

Caught up in the young couple's excitement, Emily found herself looking forward to it, and looked out the outfit she had worn at her own wedding in 1909. It was over twenty years old, but it was a style that didn't go out of date — a dusky pink two-piece with, instead of a hat, a lovely band of silk rosebuds (made by Beenie Middleton's middle daughter, who was now a milliner in Ellon, but had been an apprentice at the time). Bridesmaid Connie had been given a beautiful powder-blue crêpe de chine dress that was too tight for her mistress, but fitted the girl as if it had been made for her. Unable to afford new clothes for themselves on top of all the other expenses, Jake and Emily were content with wearing their Sunday best.

It came as no surprise to any of them, of course, that Willie would almost put a spanner in the works. Becky had been looking through pictures of weddings in the magazines Mrs Burns had given her, showing fashionable wedding parties and detailing wedding etiquette. "I don't want anybody saying we don't know how to behave," she had excused herself to her mother before breaking the appalling information that she wanted Willie to wear a kilt.

"It looks so nice in this photo, doesn't it?" she had gone on, laying out one of the books spread open at a double page image of what looked like a society wedding, or at least someone with a truly wealthy background. The guests looked like advertisements for the latest styles, like fashion plates, as Connie observed, the best man and the groom in tailored grey suits with top hats to match, the bride in a pure white confection (as befitted a virgin) with a high headdress and a long veil draped around her feet.

The two boys, one at front left and the other at front right of the picture, stood stiffly wearing the kilt and full regalia, down to the small dirks at their stocking tops. Even Emily had to agree that they looked very elegant, but they were bonnie boys, hair in place, everything about them absolutely perfect, whereas Willie . . . She shuddered at the thought of how he would look at the end of the wedding day — even at the end of the first half-hour after he was dressed. "No, Becky, I don't think that's a good idea, and besides, we couldn't afford to buy a kilt for him and all that other things."

Becky's face wore a radiant smile. "You don't have to buy anything, Mam. Mrs Burns is giving us a shot of the kilt her Tommy wore when he was about Willie's size."

When Willie was shown his outfit for his sister's wedding, he flatly refused even to try it on. "I'm nae goin' to wear a skirt! I'm nae a lassie! A'body'll be laughin' at me. Oh, Mam, you canna mak' me wear a skirt?"

Gramma McKay, there to present her wedding gift of a pair of pink flannelette sheets, shook her head at the boy for being so uncooperative but did her best to talk him round into at least giving it a try. "You never know, you might like it once you've got it on." Noticing his frown darkening, she added, "And you'll likely have the girls after you when you're looking so handsome."

It was the wrong thing to say because he didn't like girls, but she wasn't accustomed to being thwarted by anyone, not even a young boy, and went off home in high dudgeon.

Gramma Fowlie, however, did manage to talk him round the following day. "Come on, ma lambie. Just for this Gramma. Put it on to let me see how you look, eh?"

Willie loved this grandmother more than any of his other relatives, except maybe his father, so, very reluctantly, he got out the offending garment, unfolded it from its layers of tissue paper, pulling a disgusted face when his nose was assaulted by the reek of moth balls.

His Gramma fastened all the buckles that had to be fastened, fitted on the sporran and adjusted it, saying aloud as the brainwave came to her, "This is where the Highlanders kept their pistols. You ken, the men that fought for Bonnie Prince Charlie."

It was as if she had waved a magic wand. His attitude changed as he stepped towards the wardrobe mirror in the girls' room, his back straightening, his head more erect, his expression that of a brave Highlander, ready to defend the rightful king of Scotland, though his enemies called him the Young Pretender.

Gramma stood by his side, nodding, encouraging him in his moment of glory. "D'you like it?" she asked at last. "It's right comfy, isn't it, without breeks interfering wi' your legs, an' what else is in the bag?"

When he was fully rigged out in the white shirt with ruffles at the neck, the black velvet jacket and black brogues with silver buckles, the gilt had worn slightly off the gingerbread. The velvet of the jacket and the ruffles on the shirt added more femininity to the "skirt". "Do I have to wear it, Gramma?"

"Becky wants you looking smart, my pet, so for her . . . and me, eh? It's just for one day, you ken. One day's nae that lang."

And so the kilt was donned on the morning of the wedding and Willie Fowlie became one of Prince Charles Stuart's soldiers for one day . . . or part of a day. Everything was going without a hitch, but just as Willie was making his way down the ladder, one of his schoolmates spotted him and ran into the parlour to tell the other boys who were there with their parents. The Highlander was greeted with roars of raucous laughter.

Gramma Fowlie, close behind her grandson to prevent him turning and going back, was not prepared for what he did then. Unbuckling the sporran, he flung it on the floor and got himself divested of the "skirt" in spite of all the woman's efforts to stop him. She was, however, greatly relieved that he had refused to come downstairs without his drawers on, even if she had told him real Highlanders wore nothing under their kilts.

Poor Becky had to be content with the photographer placing her pageboy at the rear of the wedding group so that just his head and shoulders could be seen. Released from bondage, Willie disappeared to his attic and wouldn't come down until his Gramma Fowlie told him all the goodies would be eaten and there would be nothing for him if he didn't go down that very minute. Becky was mortified at what had happened, Emily was mortified, ashamed and furious at her son, but the rest of the party, especially the men, thought it had been hilarious. Jake was torn between having a laugh at his son's expense, being proud of him for sticking to his guns and feeling angry at him for spoiling his big sister's wedding day. He didn't worry about it after a couple of drinks, though, and carried out the duties of father of the bride and head of the house, exhorting all the other men to "Ha'e another dram. Dinna worry aboot what the wife's goin' to say in the mornin', enjoy yoursel's the nicht. We're a lang time deid, eh lads?"

They needed no further coaxing, and their wives, as they always did on such occasions, knew better than to try to rein in their men while they were drunk. Nemesis could wait until they were sober. The younger men were more interested in the girls than in the intoxicating liquor, and gradually most of them, plus an equal number of young females, would have been found to be missing if anyone had been counting them. Emily, of course, realised at one point that Connie had disappeared and tried to think which of the boys she could have disappeared with, but so many were absent that she gave up the struggle. She didn't want to show herself as an over-protective mother, and in any case, whatever her older daughter was doing, it was probably too late now to stop her. Retribution for her, her father and her little brother would have to wait until next day.

Willie, dressed in his school breeks now, was running around with the other bairns, playing hide-and-seek or tick-and-tack, or What's the Time Mr Wolf, and getting in everybody's way. Not that anybody minded, for the alcohol — liberally provided by Tom Burns — was having a calming effect on all who partook of it. Nobody at all had gone the other way, thank goodness, the aggressive way that sometimes took over.

It was well after the "witching hour" before the party began to break up. The whole house was full of cigarette smoke and the reek of whisky, which made the youngest members of the company cry because their eyes were nipping, and the mothers shepherded — almost carried — their protesting husbands towards the door. As Beenie Middleton barked to hers, "Shift yoursel', for ony sake, an' I wouldna like to ha'e a sair heid like you'll ha'e in the mornin', you drunken bugger."

Obviously accustomed to this form of address from his wife, he leered at her with a vacant grin, but she shook off the arm he was trying to slide round her waist and thrust him from her with a look of disgust.

It was wearing on for one o'clock before Emily got her brood settled down, Jake being the worst to get to bed. Connie didn't appear to be in the least hang-dog, so she surely hadn't done anything she shouldn't, Emily mused, as she took off her clothes and crept in beside her already dead-to-the-world husband. She couldn't bear to let her thoughts dwell on seventeen-year-old Becky, whose groom had taken her for a night's stay in a posh hotel in Aberdeen before their fortnight's honeymoon in Edinburgh. They'd taken the nine o'clock train and had likely been in bed for hours by now — Jackie Burns had shown signs of impatience before they left, and no doubt would have taken his way with his bride as soon as they went into their hotel room.

Emily drew in a long shuddery breath. She could only hope and pray that the poor lass hadn't had too big a shock. On her own wedding night, Jake had been gentle and loving — as he still was on the widely spaced nights when he claimed his rights as her husband — and maybe Jackie was the same, but so many other wives told a different story. She turned over carefully, her back to the grunting snores, and wished that she'd made Connie help her to tidy the kitchen before they came to bed. It was an awful thought having to rise in the morning to all that work before they could have any breakfast.

Connie was undecided whether to be glad or sorry. She *was* glad that she hadn't gone against what her mother had taught her — not to let any boy touch her until she was wed to him — but she wished she'd had the nerve to let Gordie Brodie do what he wanted. She nearly had, oh, how nearly! If he'd persisted for just another second or so, she'd have let him; it was only the thought of Mam's anger that stopped her. Plus, if he'd bairned her, Dad would have half killed her, and him, or thrown her out of the house, and she'd have nowhere to go. Gordie wasn't the marrying kind, she knew that, and he'd just wanted to be able to tell his friends she was an easy lay. Aye, she wasn't under any misapprehension about that, but she wished she'd tasted the forbidden fruit just this once. She might never get another chance.

Willie, too, was thinking, wishing now that he'd kept on the kilt. It hadn't been so bad, really. If Malcie Middleton hadn't made everybody laugh, he wouldn't have minded. He'd felt quite important being one of Bonnie Prince Charlie's soldiers. Och, well, it couldn't be helped now, and he hadn't missed much while he was upstairs. In fact, he'd seen something he supposed he shouldn't have seen and it would be best to keep his mouth shut about it. He'd been standing on his bed looking out of the skylight in his attic room, when he spotted Gordie Brodie by the coalshed, and at first it looked as if he was having a pee because the privy was occupied, but it soon became clear that he was pushing another person against the wall. Wondering if there was going to be a fight, it had dawned on the boy that the other body was a girl, and the two were so busy kissing they wouldn't have noticed if a whole army had been watching them. Willie gave a sarcastic snicher. Fancy kissing a girl, soppy devil. Nobody would ever catch him doing a thing like that. He'd no time for girls. His brows came down suddenly, as the lad bent over to lift the lassie's skirt. She hadn't been happy about that, though, and lashed out with her feet, twisting her head this way and that to stop further kisses. That was when he saw that the girl was his sister Connie, and he felt quite proud of the fight she was putting up. But what a nerve Brodie had. He wasn't a gentleman, that was for sure.

Fascinated, Willie had kept watching until her knee landed full tilt against her attacker's most delicate parts. Gordie jumped away with a yell, holding himself as Connie made her escape, and her young brother had collapsed on his bed and rolled about with laughter. Although Gramma Fowlie had come in just a few minutes afterwards to tell him to come downstairs for something to eat, and had looked surprised when she heard him gurgling, he didn't tell her anything.

Recalling the whole episode, Willie curled up under his bedcovers and soon drifted off into a deep, comfortable sleep in which he dreamed of standing beside Bonnie Prince Charlie and running forward to thrust his claymore deep into the advancing enemy, who all bore an uncanny resemblance to Gordon Brodie.

CHAPTER
EIGHT

December 1931

Jake knew exactly how his ten-year-old son felt. He had felt the same when he was that age. A bike made you feel nearly grown-up. Travelling along the roads with the wind blowing in your face and the bushes and trees whizzing past you was just like being on top of the world — no other experience could match it, but there was no money to buy a bike for the laddie. He'd been in a different position himself; having so many cousins of various ages, he got a bike handed down to him at each stage of his growing up — in addition to the hand-me-down clothes that were not quite so welcome to him. His mother had been very grateful for them, though, for money was always short for the Fowlies then, as well.

The man had been trying for weeks to think of ways to save enough for a bike. Willie was forever harping on about being the only boy he knew that didn't have a bike, and it would be a grand Christmas present. But no matter what he did or who he asked, nobody had a bicycle for sale or knew where he could get one at a price he could afford. So it was like an answer to a prayer when, clearing out an old shed that had lain unused for some years, he came across the frame of an old Raleigh, left there by some previous cottared man. But further, frantically hopeful searching produced no other parts of the vehicle, full-sized though it was. Jake decided to keep it anyway, for the rest must be lying about somewhere.

Willie himself had meanwhile been telling those of his chums who possessed a bicycle to keep their ears open. "If you hear onybody wantin' to sell a bike, let me ken," were his instructions to them. Malcolm Middleton — Malcie to all and sundry — offered to take him round the rubbish dumps on the back of his bike, and all the neighbouring farmyards, which offer Willie instantly accepted.

Thus it was that the two boys could be seen, one pedalling and the other seated on the carrier, making the rounds of the places where they might just see an old bike that somebody had thrown out. Their quest was not entirely fruitless; on one tip they found two wheels, tyres as flat as pancakes.

"Och, the rubber's fair perished," Malcie exclaimed, "they're nae use."

Willie was not discouraged. "We'll mebbe get better tyres someplace else," he crowed.

And so they took the wheels back and hid them in one of the outhouses he knew his father never used, shoving them under a piece of old tarpaulin covering something at the very back. "It's a frame, Malcie," shouted Willie, almost jumping his own height with joy. "I never ken't that was there."

Over the next few weeks, taking them well into 1932, their pilgrimage spawned most of the other parts Willie needed. The final item eluded them for six further weeks, but at last, on top of a dump they had searched in months earlier, they found the handlebars. The two boys couldn't get back quickly enough to start assembling their trophies, doing their best to keep their activities hidden from Willie's mother and father.

Jake, of course, whose own search for parts had come up with nothing more than his initial find, decided that he had wasted his time and would be best to throw it on a tip somewhere. When he went to retrieve it from his outhouse, he was astonished to find a bicycle under construction, but decided to keep the boy's ploy secret from his wife.

Keeping a lookout for his son going to school the following morning, he called him over to the paling he was repairing. "I see you've got the makin's o'yer bike," he began. Willie waited for the row he was sure would come, but his father went on, "You've done real weel, son, but I think ye'd best let me tighten up the screws and things for you."

"Was it you that got the frame?" At his father's smiling nod, he added, "You see, Dad, I want to be able to say it was just me an' Malcie Middleton that did it."

Jake guffawed. "Weel, I'm real prood o' you, lad, but mind an' tighten every screw as far as it'll go."

"We'll mak' sure o' that, Dad, dinna worry."

It was a good three weeks before the two boys were satisfied that their creation was roadworthy and started going for cycle runs together. Knowing how reckless her son was, Emily wasn't too happy about him being let loose on a vehicle he'd made himself, but he was a big laddie now, nearly as big as Jake, so she resolved to stop being over-protective. He wouldn't listen to any of her fears in any case.

She soon discovered that he was much more amenable to being asked to go to the shop in the village for anything she needed, and was there and back in less than thirty minutes. With little thought to his safety on such a rickety contraption, she sent him on all sorts of errands — although the first time she asked him to take her usual three dozen eggs to the village shop to be sold — the grocer's van had stopped coming some time ago — she was a wee bit worried about the safety of the eggs. But there had been no complaint from the shop and it became a regular task for Willie every Friday.

She felt strangely pleased with him now. As she observed to Connie one day, "What a difference that bike's made to him. I can depend on him now, for he's not as daft as he used to be."

Connie nodded. "You were aye too hard on him. He wasna as bad as you made out."

"I suppose you're right, lass, but . . . well, a leopard never changes its spots, as it says in the good book. I just wonder, though . . ." Shaking her head, she broke off.

Glad of the chance to air her little piece of good news, Connie said, hesitantly, "Gordie's asked me to his house for my supper the morra. He says it was his mother's idea." Emily's expression made her add, hastily, "I think he's serious about me, Mam, and I'm serious about him."

76

"Are you sure he's the lad for you, lass?" Emily had never taken to Gordon Brodie. He was too full of his own importance, and had treated Jake and her like dirt the few times she'd let Connie invite him there. Plus, and it was a big plus, if he was serious about the girl, he'd taken far too long to tell his folk. Still, she mused, if her daughter was truly in love, she was willing to put aside her own feelings.

Connie eyed her mother reflectively. "I've never thought he was the lad for me, Mam, but nane o' the other lads have looked twice at me."

"You should tell him you're not wanting him, then. Other lads are maybe scared to ask you out if they think you're his girl."

"You think that's what it is?" Connie seemed more cheerful.

The porch door banged open to admit Willie, who flung his satchel down on the floor before coming into the kitchen, at which his mother and sister both cried, "Pick that up!" Bending down with a scowl, he lifted the bag and hung it on the peg on the door.

Heaving a sigh, Emily said firmly, "And never mind sitting down. You know fine this is Friday, and you've to take the eggs to the shop."

"OK, but can I get a piece an' jam first?"

The two women laughed to each other as they watched him cut a thick slice off the loaf and spread it thickly with Emily's home-made strawberry jam. Then he went out by the back door, first lifting the basket of eggs which had been sitting on a shelf in the porch, the tackets on his boots making sparks fly from the stone flags on the floor.

Emily turned to Connie again. "D'you think Becky's putting on weight?"

"I haven't noticed."

"I've the feeling she's expecting."

"Ach, Mam, you're imagining things. Becky doesn't want any kids, that would spoil her figure."

"But it's not always what you want, is it? I'm sure Jackie wants a family. Most girls are expecting before they can draw breath after the wedding."

Connie gave a little giggle. "Now you're coming the bag a bit, but I'll tell you this, I hope I can find a husband quick, or I'll be past the age for having any bairnies."

"Oh, Connie, you're just a chicken yet."

"I'll be twenty-one in August."

"You've plenty time yet to have your family. Beenie was near forty-four when she had her Alice. You've another twenty years — you might end up with a whole jing-bang of babies." God forbid, she added silently.

Rebecca Burns was anything but happy about her pregnancy. The morning sickness she'd dreaded had been worse than she'd imagined, lasting for most of the day sometimes, and she couldn't bear the thought that her belly would start to grow enormous. Of course, it might put Jackie off her, which would be a blessing, for he kept on asking and she kept on refusing, and that couldn't go on for ever. He would get fed up of it, and turn to some other girl, not that it would bother her, except he might want to leave her. That would be a proper calamity. She was now part of a fairly well-to-do family, and she didn't want to lose that security.

If she could get rid of this encumbrance, she would be quite happy to remain as Jackie's wife, having the where-withal to buy what she liked and when she liked. She made a trip to Aberdeen at least once a month — Jackie had never complained about it — and that would have to stop if he decided to divorce her. Tom Burns had given them this cottage as a wedding present, so she would likely have to leave, and God knows where she would go. No doubt her parents would take her in, but she didn't want to go back to scrimping and saving for a year before she could afford to buy a new dress. No, she had better watch her step and keep hold of what she had got.

One thing she could do, though, to get her life back to what it was, get rid of this blasted infant or whatever they called it at this stage. She was just over three months late, so it should be all right. She'd heard about a woman in Tillyburnie that got rid of them for fifty pounds and no questions asked, so she'd go to her. Nobody knew about it anyway, so tongues wouldn't wag.

Having received the money for the eggs he had taken in, Willie accepted the usual long stick of barley sugar the grocer's wife always gave him. "Ta, Mrs Gill," he beamed. "See you next Friday."

With no reason now to go carefully, he swung purposefully on to his steed and rode off, cracking his whip in the air to urge it on. He had repelled several English invaders when it occurred to him to drop in past Malcie Middleton — now working for McIntyre of Wester Burnton — to show him how well the "Raleigh" was doing as a charger, and swerved into the farm road.

There were only two people in the stable yard, Malcie and the old man everybody in the area knew as the Daftie, although some thought that he wasn't as daft as he made out. He still had an abundant crop of pure white hair, and although he was missing some of his front teeth, he always wore a wide smile. He was helping the youth to polish the horse brasses, there being a show looming in the very near future. Johnny McIntyre was very proud of his Clydesdales and entered them every year; having already won many second and third prizes for various horses, his heart was set on gathering at least one first.

"Aye Malcie," Willie called.

"Aye Willie." His friend was engrossed in his task, but could still acknowledge the presence of his chum. "The bike's goin' OK then?"

"Great. I come along the road like a bird through the air."

The Daftie looked up now, nodding his approval of the vehicle, then he mumbled, "You're Jake Fowlie's loon, aye?"

"Aye."

"Your Ma mak's black puddins, aye?"

"Aye?" Willie was puzzled. What did black puddings have to do with anything?

"McIntyre killed a pig this week."

"Oh? So what aboot it?"

"I saved some o' the bleed for her."

"Oh, aye?"

"Wait a mintie."

The elderly man hobbled off and came back within the requested minute carrying a rather chipped white enamel pail. "Look," he cackled, holding it up to let Willie see inside, "Plenty there. Aye?"

The boy knew nothing about this. He loved the black puddings his mother made, but he hadn't realised that they contained pig's blood. It wasn't a happy thought. "I suppose so."

"Tak' it an' gi'e it to yer Ma wi' my compliments, but mind an' bring back the pail, or McIntyre'll gi'e me whatfor."

Willie, taller now and well on the way to being willowy instead of podgy, lifted the pail, old and battered, but like everything else in the stable and its surrounds, spotlessly clean. "I'll awa' then, Malcie."

"Watch yoursel', and go easy. We dinna want the bobby to come and tell us to shovel you up aff the road. We wouldna ken which was your bleed an' which was the pig's."

The younger boy joined in the roar of laughter as he steadied the bicycle with his knees until he could get his precious cargo hooked over the handlebars. Keeping his steed upright when all the weight was on one side was quite tricky, but at last he somehow got into a rhythm that answered his problem. Proud of his prowess, he wished that Poopie-Cecil could see him. He was pleased Malcie Middleton was watching as he set off, for he had shared the honour of creating this magnificent mode of transport.

Secure in his belief in himself, Willie fished in his jacket pocket for the stick of barley sugar Mrs Gill had given him, and discovered, to his further delight, that he could steer the bike and its load just as well with one hand as with two, and he sailed along, whistling happily.

Oh, Willie. If either of his grandmothers could have seen him, they would have told him that pride cometh before a fall, but as neither of these good ladies had any idea of what he was doing, he went on his way, considering himself the happiest, and cleverest, laddie in the whole wide world.

Coming to the stony track that led up to the Wester Burnton cottar houses, he stuck his barley sugar in his mouth in order to have both hands free to get round the corner. He took it carefully, making the left turn like a veteran of the road, and after a few precarious moments of wobbling, he picked up his rhythm again. Thankful to have made it into the home stretch, he took hold of his stick of barley sugar again and carried on a little more slowly up the track.

It had to come. There was no doubt about that. A gambling man would have deemed it a dead cert and put his very shirt on it. Willie, though, had no foreboding of impending doom, still whistling tunelessly as he imagined how impressed Malcie Middleton would be to hear how he'd coped with the tricky business of controlling a bike laden with a pail of precious goods.

He had no thought for anything else. He had no eyes for anything but a far-off vision of glory, so that he did not see the large stone thrown up by Mr McIntyre's tractor which had, only minutes before, come up this same track and had turned right into a field of turnips. All that the boy was aware of was the impact of his wheel against the boulder, of the bicycle coming apart at the seams, as he might have said, and of being catapulted over the drystane dyke on his left that marked the perimeter of the ley field, resting from crops for the second of three years.

Emily Fowlie had an uneasy feeling; not a premonition of some disastrous calamity, more a sense of something that she couldn't quite put a name to. At first, it was Jake's well-being that troubled her, yet as time passed, her thoughts travelled round the other three members of her family. Had Jackie Burns thrown Becky out for spending too much on clothes? She had warned and warned her younger daughter about that, but Becky always took her own way. But surely she'd have come home if it was anything like that? One thing was certain, of course; she wasn't pregnant. Whether she had never been, or had been and had got rid of it by some means, was something nobody could be sure about. Had Connie met with an accident at Gordon Brodie's house? But one of the workers would have come with the news. Finally, her mind turned to her youngest child, her only son, the one who had given her most trouble ever since he came into the world. Willie was always gallous, bashing at things without thinking, but always with the luck of the devil as far as the consequences went.

She glanced at the clock. He should have been back by this time though, so what was he doing? If he'd got to the shop safely, he'd have been home ages ago with the money. Whatever he was doing — some mischief or other, more than likely — he could have lost what he'd got for her eggs. She wouldn't put that past him. She could never depend on him for anything, though Jake wouldn't hear a word against him. Strangely uneasy, she set about preparing the supper. There would only be the three of them, with Connie at the Brodies'. She had got a lovely big ham shank from the butcher's van that morning, which had been simmering nicely for long enough now to add some veggies to the pot, so she set to with a will, paring, cutting and chopping. She liked to eat ham cold, but Jake preferred it hot, after his plate of pea soup. Willie, naturally, took after his father, so she had to do it their way when Connie wasn't there. When her daughter was at home, it was a case of tossing for it, or taking it turn about.

With everything cooking nicely, she sat down for a minute or two. This was the time of day she liked best; when the supper was under way and all the housework had been done. Willie was usually out playing with Poopie. No, he should get his real name nowadays since it wouldn't be all that long till he'd be leaving the school.

Goodness knows what Willie would do with himself when *he* left, she thought. He had never been interested in learning, and he wasn't particularly good with his hands — except that he'd managed to construct a bike from a lot of odd bits. Still, that wasn't enough to get him a job, and she didn't think that Jake would be able to find him work with Johnny McIntyre.

Telling herself that she shouldn't be worrying about it yet, she was brought out of her reverie by Willie limping in. Then she spotted the angry red cut on his cheek. "Have you been fighting again?" she accused, even as she stood up to attend to his needs.

"No, Mam, I fell aff'n my bike." Willie had never told his mother such a downright lie before, but he'd been thinking as he made his painful way from the scene of his accident. The blood had all been spilled, the money for the eggs had gone heelster-gowdie all over a huge expanse of nettles. He had tried to find the coins, getting his hands stung badly in the process, and he'd realised how deeply in trouble he would be if he didn't come up with a feasible story. And so he had set about concealing the awful truth. He had lifted the bits of bicycle and the severely dented pail, empty now of course, and carried them across the field until he came to the dyke at the opposite end, on the other side of which was quite a large area of moorland.

Walking in what was more or less a circle, he buried one piece of what had been his pride and joy deep in the heart of various clumps of the heather until he had disposed of everything. A degree of his guilt left behind also, he had climbed the dyke again and made his way diagonally across the field towards his home.

85

Both knees were now so painful that he stopped to find out why, and was amazed to see how badly they were scraped; and, putting his hand up to his throbbing cheek, he wasn't surprised to see it smeared with blood. He decided to admit that he'd fallen off his bike, but not to mention that the bike was no more, buckled beyond redemption. But one thing would have to be explained: where was the money for the eggs? His mother would go mad at him. Wait a minute, though. She'd likely be too busy tending his injuries to worry about money. And he could tell her truth about where it was, anyway. His hands were proof of his vain searches. The bonus was that he needn't mention the pail and its contents. She knew nothing of them. Going quietly into the porch, he opened the kitchen door and limped in — his mother's face, as she jumped up in alarm, giving him a wee bit more courage to say what he meant to say.

Emily's first action was to fetch the iodine. Her son's wound had to be made clean from any dirt and infection. It was when she made him lift up his foot so that she could see his knees better that the more serious injury became apparent. Slipping off his left boot and sock with some difficulty, she was alarmed to see how swollen his foot was. "Is it awful sore?" she enquired softly, and at his grimacing nod, she said, "I'll let you steep it in a basin for a while to see if that helps, and then I'd better bandage it."

These procedures were almost more than the boy could stand, but he managed to grit his teeth and keep from crying. At least his mother hadn't asked too many questions, and not even one about the lost money. It would come, though; he knew that.

He managed to sup a little of the soup, but was glad when Jake came in. It was Emily who told him what had happened, and after sympathising for a few moments he carried his son up to bed — with something of a struggle. "Is the bike a' right?" he asked then.

"It's a bit bashed, but it'll be fine. I'll see what Malcie says the morra."

When his mother came in to say goodnight, she asked, "What about the money you got for the eggs?"

This was the straw that broke Willie's outward composure. Tears came gushing out as he whimpered, "It fell among the nettles, and I tried and tried to . . ." He held up his still burning hands. "See?"

"Oh, bairn, you should have said. I'll get some docken leaves. That'll take out the sting."

But it wasn't only the stinging that kept the boy awake all night. His foot was giving pain such as he had never experienced before, his shoulder had also begun to ache and he felt he was burning up. Hearing his sister come in about ten, he called weakly, "Con."

Luckily, she heard him, and called, "What d'you want, Willie?"

"I want Mam."

This was so unusual a request for him that she didn't think twice about knocking on the kitchen door, knowing that, although her parents went to their box bed early, they probably wouldn't be asleep yet. Emily came out straight away, and when she felt her son's brow, she exclaimed, "Oh, my! He's burning up." After

Connie filled a basin with cold water, Emily sponged him gently.

It took well over an hour for the fever to break, but Willie was plainly still suffering extreme pain in his foot, which had swollen unbelievably now.

"He must've sprained it," Connie observed.

"Looks like it," agreed her mother. "We'd best strap it up tight."

Using a long strip torn from an old cotton sheet that was kept for mending, Emily bound the foot from toe to well past the ankle, just to be sure, and secured it with a safety pin.

Jake offered to go to the farm and ask somebody to telephone for the doctor, but Emily bade him wait until a more civilised hour. "That's two households you'd be disturbing, Johnny McIntyre's and the doctor's. Folk'll not thank you for taking them out of their beds. You'd best go back to yours and get some sleep, or you'll not be fit for anything."

Having had only two and a half hours in bed, although unable to sleep, Jake was up at half past five, and made a pot of tea for Connie and Emily, who had both sat up to watch over the injured boy. It had taken Willie a long time to settle, and he had just succumbed to slumber about forty minutes before.

Having at least got something hot in his stomach, Jake was now allowed to go to Wester Burnton Farm. There were no other houses in the immediate area that had the luxury of a telephone, nor was there a doctor nearer than in Tillyburnie, somewhat smaller than a town but a little larger than a normal village. This was approximately three and a half miles along the turnpike, and actually boasted two GPs who had to cover all the Burnton farm towns — Wester, Easter and Mains of — as well as the village itself and the hamlet of Whinnybrae, so called because the hill under which it was situated was covered with whins, or gorse to those unacquainted with the word.

"I'm sorry to bother you," Jake apologised to Jean McIntyre after making his request.

"It's no bother," she replied. "We're used to it. There's not an hour of the night we havena been knocked up at some time or other, but we dinna mind, as long as it's not for something that could easy wait. Now off you go, but you'll let us ken how the bairn is?"

"Oh aye, Mrs McIntyre, I'll dae that. Thanks."

The doctor's Morris Oxford drew up almost at the same time as Jake arrived home. "Mr Fowlie? I'm Dr Murison," he said, as he slammed the car door. A small, dumpy man wearing a creased tweed suit with a paddy hat on the side of his head, he did not give an impression of efficiency, but as the Fowlies were to discover, his looks belied his ability. Gently removing the bandage, he carefully examined the boy's foot, glanced at the stricken face and could tell by the silent grimaces that he was still in great pain.

"We'll have to get you to hospital, laddie," he said, at last. "I'm nearly sure your foot is broken, but an X-ray will show what's what."

"I was near sure it wasn't just a sprain," Emily remarked. "So what happens now? Will we have to wait for an ambulance?"

Dr Murison shook his balding head. "I've some calls to do there anyway, so I'll take him. That is if you'll help me to get him down, Mr Fowlie, and into the car."

"Aye, we'll easy manage."

But it wasn't easy. Willie could hardly stand the pain, and although he bit his lips and steeled himself not to make any noise, the odd involuntary moan came out as he was bumped down each protesting rung.

Emily, like all mothers, was quite distressed because her son was going into hospital, but more concerned that she hadn't had time to change his clothing. In fact, he had hardly anything on at all, and although the doctor had wrapped him inside a blanket off the bed, he needed something decent to wear instead of his father's old drawers that he wore in bed because there was no money for pyjamas.

"Come on, Emmy," Jake called back. "If you're wantin' to go wi' him . . ."

"No," said the doctor firmly. "It's better that she lets the professionals attend to him with no interference. Besides, how would she get home?"

He turned to call to her. "If you are looking for something for him to wear, you needn't bother. There are all sorts of things in all sorts of sizes there."

Forced to give in, she ran down in time to see her son being laid into the back of the Morris Oxford. "I'll let Mrs McIntyre know what the report is," Dr Murison smiled as he sat down behind the steering wheel. "She's quite used to passing on reports."

Emily shook his outstretched hand. "Thank you, Doctor. You'll think I'm over-anxious, but it's the first time any of my family have been in hospital."

"You're like all other mothers," he smiled.

Jake waited a moment, then said, "I'd best get started my work, lass. The bairn'll be a' right, so dinna worry. He's in good hands."

"You haven't had any breakfast. Come inside and I'll . . ."

"I couldna eat a thing. Now, stop worryin' or you'll mak' yoursel' ill an' that would finish the lot o' us."

Left on her own after Connie ran off to work, Emily had to keep busy to stop her worrying. For as much as Willie had been a thorn in her flesh all his life, she actually was experiencing what could pass as a motherly feeling towards him now that he'd been hurt. And it was all her fault for sending him to the village shop with eggs. He wouldn't have been out on that rickety old bike if she hadn't sent him. It crossed her mind then that the doctor had never asked how Willie had been hurt, though he was likely used to boys having accidents of some kind. Anyway, he said he would let them know the report, so there was nothing she could do about it now.

CHAPTER
NINE

It was nearly seven o'clock, and the three Fowlies were having supper when seventeen-year-old Andy McIntyre came with the report from the hospital. "Willie's broke his fit in three places," he began when Emily took him inside.

"Oh, my God!" she exclaimed.

"So they've put him in plaster and he'll be there aboot a week. Then they'll let him hame wi' crutches, and he'll be aff the school for a good while."

"That'll please him," laughed Jake.

"An' his shooder's badly bruised."

"Oh, thank goodness it's not broken and all," breathed Emily, then remembered her duty as woman of the house. "Would you like some of this skirlie and tatties?"

"No thanks, Mrs Fowlie, I've had my supper. Oh, an' my Da says he's gan to Tillieburnie on Sunday, so he'll tak' you to the hospital to see Willie, if you like. An' he'll tak' you back in aboot an hour."

She clapped her hands. "That's very kind of him. I'd be very grateful."

"He says be ready for twelve o'clock."

On Sunday morning, however, Emily had an even worse shock. She had decided that she wouldn't have time to go to the kirk with Jake and Connie, and was brushing down her coat when someone knocked at the front door. It was such a loud knock, like a summons for something terrible, that she was timid of answering. She was even more shaken when she beheld a policeman with bicycle clips on his trouser legs and a notebook in his hand.

"Mrs Fowlie?"

"Yes."

"Mrs Emily Fowlie?"

"Is it . . . has something happened to Willie?"

"Willie?"

"My son. He's in hospital."

This piece of information was noted down. "What is your son's name and how old is he?"

"Willie's ten — eleven in September."

"Oh." The word seemed to hold a touch of disappointment. "Do any other males live in the house?"

"Just my husband. Jake."

"Ah." This was also recorded.

"What's this all about?" Emily couldn't understand the reason for the questions. "What's my husband supposed to have done?"

"I never said he'd done nothing."

"Why are you asking about him, then?"

He looked at her sadly. "I'm nae used to this, you ken." He had lost his official way of speaking. "In a' my twenty year in the force, I've never had to deal wi' naething like this."

Slightly irritated now, Emily snapped, "Like what?"

He shook his head wearily. "Would it bother you if I sat doon?" At her sign, he plumped down on one of the old kitchen chairs and laid his peaked hat on the table. "I never thocht I'd ha'e to . . . solve a murder!" He sat back, plainly enjoying her astonishment at the bombshell he had dropped.

"A m . . . murder? But nobody ever gets murdered round here."

"Somebody has, though," he said, with quiet satisfaction. "Somebody definitely has."

"But you surely don't think my Jake had anything to do with it?"

"I'm nae sayin' that." He took a handkerchief out of his breast pocket and wiped his brow. "My God, I dinna like this for a job."

"Can you tell me anything about the m . . . murder? I'd really like to know, for I can't believe . . ."

"It's true, though, as sure as I'm sitting in this chair. I was tell't — oh, it must've been aboot half seven last night."

"Who phoned you? Are you sure it wasn't somebody playing a trick?"

"It wasna a phone call. Me an' Johnny McIntyre was in the Tufted Duck — we aye ha'e a drink an' mebbe a game o' darts, ilka Sa'urday — an' he says, 'I some think you've a murder on yer hands, Jeemsie.' " As an afterthought, he added, by way of an explanation, "Me an' him was at the school thegither."

94

"So we'll take it that this wasn't a joke, then? But what did he say, exactly?"

"He said he was gan hame fae furrin' up his tatties, that's the park next the neeps, an' he noticed this great big puddle o' bleed. He ken't he'd be seein' me in an oor or so, so he didna think it was worth phonin'."

"But where was this puddle of blood?" Emily persisted. "And why come bothering me?"

"It wasna you I was wantin' to bother, though. It was Jake."

"I still can't understand. Why Jake?"

"Well, it's like this. The bleed was on the track comin' up here."

Emily's anxious face cleared. "Now, I see. Well, I can explain that. My Willie hit a stone with his bike when he was coming home from the village on Friday afternoon and was thrown off. It'd been his blood Johnny McIntyre had seen on Saturday."

The policeman looked a little happier now, too. "That's good news, Mrs Fowlie. Oh, I dinna mean good news aboot your Willie . . . Is that why he's in the hospital?"

"Yes, he hurt his foot pretty badly."

"I'm sorry to hear that. Now, just to get my case done and dusted, as you might say, where did young Willie say he had his accident?"

"He said he was very nearly at the top. Just about home."

Jeemsie Cooper's lined brows had plummeted. "Oh, now! That pits a new look till it. Johnny says it was right aside the gate into his neep park. A good bit further doon than your Willie was hurt."

They looked at each helplessly for a few seconds, and then he said, "I did think the loon must've lost an affa lot o' bleed when you said he'd just fell aff his bike. There's still a real big puddle, you see."

"So you think somebody's definitely been killed?"

"I'm certain sure somebody's definitely been killed." He eyed her sadly and then said, "I'm sorry, Missus, but I'll need to speak to Jake. Can you tell me where I could find him?"

"He said he was just going to check the beasts were all right. He shouldn't be long, for he's going to the kirk, and I'll be going out in a wee while, for Mr McIntyre's coming to take me to the hospital to see Willie."

"That's all right, lass, I'll go an' meet Jake, and I'm sure he'll ken naething aboot this business. Off you go now, and tell the bairn I hope he'll soon be fit again."

It was only the second time that Emily had been in a motor car, but even the luxury of the dark green padded seats and the novelty of the walnut dashboard with its dainty clock and hidden ashtrays did not really register with her. All she was interested in was to hear the farmer's account of what he had seen, but his version differed in no way from that of the constable.

"I've seen plenty bleed in my time," he said, "havin' killed as many beasts as I've lost coont, but I've never seen as much outside o' the shed we use for a killin'

96

hoose. An' it fair gi'ed me a queer feelin' in my bel . . . I'm sorry, my stomach."

Emily could understand that, for wasn't she feeling the same at that very moment? It was awful to think that a murderer had been so near her home, and even worse to think that he might have been lurking somewhere on the track when Willie had been coming up it on Friday. It made her blood run cold. Needing reassurance, she said, "D'you think the bobby'll be able to catch the killer on his own?"

"Jeemsie Cooper?" Johnny roared with laughter. "He couldna catch a cauld even if he stood bare naked in a howlin' gale."

In spite of her fears, Emily couldn't help a little giggle. "You've known him a long time, of course."

"Since we were little bairns, and he's aye been slow in pickin' things up like his brain was clogged up wi' dust through nae bein' used much. God kens how he ever got into the police force."

"He must have hidden reserves," she suggested, smiling.

"They'll need to send in the big boys, though. Aberdeen, likely. They've mair experience for there's aye somebody getting murdered there. They'll soon find the bu . . ." He stopped the swearword coming out and went on, "They'll get the blighter and string him up."

Shivering, Emily considered that this man must be a bit vicious himself, but in the next minute he was making general conversation and showing so much humour that she realised that he'd been joking before — with perhaps a thread of seriousness. He left her at the hospital, where she found Willie relishing his status as a patient, and as the only person there at the time under sixty, being thoroughly spoiled.

She asked him first about how he was feeling, what the doctors said about his foot, and was suitably impressed when he said, "They put a stookie on my leg, fae my taes richt up to abeen my knee, so I couldna bend it even if I was allowed up."

"Are you in much pain?" she asked, guessing that he wouldn't be so chirpy if he were.

"Just now an' again, but it's fine in here. I just need to ask for something an' a nurse gets it for me. I think I'll get hame next week, but I'll ha'e to bide aff the school for a puckle weeks."

"That'll not worry you much," she smiled, although it did cross her mind that having him at home, incapacitated, for so long would be all the more work for her.

"It'll be great," he boasted.

"You needn't expect me to run after you like all the nurses do here, though."

She suddenly remembered that she had something to tell him, something that should arouse his curiosity and stop him thinking of himself so much. "I had the bobby up seeing me this morning."

Her son's face straightened, apprehension appeared in his eyes. "I havena been doin' naething bad, Mam."

"No, it wasn't about you. It was your Dad he asked to see, but it's nothing to do with him, either. Um, did you see any strangers, men, hanging about on our track on Friday afternoon — the day you fell off your bike?"

"I didna see naebody, Mam."

"I just wondered, because it seems . . . oh, I can't really believe it, but it seems somebody was murdered, on our track, but likely it was on Friday night, or early Saturday."

"Did you say murdered?"

"Aye, that I did. I just can't fathom . . ."

"Who was murdered? Have they found the body?"

"No, they haven't, so they don't know who it is, but Johnny McIntyre says they'll likely send detectives from Aberdeen, so they'll not be long in solving this." Willie fell silent, and didn't appear to be interested in anything else she told him; about Becky's trips to the city, about Connie's romance, plus all the gossip that had come her way.

She left when her allotted hour was almost up, but the matron beckoned to her as she went out of the ward. "I wanted to congratulate you, Mrs Fowlie, on your son. He's such a well-behaved boy, a proper angel, and always very polite. All the nurses are simply besotted by his darling curls and dark brown eyes and flashing smile. You must be very proud of him."

On the point of telling her the plain unvarnished truth about the proper angel, his mother decided not to end his reign of glory. It would stop as soon as he was discharged from here. "He says he should be coming home next week sometime?"

"Yes, hopefully on Wednesday, and we shall all miss him. He's been a ray of sunshine in our ward."

"Thank you for looking after him so well," Emily said, sorely tempted to disillusion this stately woman about the ray of sunshine, but she turned and walked away. The farmer was only about three minutes in turning up, and she was on her way home, answering his questions about her son and making him laugh about Willie's transformation into an angel. For the most part of their journey, however, they discussed the murder, wondering who the victim could be. Had either of them ever heard of any local person being missing? Had any strangers been seen in the area?

Willie didn't know what to think. There couldn't have been a murder? Not on their track? In any case, how did they know about it? His mother hadn't told him that. Maybe she hadn't wanted to scare him. She said no body had been found, so there must have been something else. His heart almost stopped as it occurred to him what that something could be. The blood? It must have been the blood! He hadn't gone back to look at it, but the Daftie had put quite a lot in the pail. Yes, the boy decided, it must have been the pig's blood, and the bobby or whoever had told him hadn't known the difference. That was a relief, anyway. Nobody knew the truth except the old man, and he was that dottled he likely wouldn't remember if anybody asked him. Malcie knew, as well, of course, but he wouldn't tell.

Yet, no matter how hard he tried to assure himself of that, there still remained a modicum of doubt. For all other lies — little, white lies, mostly — that he'd told, something always tripped him up. Somebody said something, or something happened, that proved him a liar. He'd usually been punished, but not very severely.

100

This, though, this wasn't a white lie. It was a whopping great lie, for hadn't he hidden evidence as well as giving a wrong description of the place the accident happened? It likely wouldn't be one of his parents dishing out the punishment, either. It would be the Law. The Long Arm of the Law, it was called.

He would have to confess. He should confess. The thing was, had he the courage to confess? He knew he hadn't. He would have to hope that he was never found out. He hadn't caused an awful stir, really. Just one local bobby asking questions. It would all blow past. Of course it would. The 'tecs from Aberdeen wouldn't investigate a few traces of blood that had likely vanished by now, anyway. When suppertime came, he wasn't able to eat anything. The youngest nurse, Nannie her name was, did her best to coax him to take a few spoonfuls, but had to report back to Matron that he was off his food.

Jake Fowlie was puzzled. He had sworn to Jeemsie Cooper that he knew nothing about the blood on the track, but the two Aberdeen detectives who arrived on Monday morning did not believe him. They had questioned and questioned, twisting what he said until it sounded like he wasn't telling the truth. Eventually, he had gone on the defensive, as if he were really guilty, which made things even worse.

After they left, Emily told him that she had overhead the older one saying, "We'd best get reinforcements to comb the area. We can't do anything till we find the body."

That had provided him with, at the very most, only a paper-thin veneer of hope. Jeemsie Cooper's one-track mind had thought that blood on the track meant blood on the hands of the tenant of the first house he came to — in other words he'd put two and two together and made five — but thank the Lord, the two 'tecs had the sense to see further than that.

"You ken, Emmy," Jake observed to his wife that night, "I hope they find a body, for then they'll surely see I'd naething to dae wi' it."

Because his temperature had remained high, Willie wasn't allowed home on Wednesday, and the nurses, including Matron, were really anxious about this unexplained relapse. Willie himself was living through a vile nightmare in which he could picture dozens of policemen marching into the ward, placing him in handcuffs and carrying their prisoner out triumphantly. The cruel thing was, apart from a tiny untruth about how he had lost the egg money and hiding the fact that he'd lost nearly a pail of pig's blood that his mother would have been delighted to get, he had done nothing wrong. Surely that wouldn't count against him on the Day of Judgement that his Gramma McKay often spoke about? The angel that watched over the Gates of Heaven would surely make allowances for him being so young. They couldn't not take him in . . . and send him to hell?

Then further news filtered through the grapevine of the little community, which, spread out though it was, was actually quite tightly knit together. The first to hear was Jeemsie Cooper, whose chest swelled with pride. "I ken't fine there was something," he crowed in the public bar of the Tufted Duck. "And it's stained wi' bleed. Nae jist a wee drappie, a spirk or twa, but like it was soaked in it. Aye that's the murder weapon, right enough."

He was the centre of the group of men all keen to know more. This was the first real proof, wasn't it? Nobody had really believed Jeemsie before. He liked making mountains out of molehills in his attempts to show how important he was to the force. It wasn't an empty boast this time.

The news was passed round, spreading like wildfire — or "Like the clap on the docks in Aiberdeen," as Frankie Berry, the barman, put it. In the gales of mirth that followed this, the local bobby graciously accepted all the drinks that were being laid out for him.

As is generally the case, the person on whom the news would make most impression was the last to hear, and so it was with Jake Fowlie. It was the following morning that Jeemsie came up in person to tell him. "The fork o' an aul' bike," the policeman beamed. "I bet you'd never've thocht on that."

"No," Jake agreed, "that's true enough."

"Jist covered wi' bleed."

"So you're sure that's what it was used for?"

"Dead sure. It's been sent to the toon for examination, to be sure it's human bleed, or else I'd have let you see for yoursel'."

"An' it was close by the scene o' the crime?"

"Weel . . . no," Jeemsie said, a touch doubtfully. "It was up a good bit, in the moorie, nearer your hoose."

Even this was expanded upon during the course of the day, when the various other parts of the discarded bicycle were turned up by the searchers. Around five o'clock that night, Jake was summoned by Detective Sergeant Bruce to come and inspect the finds.

"We want to know if you can identify anything," the officer told him.

Shaken to the marrow when he looked down on the pieces of rusty metal, buckled but still recognisable, Jake said quietly. "It's a bike my son and his chum cobbled thegether from bits they found on dumps."

Excitement stirred through the uniformed men. The case was getting somewhere at last.

"Your son being . . . how old?"

"Ten, but he's been in the hospital for a while. He's naething to dae wi' the murder."

"But Mr Fowlie, you say these items belong to him?"

"Aye, that's what I said."

"They're covered with blood. How do you explain that?"

Jake felt trapped, although he was sure that he had no reason to be. He couldn't understand, any more than the sergeant, how there could have been so much blood. Granted, Willie had fallen on rough ground, he'd had a lot of scratches and scrapes, but nothing to cause bleeding like this. "I couldna tell you that."

"I'm afraid we'll have to speak to the boy himself, then. Is he fit to be interviewed?"

"To be honest," Jake stated firmly, "he's nae that great. Mrs McIntyre of Wester Burnton phones the hospital every day to find oot how he is, and lets us ken what they say. He's had a high fever for a puckle days noo, an' there's nae change the day."

"He'll be able to speak to us, though."

"Can I come wi' you?" Jake pleaded, sorely afraid for his son although he was convinced that Willie had absolutely nothing to do with the murder.

The DS smiled. "I don't see why not."

They both turned as Jeemsie Cooper came puffing up holding a mangled old pail as if it were the crown jewels. "Look at this, sir. They found it among the nettles ower there." He gestured with his free hand. "It's covered wi' bleed, an' all."

"Give it here," snapped the sergeant, inspecting the item then pronouncing, "It's had bleed . . . blood in it, that's for sure. This is no ordinary murder."

"You think it was a . . . vampire?" exclaimed Jeemsie, eyes agog with tense excitement. "Killin' fowk an' drinking their . . ."

"No, you bloody fool." DS Bruce turned back to Jake again. "It's a mystery, though, so I suppose we'll need to investigate it." Signalling to two of his men, he ordered them to go round all the cottages, crofts and farms within a five-mile radius to ask if anyone would recognise the pail.

"Nobody's going to lay claim to that," one of the men protested. "It's only fit to be thrown out."

"I suppose you wouldn't know if this was something else your son picked up in a dump?" Bruce asked Jake.

"I ken naething aboot it, but he could easy have picked it up, I suppose."

"Then the sooner we see him the better. Can you come with us right now?"

The Matron almost had apoplexy when the police officer insisted on seeing her prize patient, but the man brushed aside all her protestations and walked straight past her. Beaten, she following them into the ward, hurrying past them to alert Willie that he had visitors — one of them most unwelcome.

The boy blanched and cowered down under the blankets, but Bruce barked, "Sit up, boy. I think you could shed some light on the murder case."

The Matron helped the child into a sitting position, but warned, "I shall stop you if I see he is being upset by your questioning."

The interrogation had not gone beyond the initial stage of name, age, why Willie had gone round the dumps et cetera when the ward door swung open noisily to admit the two men who had been looking for someone to identify the battered bucket. They both had massive grins over their faces. "The case is solved, Sarge," one of them laughed.

Scowling at their hilarity, Bruce said, severely, "This is a hospital. You might show some consideration. What are you trying to tell me?"

"We'd gone round about five cottar houses before we went to Wester Burnton itself, and the maid-servant took us into the kitchen where the farmer's wife was bandaging one of the workers' hands — an old man."

"And?" rapped the sergeant. "Don't make a meal of this, Black. I'm not in the humour for it."

106

"Well, to cut the story short, when I asked Mrs McIntyre about the pail, it was the old fella that screamed out, 'That's oor bucket.' It seems he gave it to young Willie Fowlie with some pig's blood for his mother. She makes black puddings with it."

Jake took over, angry at his son for not mentioning it. "So you ken't the bleed was just a pig's! You could've tell't your Mam an' me, an' saved the bobbies a lot o' work."

"I was fear't to tell, Dad. I thocht you'd leather me for losin' Mam's egg money among the nettles, an' my fit was hurtin' bad, an' . . ." He broke off as two huge teardrops spilled over and made their way down his fevered cheeks.

Matron now decided it was time she stepped in. "That will be enough. You can see how upset the child is."

Bruce heaved a sigh of impatience, or relief or anger, it was difficult for any of the others to tell, but he led the way out, remembering to thank the Matron for letting them speak to Willie. "I wish he had let the truth be known before, though. We have wasted a lot of time. In any case, now that he has got it off his chest, perhaps his fever will come down."

Which, indeed, it did. His conscience clear, Willie soon got back to normal and was allowed home the following day. Perhaps, however, a curtain should be drawn over the reception he received from his parents. His mother in particular was so disappointed in him, and angry at the deception he had carried out, that she exuded an injured air towards him, reverting, after several weeks, to their previous less-than-loving relationship.

CHAPTER
TEN

It may be anticipated that life in the Fowlie household would return to normal, even better than normal, since Willie would surely have learned a lesson from the consequences of his last escapade, but each member had his or her own reaction to what had happened.

Jake, as master of his house, felt quite rattled that he'd had no control over events, or of the opinions held by the police. Worse than that, it had hurt him badly when he learned that his son had been frightened to tell him the truth. "I thocht me an' him was chums," he lamented to Emily, "but it turned oot different."

His wife shook her head sadly. "Nobody will ever know what goes on in that boy's brain." She had lost all sympathy for her son, and she, too, was hurt that he'd been scared to admit what he had done. Their mother was the first person most boys would turn to in time of trouble, but then, she had to acknowledge, Willie wasn't most boys. Willie was a law unto himself. Or, as she had often suspected, he was spawn of the devil.

Connie, with her own worries at the time, had at first been jealous of the love and attention generated round her little brother and had tried to get affection from another source. She had been devastated by the result.

"Gordie," she had said to her escort one night, "we've been going out for a long time now, and I think . . ."

"What d'you think?" he interrupted, rudely.

"If you'd let me finish, I'd tell you," she said, miffed that he couldn't guess what she wanted to say without her having to spell it out.

His attitude changing, he squeezed her waist. "I'm sorry, Con."

"Well, I think it's been long enough." She held her head back so that she could see his reaction.

"Long enough?" His nose was screwed up in puzzlement, his brows were down. "What d'you mean?"

"I mean . . ." She hesitated before taking the bull by the horns. "I mean it's about time we tied the knot, wouldn't you say?"

This patently came as a devastating shock to the young man, whose lust-flushed face had turned a ghastly greyish-white. "You're surely not expecting me to wed you?"

"It's usual, when two people are in love." Her voice was cold. "But if you don't love me, you'd better . . ."

"I do love you, Connie. Surely you know that?"

"I know you want to bed me."

He seemed to pull his senses together now. "Of course I want to bed you. That's all I've ever wanted. I'm not a marrying man, and what you've been denying me all this time, I've been getting some other where. You can't blame me for that, Connie. You surely know a man needs a woman."

Contemplating telling him to go to hell with his other women, Connie decided not to risk the only chance she might ever have of being a wife. "Gordie," she coaxed softly, "If I let you do what you want, would you promise to marry me?"

He avoided answering this. "I've aye wondered if you loved me enough, but if you prove it, I'll be true to you. Oh God, Connie, I was just about ready to give up on you." This last being what she had been afraid of, Connie shoved her scruples behind her and let the insinuating hand reach the target it had been aiming for every time they'd been out together over the years. What did principles matter when it came to giving in or being left on the shelf?

It was two months later before Willie returned to school plus crutches, becoming the focus of much curiosity from the other boys regarding his "run in" with the police. The girls were more eager to know the extent of his injuries and how they had been received. Poopie-Cecil Grant felt rather left out of things, and mentally blamed Willie for not telling him everything before. If he had only known that his old chum was under his mother's eagle eye every minute of the day, perhaps he would have had more sympathy for him.

But the enforced extra holiday — most enjoyable at times but, at other times, almost like being on the edge of a volcano's crater waiting for it to erupt — was over and it was back to the old routine, back to the learning he detested. He'd have to work very hard to try to catch up with his fellow pupils, for he didn't fancy being kept back a class.

There had also been one big change. Mr Bremner, the old dominie, had suffered a heart attack and retired, much to the children's relief. He had been a great believer in the old maxim "Spare the rod and spoil the child", although it was a thick, tongued, leather tawse that he substituted for a cane. The new headmaster, Mr Meldrum, was a much younger, more pleasant man, who had been a member of the Flying Corps during the war, and who described some of his exploits in the air during the morning assemblies he had introduced; a big improvement on the long-winded, heavily boring sermons they had been given before.

This was not the only change, however. Mr Meldrum had a daughter, whose age placed her in the same class as Willie came back to, and she was the most beautiful girl he had ever set eyes on. Her long curly hair was darker than gold, lighter than auburn, more of a delicate pastel chestnut. Her eyes were dark, sometimes greenish, sometimes brown, framed by curled eyelashes that made them seem huge. Her nose was bordering on the snub, her mouth was a generously shaped cupid's bow, her lips somewhere between deep pink and light red. His first sight of her took Willie's breath away. He'd never had any time for girls except to torment them, but this one was nothing like the rest. Not only was she lovely to look at, she was also very clever — far ahead of any of the others in the class — plus, her name was Millicent, which was a welcome change from the Bellas, the Jeannies, the Mary Annies.

A strange wish took hold of Willie that very first day. Instead of being content to be near the foot of the class, he would get Millicent's attention by using his brain to its fullest. He could improve in his tests — even old Bremner had said he was capable of that.

As it happened, with Poopie-Cecil now in the Big School — he hadn't passed for the Academy — Willie had nobody to take his mind off whatever it was set on. He was unable to do much physical exercise for a while yet, so he used all his time to teach himself what he should have learned in his last class with Miss Bell. Mr Meldrum, of course, did not know what to expect of him, and took his progress as normal.

"Willie's surely taken a fit of conscience," Connie observed to her mother one evening, when her brother was up in his not-much-bigger-than-a-box room working quietly when he used to be rushing about all over the place and making as much noise as he possibly could.

Emily had at first suspected her son to be bent on some mischief when he was shut up there for such long periods, but several checks had found him engrossed in his school books from the last term. She had crept down again, hardly able to believe her eyes. "He's getting older," she answered her daughter now. "Maybe he's seeing sense at last."

"It'll not last long, then."

"Are you going out with Gordon Brodie again tonight, Connie?"

"Mam, don't go on about him. He does love me, I can guarantee that, and it'll not be long before he pops the question. In fact, I thought I might take him to see Becky and Jackie, to see if that'll gee him up."

"Are you sure you . . . I know I've asked you a few times, but . . ."

"Mam, the thing is, can you see any other men wanting to ask me out?"

"That's no reason to tie yourself to a man you don't love."

"I never said I didn't love him, and I'm old enough to decide what I want to do with my life."

"All right, all right. Don't fly off the handle."

Even after visiting Becky and Jackie Burns, and after admiring the house and garden, Gordon Brodie was not over-enthusiastic about marriage. "I can't help it, Con," he said, waiting until after he'd had his allowance of love-making, "I just can't see myself tied down with a wife, and the very thought of a bairn . . ." He gave a long sigh. "With my luck, it'd likely be a great squatter of bairns."

More than a little alarmed by his outlook, Connie considered ending their relationship there and then. She didn't want a husband who would resent his children, but, on the other hand, she did want a husband of some kind, and Gordie was the only available prospect. The only answer was to hope that he made her pregnant; then he would have to wed her.

Willie could not get Millicent Meldrum out of his mind. Playing football in the school yard, he spurred himself on if she was watching; he was the first with his hand up to answer her father's questions in the classroom; his day and night dreams were of her, of being alone with her, of taking her hand, carrying her satchel, of . . . kissing her. He used to shudder at the thought of kissing any girl, however old he would be, but now, just eleven years old, he would give a king's ransom to kiss Millie, as she was usually called.

He could sense her awareness of him sometimes, when he had done especially well in writing a composition, or solved a difficult mathematical problem. Her father, the dominie, was likewise appreciative of his efforts, although Willie himself didn't know that the other two teachers had expressed, in the staff room, their astonishment at the progress William Fowlie was making, whereas they had got nowhere with him at all.

So the term wore on, Willie making the initial advance one afternoon by offering to accompany Millie home as it was on his way. This led to vicious teasing from the other boys, who started to shout, "Millie and Willie, they're both really silly." One wag then started to repeat a jingle his mother had repeated once or twice to him, something that she'd heard when she was at school herself, strangely enough.

He couldn't remember all of it, but it ended, ". . . the silly scent Willie sent Millicent." This was taken up by all the boys in the Qualifying Class, as it was called, the qualification being the entry to the Academy.

Not one whit annoyed by this, Willie would take hold of the girl's hand and say, in his lately acquired perfect English, "Don't heed them, Millie, they're just big babies." Getting no response, the tormentors soon gave up, and the young pair were left to walk in peace, discussing the things that held their interest, things they hated, things they wanted to do when they grew up, but never doing what he wanted to do. He couldn't pluck up the courage to kiss her, or even to ask if he could kiss her.

Emily could not understand why Willie had changed so suddenly. It had started just after he returned to school, so could it be that the new dominie had got through to the little demon? That was the only explanation she could think of, and it didn't seem very likely to her. She wasn't complaining, though. At least she didn't have to be constantly on the boy's top for misbehaving.

The surprise came about seven weeks before the summer holidays were due. She answered a knock on the door late one afternoon to find a tall man on the doorstep. Clean-shaven, wearing a neat navy suit with a felt hat jauntily on the side of his head, his bright blue eyes twinkled at her. "Mrs Fowlie?"

"Yes?"

"I'm Herbert Meldrum . . ."

"The dominie?" she gasped, overwhelmed by the honour.

"That's right. May I come in? I have something to talk over with you."

"Oh, sorry, I should have thought. Yes, please come in. I hope Willie hasn't been up to his old mischief?"

"Old mischief? Indeed no, he is a model pupil."

Unable to believe her ears, and flustered to be talking to such a personage in her own home, she tried to smile. "If you're here to tell me he doesn't pay attention to his lessons, I know what like he is."

"No, it's not that, either. Just the opposite, in fact. Please let me explain. He is top of his class at the moment, a place fought over between him and my daughter, and he should find entry to the Academy a walk-over. As far as I am concerned, I am in the fortunate position of being able to meet any expenses which may occur for my daughter, but I wanted to find out how you and your goodman are placed."

"Well, sir, Jake's just a farm labourer, working hard to make a living. We'd never be able to send Willie to the Academy."

"Yes, that is what I expected, but I feel it would be a terrible mistake to waste such a brain . . ." He held up his hand to stop her interrupting. "There is a way round this, Mrs Fowlie. Bursaries are available for children in this situation. There is an examination to pass, of course, but William is more than capable of that. The money involved doesn't amount to much, but it is meant to help parents to provide whatever is needed for the Academy, uniform and books, for example. This is not a charity," he hastened to make it clear. "William will have earned it. Now, shall I leave you to discuss it with your husband?"

"Yes, please. I'd rather Jake heard about it."

"Of course. I shall leave this form with you, if you will return it to me as soon as you decide what to do. If you agree, both your signatures are needed, and I can fill in the other information requested and send it off."

He lifted his hat from the table and set it on his grizzled hair. "Thank you for hearing me out, Mrs Fowlie, and please stress to your husband that the boy's talents must be recognised. Good day to you."

Emily plumped down in her chair when she had seen him out. This was something she had never expected — never in her wildest dreams. Willie had always been such a lackadaisical scholar. In fact it would have taken an exaggeration of the mightiest form to even describe him as a scholar at all with his offhand attitude. What could have happened to change him?

At suppertime, when Jake was told about the momentous decision they had to make, he was as flabbergasted as she was. "But the man must be muddling Willie up wi' somebody else," he declared, shaking his balding head. "He was bottom o' his class as often as no', an' bairns dinna . . ." He stopped to think of the word he wanted, but it was Connie who supplied it.

"Metamorphose, Dad. It means change into something better."

"Aye, that's what I meant. Bairns dinna metafose like that."

"It must be Mr Meldrum that made Willie change for the better, Jake. He must be a better teacher than the last dominie."

"That's why they made him a dominie," Connie laughed. "Just sign that form and send it back. If there's been a mistake, Willie'll not pass the exam and that'll be the finish of it. Now dish up the supper, 'cos I'm meeting Gordie at half seven, and I need to wash and dress."

"Tell Willie to come down for his supper," Emily told her. She addressed her husband again. "So will we just sign this form? I want to know before Willie comes down."

"What d'you think?" he hedged.

"I think we should. Like the dominie said, it would be a shame to waste a good brain. But we'd better not tell him yet."

"Good idea."

It was only two weeks later, however, that their son was to learn the news for himself. He and Millie were walking home, slowly so that they could talk, when she said, "I'm quite excited about going to the Academy after the holidays."

Willie's heart plunged to somewhere just above his feet. They had not long got to know each other and they were going to be separated, but he couldn't let her know how he felt. It was his own fault for not paying attention to his schooling before. Now he thought about it, though, he wouldn't have been going there anyway. His father wouldn't be able to afford it. Connie had been quite clever, according to what he'd heard, and she'd never got the chance. "You'll do well there, Millie," he murmured, trying to sound as cheery as he could.

"So'll you," she laughed.

"But I won't be going."

"Of course you're going. Father's got back the reply to the forms he sent in. Four of us in our class have been accepted for entry in August. I don't have to sit the test for a grant, but the rest of you have."

"No, Millie, my dad can't afford to send me."

"Well, the grant — no, it's called a bursary — would help to pay for so much, and I'm telling you you'll be going, but you can ask my dad if you don't believe me." She flounced up her garden path, leaving the forlorn Willie standing alone.

When he got home, he went up to his room as usual to do his home lessons, but couldn't concentrate for thinking over what Millie had said. She couldn't know anything about how poor farm workers were, when her father must be making about ten times what his dad got for much harder work. She got everything she wanted, while he had to be content with what was handed to him. It would be truly wonderful if what she said was true, though. He'd be able to go with her on the bus, and they'd come back together. They would grow up together, for they'd have to stay on until they were about seventeen or eighteen.

He grinned at this prospect. Fancy him wanting to stay on at school until he was seventeen or eighteen. At one time, he'd been horrified to think he couldn't leave until he was fourteen. It just showed you. The coming of one new girl to the area had changed his whole life. He was really too young to think of love, but he knew deep down that Millie was the only one for him.

"Supper!" His mother's voice brought him out of his romantic reverie, and he jumped up to obey the summons. When they were all four seated at the table, Emily took an envelope out of her pocket. "Jake, I want you to read that till I dish up."

Willie did notice that she looked brighter than usual, no sign of the scrubbing and cooking and washing and ironing she had likely been doing all day, but he put it down to the weather. It had been the first really sunny, warm day for ages.

Looking up after a few minutes — for he was a slow reader — Jake said, "Well, will I tell him or you?"

Willie shifted his spoon a fraction. "If it's about me going to the Academy, I know I can't go."

"Ah, my lad, but that's where you're wrong," his father grinned.

"But you can't afford . . . Connie couldn't go, nor Becky."

"Things have changed since that time," Emily smiled. "Mr Meldrum said you would just need to pass a test and you'd be in. And that's a letter of —" She lifted it to make sure of the word. "A letter of confirmation. You're accepted on condition that you pass this test. Mr Meldrum says there's three of you having to try, so he'll drive you to the Education Office in Aberdeen — that's the County Office — and bring you back when you're finished, in about an hour. He's a real gentleman."

The information overwhelmed the boy, tears welling up in his eyes at the thought of such generosity, and his sister gave him a dig in the ribs. "I don't suppose it's anything unusual. Mr Meldrum'll likely get judged on how many passes he gets."

120

"No," Jake said, trying to be fair and not wanting his son's good fortune to be belittled. "That man's got all his pupils' welfare at heart, and he has to make sure the brighter ones get a good chance in life."

On the day of the test, a Saturday so as not to take them off school, the three boys were taken to Aberdeen, sat their test and given a good lunch before their headmaster drove them home again. The boys thoroughly enjoyed their meal, having been too apprehensive to eat any breakfast, something which their headmaster had foreseen.

The holidays started at the end of June, the results of the test were not made known until the end of July, so the three hopefuls had four weeks to wait. If Willie had had Millie to speak to, he would have felt much better, but the Meldrum family had gone to France for the whole seven weeks, and would not be home until a few days before schools started again. His appetite suffered and Emily could not understand why he wasn't excited about the adventure that lay ahead for him. Thankfully, the test result was favourable and the other three weeks dragged past, although several postcards for Willie came from France, so he knew he wasn't forgotten.

Willie had stopped being the focus of attention in his own house on the day Connie announced that she and Gordon Brodie were going to be wed. Jake was pleased for her, but worried about the expense. Emily was less than enthusiastic, guessing at first that it was desperation not love that had made her accept this man, but the hastening on of the wedding made her suspect that it was even worse than that.

Gordie put up no pretence. He made it widely known that it was only the expected but unwanted child that was making him take this step and, although Jake would willingly have thrashed him within an inch of his life and then thrown him out, Emily held him back.

"We can't have him going around telling folk you've attacked him. No, Jake, we'll just have to put up with it and pray he doesn't treat our Connie badly. At least he's doing the right thing and giving the child his name."

She didn't altogether convince her husband that violence would do no good; a dozen times a day she could hear him muttering, "I shoulda kicked the bugger's erse, that's what I shoulda done."

Sometimes wondering if they should have forbidden the wedding, she had to remind herself that Connie was well into her twenties and could, by law, do as she pleased, though what pleasure she would get from being wed on that lump of — she hated even to think the word, but "shite" was the only way to describe him. It wouldn't be love that her daughter would get from him, it would be endless heartache, for it was well known that he had other girls.

Willie was too wrapped up in his own blossoming "friendship" with Millie to notice what was going on. He did wonder why Connie wasn't having a nice wedding like Becky's, but she had always been different, and if a registry wedding was what she wanted, it was really nobody's business. His own life was very comfortable, thank you. It couldn't be much better, really, for Mr Meldrum only drove them to the Academy and they had to take the bus back, which meant, of course, quite a walk from the turnpike. They had progressed from going hand in hand to arms round waists, which was very satisfying, yet sometimes just lately he had felt the need of something more than that — what exactly, he didn't know. A few kisses, maybe? But they were too young to be kissing.

The lessons they were getting at school were much harder than in the school at Burnton, but so far he was coping. He and Millie weren't in the same class, worse luck, as boys and girls were kept separate, and he missed the excitement of competing with her in a friendly way, but they had got into the habit of discussing the homework they had been given.

As the months passed, Willie had a spurt of growing, and before she knew it, Emily saw that he was taller than his father. Taller and fitter. He had a healthy tan from walking so much, his cheeks were rosy. He still had a little tuft of hair at the back that refused to lie down, but that didn't detract from his appearance. She surprised Jake, one evening, by saying, "I can't get over how grown-up Willie is now. He's quite the young man."

Watching the steam rise from his socks as he held his feet out to the fire, Jake nodded. "Aye, he's big enough now to dae the diggin' for me here, an' some o' the other hard jobs, as weel."

"I was thinking he could chop sticks for me and do some other little jobs."

"It's time he was workin' for his keep. I'd to work for my Da fae when I was aul' enough to lift a spade."

The youth himself was not enamoured of these ideas when they were presented to him. "I've got hours of home lessons, Mam." Recognising the displeasure on both his parents' faces, he added, "I'll do what I can, then, and full time in the school holidays. Will that be enough?"

Sighing, Jake laid down his empty teacup. "We'll see how it goes, but me an' your Mam's nae gettin' ony younger, you ken, an' I need to be fit enough to work for McIntyre or I'll get the sack. I aye hoped you'd tak' ower the keeping o' this place, that's why I wasna keen on you startin' the Academy. You dinna need to ken the geography o' the world for that; nor workin' oot great lang sums. An' what good's Latin gan to be to you? Now, if they was learnin' you how to plough a straight furrow that would be . . ."

"No, Jake," his wife broke in, gathering up the dirty dishes. "Learning's never a waste. It's surprising the kind of things that could come in handy."

Feeling a rush of shame at the memory of his old school chums, who'd all had to help their fathers since they were fairly young, Willie said, "I'll do as much as I can, I promise. I'd have left the school if I could, but seeing I've got the bursary, we'd have to pay back what we've already got."

Thus it was that Willie found little time to dream from then on, and was forced by his conscience to go straight home every afternoon. "I hardly get a proper chance to speak to you," Millie complained one day as they said goodbye at her gate. "I miss our wee chats, you know." Hesitating, she looked at him in a way that made his heart speed up. "I miss you, Willie."

"And I miss you, Millie."

Despite their sadness, they both smiled at the Willie/Millie rhyming, then the girl whispered, "We're meant for each other, Willie, so don't go looking for anyone else." With a quick movement, she kissed him on the cheek, turned and ran into the house. Thunderstruck, Willie kept standing, wishing that he could return the kiss; wishing that he would never have to wash his face again; wishing that he didn't have to go home. But he had made a promise.

It was difficult fitting in everything that he was expected to do, and his teachers began to take notice of the difference in his homework. "Did you do this exercise before rushing out with your friends?" the Latin master asked one forenoon.

"No, sir, I never have time to go out with any friends."

Because every teacher dished out work for their pupils to carry out at home, it often meant Willie sitting well into the night, but he did not want to admit that he had his chores for both parents to do first. And so the time flew past.

Although Connie had persuaded Gordon Brodie to marry her because she was expecting, she was still terrified about it, even now. She'd been disgusted at the way Gordie had treated her since the very day they were wed. All the old wives' tales about men being like beasts in the bed hadn't been strong enough. Her husband had practically torn her apart on their wedding night, making her bleed copiously although they had done the deed many times before it was legal.

"That's what happens," he had snarled. "What did you expect?" Then he'd just fallen asleep, one leg still lying heavily over both of hers.

It had taken her some time to extricate herself from the shackle and creep to the kitchen to clean herself. She had wished that she didn't have to go back to bed, but where else was she to go? In any case, she had married the man and she'd have to put up with him.

She couldn't put it out of her head, though, and had been lying on her back for only about ten minutes when he hoisted himself on top of her again. The act didn't take so long this time, but the result was exactly the same — groom instantly dead to the world, bride pinned down. She had got used to this pattern, of course, although it had been a hundred times worse in the two weeks they lived with her in-laws until their little house was ready, sleeping in the bedroom next door to them.

"Gordie," she'd whispered as the bedsprings started to creak noisily, "what if your Mam and Dad hear us? What'll they say?"

He had rammed into her as hard as he could. "What can they say? It's what every man and wife do. They did the same theirselves — still do, for I've heard them at it."

Looking back on it now, she knew she had been ignorant of life. Her parents must have done it, they had three children as evidence, but surely Dad hadn't been as rough as Gordie. He couldn't have been; he was a different type.

When they had been offered the tiny cottage, isolated from any of the other houses and left vacant when an old woman died, she had hoped that she would feel better, since Gordie would be free to make as much noise as he wanted. He had been getting more and more vicious, however, until she felt, sometimes even wished, that he would accidentally kill her.

Over the last few months, it had got even worse. He started going out every night, with his mates, he said, but she had her doubts. He didn't have the money to go drinking every night, and not come home until after midnight, so drunk he could hardly stand, sometimes. Besides, the Tufted Duck closed at half past nine, so where did he go after that? She was so upset and confused about this, she was forced to confide her fears to her mother on one of her visits.

Emily had given her the opening by remarking anxiously, "Are you sure you're feeling all right, Connie? You're looking real pale. Is Gordie treating you right? I know you're carrying, and I know he hits you for I've seen the bruises. I'm not blind you know. You can't go on like this, Con."

Sighing, the young woman had told her everything, from the agonies of the wedding night, the repeated onslaughts, the abrupt cooling off followed by the nightly absences. "I think he's seeing somebody else, Mam," she ended, her voice unsteady.

"Oh, Connie, my lovie, I was some feared for this. I could tell Gordon Brodie was a man that needed a woman whatever happened. There's a lot of men like that. They go at their wife till they've bairned her, then when the poor lass gets bigger an' bigger, they look for somebody else to pleasure them. I've seen it happen over and over again, and if I'd my way, I'd castrate the lot of them."

Her brows down, Connie said, perplexed by the unfamiliar word, "What does castrate mean?"

Emily shrugged but answered as honestly as she could. "It means they should have their . . . balls cut off."

Her daughter's eyes had shot open in amazement. "Mam! I've never heard you saying that word afore."

"No, and you'll likely never hear me saying it again."

Becky Burns had made up her mind at last. She had been considering it for some time, and was finding life with Jackie more and more tiresome. She knew that her mother would tell her she was lucky to have such a good man, so fond of his home, so loving towards her, but she didn't want a namby-pamby man, she wanted a real he-man, a man like Clark Gable, a man that would rough her up a bit; not too much, though. Not like Gordie Brodie was doing to her sister.

She had been fully aware for some time that her in-laws weren't happy about the kind of woman their son had married. She knew they had been looking forward to having grandchildren but they'd had that! There must be a way out!

She approached Jackie's father first. He was a fair man, and might be only too glad to agree with what she suggested. To her astonishment, her assumption had been spot on, and within two months, she was on her way to America, with a cheque for one thousand pounds in her purse to see her through until she was able to look after herself — on condition that she did not contact Jackie in any way.

"I know this will break his heart," Tom Burns had said, "but he'll get over it, and I'm sure he'll find a better mother for the children he wants."

Her own parents, of course, thought she was mad, exchanging a good, loving husband for the unknown man she was hoping to find in a far-off country, and taking what amounted to a bribe for doing it.

As her father said, "You'll be back within a year, begging poor Jackie to forgive you."

"No, Dad. I need excitement. I need the love of a proper man. I need my freedom."

Emily frowned to let her husband know not to say any more. Becky had always been headstrong, and she would have to learn for herself that you can't always get what you want in life, that you should learn to want what you do get. "So when are you leaving?" This wasn't just one of her chicks flying the nest, both her daughters had done that already, but this one, this flighty younger one, was taking herself to the other side of the world, and they might never see her again.

"Tom Burns has booked my passage, and I sail from Greenock tomorrow."

"Tomorrow?" Emily's hand flew to her heart, but Jake held out his arms to his daughter and she ran to him with a cry. "Oh, Dad, I'm sorry, but I need to prove myself. You must see that."

He kissed her cheek and she moved towards her mother. "Mam?"

The pleading on her face made Emily gasp with emotion, but she hugged the young woman for several moments. "Look after yourself, Becky," she managed to say, "and be sure to write and let us know how you get on."

"I will, Mam, I promise." The noise of a vehicle drawing up at the door made her glance out of the window. "Here's the car Jackie's father said he would send. He's been ever so good." She ran out, and waved airily to them as the Sunbeam Talbot glided away, making very little sound even on the rough stony track.

"It must be nice to have money," Emily commented bitterly, "dishing out a thousand pounds when you feel like it. If we could have done that, d'you think she'd have come back here to live?" Her voice breaking altogether, she slumped down into her chair at the fireside, and Jake's heart was breaking into so many small fragments that he could give her no comfort. All he could think of was that if his daughter hadn't kept the news of the mess she had made of her life until the very last moment, he might have managed to talk her out of this final step.

CHAPTER
ELEVEN

1936

Connie Brodie rose early. Her husband had come home in the early hours of the morning, as drunk as she had ever seen him, and had looked at her as if he couldn't stand the sight of her, a look he had perfected to a T over the few months he'd been a husband.

"Jeez, Con," he'd mumbled, "you're as fat as a bloody pig. It's nae wonder I've had to get a nice bit o' stuff to . . ." He leered at her conspiratorially.

She knew he was waiting for her to row with him which would give him an excuse to hit her, so she kept as calm as she could.

"She was the bees' knees," he persisted, baiting her. "Lovely slim body, but paps as soft as a quilt." He kept eyeing her, waiting for the explosion, but she had learned a lesson from his previous assaults. "You're nae jealous? Damn fine wife you are." Stumbling towards her, he let fly with his fist, almost overbalancing with the effort.

Even knowing that her silence was riling him, she was determined not to give in. Another punch with the same force would have him off his feet altogether, and she would just leave him lying on the floor. Unfortunately, it was a series of punches that he inflicted on her — her face, her chest, her stomach — before he keeled over and she left him lying. Weeping softly, she poured some warm water into the basin and dabbed her battered face and breasts, wishing that she'd had the presence of mind to protect her unborn child with her hands.

When she heard movement behind her, she waited for the next attack, but her lout of a husband didn't even look her way as he staggered outside. Her legs were shaking now with relief. She needed a cup of tea, and then she would go back to bed for a while. Gordie wouldn't likely be back until midnight or later. It took ten agonising minutes before she was able to sit down in her armchair, and before she had drunk half her tea, she had fallen fast asleep; a sleep so deep it was almost unconsciousness.

Gordon Brodie had a morning of ups and downs. It hadn't started well, with his bitch of a wife looking at him like he was shit and never saying a word, but he had soon sorted her out. A few wallops now and then did her good, and that great belly of hers made him want to spew. He didn't want to touch her nowadays, so he had to look for satisfaction elsewhere. He hadn't gone to work; how could he with this passion eating at his vitals? By a stroke of luck, he'd suddenly recalled a woman he'd dallied with off and on, who was always ready to open her legs for him. But not today. "I heard you was a married man," she'd barked at him, "an' I'm nae wantin' blamed for splitting up a man and wife."

132

"She's expectin'," he'd explained, hoping that would change her mind.

"You canna get her an' you come rinnin' to me? Well, nothing doin', you randy swine, so aff you go an' dinna come back. I can get plenty ither men, better nor you."

He had very nearly hit her, but had thought better of it. She was a hefty piece and could likely knock him flat with one finger. He had wandered about for a while, round and round in circles trying to think, and then gone into the hotel bar. It was just after eleven and the Tufted Duck didn't close till half two. Nursing a pint, he looked around him. As usual during the day, the customers were mostly old men, but three women were sitting at a table in the corner. None of them looked any great shakes, but beggars couldn't be choosers, so he sauntered over with what he believed was a smile to charm the birds off the trees. "Hello, ladies, my luck must be in the day."

"Bugger aff," retorted the female in the middle, not bothering to remove the cigarette dangling from her thickly painted lips.

His face flushed with fury. "Well, that's nice, I must say. I was just makin' conversation, but if that's how you feel, you can shove your heid up your backside."

"An' you can tak' a runnin' jump at yoursel'. You think you're something, but you're jist a big round O."

This came from the youngest-looking of the three, still not very young, but just that little bit more attractive than the other two. Her hair, although the same peroxide blonde as theirs, curled neatly round her face, her skin was less mottled, her neck less craggy, but she had spoiled her chances with him.

He turned to the last one. "Would you care for a drink?"

"Would I nae?" she cackled, setting his teeth on edge. "I maistly only tak' brandy, but I canna afford it the day." She drained the last few drops from her half pint of beer and sat back expectantly.

Growing more frustrated by the minute, and guessing that the woman had hardly ever drunk brandy in her life, Gordie nevertheless put his order to the barman, whose smirk came dangerously near to earning him a punch on the mouth, but Gordie turned away in a few seconds with the two glasses in his hand. Sitting down next to the chosen recipient of his attentions, Gordie wondered if he was doing the right thing. There must be other women, more personable women, who would be glad of his company. "So? How's things goin' wi' you?" This was his usual opener, in the seductive voice that generally worked wonders.

"Ach, well," she simpered, "aye busy. Hardly get time to draw a breath, some days."

He nodded. "Aye, I'm the same myself some days, but . . . um . . . well, I find myself at a loose end for the next hour. Would you . . .? Would you be interestered in . . .?"

"Ach, Maggie," interrupted the personage in the centre of the three, "tell him tae get lost an' leave us to enjoy wir drinks in peace."

Indignant at being thwarted when he was almost certain he had made an impression on his prey, Gordie ignored her. "Listen, eh, Maggie? I'm prepared to pay. I am not after anything for nothing."

She regarded him scornfully. "You listen, Mister. Me an' my friends is just out for a few quiet drinks. We've had enough o' men like you that think they're God's gift to weemen. I tell you, I wouldna want you supposin' you came free in a ha'penny lucky bag."

Outraged, he adopted an upper-class drawl. "There's no need to turn nasty. I was merely suggesting . . ."

It was the farthest away "lady" who said, imitating his mode of speech, "An' I'm merely suggesting that you make yourself scarce, my fine fellow. You can surely see you're as welcome here as a dose of the pox."

All three females fell about laughing. "Oh, my God, Nettie, you're a richt ane," screeched one. "A dose o' the pox! That fits him richt enough."

Conscious of being the focus of all eyes in the room, Gordie whipped round and stalked out as if he had to keep an urgent appointment. It was the first time he'd ever been treated like this. Oh, he'd been refused before, but always with what sounded like a legitimate excuse. He tottered on for a few hundred yards with no notion of where he was going before realising that the brandy had combined with what he'd had the night before, and he was in no state to go anywhere. Nodding wisely to himself, he made up his mind to go home. He could vent his wounded pride on his wife. She had likely recovered from the punching he'd given her earlier. His spirits lifted as it crossed his mind that what he had already done to her could, with any luck, have resulted in her losing the blasted baby she was carrying.

It was bad enough trying to keep a wife as well as himself, without another mouth to feed.

His step lightened, his head came up and he felt ready to face whatever names Connie called him. Or her mother, if she'd managed to get word to her, somehow or other. He just hoped Jake Fowlie hadn't been told.

As he drew nearer to the old cottage that was his home, an icy shiver suddenly ran down his back. He halted for a moment, wondering if this was a warning of trouble, then, assuring himself that it must have been "somebody walking on his grave" as the old saying went, he marched as jauntily as he could up the long path. The house was hidden for most of the way by a row of silver birches, but after passing them he saw that everything looked perfectly normal and felt much easier. The drink had made him imagine things.

Ready to excuse his drunken state, he opened the kitchen door to find his wife asleep by the fireside. "Get up, you lazy bitch," he roared. "I'm needing something to eat."

Hardly allowing her to recover her senses, he lunged at her, yanked her to her feet and bared his teeth when she let out an involuntary moan. "So you're nae ignoring me this time? Let's see how good you are, though. Nae mair pushing me awa'. You're my wife and you've to dae what I tell you."

Her composure was too much for him. What right had she to criticise him? He was the man of the house; she was only one of his chattels. "You want some mair, do you?" he snarled, taking the back of his hand round her ear.

She knew she should hold her tongue, that whatever she said would rouse him to further anger, yet she wanted to prove that she could stand up for herself. "Man of the house? You? What have you ever done for this house? I've done everything myself; I've cooked, kept things clean; I've . . ."

Losing all control of himself, he kicked her low down on her belly, and she sank to the floor in agony, but he still had not finished with her. Although he could see that she was fighting for breath, he kicked her over and over again until she lay completely still. "That'll learn you to defy me!" he cried, suddenly collapsing into his usual chair. Why should he not have a rest as well as her?

Connie crouched behind the old couch that had been left in the old cottage, hugging her bruised body for comfort. It wasn't the first time Gordie had hit her — he seemed to take great delight in using her as a punchbag — but this was the worst yet. Whimpering, she closed her eyes to shut out the bare walls, the patches of black where the damp had taken a grip. Her brain didn't seem to be functioning properly — she couldn't remember exactly what had happened — but she did know that this was no place for an infant to be born. Then the thought crossed her mind that maybe it wouldn't be born alive anyway. Its father was doing his best to make sure of that.

When he had first learned that she was expecting, he had wanted her to get rid of "what was in her belly" but

137

she had flatly refused and said he'd have to marry her, otherwise her father would knock him senseless. He had threatened to swear that the child wasn't his, that she'd been with another man. She had just laughed at that, and said her father wouldn't believe him. Then he had got more persistent and said he knew some old crone who specialised in abortions, but she had held out against that, as well. Now he was doing his best to dispose of it himself by battering her almost every day.

The pain in her stomach intensified suddenly. Sharp and deep, over and over again, as if her body was protesting at something. Her eyes shot open as her head cleared. Oh, God! The baby must be coming early, and there was nobody here to help her — or near enough to hear her if she shouted.

She would probably be better to get herself to bed, though, if she could manage to get the rubber sheet and some towels from the press. Finding it impossible to get to her feet from this position, she heaved herself on to her knees with great difficulty. After several attempts, she discovered that she still couldn't stand up, but never mind. She could crawl, couldn't she?

But even crawling wasn't so easy, not trailing this cumbersome lump along with her. Her first target, the towels and rubber sheet, was another impossible task, being on the second shelf from the floor, but she persevered in fits and starts, stretching that little bit nearer each time. At last her flailing hand touched something, and a quick tug brought a cascade of towels and, thank heaven, the rubber sheet on top.

So far, so good, but how to take just what she was needing? That was the problem. Her brain incapable of finding an easy answer, she shoved the bundle forward with her chin, for she needed both hands on the floor to keep her steady. Her load gradually lessened, as she inched forward, leaving behind her a trail of items that had worked loose.

She had barely reached the door of the poky bedroom when she found that she could go no farther. All her efforts to reach up and turn the knob came to nothing as she lost consciousness and collapsed on top of two towels — all that were left.

Some hours later, Gordie woke up wondering, for a moment, where he was. One glance round made him recall a little of what had happened. The kitchen looked like a battlefield, with things lying about, furniture overturned, broken ornaments everywhere. But all that was the result of the quarrel he'd had earlier with his wife, so why hadn't she tidied it up? She was usually real fussy about keeping things tidy. Where the hell was she anyway? Gone back to her bed like enough, the lazy slut. She'd left the door into the lobby wide open as well, not much wonder the place was getting cold.

Steadying himself against the table as he stood up, he shook his head to clear the cobwebs, and picked his way carefully over the well-worn linoleum. When he saw his wife lying on the lobby floor, a pang of — not conscience, more warning of something not quite right — smote him, and he bent down to touch her. Feeling no pulse sobered him quicker than a pail of cold water in his face would have done, and he stood in dismay, trying to think what to do.

God Almighty! He hadn't expected this! His brain was still too fuzzed up with drink, last night's as well as today's. He needed to get a proper sleep to clear it, but how could he get to his bed with this thing in his way? He didn't fancy stepping over his dead wife. Turning round with the intention of going outside, round the back and climbing in through the bedroom window, he suddenly became conscious of someone coming up the path. It was only a glimpse through the kitchen window and, without taking time to find out who it was, he pivoted round on his heel. Leaping over the obstruction, he ran into the bedroom and pushed up the window. Fear of discovery gave him unsuspected agility and he clambered out with no difficulty and ran off.

CHAPTER
TWELVE

As Willie and Millie were standing at her gate, lingering as they always did, but unable to take the next step in their relationship, her father came running round the corner of the house. "I'm glad I caught you, William," he smiled. "Would you mind coming into the garage with me?"

Puzzled, the youth glanced round at him. "I can't stay long, sir. I've got my chores to do at home, as well as my homework."

"I hadn't realised that you were expected to help your father. It must be very difficult for you to keep up with everything."

"Yes, sir, but I'm coping . . . just." He gave a wry grin.

"Perhaps I shouldn't do what I meant to do." Mr Meldrum hesitated, and then seemed to come to a decision. "No, I do not see why I shouldn't. I was clearing out some rubbish — it gets so cluttered, you see — and I spotted my old bicycle in the corner. It's still in quite good condition, for once I bought the Ford I became used to driving around and saving my energy."

Wondering what was coming, Willie waited patiently. If the man wanted help to pump up a tyre that would be fine, but he didn't have much time to spare.

"I can see you're puzzled, my boy, so I won't prolong the agony any longer. I would be glad if you will take the bike off my hands. It will go to rack and ruin if it hangs up there much longer, and to be honest, my cycling days are over."

Unable to take in the offer, Willie helped him to lift the Raleigh off the hooks on the wall. It looked good, much better than the one he and Malcie Middleton had put together. In fact, apart from the thick layer of dust there, and the cobwebs between the brakes and the grips of the handlebars, it looked almost new.

"Well, what d'you say, William? Can you find a use for it? I'm sure Millie would be glad of company on her outings . . ." His eyes twinkled as he added, "That is, if you can give her some of your time."

Wishing fervently that he could give her all of his time, Willie couldn't help blushing. "It's very good of you, Mr Meldrum, but I can't accept it."

"If you mean you have no wish to go cycling with my daughter . . ."

"Oh no, sir, it's not that. In fact there's nothing I'd like better, but I really don't get any time off."

"You could always cycle to school. That would save your bus fares home and me the journey in the mornings. I think I had better remind your father that all work and no play makes Jack a dull boy, and that goes for girls, too. My Millie needs some relaxation, something to look forward to each week. Perhaps on

142

Sundays?" He seemed pleased to note the glance the two young people exchanged. "Take it with you, my boy, but check it over thoroughly before you venture out on it."

Recalling what had happened when he had not been very thorough in checking over a bicycle, Willie silently vowed to be extra particular this time. After thanking his old headmaster he wheeled the vehicle down the path, with Millie walking alongside him. "It's very good of your father," he told her, "and I'd give anything to go out on runs with you, but cycling to school and back will give us a wee bit more time together."

"That's what I was thinking." Smiling mischievously, she stood on tiptoe and kissed him full on the mouth.

The boy's heart was still beating double-quick time when, pushing the bike, he passed the end of the lane to Connie's house and it occurred to him that he had better go and see how she was. His mother had said his sister wasn't feeling very well yesterday, though she still had a couple of weeks or so to go before the baby was due. It wouldn't take long. Just a quick call so that he could give Mam a report.

Making a detour to the tiny cottage, he propped the bicycle carefully against the wall, and knocked on the door. Because the house was so isolated, Connie always kept it locked. Waiting a few seconds, he knocked again, his usual rat-a-tat-tat so she would know who it was. Still getting no answer, a deep apprehension swept over him. She wouldn't be out on her own, and Gordie was hardly ever there, so something must be wrong.

Walking round the gable end, he peered in at the small window in the lobby but could see nothing and carried on round the back. There was a net curtain on this window, for privacy Connie said. He knew she wasn't happy living here, for she had often told them she felt nervous because it was so lonely. Because of the net, he couldn't see in, but the sash window was a good bit open. It only needed a slight push up and it was enough for him to get in.

Reaching the sill took a bit of manoeuvring, but he did eventually succeed in getting his leg inside. Unfortunately, he didn't see the big Victorian-type vase sitting on a small table beside the window, and accidentally tipped it with his foot. The crash made him lose his hold and down he went, too. The resulting noise made him absolutely certain that the house was empty. Nobody could have slept through that.

Getting to his feet and gingerly touching his leg to find out if he'd done any damage to it, Willie looked around him. The room was spotless, apart from the mess the vase had made, the bed was in pristine condition, and nothing else seemed to have been touched. He had better check in the kitchen, and if his sister wasn't there, goodness knows where she could be.

He was assailed suddenly by a shiver going down his spine. Something was wrong — he was sure of it. Gritting his teeth, he opened the door from the bedroom into the little lobby and nearly stepped on a bundle of . . . He jumped back in alarm as he realised that it wasn't a bundle of anything. It was Connie!

144

Bending over, he touched her brow. Not stone cold, but too cold to be . . . There seemed to be a lot of blood on the floor but he kept his eyes averted as he stumbled through the kitchen, over the towels strewn in a kind of trail, to unlock the door. He had to get air or he would pass out. There was nothing he could do to help his sister, nor the bloodied thing lying between her legs.

Once outside, he drew long breaths of fresh air until he felt a little more composed, then he sat down on the low wall that girdled the front garden. What should he do? He felt so useless, and it would take him ages to walk home. Remembering the bicycle, he turned to look at it. It looked in perfect order. Should he chance it? Getting to his feet, he went over to feel the tyres. Hard as rocks. Mr Meldrum must have checked them himself, despite the cobwebby handlebars.

His power of thought practically exhausted, he had one thing in mind now — to get home, as quickly as he could. He was still only fifteen and couldn't deal with what had happened. As he was setting the bicycle upright, he caught a movement out of the corner of his eye, and stretching so that he could see better round the end of the house, he saw a man coming out of one of the outhouses at the far end of the back garden, quite an extent considering the size of the tiny cottage. This person was looking furtively about him and, having made sure that no one was near, he ran like the wind, vaulting the wooden fence and carrying right on into the wood behind.

At first, Willie thought nothing of this. Connie had often said she was sure there were gypsies, or tinks, hiding somewhere near. She had missed various items of clothes from the washing line, and she'd been almost sure that her hens would have laid more eggs than she found.

Then another thought occurred to him, making him feel sick. It was no gypsy he had seen, nor a tink. The man was well-dressed, and reminded him of somebody. It had just been an impression he'd got, since he hadn't seen much of the man's face. He'd had a quick glance to his left and then to his right, but he hadn't looked straight ahead. If he had, Willie thought now — the slight impression he had before crystallising into a certain recognition — he'd have seen his young brother-in-law watching him.

But why had Gordie Brodie been skulking about in a shed? Why had he been so afraid of being seen? At that moment, a flash of inspiration hit him, practically taking his breath away. It must have been Gordie who had killed Connie! Not must have, though. It was!

Unable to cope with this thought, Willie jumped on the bicycle and made for home. It did not take long. It took him longer to make his father understand what he was saying, but at last Jake, not believing that his daughter was dead but recognising that his son was too shocked to be of any help, set off on foot for the farm, to ask Mrs McIntyre to phone the doctor.

Jeemsie Cooper had been enjoying a breakfast of ham, eggs and toast, very acceptable because it was so late — he'd spent most of the night helping Johnny McIntyre to round up the sheep that had managed to break out

146

of their field. The little blighters, some of them not so little, had led them a merry dance before they were all captured, even though there had been about seven or eight men all engaged in the hunt. Still, that was another job well done, and he'd have a few hours to catch up on his lost sleep. Demolishing his last bit of toast in one mighty mouthful, he couldn't help grinning. From catching lost sheep to catching lost sleep, that was really clever. He must remember that; it would be a good conversation piece, for he was never very good at making witty conversation.

Yawning, he got to his feet and moved over to his easy chair by the fire. His mother would be busy with her housework and the outside chores, so she wouldn't likely be in the kitchen again till it was time to make some supper. He put his feet, already bootless, up on the fender stool, shifted the cushion at his back to a more comfortable position and shut his eyes.

Some time later, Bella Cooper peeped round the door, having guessed that her son would be asleep. Poor lad, he needed the rest, so she withdrew with the same silence, but only another fifteen minutes had passed when someone hammered on the door. She hurried to answer it, hissing as she opened it, "Stop that noise. You'll wauken my Jeemsie an' he's been workin' a' nicht."

A breathless Andy McIntyre shook his head. "You'll ha'e to wauken him, fitever, Mrs Cooper. He'll ha'e to go to Gordie Brodie's hoose — you ken, up the glen. Something affa bad's happened."

Unwilling to believe that any incident would be bad enough for her to rouse her son, she bridled. "What kinda something?"

"Jake Fowlie says his lassie's been murdered."

"But he canna be sure she's deid. He's nae a doctor."

The boy shrugged. "My ma's phoned the doctor, so he'll be there. Ony road, it wasna Jake that saw her. It was his laddie."

Her mouth gripped, still unconvinced, the woman went into the kitchen and shook Jeemsie, still deep in the arms of Morpheus. "Jeemsie! Jeemsie! You're needed at Birch Cottage. Andy McIntyre says Connie Fowlie's been murdered." She used the girl's maiden name, as was the custom in the area.

Her last word spurred the man into action. His eyes barely opened, he sat up to put on his boots. "Who says she's been murdered? Ordinary folk canna mak' that kinda decisions. That's the police's job."

"It wis Jake Fowlie said it, but Andy says it was Willie that found her."

"Willie Fowlie." Jeemsie let his hands drop. "Kennin' him, he could be tellin' lies. He wasted hours o' police time wi' yon last cairry on."

Bella had had more time to consider this side of things. "No, Jeemsie. This is different. Last time, there was never nae body found." She left it that. It was enough for her son, however. "Right enough, Ma. If Connie's just a body, it must be murder. I just wish I could be sure."

Saving any further conjecture on anybody's part, Doctor Murison was already there and had pronounced

148

the victim dead. "As a result of a horrendous attack," he told the two men who had beaten him to the house, McIntyre having taken pity on Jake and driving him there himself. "Sadly, the infant has also suffered severe injuries, so it is just as well that it did not survive."

Studying the carnage, Jeemsie wished that he had phoned for assistance before leaving his own home, but he hadn't wanted to place himself in a position liable to ridicule, and would have to cope unaided until he could report the crime. He took his notebook from his pocket, took out the pencil he always left inside, and began his investigation. "Who found the body?"

Jake stepped forward. "My son Willie."

"And you're prepared to believe him, after what happened that other time?"

"I didna believe him at first," Jake admitted, "but I did believe she'd been hurt, so I went to Wester Burnton to get somebody to phone the doctor."

Murison lifted his bag from the floor. "I must get on, I have patients waiting." He addressed Jeemsie now. "You will arrange for the removal of the body, I presume?"

The policeman looked stunned. "I'll need to phone for assistance, but there's nae a phone here, is there?"

"No," Jake supplied, "nothing nearer than Wester Burnton."

Johnny McIntyre, Good Samaritan that he always was, chipped in, "I phoned Aberdeen afore we come here, Jeemsie, so they'll be well on their way. I need to be gettin' back now, though."

Waiting until the two men had left, the PC muttered, "It was kennin' it was your Willie that reported it, that's why I didna ring Aiberdeen. I thocht it was another caper, like the last time."

"He was only a bairn that time," Jake said, indignantly. "He was fear't to tell."

"He's maybe fear't to tell this time, an' all."

"What d'you mean by that?" Jake was scowling. He was finding it hard enough to hide the grief for his daughter that was doing its best to consume him, without having aspersions cast on his son.

"Take it whatever way you like, but it seems suspicious to me that he ken't she was deid, when he'd never seen a deid body afore. You see what I mean? Of course, he could've just been guessin'. Either that, or he's the murderer."

His face almost purple with anger, Jake shouted, "Dinna spik bloody rubbish, man! He wouldna kill his ain sister. He wouldna kill onybody! He tell't me aboot it, for God's sake, and he wouldna tell if he'd done it his sel', would he?"

"Jake," murmured the policeman, trying now to pour oil on the troubled waters, "I dinna ken what your Willie would've done." He was completely at a loss. Word had been sent for help to solve a murder, when he, who should have been first on the spot, had arrived there last. And he hadn't one single clue as to who had done it. He eyed the other man hopelessly, then mumbled, "I'm sorry for saying it, Jake, but I canna think on ony other solution. Can you?"

Jake rubbed his rough hand over his even rougher chin. "I canna say as I can, but there must be some explanation." After standing deep in thought for some moments, he suggested the only thing that occurred to him, surprised that the bobby hadn't thought of it himself. "You could ha'e a look round an' see if you can catch the criminal. He could still be skulkin' aboot outside."

"That's a good idea. There's not much I can do here, till the Aiberdeen boys come."

Realising that there was nothing Jeemsie Cooper could do anyway on his own, Jake muttered, "I'll gi'e you a hand."

The two men decided to split up and thus be able to cover more ground, and each went off in a different direction. And so it was that, when the police van arrived at the cottage, the only occupants were the two corpses.

Dod Bruce, the Detective Inspector in charge — Johnny McIntyre had stressed that it was a murder and not a hoax — jumped out first, the three PCs following him. "Reid, you come inside with me," he ordered, "and Cormack and Dunne, you search all the outhouses and the immediate surrounding area."

The indoors investigation yielded no clues; the outdoors crew having the same result except for coming across Jeemsie and Jake. The four disconsolate searchers returned to admit defeat. It was only then that Jake remembered that his wife had been left to comfort Willie, when her own sorrow must be breaking her heart. Connie had been her oldest child, the one on whom she had depended most. He himself had not had time to come to terms with it, even seeing his lovely daughter lying on the floor like that hadn't hammered it home to him.

Feeling as if the weight of the world was on his shoulders, he addressed the DI. "I'd better be getting home to my wife."

Bruce barked, "And who are you, exactly?" obviously annoyed that a mere civilian was intruding on a murder scene.

"He's the victim's father," Jeemsie explained. "It was his son that found the body."

Bruce relaxed slightly. "All right, Mr . . .?"

"Mr Fowlie," supplied Jeemsie.

"Right then, Mr Fowlie, you are at liberty to go home, but we will have to take statements from you and your son later."

"Yes, of course." Jake turned away.

On his way home, it occurred to him that Emily wouldn't know for sure that Connie had been murdered. Possibly, she was still be clinging to the hope that Willie could be mistaken, that her daughter could have regained consciousness and would be all right. Her husband would have to disillusion her, Jake mused. The man who loved her most would have to tell her the truth, to break her heart. Oh, dear God! His poor, poor Emily. To lose a second daughter so soon after losing the first.

Emily was sitting by the fire with Willie on her knee, although he was already taller than she was. She had

never held her son so closely since he was a baby —
had hardly ever had her arms round him at all — but
she needed his body against her for comfort as much as
he needed hers. Jake's heart was pounding as he looked
on them, but Willie jumped up and came to him. "Dad,
Connie *is* dead, isn't she? Mam doesn't believe me."

"Aye, lad, I'm sorry to have to say Connie's dead.
God kens who did it, for Jeemsie says there hasna been
ony tinks or gypsies ony place near here for months."

With tears coursing down his cheeks again, Willie
said, "Dad, it was Gordie."

"Gordie? No, loon, you canna think that."

"I dinna think it, Dad, I'm sure it was him. He'd
been hiding in one of the sheds, and I saw him coming
out, and looking from side to side to make sure nobody
could see him."

"So how did he nae see you, if you saw him?"

"I was at the front of the house, at the corner of the
gable end, and he never looked in that direction, and he
jumped the fence and ran away into the wood."

"But he wouldna kill his ain wife. He would never
have hurt her even."

At this, Emily raised her tear-ravaged face. "Aye
would he. He's been ill-using her ever since they were
wed. He's an animal."

Although upset that she had told him nothing of this
before, Jake only commented, "The pair o' you had
better tell the 'tecs all that when they come askin'
questions. That'll let them ken there's only one
suspect." His sorrow for his daughter, his black rage at
his son-in-law, his compassion for his young son who

was obviously still in shock, suddenly merged into an emotion he had never experienced before, overwhelming him in its intensity. With no warning, he spun round and strode out, his one wish to be alone in his bottomless misery.

Gordon Brodie had sobered up more quickly than he had ever done. Even the sight of his wife's bloodied body and that of his child had not had the same effect. It was his shock on seeing somebody coming towards the house when he had been feverishly searching for the means of concealing his crime that had panicked him. He hadn't even had time to pick up the pieces of glass and china that were scattered over the floor, he had been perilously near to being caught. He had meant to hide the bodies somewhere and leave the place spotless, explaining Connie's absence by saying she was going to her mother's house for the birth, but something must have changed her mind. Then, if they'd questioned him further, he'd have sworn he didn't know where she'd gone.

Now, he was a fugitive from justice. Nobody would believe any denials he made; and there were those three women in the Tufted Duck. But wait! They might come in handy, mightn't they? They would vouch for him being there at what could be the time of the deaths. They would give him a perfect alibi. He had gone out to get drunk because his wife had said she wasn't coming back to him after the baby was born. That was reasonable. But he'd rather he managed to get clear away and didn't have to say anything. He'd been lucky

154

to sneak into this old shed they had never used, and he hadn't heard a sound since. Whoever had come to the cottage had surely gone away again when he got no answer to his knock. So the bodies hadn't been found yet, and it would be safe to make his escape, though he'd no idea where to go. Hopefully, something would come to him.

Peeping round the rickety door and seeing nobody, he decided he may as well run for it now. Jumping the low wooden fence, he raced into the wood. If he just got clear of this area before the police came looking for him, he'd be happy. They would come looking for him, that was an absolute certainty. The husband was always the first suspect. They would spread the net, of course, when they couldn't find him, but by nightfall he should be far enough away to be safe. He could start a new life somewhere else, change his name and get married again if he felt like it.

Unfortunately, it did not enter his head that his flight would pin the murder on him quicker than any evidence could do.

It was the following morning before the detectives came, yet after a whole night of individually going over what had happened, not one of the Fowlies felt any easier about being interviewed. Willie's statement naturally held their attention most, and DI Bruce questioned him repeatedly, trying to find a chink in his story, but finally having to accept it as the truth. "Thank you, Willie," he said. "I'm sorry if I gave the impession that I doubted you, but we have to be absolutely sure of our facts before we can accuse anyone, and have a case that will hold water. As it is, there is still a lot of work to do. We must discover his movements over the whole day, and of course, locate him, which we will do, no matter where he is hiding." Rising to leave, he remarked, "And Mr Fowlie, Mr McIntyre says you do not have to return to work until you feel ready. This has been a terrible ordeal for your family, and they need you."

It was Emily who answered, her voice unsteady but determined. "That's very kind of him, but tell him Jake will be back tomorrow. There's really nothing he can do here."

As soon as the two men left, she made both Willie and Jake go back to bed and busied herself with the housework as being the only way to take her mind off the tragedy. It didn't work, of course.

CHAPTER
THIRTEEN

1938

Connie's murder three years earlier had badly affected all the Fowlies. Jake had been working every minute of the day, refusing to let Willie leave school to help him. "I'll manage mysel'," he snapped. "I'm nae a decrepit aul' fool just yet." Willie was torn between grief for his sister, who had been the only one ever to show him true affection — apart from Gramma Fowlie, who was now crippled with arthritis — and yearning for the education he knew he was capable of. Emily was most affected. Not only had she lost her elder daughter for ever, Becky had written nothing since her arrival in America. To cap it all, her own mother had gone to live with her other daughter in London. She had never been all that friendly. She had been against Jake from the very start, but she was the only relative Emily had had in Scotland. She had withdrawn into herself and still showed no interest in anyone or anything. But life seemed to go on around her.

When the results of the examinations came out, both Millie Meldrum and Willie had passed every subject with flying colours. Millie was jubilant, and the elated Willie had grabbed her round the waist and whirled her round in front of students and masters. The denouement had come when he arrived home. "I canna afford to put you to University," Jake said, "so put it richt oot'n your heid." A tentative appeal to his mother was met with silence, and Willie knew that the subject was closed.

Millie threatened her father that she wouldn't go if Willie couldn't go, and there the matter may have remained if Fate had not taken a hand. Mrs Meldrum, who generally paid little attention to what her husband and daughter talked about, suddenly observed, "Why can't you pay for Willie at the Varsity like you've done for him at the Academy? What the bursary didn't cover, I mean."

"My dear, it's an entirely different situation," her husband replied, but she had given him cause to think. Not being a man to dive at things without thinking, he gave it some deep consideration, and at last came up with a solution. It would all depend, of course.

Willie offered his services to his father for the holidays, with the promise of looking for a job for himself later, and having been refused — Jake's way of making up for not letting him go to University — spent the next two weeks going cycling with Millie. Their favourite destination was a small loch, its grassy banks concealed from prying eyes by bushes. It was too good a place to waste, and the two young people took full advantage of it. Millie took a picnic with her, and they would sit on the lush, velvety grass for an hour or more sometimes, the talking and eating periods getting shorter as they spent more and more time telling each other of their love.

It was difficult for Willie to think that he would hardly ever see Millie after she started at University, and not only that, she would likely fall in love with some other boy. She laughed at him for saying this, and sometimes countered it by saying, "I'll never look at another boy, but maybe you're wanting to get another girl. Is that it?"

They were lying side by side, in a good position for kissing, so he pulled her towards him and kissed her as neither of them had kissed before. Time passed unnoticed, each experiencing emotions that they were aware were fully adult, and not knowing what to do. Desperate as he was to show her how much he loved her, Willie pulled back suddenly. It wouldn't be right. They were too young to take on the responsibility of the child that could result from his ignorance.

She seemed hurt as they looked at each other, but he could only say, "No, not yet, Millie."

"You don't want to?"

"Don't ever think that," he burst out. "Of course I want to, but we'll have to wait until I'm earning enough to support . . ."

"But you'll be coming to University, please, Willie? Please?"

"I wish I could, my darling, but I'll have to work for a living."

Jake was astonished to see Mr Meldrum on his doorstep at nine o'clock that night. He had not long finished his supper, working until darkness fell, and was sitting in his shirt sleeves and galluses. "Come in, sir," he said, deferentially, for he was well aware that this man had paid for many items Willie had needed at the Academy.

"Is William in? I want to be sure that he doesn't hear our conversation."

"Aye, Willie's in, but he's up in his room readin'. He'll nae hear what you have to say. When his heid's in a book, he's dead to the world."

"It's about Willie, you see, Mr Fowlie. My daughter tells me that you don't want him to go to University."

"It's nae that I don't want him to go," Jake said carefully, looking at his wife and pleased to see that she was listening.

"I understand, but I still feel that it is a shame for him to waste such ability as his."

"I canna afford to put him, and that's a fact. If you're thinking on offering to pay for him again I canna accept."

"No, Mr Fowlie, I am not exactly offering to pay for him. What is being offered is . . ." He pulled a face and followed it by a mischievous smile. "I've been talking to the Reverend Fyfe, who said he knew that your William was a very intelligent boy. When I explained that he had enough qualifications for University, but that he couldn't go because of your financial situation, he made the offer to me and saved me having to ask. We will go fifty-fifty on all William's expenses."

"I've had enough charity," Jake exclaimed, thumping his fist on the arm of his chair. "You ken I'll never be

160

able to pay you back, an' I canna be in debt to the minister as weel."

"You misunderstand, Jake," Mr Meldrum soothed. "Neither of us want to be repaid. We are both very fond of the boy and would hate to think of him losing his rightful place in the world. Please try to see it from his point of view. He is so clever, there is nothing that he couldn't tackle and do well. He could be a doctor, a minister, a schoolmaster, a politician even. There is no limit to what he could achieve — if you will only allow him his chance."

Emily spoke now, for the first time. "He's right, Jake. We've both known for a while that Willie could go on to better things, but I've been as big a stumbling block as you, and now he's on the doorstep to a good career, we have to give him the chance."

Mr Meldrum beamed at her. "Thank you for this, Mrs Fowlie. You will never regret it."

She gave a wry smile. "I wouldn't be too sure of that, though. Willie has always been a puzzle to me. My mother-in-law used to call him a wee nickum, and so he was, always full of mischief, and maybe he always will be, but I can't stand in his way now."

"May we keep it a secret between us until tomorrow?" he asked. "As you possibly know, my daughter and your William have been seeing quite a lot of each other lately, and I'm sure she would love to be the one to tell him the good news."

Jake nodded. "So be it, but I'll make sure Willie pays back every penny you spend on him. Be sure o' that, Mr Meldrum, you an' the minister baith."

"If he graduates with honours, that will be all the payment we need. It's been good having this little chat with you, but I must bid you good day. No need for you to get up," he smiled to Emily as she made to stand. "I can see myself out."

Husband and wife looked at each other when they heard the door close behind him, Jake raising his eyebrows as he said, "Well, that was a surprise, but I'm nae that keen on the idea o' bein' beholden to him and the minister."

"They're doing it for Willie," Emily sighed, "and while I wonder if they'll come to regret it, I'm grateful to them for it. At one time, I'd never have thought he had it in him to go to the Academy, never mind the University, but give him his due, he's worked hard and he deserves to get on."

When Willie came downstairs about half an hour later, he sat down in silence for a few moments and then burst out, "I've been thinking, Dad. You know I'm not that keen on working on the land?"

Puzzled at what his son was about to say, and half believing that he had been eavesdropping on the conversation with Mr Meldrum, Jake just nodded.

"What if I was to give it a try for — say a couple of months, and if I said I still couldn't face it as a full-time job for life, or if you thought I was useless, would you let me look for another job for myself? Something I felt I could be happy at?"

If his mind had not been so engrossed in his own thoughts, he might have seen the conspiratorial look that passed between his parents, but he did not recognise it. "I'll work really hard for you, Dad, I'll give it a good try, I promise."

Stifling the urge to put his son out of this uncertainty about his future, Jake managed to say, "Aye, well, we'll wait an' see what happens, eh?"

"OK. I'd better start tomorrow, then." He was clearly anxious to get to the end of the next eight weeks, but recalling what was going to happen the next day, Jake said, "Ach, we'd be as weel leavin' it till Monday."

"Thanks, Dad, and if tomorrow will be my last free day for a while, I may as well make the most of it."

He set off on his bicycle, kept spotless and in good running order, just after nine, his heart singing as he took care not to hit any of the large stones that always seemed to litter the track down to the road. This part of Aberdeenshire was mostly stony ground, evidence of the scree taken down by the glaciers making their way down the mountains to the sea at the end of the Ice Age. However often the farm labourers tried to clear them off, there were as many again the next time the fields were ploughed.

At Burnton schoolhouse, the three Meldrums were just finishing breakfast, and Willie apologised when Janet, the little maid, showed him in.

"It's all right, my boy," grinned his old headmaster, "There's no need to apologise for being early. It is we who should apologise for being such sluggards." And his wife added, "Don't bother clearing the dishes, Millie, Janet and I will easily manage."

Willie did not have time to speculate as to why the man and his wife looked so pleased with themselves;

163

Millie had jumped up from the table and was dragging him outside. "Bye Mum. Bye Dad," she called, picking up the small picnic basket as she went through the hall.

She looked so lovely, so happy, her dark blue eyes dancing, her goldie hair blowing in the breeze, that Willie found difficulty in fixing the basket to the carrier on the back of his cycle. What he wanted to do was grab her and kiss her until they both ran out of breath. But he couldn't do that in full view of the dining room window.

"Could we go to Carter Loch?" she asked, as they set off. "I've something to tell you, and that's as good a place as any."

"Something good, or something bad?"

"Something good — well, I hope you'll think it's good."

"I've something to tell you, as well," his smile was forced. "But I'll let you go first."

"When we get there."

Their journey took them the best part of an hour, but neither of them minded. They loved the fresh smell of the pine trees on either side for some miles, the rainbow colours of the wild flowers on the grass verges, masses of foxgloves swaying in the wind, patches of blue forget-me-nots, white Stars of Bethlehem, sorrel. "When I was little," Millie told him, "we used to play at shops, and we used the red bits of sorrel for mince."

He wished he had known her when she was a little girl. "Poopie and I just used to play cowboys and Indians."

"Poopie?"

164

"Don't ask."

"I am asking. Why was he called Poopie? It wasn't very nice."

"No, you're right, and it was why you thought it was. He couldn't help it."

"What a shame. Was he a nice boy?"

"He was my best friend for years. He's a year older than me, but he didn't pass the qualifying exam, and we don't see so much of each other now. Last time I saw him, he was working at Easter Burnton as ploughboy."

"You shouldn't lose touch with him, though. Try to see him again."

"I do sometimes see him, but just long enough to exchange a few words."

They had passed the old mill, not in use for many years, and the grass and weeds were practically blocking it from view. Without thinking, Willie remarked, "There's a story that two little twin boys fell in the mill race and were drowned. They had been picking wild rasps. Look, you can still see them growing there."

"Oh, that's really sad. Let's speak about something different."

"I'm sorry." He very much regretted it, for her shoulders had slumped, and there was a general air of sadness about her. He searched for something to cheer her and spotted something ahead that might do the trick. "See this old hut coming up. They say that was used by men making illicit whisky. They kept their stills hidden in there, so the Revenue Men wouldn't catch

165

them. There was a lot of that going on round here at one time, and poaching." She seemed happier again, he was glad to see. "They say the Covenanters roamed about this area, as well."

"I suppose there are stories like that wherever you go in Scotland. I'm quite interested in history, but so are you, of course?"

"Yes, I am. I like to read about the past. If I'd been able to go to the Varsity, I would maybe have aimed at being a history master somewhere, but ..." He shrugged his shoulders.

On the point of telling him her news now, Millie was glad to see the start of Carter Loch just ahead. "Well, here we are," she said, slowing down as they mounted the grass and pushed the cycles slowly and carefully between the clumps of heather and other low bushes until they reached their favourite spot — secluded and sheltered, and carpeted by mossy grass that was very comfortable to lie on.

First opening the straps that held the basket, Willie set it on the ground, laid his cycle carefully down beside it and then helped Millie with hers. Then they spread their jackets out, although there had been no rain for some time and everything was bone dry. He helped her down first and then sprawled by her side. "Will you tell me your news now? Or shall I go first?"

She regarded him thoughtfully, yet her eyes soon began to dance again. "I think you should go first."

So he told her what he had suggested to his father and the response that he had received. "So this is the last day we'll be together for I don't how know long.

But I'll surely get a day off now and then." He felt saddened that she was not looking disappointed, and decided that he didn't really want to know what she had to say, all about the university, he presumed.

"Well, now it's my turn," she began, sounding far too cocky for his liking. "I've been studying a railway timetable, and it's not handy going to Aberdeen by train."

Wondering why she bothered to tell him this, he muttered, "So what are you going to do?"

"Dad says the bus isn't much good, either, but his sister has a large house in the Spital and she has offered to take us."

"No!" he said, sharply. "Don't include me. I've told you I can't go."

She laughed gaily. "I know you have, but arrangements have been made."

"They'll have to be unmade, then." He was disappointed in her, hurt by her determination to ignore his position. "I can't go and that's final."

She didn't seem in the least perturbed by his persistence. "But, Willie, you don't know what I know."

"Stop joking, Millie! It's not funny."

"I'm not joking." She looked round into his face, then stroked his cheek. "I wouldn't do that to you, my dearest. But it's been arranged by my father and the minister that they'll pay all your expenses."

He shook his head mournfully. "My father won't agree, and anyway, even if he did, I couldn't accept such an offer."

"But they really believe you deserve it, and you surely aren't going to let them down?"

"You make me feel bad about it, but I really can't. Not only would it be my fees, but books, and now, you're telling me, board and lodging to your aunt."

"She doesn't want us to pay. She's got plenty of money. Her husband was a skipper and left her very well provided for."

"But I can't . . ."

She rolled over to stop him with a kiss, a kiss that lingered, was repeated over and over again, and he knew he had been overruled. He could not argue against her now, he would have to accept and be grateful to all the people who were making his dream possible; it would be up to himself to make it come true. He would actually be starting his first year at Aberdeen University with Millie at the beginning of October, 1939.

Part Two

CHAPTER
FOURTEEN

Willie had worked on his father's plot of land for most of the summer, with one day off every week, which he spent with Millie, but things changed somewhat on the third day of September, when Neville Chamberlain announced that Britain was at war with Germany. Many of the young men in the Burnton area were fired with patriotism between then and Christmas and volunteered to fight for their country. Poopie Grant — Willie could never get into the habit of calling him Cecil — came to say that he'd made the decision and had to report at the Scottish Horse base at Perth.

"I wish I could come with you," Willie told him, "but I'm tied hands and feet for the next four years."

Poopie grinned. "The war'll likely be ower by that time. We'll beat the Jerries afore you've finished your first year, I'm damned sure o' that. I'll let you ken every time I get hame, so we'll see each other sometimes."

"I'll miss you, Poopie," Willie muttered, feeling quite sad at the idea of them parting. Although they hadn't been as close during the past few years as they had once been, there was still a deep bond between them. After recalling their younger days, and all the trouble

Willie had been in, the other young man took his leave with a cheery, "I'll never ha'e anither pal like you."

"Neither will I," Willie assured him, and it was true, he thought. They had been little boys together, they had done everything together. It was just a pity that Poopie hadn't had the brains to pass the qualifying examination.

Neither of the two young people liked Aberdeen at first, but they soon got used to it. Millie's Auntie Sophie was a tall, slim lady who wore her hair in the fashion of the 1920s rather than the longer style of the present day. At first sight, Willie thought she would be severe and grim, but how wrong he was. Sophie Chalmers was full of fun, and didn't lay down any rules.

"I trust you two to behave yourselves," was all she said, and of course, they had to, anyway. They did not have time to do otherwise, for they were kept at it until late in the evening, Millie concentrating on English on her Arts course and Willie taking History on his, so they had no subjects in common.

There was a shortage of lecturers after a while, when many were called up or went voluntarily into the services. Gradually, too, the number of male students drastically reduced, a sore point with Willie, who felt that he could not give up the chance he had been given to improve his prospects. It would be like throwing his sponsors' largesse back in their faces. He made no mention of his feelings to Millie, although his conscience pricked him each time he entered a huge lecture hall, where row upon row of seats sat empty, while the rest were occupied mainly by females. He wasn't the only young man there, though, which did salve his guilt a little.

One thing cheered him. Walking twice daily through the entrance to Marischal College, his heart filled with pride. This was said to be the largest granite building in the world, and it was absolutely magnificent. Looking up at the hundreds of intricate minarets and granite figures which decorated its façade, it was impossible to imagine the amount of hard work that had gone into the making of them, especially at a time when modern-day machinery and tools had not been invented. When the sun was shining it was a sparkling, silvery edifice as impressive as any royal palace. He would be forever grateful to the men who had made it possible for him to study there.

He and Millie went home for Christmas, and he felt obliged to help his father as much as he could. Jake's back was getting bowed, his hair was fast disappearing and what was left was pure white. He wasn't that old, Willie mused one day. Born in 1890, he would only be fifty on his birthday in May but he'd had a hard life with a son who had not helped him enough. His mother wasn't much better, of course. Her hair was still as thick as ever, but it was pure white, too, and there were deep wrinkles on her brow. He was likely the cause of most of them, he thought, sadly. He'd given her a lot of worry when he was young, and then there had been the trauma of Connie's death. She had never really got over that, and likely wouldn't until Gordon

Brodie was caught and paid the penalty for what he had done.

Becky hadn't helped her mother's health, either. They had never had another word from her since she'd left Jackie Burns in search of a better life in America. More than likely, she had got in tow with some shady character who had promised her the earth and given her nothing when it came to the point. Or she may have found another husband and could be saddled with a string of kids. Knowing Becky, she could even be on to her second or third husband by now. It's what they did in America.

Willie was very pleased when Poopie Grant turned up one evening and they went out together for a drink in the Students' Union. Willie plied his friend with questions about his initial training but, although Poopie did answer them, he didn't seem overpleased with himself. "Six weeks o' drill and route marches," he moaned. "Blistered feet an' broken back. It's nae human. An' the food! Nae fit for pigs."

Willie smiled. "Ach, come on, Poopie, you're pulling my leg. It can't have been as bad as that."

"It was, Willie, I swear it. You should be glad you couldna join up. But we'll be sent overseas come time, so that surely winna be so bad."

It would probably be much worse, Willie reflected. It was just as well that Poopie wasn't all that logical.

The "glorious retreat" from Dunkirk absorbed everyone's interest over the summer, many wondering how it could be called "glorious" when "retreat" usually

174

meant "defeat", but the die-hards would explain how it had been an almost impossible rescue of the troops who were cornered like rats in a trap, yet got away. It was the main talking point in pubs, after church services, at all times when people got together.

Then came the Blitz, which, although it mainly concentrated on London, also affected parts of several large cities in southern England. Rural Aberdeenshire did not come under attack, although many Scottish cities and towns were to receive the Luftwaffe's unwelcome attention before long, as were cities in all parts of England.

Fraserburgh and Peterhead, both important seaports, were the nearest recipients to Tillyburnie and the Burnton area, and Aberdeen itself was to become known as the most frequently bombed city in Scotland, although it did not suffer the same amount of damage and casualties as Glasgow and Clydeside.

Willie made a point of doing some work in his father's large garden every weekend as well as in his holidays, but claimed the occasional Sunday to go cycling with Millie. During term they had little time for pleasure, occupied in writing essays and theses until well into the mornings, but they were both quite content for it to be like that.

In October 1940, both Willie and Millie discovered, to their great delight, that they had passed all their first year exams. "They'd probably been easy, being the first," Millie observed as they looked at the notice board. "They'll get harder as we go on, no doubt."

The questions did get harder, and the day-to-day work, but they persevered, surprising themselves by how well they were coping.

On the Easter 1941 vacation, Willie heard with dismay that Poopie Grant had been sent to the Middle East. "Poor Poopie," he said to Millie when they managed to get an hour together. "He doesn't know what's in front of him. I've heard it's killing fields over there, but his Mam says his letters are cheery enough, when he manages to get time to write."

"Don't worry about him, Willie. He can probably take care of himself."

"You don't know him." With all his heart, Willie wished that he could be there to protect Poopie, as he had done when they were small.

It was in May of the following year, on a beautiful sunny day, a soft wind blowing gently, that Willie heard the news. On his way to his first lecture, he was quite pleased to see Malcolm Middleton in the Gallowgate, although he had no idea what had brought him there. Millie wasn't with him because she didn't have a class until 11 o'clock, so he stood up to have a chat with his erstwhile chum — the joint assembler of the old Raleigh bike that had caused Willie — and PC Jeemsie Cooper — so much trouble.

"I suppose you've heard aboot Poopie Grant?" Malcie asked, eyeing Willie to see his reaction.

"What's happened to him?" Apprehensive anxiety swept into his very being.

"He's been killed. Oh God, Willie, I'm sorry, I thought you'd have heard. That's why I was comin' to see you. Are you OK?"

"I'm a bit shaken," Willie admitted. "I hadn't heard, and Poopie and me — we were like brothers, in a way."

"Aye, I can mind on you stickin' up for him at the school, and him a year aulder than you. You did his fechtin' for him, an' all."

"Not this time." He felt bitter. Why, oh why, hadn't he just said to hell with everything and joined up along with Poopie? "I'd better go, Malcie, or I'll be late."

Malcolm carried on up the hill, Willie continued going down, but just before reaching Marischal College, he turned right down Upperkirkgate. With no destination in mind, he trudged onwards across the junction with St Nicholas Street and up Schoolhill. As he passed Robert Gordon's College, a private school for boys, he remembered that the Gordon Highlanders' Drill Hall was just round the corner. It was also their Recruitment Centre. It was a sign, wasn't it? He hadn't consciously planned it, but why should poor Poopie give up his life while he was cowardly hiding in huge lecture halls in the University, making excuses for not answering the call to arms? Why couldn't he go? Why should he care about other people? If he wanted to go to war, nothing should hold him back.

A little farther along, standing in front of the Cowdray Hall with its granite lion in the corner, a memorial to those killed in the Great War, he struggled with his problem. He was being kept back by the fact that two honourable gentlemen had been willing to

177

support him in getting the best of education, which would enable him eventually to choose whatever career he fancied, but was that enough to tie him to them for years? Wouldn't they be just as proud of him if he went to save the entire country from annihilation by the Germans? Should he wait until he next went home and ask his parents' permission? What if they said no? How would he feel then about doing nothing to atone for Poopie's death? He would never forgive himself, that's what. His mind finally made up, he turned into Blackfriars Street and on into the Recruitment Centre.

More than half an hour later, he emerged from the rather dingy hall, where a burly sergeant had asked him several direct questions that he was able to answer to the man's satisfaction. Then he'd had an embarrassing medical examination, and had passed that also. Whatever happened now, he had signed on as a Gordon Highlander, and no one could alter that. He marched out as though he were already wearing the kilt, back to Marischal College to inform the office of his decision.

It was easier than he had expected. The secretary smiled wearily. "You're the third one this week, and I'm beginning to think I'll do likewise. The trouble is, I haven't the nerve to tell my lady friend."

His lady friend. Willie had completely forgotten *his* lady friend. What on earth would Millie say? Rather than face her in the quad, he made for her Auntie Sophie's house in the Spital, hoping that he wouldn't meet her on the way. He had a quick glance at the watch she had given him as a Christmas gift. Five to eleven. It was safe enough. She'd be in the lecture hall by this time.

Sophie Campbell was astonished to see him back so early. "Are you not feeling well?" she asked solicitously.

He attempted a smile. "I'm feeling better than earlier on. I've just enlisted in the Gordons."

"You've done what?" she gasped. "Does Millie know?"

"Not yet." He told her what had happened to make him take the momentous step.

She listened with interest, then asked, quietly, "You and this Poopie? You were very good friends?"

"Yes, very good. I was the strong one; he was always the weak one, and I've let him down. I wasn't there for him." At last his grief for his boyhood chum overwhelmed him and he sank on to a chair, put his arms on the table and burst into a paroxysm of tears.

"Oh, laddie," Sophie consoled, "don't take it so badly. The two of you had drifted apart and you couldn't have protected him from harm all his life."

He tried to pull himself together. "I know, I know, but I can't help feeling I was still responsible for him . . . and now . . . and now . . ." The tears came again, but with less force. "I'm sorry, Sophie. Just give me a minute. I'll get over it."

"Will you be all right if I go out? I've nothing in for your lunch."

"I'll be fine, but don't worry about me. I think I'd best go home."

"I'll have to get something for Millie and me for tea anyway. Are you sure you won't wait and tell her what you've done?"

"I can't face her yet."

"I can understand that. Lock the door if you go off before I come back. You've still got the key I gave you?"

"Yes, and I'll put it through the letter box. Thanks for everything you've done for me." It came to him then that this was another person who had helped him financially. "I just wish I could pay you for my board and lodgings."

"Don't be soft. If I can't spend my money the way I want, what's the world coming to?"

It was some time after she left before he washed his face and packed his belongings. There was a train at five past two, and he would just have time to catch it.

The fifteen-mile journey took quite a time because of the number of stops on the way, but at last it steamed into Udny Station, the nearest he could get by rail to the Burnton area. Lugging his cardboard suitcase, seemingly heavier now than when he had gone to Aberdeen first, he set off to cover the three-and-a-half-mile gap, but fortune smiled on him. Just as he was beginning to think that he couldn't walk much farther without a rest, a tractor drew up alongside him. "Can I gi'e you a lift, Willie?"

The young man had hardly enough breath to answer Johnny McIntyre, who jumped down, hoisted the case on to the back of the tractor then jumped up again and held out his hand to help Willie. "I was sorry to hear aboot Poopie Grant," the farmer said then, kicking the feet from under his passenger's hold on his emotions. "Losh, Willie, I didna mean to upset you."

After a few seconds and having bottled his grief once more, Willie said, "I wasn't there for him. I wasn't there for him." He looked round into the other man's face. "I wish I'd joined up with him, but I enlisted in the Gordons this forenoon."

"Well, it'll not help Poopie, but it'll salve your conscience. I suppose it's the best thing you could have done. Dinna blame yoursel', lad. It would've happened whatever."

"You're a believer in Fate, then?"

"I am that. Oor lives are drafted oot for us afore we're ever born."

"Maybe that's true, but I feel better for having done something positive. As you say, it won't help Poopie, but it might help the war effort. Not that I think I'll make any great difference," he hastened to add, "but at least I'll feel that I'm being of some use."

"Aye, you're right, Willie. If every young man felt like that, we could wipe the Jerries aff the face o' the earth the morra."

Willie was a little surprised to find himself smiling as he walked up the track. He had thought he would never smile again. But there were still his parents to face, and they wouldn't adopt McIntyre's realistic outlook.

He walked into the house without knocking, as he had always been in the habit of doing — it was his home, after all — and was amazed by his mother's reaction. Her face had blanched, her hand had lifted to her chest, her mouth had fallen open.

"Willie! What's wrong?" she managed to gasp.

"I'm sorry, Mam, I didn't mean to . . . I never thought . . ."

"You never think, that's the trouble with you," she murmured. "Why are you here? Has something happened?"

He felt his throat closing again. She wouldn't understand, but he would have to tell her. "I've volunteered for the Gordons."

"You've what? Have you gone out of your mind? What about University?"

"This is more important, Mam. I need to go. Surely you can understand?"

"Has this anything to do with Cecil Grant? I suppose you know about him?"

"Yes, I know. That's why I did it. I always looked after him, remember, fought his battles for him, protected him . . ."

She ended the sentence for him. "So you feel responsible for his death?"

"Exactly. I'm glad you see it my way."

"No, I don't see it your way, but I guessed that's what your twisted mind would think."

"It's not twisted, Mam. If I'd been there, I'd have looked after him. I'd have made sure nothing happened to him." He could feel the tears gathering again. "I'd better go and tell Dad, though he likely won't be pleased, either."

Getting no answer, he stood up and went out, not knowing exactly where to find his father, but letting his eyes scour around hopefully. He had no luck until he saw him hammering in a gatepost at the far side of the ley field.

"Good God, Willie!" Jake exclaimed. "What are you daein' hame the day?"

"You'll likely have a fit when I tell you, Dad."

"Weel, come on then. Best get it ower wi'. Have you been expelled, or whatever they cry it? Sent doon? For daein' something you shouldna dae?"

"No, it's nothing like that. I . . ." He hesitated apprehensively.

"Oot wi' it, lad. I havena a' day to waste."

As if taking a running jump at it, Willie drew in a deep beath and blurted out, "I joined the Gordons this morning."

"You what? Are you mad? You canna gi'e up your chances like that!"

"I don't care about my chances. This is more important to me."

"Mair important? But it's nae jist yoursel' you've to think on, it's the two men that made your education possible. Were you nae thinking on them?"

"They'll understand. At least, I hope they will, but even if they don't, I still have to go."

"Still have to? So somebody's makin' you go? Some lassie, mebbe?"

"A laddie, Dad."

"Ah! I think I see noo. Poopie Grant? You want to get revenge for him? No, wait a minute. I've got it. You think you should have been wi' him?"

"Aye, Dad. That's it."

For a moment, Jake screwed up his face, trying to come to terms with this; whether to reprimand his son for being rash, or to be proud of him for wanting to fight for his country. An old soldier himself, he opted for the latter. "Aye, weel, you're a brave loon, but I wouldna like to be you explaining to the dominie and the minister. They'll nae be pleased."

"I'd better go and get it over with."

"Aye. Eh, does your Mam ken yet?"

"I told her first. She's not happy about it."

"No, I'm damned sure she's nae. Off you go, then, an' I'd best gan in an' try to soften her a bit."

Judging that the dominie would be home from school by now, Willie went straight to the schoolhouse and pulled the bell determinedly. "I want to speak to Mr Meldrum," he told Janet. "It's important."

The little maid seemed worried. "Is it something aboot Miss Millie?"

"No, it's not. Why did you think that?"

"There's been raised voices in the parlour since the master came home, so I thocht Miss Millie was ill or . . ."

"Nothing's wrong with Miss Millie. Now, will you show me in?"

She knocked timorously on the door before announcing, "Willie Fowlie wants to see you, sir."

"And I certainly want to see him."

Janet held the door open and Willie, realising that the man already knew, walked in on legs trembling with apprehension of what was to come. "I take it you've heard, sir?"

"You take it correctly, William. What tomfoolery are you up to now?"

184

"It's not tomfoolery. I've volunteered."

"For the Gordons. Yes, I know that, too. First, my sister telephoned me with the news, and some time later, my daughter called — in a state of great disress, I may add. What on earth were you thinking of?"

"I'll try to explain." Willie gave his explanation, plainly and simply, stressing the part he had played in Poopie's earlier life.

"So you feel it your bounden duty to atone for the years you ignored him?"

Mistakenly believing that the man's searching gaze meant sarcasm, Willie went on the defensive. "I didn't ignore him, Mr Meldrum, but circumstances were such that we didn't come in contact so much. If I hadn't gone to the Academy and on to University, we'd have seen each other every day."

"So, you put the blame on me?"

In his precarious emotional state, the youth failed to see the twinkle in his benefactor's eyes. "Oh, no, I didn't mean that, I'm sorry. It was something I'd never thought possible, and I'm very grateful for the chance you gave me." He broke off, searching for words to express himself.

It was Mrs Meldrum who took over. "Stop teasing him, Herbert. Surely you can see how badly his friend's death has affected him, I can quite understand how he feels." She turned to the young man. "In fact, William, I admire you for what you did this morning. Not many people would give up everything they hold dear because of their boyhood principles."

"Yes, indeed, Margaret. I am sorry, William. It was unforgivable of me to make light of things. I do understand how deeply you feel, and, although I must admit to a degree of disappointment that you are forsaking education for what you consider your duty, I do, however, wish you well."

"Thank you, Mr Meldrum, and you, too, Mrs Meldrum," Willie croaked, trying to hold back the tears that were on the brink of overflowing. "I feel awful about you wasting your money on me, and I promise to repay you after the war." He stood up to leave.

Reaching over with his hand held out, the man said earnestly, "Look, my boy. I want nothing paid back. What you have learned so far will not be wasted. It will remain in your mind for ever. It will give you a different perspective on things. It has shaped your life for the better."

Having made the expected gesture, Willie turned to the man's wife. "I must thank you, too, Mrs Meldrum, for seeing things my way."

She gave a small laugh. "My pleasure. No, Herbert, don't get up, I'll see William out."

At the outside door, she said, seriously, "I'd like to ask you something, if you don't mind, William."

"I don't mind."

"I want to know how you feel about Millie. She was really upset when I spoke to her on the phone earlier. She loves you, you know."

"I know, Mrs Meldrum, and I love her, but I would never be happy again if I didn't do what I feel is right.

Please tell her I'm sorry for hurting her and we can get together again after the war — if she still wants to."

"Dear boy, you can tell her yourself. She was going to be taking the bus from Aberdeen at five to six, if you want to come back?"

This was something he had wanted to avoid. He didn't think he could bear actually having to say goodbye to her. He loved her so much that the thought of leaving her was tearing at his innards, and he couldn't back out of his commitment to the Gordon Highlanders now. If he didn't make the effort to see her, though, Millie would think he didn't love her at all, which would hurt her even more. "I'll meet her off the bus, though I don't think it's a good idea. It'll be torture for both of us."

The woman patted his shoulder. "Please don't worry about it. Millie will find comfort in the fact that you do love her, even if you have to leave her. Now, what are you going to do until it's time? You can come back inside and wait?"

"No, I'll go and tell the minister what I've done. I'd better get that over."

"Good luck, then, William." She gave him a quick kiss on the cheek.

It wasn't far to the manse, and it was quite near where Millie would come off the bus, so he didn't hurry. He wanted to be in complete control of himself for this meeting, and while he walked, his mind returned to Mrs Meldrum. He had never really spoken much to her before, and he couldn't get over how like Millie she was. Or should it be the other way round?

She was not quite as slim as her daughter, but not at all plump. Her hair was perhaps a little darker and not so wavy, her eyes were the same deep blue.

To his immense relief, the Reverend Fyfe was as understanding as Mrs Meldrum. "I congratulate you on your sense of loyalty to your friend," he beamed. "Most people lose touch with the friends they had when they were children; one side or the other makes more of his life, creating resentment on the part of the one who has not done so well."

Willie shook his head. "It was the opposite way round with Poopie and me," he said, ungrammatically, for, at present, that part of the learning he had striven so hard to master had vanished along with everything else he had learned. "I was lucky to have the brains, and luckier still that I was recognised to be worth two men paying for my further education. Poopie would never have been anything other than a hard worker, but he was never jealous of me. He never even hinted that life wasn't fair, yet . . ." He gulped but carried on, ". . . life hasn't been fair to him, has it? He was a decent person, the very best."

"Yes, William, I quite agree with you. Life is never fair, as we see it. The old saying 'Only the good die young' is very often true. It would seem that God takes pity on a person who considers others although he has not much to be grateful for himself. The gates of Heaven are opened for him to enter, to leave the cares and woes of the world behind. Look on it that way, my boy, and you will begin to feel better."

"I can see what you mean, Mr Fyfe, and I will try, but it's not just Poopie's death that I've to contend with. I feel I've let you and Mr Meldrum down, too, yet I know perfectly well that if I stayed on at the University my heart wouldn't be in it."

"William," the old man leaned forward to pat his arm, "I do understand, and you must try to understand that you are under no obligation to me. I did what I thought was right, with no pressure from anyone, but you have not made me lose faith in the human race because you have not taken full advantage of it. You did what you believe is right, and I am sure Herbert Meldrum feels that way about it, too."

"Yes, he more or less said that."

"So forget about it, and enter your new life with vigour. Set your mind to it, and there is no doubt that you will do well. Remember that you go with my blessing."

Overwhelmed by grief for his childhood pal, gratitude towards the two men who had gambled on him and lost and growing concern as to the outcome of his coming meeting with Millie, Willie had left himself no time to plan what to say. He would have to take things as they came, just as he had done so far.

The sun was still glowing red low in the sky as the bus from Aberdeen drew up outside the church. Millie Meldrum, the only passenger to alight, gave a glance around when she stepped down, her face lighting up when she saw Willie waiting. "I wasn't expecting you to meet me."

189

"I thought I'd better," he replied, suspecting that this was going to be the hardest interview of the lot.

"You don't have to explain anything. Auntie Sophie told me."

"I'm sorry, Millie. As soon as Malcie Middleton told me about Poopie, I knew what I had to do, so I did it."

"Would you like to go for a little walk with me before I go home? I'd really like a little while with you on our own."

His heart sank. He wasn't prepared for this. Being alone with her for some time was a different thing from the five minutes he had visualised, but he supposed he owed it to her, though it would no doubt whip up his mangled emotions to fever heat and turn a knife in his heart.

As they passed the last gas lamp on the short street, he noticed the strain on her face for the first time, but he walked doggedly on without saying a word. He meant her to set the direction of their conversation, and at last, she murmured, "Can we sit down somewhere, Willie? It's easier to talk, don't you think?"

"I don't mind."

She had obviously been giving this some thought earlier. "Up the Ellon road a bit?"

He knew the place she had in mind; they had often chosen this secluded spot when they were walking out together, and he began to wonder if he could remain logical, could fight against the passion he could already feel buiding up at the thought of being close to her. The dusk was gathering momentum, just a slight line of red on the horizon where the sun was fast disappearing

190

altogether. It was the kind of evening that they used to like best, sitting on the springy grass, hidden from sight of the road or any peeping householder. Having no coat, he removed his jacket and spread it out for her to sit on.

"Thanks, Willie. And before we say anything else, I'm not angry with you. I know how you've always felt about Poopie, and maybe you blame me for keeping you apart?"

"I've never thought that, Millie. It was developing circumstances, that's what did it."

"I don't relish the idea of you leaving, but you must stick to your principles, I can see that. It'll be a few weeks yet before you go, though?"

He looked away. This was the devastating bit, for her as well as for him. "I've to report at Woolmanhill at 10a.m. tomorrow."

Her shocked gasp was so loud that he turned to face her again, and even in the gloom he could see that her face had blanched. "I'm not all that happy about it, either."

"But I thought . . ." She stared into his eyes, her tears threatening to overflow. "I thought you'd have at least this weekend — till Monday anyway. Oh, Willie, I can't bear to think . . . Is this the last time I'll see you till you get leave?"

It was hard to bear his own agony now, but trying to bear hers too was far worse, and his arms went out automatically to hold her, to comfort her, to let her see that he still loved her as much as ever. "Oh, my darling, darling, Millie," he groaned "Don't cry. Please don't cry. I can't bear to see you like this." He held her tightly, her deep sobs shaking his body as well as hers.

In spite of the resolution he had made not to kiss her, in case it led to more serious actions, he soon discovered that her lips trembled against his, but calmed after a few seconds. By this time, of course, it was too late to stop their youthful emotions taking over, youthful perhaps, but even more fierce than if they had been a mature man and woman.

They lay for over two hours, affirming and reaffirming their love for each other, that they would remain faithful for ever, that nothing would drive them apart. "You'll marry me when you come home on leave?" she asked, pride lost in this all-consuming love.

Sighing, he sat up. He had not foreseen this, but even in his present state of euphoria, he could see the pitfalls of such a marriage. "No, Millie, I can't tie you down like that. I might be killed."

"You won't!" she cried. "I won't let you be killed. I'll be praying for you every minute of every day, and God has never denied me anything, ever."

He did not point out to her that it was her father's position as a headmaster which had given her everything she had ever wanted; that was the main reason for his decision to wait. If he were killed, she would believe that God had forsaken her, and that would be worse than anything. "I promise we'll be married as soon as the war is over," he vowed, "and I won't change my mind about that. It surely won't be very long now, anyway." He got to his feet and held out a hand to her. "I felt you shivering just then, it's time to go. It's getting chilly."

"I'm not cold," she protested, but stood up obediently, casting a quick look at her watch. "My God, Willie, it's nearly midnight! I'll get hi-mi-nanny when I go in."

Willie grimaced. "Your father'll likely tear me to shreds; a bad influence on his darling daughter."

They hurried as quickly as they could, but heard the kirk clock striking the witching hour as they were practically at her door. He sighed resignedly. "I'd better wait and get what's coming to me."

No one appeared, however, and when Millie turned the door handle, she found it unlocked. "They trust us," she whispered, giving Willie a loving kiss before she went in. "You'll write?"

"Every day," he promised.

"So'll I, once I get your address."

No one had waited up for him, either, he found, and guilt swept over him as Millie's words came back. "They trust us." They hadn't been worthy of such trust, though. He felt thoroughly ashamed but he had no time to dwell on it. He had to get up in the morning and catch a train back to Aberdeen.

Neither of the lovers slept well. Willie was worried about what he had let himself it for, both as a result of volunteering and of his behaviour that evening. Millie was thinking of how she could get Willie to change his mind about marriage. If the war lasted for years, like some of the old folk thought it would, he could fall in love with another girl, someone he might meet wherever he was sent to.

CHAPTER
FIFTEEN

During his initial training in the fairly new Bridge of Don Barracks, on the outskirts of Aberdeen, Willie decided not to give Millie his address, telling her that they had been instructed just to write "Somewhere in Scotland". If she knew where he was, she was liable to come to see him, and there was no time for visitors; no time for anything but route marches, drills, eating and sleeping. He hardly had time to write to her once a week — just once in two weeks to his mother.

Realising that Willie's time would be fully occupied, Millie made no complaints. She was excited about what she planned to tell him when he came home on leave. At first, she had hoped that it would be the truth, but it hadn't worked out that way. She still intended telling him she was pregnant, and hoped that the miracle would take place during the next time he was home. If she had anything to do with it, they would be coupling every night, so saying she was pregnant beforehand would merely be jumping the gun a little bit. Willie, being the honourable, decent person he was, would have to marry her. Then, if it happened the way she wanted, she could easily tell him, when the infant was born, that it was late. Nobody would ever know otherwise. It was all so simple, and no harm would be done.

Margaret Meldrum was keeping a strict eye on her daughter. It was all very well for Herbert to say that even if the young couple had been together that night until midnight, it could have been perfectly innocent. From what she knew of men — and she'd known a few before her marriage — none of them, including her husband, would have let such an opportunity pass without at least trying. It was only when the girl did not feel the same way that their efforts had not succeeded, and she was practically sure that Millie was as much in love with Willie Fowlie as he was with her. But the weeks had gone past and the girl had ovulated every month as usual, so she definitely was not in the family way, thank goodness. It wasn't that, as a mother, she had anything against Willie as a son-in-law, but it would be preferable if the girl finished her University course and had her MA degree under her belt. That would always stand her in good stead if she ever had to earn a living — most unlikely, but you never knew.

Emily had also been suspecting that she might become a grandmother sooner than was practical, long before she felt like it. Her son had been in trouble of one kind or another throughout his childhood and into his teens and had only really calmed down since he got involved with the dominie's daughter. It had been very obvious for some time now that they were in love, or it would perhaps be more correct to say they were besotted with each other, and being together in the dark, until after midnight, on the night before Willie left, there was nothing surer than they had taken full advantage of the situation. But nothing untoward appeared to be happening at the schoolhouse. Millie came home for the odd weekend, and there wasn't the slightest sign that she was expecting.

Willie had found it fairly easy to get on with his comrades, some of them volunteers like himself, but mostly conscripts. It was simple to pick out which category each man belonged to; the cheery, eager-to-get-waded-into-the-enemy sort had enlisted voluntarily; the moaners, chip-on-the-shoulders kind had been taken against their wills. He did realise that there were exceptions to both categories, but as a general rule, this was the case.

It was natural, then, that they drifted together, like with like, and formed several small groups. Willie found himself making a sixth of one set, four lads from Inverness who, pals since schooldays, had been joined on the train by a boy from Elgin, all on their way to report in Aberdeen.

Gradually, as was also natural, the four original pals left the other two more and more often by themselves, and thus it was that Pat Michie and Willie Fowlie became inseparable. Through all the drills, the target practice and route marches, Willie looked after his friend, who reminded him very much of poor Poopie Grant. He, too, was shy and timid, afraid of asserting himself, and when any of the corporals or sergeants picked on Pat for not doing something correctly, it was Willie who stuck up for him. One sergeant, especially,

196

seemed to find delight in holding Pat up for ridicule for his poor performances in the skills they were being taught, and constantly laughing at Willie for trying to defend him.

"Who d'you think you are?" he sneered one day. "A puffed-up Mammy's boy? Little Lord Fauntleroy? A Nancy-boy student that thinks himself better than anybody else?"

Willie saw red at this, and without stopping to think of the consequences he lashed out with his fist, taking the sergeant completely by surprise. "I'll soon show you who's a puffed-up Mammy's boy," he snarled, "and I'm not a Nancy-boy because I stick up for a pal. I can recognise a bully when I see one, and you can put me on a charge if you want to. It's been worth it."

To his astonishment, the sergeant spun round on his heel, rubbing the jaw that had suffered from Willie's attack. The men who had stopped what they were doing to watch had all expected to see him being marched off to spend some time in the glasshouse, and ran up to slap him on the back.

"Good for you, Fowlie."

"You showed him."

"What a beauty of a punch!"

"You damn near KO'd him."

When the clamour died down, and another sergeant came to finish the drill, he purposely avoided catching Willie's eye. The expression on his weatherbeaten face, however, was almost as if he admired what the recruit had done but could not tell him so. Pat Michie's gratitude went much further, and was so embarrassing that Willie had to laugh off his "heroism". He felt much happier now than he had felt for some considerable time and couldn't understand why until it dawned on him one night in bed, that he had defended another human being weaker than himself as he used to do with Poopie Grant. It didn't quite make up for not saving his boyhood chum from his final ordeal, but it was certainly helping.

What Poopie had told him about his basic training was as near the truth as he could have got, Willie discovered. Route marches, hours of drill, weaponry instructions, guard duty — and only a few hours' sleep every night on a most uncomfortable trestle bed. In the morning, before the crack of dawn even, the bugler took a delight in loosing off Reveille, and there followed a mad rush to the ablutions.

Although he was well aware that his manner of speaking earned him the nickname "Clever Dick", Willie didn't care. They could make fun of him as much as they liked; at least they would not be able to find fault with his stamina. He hadn't been a molly-coddled child. He'd been brought up in a working-class household, with probably a lot less going for him than some of the others. No amount of drills or marches would be too much for him. He was there to do everything that was asked of him, and to work off the guilt over Poopie's death that he was certain would eat at him for years. Only when he had done something of outstanding bravery would he feel free of that guilt.

When their basic training was almost over and they were given the dates of their first leave, Willie purposely did not tell Millie in his letter exactly when he would be arriving home. He merely wrote, "on the 23rd", and hoped that she wouldn't try meeting every train and bus. As it happened, his whole unit had been posted to Redford base outside Edinburgh because there had been an invasion scare.

It was more than a week later, then, that he swung his kitbag off the train at Aberdeen and went straight to the large destination board in the centre of the Joint Station, so-called because all the smaller railway companies — North of Scotland, Highland, London Scottish and so on — had amalgamated into one terminal for the London North Eastern Railway. Learning that the first train to go through Udny Station was not for three hours yet, he wandered over to the small tearoom to have some sustenance. The short journey from Redford to Edinburgh had been bad enough with about forty soldiers going home on belated leave more than filling the labouring bus, but the train from Edinburgh to Aberdeen had been a thousand times worse. It had apparently been packed from London, with more and more travellers, civilians as well as servicemen, joining at each stop on the way north. Why hadn't they paid heed to the posters up all over the place — "IS YOUR JOURNEY REALLY NECESSARY?"

By the time he had boarded the train there were no seats whatsoever, hardly any room in the corridors, with somnolent bodies packed like sardines, even in the toilets, although quite a fair amount had got off when he got on at Waverley. After Dundee, however, the crush thinned out, and gradually most of the remaining passengers had found a seat. He hadn't been lucky until they stopped at Montrose, and by Jove he was glad of the rest.

Realising that the small café had filled up, Willie took himself out to one of the seats provided in the main part of the station, and thankfully stretched out with his kitbag as a pillow. Two and a half hours later, the bustle of moving travellers alerted him to why he was there, and with a weary sigh, he got up and made his way to the gate of the platform he needed. For a scary moment he could not find his travel warrant, then he recalled, with a rush of relief, shoving it inside his cap for safety, and in another few minutes he was seated in the short train that would take him to Udny Station.

Very soon, the clickety-clack, clickety-clack, the accompanying choo-chooing and the rhythmic swaying motion lulled him to sleep again. Only the stationmaster/porter's strident bawl of "Udny! Udny!" brought him abruptly back to consciousness.

After telling his father something of what he'd been doing, and answering his mother's questions as best he could without mentioning the gruelling instructions he'd had in the use of rifles, bayonets and other types of weapons, including grenades, he spent most of his first two days catching up on lost sleep and giving Jake a hand with whatever task he was doing. It was quite a comfortable feeling to be working alongside his father, but he knew that he wouldn't have enjoyed it as a full-time job. He spoke now of things he couldn't tell his mother; of how he was tired of training, of how much he wanted to be fighting the enemy not wasting time on cleaning latrines; of standing guard duty; of having to knuckle under the blatant bullying of some of the sergeants.

"But you must've ken't the army wasna a place where you could dae what you liked," Jake reminded him. "There has to be discipline. There has to be training, or how would you ken what to dae if we was invaded? Your Mam was maybe right. I wasna hard enough on you when you was little."

"She was likely right," Willie laughed. "I suppose I must have driven her mad with the things I did."

"Aye, well," Jake admitted, "but you wasna a wicked laddie. You never meant to hurt naebody. You was just illtricket, like a lot o' ither loons."

Discussing the scrapes that the boy had got into — the shoe polish, the hens, the kitten, the schoolboy fights, the episode with the bike that had precipitated a murder hunt — they had been laughing until that last incident reminded Willie of the real murder that had followed some years later. "There's never been any news about Gordie Brodie? He's never been found?"

His face sobering, Jake shook his head. "Never a word. I think it's been swept under the carpet."

"But the police know he killed Connie. I told them myself."

"I ken it was him, an' Jeemsie Cooper's sure it was him, but the 'tecs . . . They've got it into their heids you just *thocht* it was him you seen. They think you was ower young to be sure, an' they've stopped lookin' for him."

"I haven't stopped looking," Willie declared. "Everywhere I go, I keep an eye out for him. He can't escape for ever."

"I hope you're richt, but for ony sake dinna say onything to your mother. She's never got ower it. An' Becky's never written, so she doesna ken where she is, an' you're nae exactly . . ."

Ashamed at neglecting such a duty, Willie promised to write more often. He hadn't really thought about his mother's situation. Not one of her three children left to comfort her in her encroaching old age. She couldn't be much more than fifty, yet she looked a lot older. Was he really the cause of all those wrinkles on her brow, of her steadily increasing grey hairs, of her dull, weary eyes?

Having run out of conversations to have with his parents, Willie started a round of visiting. His first call was on Beenie Middleton, the woman who had brought him into the world. She, too, was looking much older, but her face lit up to see him. "Come awa' in, laddie, the kettle's just bilin'. Did you ken my Malcie's been called up? He's in the Ordnance Corps, but he's nae affa happy."

Remembering Malcolm Middleton's history of long periods of doing nothing between extra-short terms of employment, Willie wasn't surprised to hear this. "He'll get used to it, though. It's not such a bad life."

"You must've ken't a big difference, though, you being at the university an' a' your learnin'. Was you nae surprised? Did you nae feel let doon?"

"I suppose I did, for a while, but you've just got to tell yourself if that's the way it has to be, that's how it's got to be. We're all in the same boat."

"My Malcie doesna like hard work, that's what's wrang wi' him. He's a lazy bugger, just like his Da." She roared with laughter now.

Willie knew that her husband had always been a drunkard and had never held down a job for long until he'd come to Wester Burnton, where he seemed to have come to his senses as far as work was concerned, though he still liked a good drink.

After about an hour, he bade Beenie goodbye and promised to come to see her again if he had time. He headed next to Mrs Grant's house, passing several cottages, outside one of which were two dirty-faced little boys intent on their game of marbles, or "bools" as Willie knew they were called here. Outside another were three dainty little girls in bare feet tucking their dolls into cardboard boxes for cots, he presumed, or maybe prams. It was great what a child's imagination could do. He felt a flash of resentment at the detectives for not believing what he'd told them. He had been fifteen years old, not a child. At any rate, not young enough to be imagining seeing somebody who wasn't there.

Last in the group of this six of the houses provided by Johnny McIntyre for his workers and their families, was the home of the Grants. Willie had swithered about going there, although he knew he should tender his condolences to Poopie's mother. There was a two- or three-year-old sitting on the doorstep eating a thick slice of bread, his mouth already covered in jam, and he wondered if this was a grandchild or fostered. He could vaguely remember that Tibby Grant had occasionally taken care of other people's children in cases of illness or families being split up.

The boy's eyes followed him as he opened the gate and walked up the long garden path, staring up at him silently as he knocked on the door.

"Hi, kid," he said, pleasantly. "Were you hungry?"

His only answer was a nod, but it didn't matter, as Tibby came to the door cleaning her floury hands on a huge white apron — or, to be absolutely accurate, on a white apron liberally spotted with red jam and brown stains that could have been gravy. Her straggly grey hair had escaped from most of its hairpins and was inching down her crepey neck.

"Oh my God!" she exclaimed. "Willie Fowlie! Oh, loon, it's good to see you. You're lookin' weel. Life in the Gordons must be agreein' wi' you."

"Nae so bad," he laughed, lapsing into his old way of speaking. He felt an affinity with this woman, more than he had ever felt for his own mother, and to be truthful he had probably spent more time in this house than in his own when he was a boy. "How are you, Mrs Grant?"

She eyed him reflectively. "I could say I was fine. I could even say I wasna so bad, but the truth is, I just tak' each day as it comes. I dinna like bein' on my ain for ony length o' time. I need to feel somebody's near me, auld or young, it doesna matter. That's why I foster bairns. I've had three fostered on me since Poopie . . . but I've got my Daisy's twa the now till she's on her feet again efter this last ane. Leslie, that's him playin' oot by, he's the youngest, and Greggie, her auldest, he's at the school."

Her eyes losing the faint sparkle that had appeared while she was speaking of her grandsons, her voice trailed away, but with a start, she said, "Dinna mind me, Willie, lad. It comes on me that sudden whiles. I've gotten ower him, richt enough, but there's never a day gans by that I dinna think on him."

"It's only natural, Mrs Grant."

"Losh, Willie. You surely ken me weel enough to cry me Tibby. Good God, loon, I've dichted your neb, I've cleaned your scratted knees an' put iodine on them, I've gi'en you boseys when you fell . . ." Her voice wavered slightly. "Willie, you was like anither son to me, an' I'm gled you still want to come to see me. You're a good loon, a real good loon, an' I ken fine it was for my Poopie you gi'ed up your education and jined up."

He put out his arms to hold her when she burst into tears, patting her back and making soothing noises. He knew exactly how she was feeling; hadn't he felt like this ever since he'd heard about his old pal's death? In that moment, as his own tears overtook his fragile composure, it dawned on him that while he, a young man, stood with his arms round a woman who must be around sixty, at least, this must be the first time either of them had been able to show the full, shattering depth of their sorrow for the soldier both of them had loved, in spite of all his faults.

It was fully five minutes before the woman drew away. "My, Willie, I dinna ken what you must be thinkin' o' me. I'm a silly, sentimental aul' fool."

"You're not silly, Tibby, and you're not old nor a fool. And there's nothing wrong in being sentimental," he assured her. "The world would be a better place if more people showed some sentiment now and then."

She wiped her nose with a hankie that had seen better days. "Well, maybe you're right, lad, but there's a time and a place for a'thing, as the minister said to the verger when he catched him peein' on the roses." She dashed away the last vestiges of her tears and gave a raucous laugh. "Your Ma would ha'e a fit if she heard what I'm sayin' till her darlin' boy."

"I'm not her darling boy — never was. It was her two girls she loved."

"Poor wumman. She hasna had her sorrows to seek, has she? She's lost them baith, and I tell you this: I dinna ken how she got through that." Clearly wanting to avoid further dips into the slough of despond, she said, brightly, "What say you till a bowlie o' broth?"

"Aye," he grinned. "A bowlie o' broth never goes wrang."

And so they enjoyed the thick soup — the kind that a spoon could stand up in — reminiscing about the things the two boys had done, and finding themselves laughing as heartily as they had been weeping a short time before. There were also little lapses into the sadness again, when other bits of the past came up, but on the whole they kept the light-heartedness throughout.

The old wag-at-the-wa' showed six o'clock before they noticed the time, even though Tibby's older grandson had come home from school and the younger one had come in twice for a "piece an' jam". It was as though they were small interruptions that didn't really interfere with the conversation. But the young man got to his feet now. "I'm sorry Tibby, but I'll have to go. I've been out since breakfast time."

She, too, stood up. "Aye, your Ma'll be wonderin' where you are, but you ken this? I've really enjoyed your visit. It's cheered me up like naething else would've daen. I canna thank you enough for mindin' on an auld wife."

"I've really enjoyed it as well, Tibby, and if I've got time I'll come again before I go back." He held out his hand at the door, but she grabbed his shoulders and kissed him on the cheek.

Not another word was spoken, and he walked down the path patting the boys on the head when they came running up to ask their grandmother if their supper would be long.

He heard the door being shut, but his heart was much lighter on his way home than it had been when he left in the morning. Emily, of course, was curious to know where he had been, and he told her most of what had been said in both houses. "I think Beenie's a bit worried about Malcie. He doesn't like the army, and you know what he was like. I think she imagines him deserting and being put in prison, or something like that, but Malcie always manages to come out smelling of roses, doesn't he? Not like poor Poopie."

"And how did you think Tibby was managing?" Emily wanted to know.

He didn't tell her anything other than, "She says she's fine, but I think she's putting a brave face on it. We had a nice long chat, put the world to rights."

Emily couldn't help but smile at this. "You two would be able to do that, right enough. You've both got plenty to say."

Jake came in at that moment, and the two men discussed the fortunes of the war, criticising this general for his tactics, that one for not having thought out his plan properly, occasionally praising some small victory over the Germans, until Emily said, rather sourly, "That's enough war talk. It's bad enough getting it all the time in the paper and on the wireless, but not at my own table."

Jake winked at Willie, and then said, in an exaggerated English accent, "So what do you think of the price we're getting for potatoes now?" which made the two men double up, but Emily drew in her lips. "If you think that's funny, you've got minds like ten-year-olds."

Willie toyed for a second with the idea of telling her Tibby's joke about a verger, but decided against it. His mother would definitely not see the funny side of that.

The next day was Friday, so Willie deliberately kept away from anywhere near the Meldrums' house. He didn't want to see Millie, especially when he hadn't arranged to meet her, and she could be home for the weekend some time today. He asked his mother to make a few sandwiches for him and he filled a flask with tea, then spent an hour cleaning his bike. He had to get away by himself. He had to think things through, without interference from outside, and that included his parents and Millie. Especially Millie.

As he pedalled off in the opposite direction from her house, he reminded himself that he had made a big mistake on the night before he had to report to Woolmanhill, a couple of months ago now, and had been very lucky to get off Scot free. If he had made her pregnant that night, it would have been the end of her career, the end of his peace of mind, and the only way to prevent it happening again — as they were so often told in the lectures they got — was celibacy. No hanky-panky. No letting your dick rule your heart, as one officer had so basically expressed it.

Recalling the man who had said it, Willie wondered if the old codger had ever been in love with a woman. It didn't seem likely, otherwise he wouldn't imply that celibacy was easy. It certainly wouldn't be easy for William Fowlie. It was the other way round with him; his heart seemed to rule his dick, though that probably made no difference.

He cycled on for quite a while, deliberately avoiding the Cooper Burn or Carter Loch. He had no wish to revive impossible-to-be-repeated memories. He did find an ideal place; a little dell on the fringe of a wood, where he could sit — or lie if the mood took him — in perfect solitude and peace amid the firs and larches.

Having spent most of the night trying to come to some decision about his life, he dozed off minutes after lying back with his jacket as a pillow, and woke up quite some time later, refreshed and ready to face anything. Yes, it would be best to steer clear of Millie Meldrum until the war was over. The way things had been, he couldn't concentrate on what he was supposed to be doing, and, for a soldier, particularly a Gordon Highlander, that was no good. He had to be alert at all times, ready to repel invaders, ready to be sent abroad to face the enemy, just ready for anything. If only they would send him overseas, it would be so much easier, but no doubt that would come — eventually.

When he went back, things could have completely changed, although the battalion surely wouldn't go overseas without him? No, no, that was impossible, unthinkable. He had a duty to carry out, and God himself wouldn't stop him.

He gave an abrupt laugh. What was he going on about? He had only just passed his initial training, so he wouldn't be sent overseas for a good while yet.

Feeling quite hungry now, he fished in his haversack for his sandwiches, removed the cup from the flask and filled it with tea. He thoroughly enjoyed his solitary picnic; his appetite had come back since he'd made his decision, his day had not been wasted. He could make another round of visits to old friends; he'd face them now with a clear conscience. He hadn't yet gone to see

Johnny McIntyre, and he might chance going to the Meldrums; he could tell them that, although he loved Millie with every fibre of his being, he thought it would be best not to see her until the war was over. It would make things easier for everyone.

A heavy burden having been taken from his shoulders, he took a walk, stopping here and there to watch the wildlife, the rabbits, the birds, none of whom had any knowledge of humans and were all the more friendly because of it. At one point, even a deer came near him, not quite up to him, just keeping abreast of him as he went along the edge of a burn. The hind was so lovely, he wished that he had a camera, her huge eyes regarding him shyly, her head erect, but very, very timid. If he made the slightest move towards her, she slewed away until she felt safe and then inched her way back. He was so amused by this that he made several feints, but she tumbled to his trickery and stood her ground.

"Good for you, lass," he crooned, holding out his hand to her, but she gave a small whinny and ignored it. A noise from inside the wood made her turn slowly and pad away, leaving him wondering if her lord and master was waiting for her. The thought that a rampant stag might have appeared at any moment and attacked him for dallying with his mate was not at all pleasant, and he thanked his lucky stars that he had not been the target of a charge.

This episode seemed to him to be a good omen for the future, and he wandered back to his picnic site slowly, to prepare for taking the road again.

CHAPTER
SIXTEEN

It was inclined to be drizzly the following morning; the sky grey and forbidding, the wind, as Jake put it, "Ower lazy to gan roon' you, so it gans richt through you." Considering what would be his best option, Willie plumped for doing some more visiting. It would be better than being cooped up in the house all day and having to answer his mother's scarcely veiled questions about his relationship with Millie. Closely wrapped up in his heavy greatcoat and cap with its "Bydand" badge well up for show, he opened the door and prepared to step outside.

"You're not going out in your bare legs in this weather?" Emily demanded. "You'll catch your death of cold. Put on a pair of trousers, for any sake."

His forced sigh, short and vehement, showed his annoyance. "I tried on all the three pairs I had, and none of them fit me any more. I was like a sack of tatties tied in the middle and I'd have died of strangulation before I'd got as far as the road."

"Would a pair of your father's not fit you?"

"Ach, just leave me, Mam. I'm not a kid now, and I stopped wearing hand-me-downs ages ago."

"Don't expect me to dance attendance on you, then, if you land up with a chill."

"Cheerio, Mam."

He strode out, closing the door behind him with perhaps a little more force than was necessary, and coming off the track on to the road, turned in the direction of Wester Burnton. If he saw Johnny McIntyre on his way there he would stop and have a news with him, and then go on to the farmhouse, for Mrs McIntyre had always been very kind to him. Breathing the caller air deep into his lungs, he felt on top of the world, not exactly master of all he surveyed, more like renewing acquaintance with every blade of grass, every stone, every tree — not that there were many trees, for the Buchan area of north-east Scotland had been blasted by strong winds for so many centuries that in some parts only a few stunted examples remained. Of course, there were woods in other parts, grand examples of a glory that once was, but the most interesting bits to him were the standing stones, from which archaelogists could prove that life in quite an advanced form had been present here for thousands of years.

"Hey, Willie!"

He started in surprise, so immersed in his own thoughts that he hadn't seen the two men in the field he was passing. "Aye, Mr McIntyre," he called back.

"You're hame for a while, then?"

"I go back on Monday."

"I'd like fine to ha'e a wee blether wi' you, loon, but I'm real busy the noo. I tell you what, though, you go in and ha'e a few words wi' the wife. You and her aye got on fine, and I should be in aboot half twelve. We can ha'e a drappie denner then I'll tak' you farever you want."

"That suits me, Mr McIntyre."

"Godamichty, loon. I stopped bein' Mister McIntyre years ago, and I maistly gets cried Wester, and sometimes, jist WB. The younger generation dinna show ony respect to aulder fowk, though there's nae mony left nooadays."

Walking towards the farmhouse, Willie thought over this last remark. The war had certainly brought changes to the workers, but he hadn't given a thought to how it had affected the bosses. He'd heard tales of the farmers making pots of money by growing the crops they were told to grow by the Ministry of Agriculture, and good luck to them, but he hadn't remembered that most of the young men, the fit, the willing, had been taken by the War Ministry and that it would be the older, unfit, willing but not so able, that were the mainstay of the farming communities, helped by the under-eighteens.

Cutting off a corner by vaulting a drystane dyke, he made his way more circumspectly to the back door of the farmhouse, where Maggie McIntyre exclaimed with delight, "Willie Fowlie! Now you're a sicht for sair een."

She bade him come in, settled him on a wooden chair and filled a large enamel mug with tea that she assured him was freshly made, and its taste proved her claim. She didn't quiz him in the way his mother had, but he found himself telling her things he hadn't told Emily, and, following that, she acquainted him with facts about the locals that his mother had never mentioned; indeed, perhaps did not even know.

Before they knew it, the farmer was in for his dinner, although he was more inclined towards asking what Willie's basic training had consisted of. At last, he said, "My God, it's half three already, and I've still got a few thingies to finish, but if you can hang aboot for an 'oor or so, I'll run you hame."

"No, you're fine. I'll easily manage to walk."

"Go roon' and ha'e a chat wi' my new milkmaid, an' I'll nae be lang."

Willie interpreted the twinkle in the eyes of both the man and his wife as evidence of the new milkmaid being either a raving young beauty or a decrepit old hag, but was certainly not prepared for the person he saw cleaning out pails and jugs at the big sink in the dairy. "Oh, it's you, eh . . ."

He never knew how to address the poor man, for he didn't want to call him "Daftie" like the men used to do. "Are you helping the new milkmaid?"

The tired old eyes brightened a little. "It's Willie, isn't it?" He gave a little chuckle. "Nae milkmaid. Jist me."

"You must be the milkmaid, then. That's good. You must be real proud of that?"

"Aye, real prood. Mester Mac says I'm daein' a grand job, and the wife says the same."

Willie felt a shiver of horror going through him. Surely this man hadn't taken a wife? Who on earth would have him, anyway? Fortunately, before he said anything, it occurred to the young man that he meant the farmer's wife. Trying to find a solution to the name business, he phrased his next question carefully, leading up to what he wanted to know. "You'll be missing Malcie, I suppose? Now he's in the army."

"In the war." The old man nodded. "Nae my war. Your war."

"That's right. What were you in the last war? What did they call you?"

With an obvious great effort, the old man stood to attention, his right arm up in a smart salute. "564351 Corporal MacLauchlan, L., sir. Rank, name and number, that's all." His body caved in once more, his eyes lost their momentary illumination.

"Fancy you remembering that," Willie said, honestly impressed. "What did your fellow soldiers call you? You see, I need to know what name I should give you."

"Lachie, maistly."

"Oh, I see. Short for McLaughlan?"

"No, my name *is* Lachie — Lachlan McLaughlan, corporal in the Seaforths."

Willie was astonished, but the flash of lucidity had completely gone, and the old man's next words were, "Poopie's awa' an' a'."

The impediment that usually came into Willie's throat at any mention of his old friend almost choked him, but he managed a slight nod.

"A richt quiet loon, Poopie."

"Yes, he was." Get yourself out of this hole, he told himself. "Do you like being a milkmaid, Lachie? Do you take in the cows and milk them, as well? And what about the butter?"

216

"The wife still mak's the butter. I separate the cream for her, then she churns it, and I tak' the buttermilk. A' the wives like buttermilk for makin' scones an' pancakes."

"Mrs Mac's a real hardworking woman, but I'd have thought she'd enough to do in the farmhouse, without making the butter, as well."

"Aye, Mester Mac's aye gettin' on till her — daein' ower muckle."

Much to Willie's relief, "Mr Mac" came round the corner at that moment. "What d'you think o' my milkmaid, then?"

Willie smiled. "Lachie's better than any young lassie, I'll say that. Well, cheerio, Lachie, I'll see you next time I'm hame."

In the car, McIntyre said, "He's good, but why Lachie? Where did you hear that? It suits him."

"It's his real name. Lachlan McLaughlan. He told me he was a corporal in the Seaforths."

"McLaughlan? Aye, there's something familiar aboot that. I was only a bairn when he came to work for my father, but by the time he came back from the war — and it was a year or so efter the Armistice for he'd been in some kind o' home — Father had died and the name never came up. As you ken, a lot of folk ca' him the Daftie, but he's nae so daft."

"No, he's not. He surprised me right enough."

McIntyre drew in to a quiet spot for a few minutes, for a "blether", but mostly about how his workers had been called up, or had volunteered, and how difficult it was to find replacements. "Damn near impossible," he said, vehemently. "And the worst o' it is, nae a' the men'll come back. Oh, loon, I'm sorry. I shouldna be saying things like that to you." He switched on the engine again, and drove the short distance to the cottar houses. "Look after yourself, Willie," he said, letting his passenger out, "and jist remember this. Never volunteer for onything."

"I'll remember," Willie smiled, having made up his own mind weeks ago that the only way to get on would be to volunteer for everything that was offered.

His mother, of course, wanted to know where he had been and was quite surpriseed that he had spent a whole day at the farmhouse. "You're hardly ever here," she complained. "Your own father and mother, but you'd rather be speaking to strangers."

Jake's brows went down. "Go easy, lass. He did spend his first few days here, and tell't you everything you wanted to ken. He needs different company sometimes, an' he still hasna been to see the Meldrums. Millie's been hame since Friday nicht, an' she aye gans back on the Sunday efterneens, so you'd best see her the morra mornin'."

"To be honest, Dad," Willie said, uncomfortably, "I'd rather not see her."

Emily opened her mouth, obviously with the intention of asking why, but Jake stepped in. "It's up to you, of coorse, but I'd advise you to think aboot it."

Willie did think about it. He puzzled over it all night, longing to see the girl he loved with all his heart, aching to hold her in his arms, but afraid that in his lust, he would hurt her, or even worse, bairn her, as the Burnton

218

women would say. Either way, she would probably want nothing more to do with him. No, it was better not to place himself within reach of such temptation.

He still hadn't gone to see the minister, but he'd be busy on a Sunday morning, so that call would have to wait until afternoon. He had promised to call in to Tibby Grant again if he had time, and he should really go and see Gramma Fowlie. Yes, that's where he should go.

Looking out from the skylight in his small upstairs bedroom on the Sunday morning, the weather did not look all that promising, but Willie would have gone out if it had been lashing rain or drifting snow, even a Force 9 gale. As it happened, by the time he had washed and shaved and had his breakfast, the sun was making a fair attempt at shining, the grey sky had almost cleared. Emily was already dressed in her Sunday clothes, Jake was polishing his Sunday boots, both obviously going to church. Willie knew that his mother was half expecting him to join them, but he just wasn't in a churchy mood, and as he sat down at the table, he said, "I promised Gramma I'd go and see her, so I may as well go. It's a fine day for a walk, and she'll be looking for me." He noticed his mother drawing in her lips, but she said nothing.

It was Jake who said, as he took his greatcoat off the hook on the kitchen door, "Will you be hame for your dinner?"

Emily seemed to come to a decision. "I've a whole pot of stew and carrots. If you wait a minute, I'll put enough in the flagon to do you and your Gramma."

"Thanks, Mam, that'll be great. I should think I'll be home for my tea, though."

His father winked at him in satisfaction as he went out carrying the container inside a shopping basket, where it sat quite steadily.

He spent all forenoon with Mina Fowlie, whose body was beginning to cause problems — legs unable to walk more than a step or two, feet crippled by corns and bunions, knees that creaked as she walked, hands curled by arthritis — but there was nothing wrong with her tongue, and she chatted away twenty to the dozen, laying bare her neighbours' secret romances that were the talk of the place, the rumours of somebody's sticky fingers that everyone knew about except the police, the row between the kirk organist and the leader of the choir. He didn't know any of the people, but he found her way of telling the stories very amusing, and the pair of them chuckled like mischievous schoolkids.

Just before twelve o'clock, which he knew was her regular dinnertime, he emptied the flagon of stew into a pot and heated it on the fire — she still hadn't had gas or electricity installed — and they sat down to eat at only a few minutes past the hour. "I havena any tatties," she had told him earlier, "for I was gan to ha'e cheese and breid, but I got a new pan loaf fae the baker's van yesterday, so we can ha'e a chunk o' that to dry up the gravy."

Anyone not acquainted with the niceties of the Doric tongue might think breid and loaf are the same thing, and so it can be at times, but in this case, Willie knew that by breid his grandmother meant oatcakes, which

220

spread with butter made an ideal accompaniment to the crowdie cheese made on most of the farms. She made him cut two "doorstep" slices from the loaf, thick slices that they broke with their fingers to soak up the gravy.

After eating an apple each for pudding, the young man washed the dirty dishes, flagon and pot, and then said, "I want to go to see Mr Fyfe, the minister at home, you know, so I'd better go soon, or else he'll be busy with the Young Communicants, maybe, or a Bible Class — and then it'll be time for his evening service."

"Aye, they're gey hard worked on the Sabbath," she grinned, "but some o' them dinna dae muckle for the rest o' the week."

"Oh, I wouldn't say that. There's weddings and christenings . . ."

"An' frunials, but that doesna tak' six days, does it?" She giggled to show she wasn't serious.

"You're an awful woman, Gramma."

"It's either that or gi'e up an' let the undertaker get anither frunial to dae."

"No, no, don't say that. You've been the backbone of my life, Gramma, so don't even joke about something like that."

"You're richt, laddie. I'm makin' fun o' men that are dedicated to God. They do a lot o' good work, giving folk comfort in a time of need, just bein' there for them is a blessin' sometimes."

"I'd better be off, but remember, I need you to be here when I come back next time."

"I'll dae my best, but you ken, Willie, naebody has the power to escape the Grim Reaper. When your time comes, you have to go, and the trouble is, you never ken when your time is comin'. An' maybe that's a good thing."

Very emotional now, he bent his head to kiss her cheek when he shook hands with her, and, his eyes blurred with tears, he narrowly avoided walking into the door on his way out.

The Reverend Fyfe greeted his visitor warmly. "Sit down, my boy. I half expected to see you in church this morning with your parents, but . . ."

"I went to say cheerio to my grandmother."

"Yes, so your dear mother said. Well, that was a charitable thing to do. Many of the younger people today have no time for their grandparents, or indeed for anyone over the age of forty. Now, tell me about your training. You know, I would have quite liked to volunteer as a chaplain again, but my age is against me."

They chatted companionably for the next hour and a half — the older man wanting to know if Willie's education had helped him in his present situation, to which he gave a fictional affirmative reply, and then Mr Fyfe said, "I know a white lie when I hear one, but rest assured. Your time at University will not be wasted when you come out of the army. It will stand you in good stead to find a decent job, a good career. Have you been to see Millie Meldrum yet?"

The abrupt change of topic disconcerted the young man. He wasn't prepared to discuss this side of his life, but the other man had noticed. "I am sorry, my boy. I didn't mean to pry. Now, I'm afraid we will have to stop there. I take a Young Communicants' Class at half past three; not that many attend, but even adding two or three new members to our congregation is a worthwhile cause. Thank you for coming to see me, William, and I wish you luck in your career in the Gordon Highlanders. A really fine regiment, with a long history of gallantry. God bless you."

They shook hands and Willie went down the path on to the road, wondering if he should chance going to the schoolhouse, or if it was too early and Millie would still be there. He decided against going and made for home, deciding at the last moment to spend a little more time with Tibby.

As always, she welcomed him warmly, but cannily avoided even the slightest reference to the tragedy, confining herself to giving him little tidbits of gossip regarding mutual friends and acquaintances. "Beenie says Malcie'll be hame some time the morn, so you'll just miss him. She says he's settlin' doon now, an' nae afore time. He's aye been a big bairn, nae happy unless things is gan his way, but the army was the best place for him. They'll nae tak' ony o' his nonsense. It'll be the makin' o' him — you wait an' see."

He smiled a little wryly. "I bet you say the same about me."

"Na, na, laddie, you've aye been a different type. You never expected things to be handed to you on a plate. I ken you werena happy at the dominie sub ... eh, subsiding — is that the richt word? — your education."

Stifling a grin, he said solemnly, "It's sub-sid-ising, but you're right. I wasn't happy. I like to work things out for myself, then I've only myself to blame if anything goes wrong."

"Aye well, that's a good enough reason, I suppose, but you'd mak' things easier for yoursel' if you sat back an' let somebody else tak' the responsibility." She uttered a screech of laughter here. "Oh, would you listen to me? Fowk would think I'd swallied a dictionary. Me that's never picked up a book in my life." She looked at him askance. "I suppose you think I'm a richt dunce. You see, I canna read. I was the auldest an' I was kept aff the school every time my mither had a bairn, and my faither was a randy auld bugger . . ." Another howl of laughter.

Understanding, Willie laughed along with her. It had long been a common occurrence amongst the farm labourers' families — the first-born female child was expected to be a sort of second mother to the younger siblings, and was thus deprived of a decent schooling. There was only one thing he could think of to say. "At least you were well prepared when it came your turn to run a house and a family of your own."

"You think like an auld ane, d'you ken that? Govey Dick, you'll mak' a damn good man to some lucky lassie some day, be she Millie Meldrum or somebody you havena met yet."

He gave a hearty laugh at this. "Tibby, you're fishing now, but I'm not rising to the bait. I'm making no commitments until the war's over, but I promise you, when I do, you'll be among the first to know."

After another half-hour or so of banter, he took his leave, kissing her cheek as he shook her hand, something he never did as a rule, not even to Emily.

Coming to the Middletons' house, he decided that he had better say goodbye there, too. Although Beenie and Tibby were the best of friends, there still existed a shred of one-upmanship between them, and it would probably cause trouble if he spent so much more time with one than with the other. "I jist wondered if you'd have time to come an' see me again," she beamed, plainly pleased that he had bothered. "It's a pity you'll nae be here to see Malcie, though."

"I know, but that's life, isn't it? Anyway, tell him I was asking for him."

"I'll dae that, and he seems to ha'e settled in, noo. I'm sure he'll be a different loon efter the war. Mair content and nae forever grumpin' aboot things. He was aye a moaner, my Malcie."

"I got on all right with him. He never moaned to me."

"He ken't you was cleverer nor him, and you'll end up a lot better aff than him. He'd aye keep far in wi' onybody like that. An eye oot for number one, you could say."

"There's nothing wrong in that," Willie laughed. "If we don't look after number one, nobody else will."

"Aye, but you've got the brain for it. He hasna."

"Malcie'll get on all right. You don't need to worry about that."

"You ken this, Willie? Every time I see you, you mak' me feel a lot better. You've got something aboot you, I canna describe it, but you'll go far, loon. I'm sure o' that."

"That's good of you, Beenie, but I'll have to go now, or Mam'll fly off the handle at me for bein' late for my supper."

"Your Mam doesna ken when she's weel aff. Bye bye, then, an' haste ye back, as they say."

"Bye, Beenie, and I'll see you next time I'm home."

Contrary to his expectations, Emily asked no questions, but he told her anyway about his various ports of call. It was Jake who said, "So you didn't go to the schoolhouse?"

"No."

The matter was left there, the parents rather disappointed that their son hadn't bothered to visit the man who had done so much for him, the boy himself doubting if he had done the right thing. Whatever, it was too late now to do anything about it.

CHAPTER
SEVENTEEN

Although most of their day was occupied in going over and over what they had been taught during their basic training, the young men did have some time to relax. The majority made straight for the nearest dance hall, with the intention of finding a girl friend for the evening, or, with the same end in view, to the nearest public house. At least two of the relatively new recruits, however, were not interested in girls. Willie Fowlie and Pat Michie had their own way of filling the time — exploring the local area, enjoying a chat whilst having a bracing walk and rounding things off with a quiet drink in the pub.

The problem with the last option was, of course, coming in contact with the opposite sex. Each of them found it hard to cope with this. As Pat confessed after their first awkward visit, he had never had anything to do with girls. Willie, on the other hand, was so involved with one girl in particular that he had no wish to take up with another; he had, however, a longing to find the right girl for Pat. Once that mission had been accomplished, he could discuss his own romance with his pal without feeling at all embarrassed.

Willie found great difficulty in writing to Millie. His remorse for not once going to see her was so deep that he didn't know where to begin. How could he tell her that he loved her too much? It would really be a pathetic excuse without explaining what he meant. How could she possibly understand what happened to him when he was close to her? She would despise him for not being able to control his lust. But the thing was, it wasn't just straightforward lust; it was a truly wonderful love for her that sparked off a desire that wouldn't be denied. Even that, though, was pathetic. She would be disgusted at his cowardly attitude, and wouldn't want to have anything more to do with him. The only thing to do was to keep away from her, but to let her know in his letters — not as frequent as before — that he still loved her with all his heart.

He did contemplate discussing his problem with Pat Michie, but although his pal was a little over a year older, he had never, by his own admission, been attracted to any girls and would thus never have been anywhere near this situation. But it might be a good idea to get him interested in the feminine sex. If they started going to places where they would meet some decent females, there was always a chance and once Pat experienced the temptations, he'd be better able to give advice on how to avoid them.

Edinburgh being fairly near, this was their new stamping ground. Instead of going for walks to admire the countryside, as they had been doing until now, they frequented dance halls and tearooms on the hunt for feminine company. Willie had ruled out pubs. Really decent girls didn't go drinking.

The two young men, both inclined to be too shy to make inconsequential conversation, had no luck on their first two visits to the capital — one to a small tearoom in the Grassmarket, one to an even smaller café in Rose Street — but when, as a last resort, they tried a quiet little pub in a side street, they had only been sitting in a corner for a few minutes when two WAAFs came in. While one disappeared, probably to the Ladies, the other had a quick look round and then came over and addressed Pat shyly. "Excuse me, are these two seats taken?"

A red wave running over his cheeks, he mumbled, "No, they're not."

She plumped down next to him. "Thank goodness! We've been trailing round for ages looking for a decent place. All the rest seemed to be full of Yanks, loud mouthed, gum-chewing Yanks that think they're God's gift to women."

"I take it you don't like them," Pat ventured.

"Can't stand them. They think a pair of nylons is their password to heaven." She laughed at his puzzled expression. "They think they can exchange nylons for a girl's virginity."

"Oh." His face was now a deep shade of puce. Never having had any dealings with girls, he had no idea what nylons were, but he did not dare to ask. "We don't have nylons to give away."

"I'm glad to hear it." She waved to the other WAAF who had been held up by a raucous crowd of sailors.

"Over here. This is Josie," she went on by way of introduction, "and I'm Dot."

Pat did the needful. "He's Willie and I'm Pat."

Dot, the tallest one, raven-haired and rosy-cheeked, with dancing brown eyes and a happy smile, went to the bar for their drinks, leaving Josie, mousey-haired, pale complexion, serious eyes, looking like a scared rabbit at being alone with the two men. Surprisingly, it was the older lad who tried to soothe her fears, smilingly informing her, "Willie and I are stationed in Redford. We haven't been there for very long, but we've discovered a few nice walks already. If you're interested, we could show you, some time."

Both his face and hers were flushed now, but she nodded. "That would be great. Dot and I love walking, but we've been a bit scared of going on our own, with so many Yanks about."

Pat grinned, seemingly finding it easier to make conversation now that he had started. "Thank goodness at least some girls don't fall over themselves to make up to them."

Grinning too, Josie shook her head. "They think far too much of themselves for me. Even Dot doesn't like them, and she's more a one for boys than I am."

"Have you and Dot been friends long?" Pat asked now.

"We went to school together, and joined up together, so we're pretty close." She turned as her friend came back with two glasses of tomato juice. "I was saying we've been pals a long time."

230

Josie kept on talking to Pat, to whom she was clearly attracted, Willie was glad to see. "You two are Scotch, aren't you?"

"Scots, yes we are. Willie's from a wee place in Aberdeenshire called Tillyburnie, and I'm from Elgin, a bit farther north."

"Dot and I are both from a wee place . . ." she imitated his accent, ". . . in Wiltshire called Mere. Not far from Stonehenge. I suppose you've heard of that?"

"Never been there, but I have heard of it."

Dot suddenly lifted her glass and went round to sit next to Willie. "We may as well get to know each other. That two look as if they've forgotten we're here."

He smiled, but felt at a loss. It was all right for him to plan for Pat to meet a nice girl, but he hadn't taken into account that the nice girl may have an equally nice friend. He did not want to cause any more problems in his life, but he could hardly ignore her. "Before we go any further," he began, hesitantly, "I'd better tell you I have a girlfriend at home. I'm going to marry her once the war's finished."

She beamed happily. "That's good. I've got a boyfriend, Brylcreem boy, who, like you, wants to wait until after the war to get married. I thought he wanted to be free to have a good time with the girls, so I hope he's as honest as you. I admire you for it, and as long as we know it's all above board, we'll get along fine."

It was an ideal arrangement, as far as Willie was concerned, even when a niggle of conscience warned him that even a platonic friendship could go badly wrong if one of the pair got serious about the other.

231

Still, there was little likelihood of that, since both of them had a true love waiting in the wings, so to speak.

"Some people think Josie and me are an odd pair — one shy and quiet, and one, me, who speaks far too much."

"Josie's been managing fine on her own up to now," Willie observed, "and so has Pat. He's usually tongue-tied if a girl as much as looks at him."

"So you're usually the one with more to say?"

"Not really." Casting a quick glance round, he was pleased to see that Pat and Josie were still carrying on a quiet conversation on their own. "They're getting on, anyway."

"Thank goodness. Sometimes it's like pulling teeth to get a word out of her, but she seems to like Pat. Have you two known each other as long as Dot and me?"

"No, we just met when we were doing our basic training."

They had split naturally into two couples, and while the other two were finding out about each other, Dot and Willie discussed their romantic partners. He gave her a brief account of how Millie and he had met, had liked each other from the very start, how liking had grown into love. He did not mention that she was still at University as far as he knew, nor give the reason for his voluntary enlistment.

Dot gave him an equally brief account of how she and Paul had met — both had worked with the same firm since they left school — and how their liking had also become deep love. "So that's everything out in the

232

open," she grinned, at last. "We can enjoy ourselves without anything silly happening. Yes?"

"Yes." He shook the hand she held out. He liked her, could maybe have more than liked her, but it was better this way. Far better.

When the barman shouted "Last orders" they quickly emptied their glasses and stood up to leave, Dot turning to Josie and saying, "We'll catch the quarter to ten bus if we put a step in."

It was Pat who said, sounding quite disappointed, "Can't we walk you back to your billet? We won't mind how far it is, eh, Willie?"

Willie gave an exaggerated bow. "We'd be delighted, ladies."

"It's too far," Dot said, firmly. "In the opposite direction from where you've to go."

On their way outside, Pat and Josie tried to arrange a date, but were having great difficulty because their times off duty did not coincide. At last, however, they came to an agreement. "Half past seven next Saturday, here?" Pat's eyebrows were raised in hope.

Willie felt obliged to issue a note of warning. "There's rumours of us being posted, remember? We might not manage to get word to them in time."

"Good thinking," Dot agreed. "Well, we'll leave it at that. Next Saturday, but if you don't turn up, we'll know you've been posted."

Willie was saddened suddenly by the fraught look that passed between Pat and Josie. They were obviously attracted to each other, but service personnel had really no right to be planning ahead — not during a war. He

233

did yield a little, though, by allowing the pair to fall behind as they walked towards the bus stop, to allow them a little privacy.

As it happened, the rumours of a posting were true, and the Wednesday found the two young men en route for a new destination. Their days, and nights as often as not, were spent on manoeuvres, the Yorkshire moors being ideal for testing the stamina of these young lads. They were gruelling times, purely to discover how they would survive under great pressure. Thankfully, it was never a case of one man being on his own. They worked in groups, each group at war with the other, divided into sets of six, four or even two, which was the hardest of all. Sleeping where they could find a place, eating the hard tack rations provided for them, stalking the enemy while trying not to show themselves. It did no good to moan to the umpires who went round them at unspecified intervals to check that all the combatants were still surviving. These veterans had survived the last war and had no sympathy for any namby-pamby youths. Willie was determined that he and Pat would not cave in, no matter how bad the circumstances became, but it took much persuasion at the outset to make his friend see how important it was to pass every test set for them. There came a point, however, when fighting the hardship was all they had to live for; nothing else mattered.

It came to an end at long last, and those who had not been "wounded" and sent back to the "hospital" set up in a local school, were conveyed back to their camp by lorries, triumphant at being real survivors, and ready to boast to the men who were about to start on the scheme that, "It was nothing. A dawdle."

After his first, aborted-successful attempt at fraternising with the opposite sex, Pat felt rather easier with girls now, but, although they chatted up several in Yorkshire, he never let his feelings get the better of him. Willie was soon telling him about Millie, giving the excuse he had recently invented for why he couldn't go home on leave: that she had been getting far too serious for his liking. He did feel guilty for putting the blame on her, but how could he admit to his own failing? "I don't want to fall out with her," he said, earnestly. "I really do love her, but as for marriage — not yet. The thing is, she's so determined, anything could happen."

"It wouldn't be any hardship to marry her, would it? That's what you want, anyway, isn't it?"

"Yes, by God, that's what I want, but you don't understand. Her father's the headmaster, was *my* headmaster, and there's other reasons I can't . . . Oh, it's impossible to explain, but I'd rather not go home for a while. I think I'll get a warrant to Edinburgh. I liked it there when we were at Redford."

"I liked it as well. If I get leave at the same time, would you mind if I came with you?"

"No, I'd be delighted, but wouldn't you rather go home? Your mother would . . ."

"My mother wouldn't mind. She's very understanding."

As it happened, their leaves did not coincide, and Willie spent his ten days in Edinburgh on his own. It would have been better if he'd had some company, but at least it gave him plenty of time to think, mainly when he was walking between the various "sights". Before the war, these tourist attractions would have been besieged by holiday-makers, but they were now being visited by groups of foreign servicemen, the Americans in particular loud in praise of the ancient buildings and their history.

Willie generally spent around an hour or more every evening in one or other of the quaint drinking establishments, finding himself regarded as a mine of information since, with his previous interest in history, he could answer most of the questions they fired at him because he was "Scotch". He explained the religious hatred between Mary, Queen of Scots and John Knox, and related the story of Jenny Geddes throwing her stool at the preacher in St Giles Cathedral because she did not agree with what he was saying. In the Palace of Holyrood House he showed them the small room in which Mary's jealous husband, Lord Darnley, had killed Rizzio, her musician, who was suspected of making advances to the Queen. One of the GIs gave a long whistle at this. "Geez! That's even better than anything Hollywood could produce, and it's *real*."

They always wanted to know more, and as Willie smilingly obliged one night, he realised that he hadn't once thought of Millie and his love for her while he was "lecturing". But it wasn't a case of "out of sight, out of mind", he decided, when he was lying in his room in

236

the small, but perfectly adequate hotel he had found. It was more a case of love versus his interest in the past. If she were here with him, he wouldn't be wasting his time teaching Americans about the history of Scotland.

When he returned to Yorkshire, he had to wait until Pat came back from his leave before he could entertain him with the silly questions he'd been asked by his "pupils", and the general lack of knowledge they had had about Britain as a whole. But it was evident that Pat was still pining for Josie. They had known each other such a short time that they hadn't thought to exchange service numbers or addresses, or even surnames, so there had been no correspondence between them. The experience had, however, given him a deeper insight into the pitfalls of love.

As Willie said without thinking, "When I was with Millie, I couldn't even look at her without wanting to . . . ravish her." He came to an abrupt halt, looking at Pat shame-facedly. "No, that's not strictly true, but I do get fired up."

"That's only because you're not seeing her all the time," his friend suggested.

"It'd be worse if I were seeing her all the time."

Shortly after this, their battalion was sent even further south. "Maybe the next move'll be across the Channel," Willie observed hopefully as they unpacked their kitbags in Aldershot. "It seems to me that's what they're aiming for."

"I doubt it." Pat did not look in the least thrilled at the prospect. "No British troops have been sent to

Europe since Dunkirk. If we do go overseas, it'll be farther afield than that."

"Wherever, I'm ready for it."

Their next few weeks were mostly spent apart. Willie volunteered to be a stand-by dispatch rider, and went through a gruelling training course. "One of the instructors let something slip today," he told his friend one evening. "Apparently they're training us in case the official dispatch riders are wounded or killed and there's nobody available to take over. It looks to me as if we *are* heading for active service somewhere." But no other rumours surfaced, and the daily life of these Gordon Highlanders went on as usual.

CHAPTER
EIGHTEEN

Just over four months after Willie's last leave, he and Pat were both allowed another ten days, but Willie was still unwilling to go home. "You know why," he told Pat, shy of elaborating again. "I want to sort things out in my own mind. You know, I want to be sure."

"I don't know," Pat admitted. "I've never had a real girlfriend — for long enough."

"We'd better get you over that hurdle as soon as we can," Willie laughed.

"I don't know if I want to." After a few moments of silence, Pat burst out, "Anyway, I've been thinking. Why don't you come home with me? My Mum won't mind. She'll be glad to see I've made a close friend at last."

"But she won't want an unexpected visitor turning up."

"She'll be glad, I tell you. Get your warrant made out to Elgin."

Although it made him feel like some sort of deserter, a traitor to his family and to Millie, Willie did as he was asked and Mrs Michie did make him very welcome. "Pat's always been such a loner," she confided. "I've been really worried about him. I thought for a while he might be . . . you know . . . but I can see you're definitely not one of those." She put a hand on her hip and minced a few steps, giggling.

Chuckling, too, Willie said, "No, I'm not one of them."

During the days, Pat took him to visit some of his numerous relatives and showed him around the area, spending almost a whole day in Cooper Park, an hour of another afternoon taking advantage of the solemn peace and quiet of the cathedral. They spent most evenings in one pub or another, enjoying the attention that the women and even the older men were paying them. It was heady stuff, and Willie was glad that Pat was entering into the carefree spirit that seemed to abound. Knowing that his pal was enjoying himself too, he took a glance round the bar; not many young men — they'd all be in the forces — but still some thirty- or forty-somethings, married men, likely. Hearing what was more or less a familiar voice, he turned to see if he could recognise the owner — and froze.

He wasn't aware of making any sound, but Pat had sensed something. "Are you all right?" he asked, anxiously. "You're as white as a sheet."

Instead of answering, Willie grabbed his arm and hurried him outside. "I've had one helluva shock. I just saw somebody I know."

"You don't want him to see you?"

"No, by God, I don't! Pat, is there a police station anywhere near here?"

"Not far. I'll show you."

Nothing was said as they made their way there. Pat was desperate to learn what had upset his pal, but he

240

could see by Willie's set face that he would be told nothing even if he asked, and had to wait until they were talking to a police sergeant before his curiosity was in any way satisfied.

The first question to Willie was, "Do you want to report a missing person?"

"Not exactly. I've just found a missing person."

"I don't understand."

"He's been missing for a good few years now, but I've just seen him in a pub round the corner."

"Did you make sure he really was the person you think he is?"

"If I had, he'd have bolted." Willie drew a deep breath and spoke the words he knew would put a different perspective on the matter. "He's wanted for murder."

In other circumstances, the officer's expression would have made him laugh, but Willie was in no mood for laughing. He had waited for at least five years for this and he wasn't going to let even a sergeant of the law let Gordon Brodie slip through the net.

"A murder? And whose murder might that be?"

It became obvious to Willie that the man thought he was drunk. He had certainly had a couple of drinks, but he would have known that falsely prim voice anywhere, in any condition, drunk or sober. "My sister's. He battered her to death, and her unborn baby. Phone Aberdeen if you don't believe me. It was detectives from there that were working on the case. They were positive he was guilty, but he'd managed to escape before I found her body."

"So you found the body, eh?" The sergeant massaged his chin as he debated on this information. "Well now, you must've been just a young laddie at the time."

Willie was stung into defensive anger by the man's sarcastic tone. "I was only fifteen, but I'm telling you the Gospel truth."

"Wait there."

He left them standing at the counter, with a young bobby eyeing Willie as if he were Jack the Ripper. "You're safe enough," he said, his voice a touch bitter. "I'm not mad, I'm not drunk, I'm doing my best to get a vile criminal brought to justice."

The PC relaxed a fraction and remembered his duty. "I'd maybe better take your name and other particulars."

"My name is William Fowlie and I live in Tillieburnie, Aberdeenshire. My father works for John McIntyre, farmer at Wester Burnton. My sister's name was Constance Fowlie, married to Gordie — his right name is Gordon — Burns, and he . . ."

Before he got any further, the sergeant returned, looking grim. "I got his name —" began the young constable.

"Come through, sir." The sergeant raised the flap and held up his hand to Pat. "Just this gentleman, I'm afraid."

"I'll wait." Pat tried to sound as if waiting for unspecified lengths of time was quite a normal thing for him to do, although he was quite disappointed at being left out. How much longer would it be before he knew exactly what was going on?

It was after midnight before the exhausted young men made their way back to Mid Street, where Mrs Michie was anxiously waiting. "It's nearly three hours after closing time," she said accusingly. "What on earth happened to you two? Did you get in some sort of trouble?"

Pat looked expectantly at Willie, who nodded wearily. "It wasn't Pat's fault. It was mine. It's a long story, and I've gone over it dozens of times at the police station, but if you . . ."

"The police station! My God, Willie, what did you do that the police arrested you?"

"He wasn't arrested, Mum," Pat corrected her. "Let him tell you — you'll be surprised."

"I'll make a fresh pot of tea. Carry on, Willie, I'm listening."

He made the story as short as he possibly could, giving the stark facts of the actual murder as the detectives had pieced it together, and neither of his listeners interrupted him. Throughout the telling, he had twisted his hands together, rubbed his chin, wiped his sweating brow with his khaki handkerchief, several times each. But not once had he taken a sip of his tea. It was as if he were actually living the time again, the awful trauma he had suffered as a fifteen-year-old.

Coming to the end, he looked at his hostess. "I told them I'd be here for the next three days, for the Aberdeen 'tecs will want to speak to me. I hope that's all right, Mrs Michie?"

"Yes, of course." She could see that he was at the end of his tether, and added, "Did they not offer to take you home? They'll have to speak to your father and all the other people that were in the house where it . . .."

"They did offer, but I said I'd rather stay here. I didn't want to go home because . . . well, because of a girl. She's my girlfriend, but . . . Oh, I can't explain. It would sound so silly."

She looked at her son. "Pat, I think you should go to bed. I'd like to speak to Willie on his own."

Trusting her not to upset his friend, Pat did as he was told, and she turned again to Willie. "I won't make fun of anything you tell me, so if you feel like getting it off your chest . . .."

His emotions in a state of deep turmoil, he was glad to tell her about Millie, how clever she was, how much he cared for her but was worried about being near her. He didn't expand on this, but the woman, understanding his problem, nodded sympathetically until, with a heave, he burst into tears. She moved over to sit beside him on the old couch, and when he turned and laid his head on her shoulders, she let him sob his heart out.

"It's all right, my lamb," she assured him after a few moments. "Let it out. You'll feel better for it. It's not good to bottle things up."

At last he drew away from her, but he did feel better, not fully realising that his tears had been for Poopie Grant as well as for Connie, with a fair modicum of the self-pity he felt at having to keep away from Millie Meldrum. "Thank you, Mrs Michie," he murmured. "I'll never forget you."

"I hope not," she smiled. "I hope you'll come back with Pat on your leaves till you make up your mind

244

about your Millie. If you ask my opinion, though I know you'd rather not hear it, but I think she'd be pleased if you did make her pregnant. She sounds a nice lass, and . . ."

He gulped. "It's her father I'm worried about."

"Ah well, I can see what you mean there, but he must think a lot of you when he was willing to pay for your education."

"Not after I flung it back in his face."

"I'm sure he still likes you, deep down. Time does make a difference."

"Maybe, but there hasn't been enough time yet. Um . . . is it all right if I come here on my next few leaves, even if Pat doesn't get off the same time as me?"

"I'd be delighted to have you, Willie lad, but your mother must be missing you. You should go and see her."

"She wouldn't be missing me. She's never loved me, I wasn't a well-behaved little boy, you see. I got into all sorts of trouble, and she didn't love me like she loved my two sisters."

"No, no, I think you only imagined that. Well, whatever, off you go to bed, and we'll see what the morning brings."

The morning brought two detectives from Aberdeen, anxious to give them the latest news. "We contacted the Inverness police to pick up Gordon Brodie, and he is now in custody, awaiting trial. This will not take place for some time, as we have a lot of facts to collate, a lot of evidence to reaffirm."

They drove him to the Elgin police station and went over everything he had told the sergeant the night before. He was tired because he'd only had about an hour's sleep, but he was relieved to gather that they were taking his story as true, and that Gordon Brodie's alibi that he had been in the Tufted Duck from opening time in the morning until late afternoon had been proven false. The three women he had hoped would be the means of clearing him testified that he had come in around one, and left before the official closing time at half past two in the afternoon. The officers knew, and knew that Willie knew, that even after the pub was supposed to close, many customers remained sitting until it opened again at half past five. The wanted man had not come back then, nor at any time before the final closing hour of half past nine.

As Pat observed on their way to his home, "He's for the rope, then."

His emotions as raw as they had been that day five years earlier, Willie said nothing. Hanging wasn't good enough for the man, but what was the alternative? A life sentence? Murderers very seldom had to serve their full term, and were frequently released after only a few years; unless, of course, they were sentenced to hang. He was positive of one thing. Should Gordon Brodie get out early, and he, Willie Fowlie, brother of the wife the man had so brutally slaughtered, ever ran into him, he would kill the devil with his own bare hands. He had been assured that someone would let his parents know that they would have to be interviewed, and probably Jeemsie Cooper, the doctor and Johnny McIntyre. They could vouch for the mayhem Brodie had created, the mess he had run out on, the heart-rending sight of Connie's broken body — and that of the child who had been forced out of her — lifeless.

Until it was time for them to leave, he did his best to remain cheerful in front of Mrs Michie, even knowing that she would have given him the comfort he craved. He still felt thoroughly ashamed of his weakness the night he'd recognised Brodie. The whole traumatic incident had come flooding back to haunt him. He ought to have gone to see his parents, he knew that, but he couldn't face their sorrow as well as his own. Once again, he needed to get away, to leave all the bad memories, to get back to some sort of normality. It wasn't Millie who was keeping him away this time. He had not given her one thought since this business started, except maybe he'd just mentioned her name to Mrs Michie. He couldn't remember everything he'd told her — he'd been in such a state.

There was no trial. Gordon Brodie broke down and confessed after many, many hours of interrogation, putting up only one excuse for what he had done. "I'm a man that needs a woman, and . . . the wife I picked didn't like sex."

"And that's why you killed her?" The Chief Inspector was plainly shocked.

"That was part of it. I'd given her a bit of a going over and then I went out to get a drink to cheer me up. I did ask a woman I used to know, a prostitute, to help me out, but the bitch refused. Then another one turned me down in the pub, and they were all laughing at me. By this time I was drunk and mad with rage, so . . ." He stopped, shrugging as if his ensuing actions had been inevitable.

Emily wrote to tell Willie what she had been told, but he later received an official communication from the Procurator Fiscal informing him that he would not be required to give evidence and explaining why. "The prisoner was discovered dead in his cell one morning, having hanged himself by tearing his bedsheet into strips. There will thus be no need for you to appear as a witness."

"I bet you're relieved at that," Pat Michie said when he was told.

"I can't help thinking what a coward the man was," Willie muttered. "He could beat another person to death without batting an eyelid, but he couldn't face death by hanging, for that's what it would have come to. No, he ended it himself, and I bet I'm not the only one to feel cheated."

CHAPTER
NINETEEN

Having thought it over ever since he left Elgin, Willie had decided, much to Pat's surprise although he made no comment, that he still couldn't face going home on his next leave, although he did feel guilty about it. He had never really given a thought to his mother's feelings, and she must have been quite hurt by him keeping away. He'd had no reason to neglect her, she'd never actually been nasty to him, it was just this stupid chip he'd had on his shoulder about her loving his sisters more. And his father certainly hadn't done anything wrong, so he didn't deserve being ignored, either. Worse still, of course, was his attitude towards Millie. It wasn't her fault that he was afraid to be near her. It was entirely his fault, the way his love for her turned him into a sex-mad beast. He pulled his wandering thoughts to a halt. What was wrong with him? Surely he had the will-power to step back from crossing the line? But he had no faith in himself, that was the trouble.

Time passed, noses to the grindstone while being taught an entirely different type of warfare from that they had learned before. It was one routine by day, another on any free nights they had. The two young friends, Willie twenty-one and Pat twenty-two, declared no interest in the opposite sex, and were quite content to be in each other's company all their waking hours. Their sleeping hours were, of course, filled with dreams of girls; Willie's of the only girl he had ever, and would ever, love, and Pat's of the first girl he had ever had feelings for.

They had to endure much teasing from their comrades, who all took it for granted that, since they spent so much time together, they were "cissies". Even when that teasing became bawdy, even disgusting to them, Willie and Pat ignored it. Their tormentors wanted them to rise to it, to demean themselves by denying it so forcefully that the accusation should be proved true. Nothing came of it, however, and the only quarrels that cropped up were between two lads both after the same girl, or about some imagined slight that someone could not let pass. The usual behaviour when young men are cooped up together.

On Willie's next leave, he opted to go to York. While on the moors, they had never had a chance to visit the city itself. There was plenty of history to explore there, and although he knew some of it, he wasn't very familiar with it. He did feel bad while he was writing to Millie to tell her this, and knew that it would make her very sad, but he still couldn't trust himself to be with her. She could only have a year or so, maybe less, before she would be graduating with an MA Honours degree. If only he could be at the same stage — but he had given up any chance of a degree.

250

This was the very first time that he had given any thought to what he would do after the war. He wouldn't be qualified to teach. He knew nothing of any other career. The only other thing he knew about was farming, and not a great deal about that. Well, that would ring the bell for Herbert Meldrum. He would no more let his daughter marry a farm servant than let her marry a circus clown. Great God! Why hadn't he taken time to think out this side of things before he'd jumped in and signed up for the Gordons? He'd been far too impetuous, but he'd done it for Poopie. Yes, he *had* done the right thing — however long he'd have to wait to prove it.

His ten days in York were very satisfying. He spent much time in the Minster, letting his mind go blank and soaking in the peace first, and then observing the other visitors walking round quietly, wondering where they came from, why they were there and hoping that they were finding as much comfort as he was. Easier in his mind, he made a round of some of the other places he had read about, happy actually to see them and learn more about what had happened there in the dim and distant past. As in Edinburgh, of course, the city of York was liberally sprinkled with servicemen and women, including quite a few US personnel, but they didn't seem to be so brash, and having no knowledge to pass on to them, he merely smiled at them in passing.

He felt completely rested when he returned to his unit, even starting to wonder why he had kept away from his home for so long, and by the time Pat returned from Elgin Willie was determined to go home next time he was on leave.

And so, for another few months, the routine was much the same as before, until, with no warning or any explanations, they were moved in convoys of trucks to the south coast of England. Now the rumours began to fly that they were about to be posted abroad, but nothing definite was announced. Willie had imagined that it would be embarkation leave this time, but no reference of it was made by the time he asked for his warrant to be made out to Tillyburnie. He felt quite disappointed, and most of his comrades obviously felt the same, if their complaints about being "stuck in this bloody hole till the end of the war" were anything to go by. He wrote to his mother, advising her of the approximate time of his arrival, and after struggling with his conscience, sent a short note to Millie.

On the morning of his departure, it was announced that this was indeed embarkation leave, and that all ranks would be given their full quota of furlough, which they took to mean that it could be a few weeks yet before they were sent overseas.

His journey home was long and arduous. Portsmouth to Waterloo was bad enough, then several hours to wait in King's Cross for a train to Aberdeen, then some hours sleeping on a bench in the Joint Station for the first train on Monday morning to get him to Udny Station, and another hour and a half before he could get a bus to Tillyburnie village. Having set off in the early hours of Sunday, it was almost noon on Monday before he staggered up the track to his home.

252

Emily did not make a fuss of him — he hadn't expected her to do so — but packed him off to bed as soon as he supped the broth she gave him. She could see that he was too tired to eat anything else. She had many questions to ask him, mostly about why he had never come home again, but she and Jake both had to wait, for their son slept round the clock. Emily had gone up several times to check on him, and had been surprised by the unusual tightening of her heartstrings when she looked down at him, his dark lashes curling on to his haggard cheeks, his hair cropped shorter than she had ever seen it. "He's sleeping like a baby," she told Jake when he came in for his supper. "Sounder than he ever did when he *was* a baby."

Her husband said nothing — it was the first time he had ever heard her speak of their son with a catch in her voice — but he was pleased at her reaction. Was this the dawning of motherly love for the boy?

After supper on the Tuesday, Willie fended off their questioning by saying, "Don't ask. I'd an awful lot on my mind that I had to figure out, and that's all I'm saying."

His father made one brave try. "But surely you could have done your thinking at home?"

"No, Dad, I couldn't, but I've more or less sorted myself out, and I may as well tell you, I'm on embarkation leave. It'll likely be a few weeks yet before we're sent overseas, but I'm really looking forward to it."

Emily opened her mouth, but Jake frowned at her. He could see that the lad was set in his mind.

And so the first three of his ten days of freedom had passed before Willie recovered enough to get out and about. On the Wednesday, he visited Beenie Middleton and Tibby Grant, both of whom made him very welcome. Beenie told him that Malcie was in the Middle East with the REME, where he had been transferred after the reorganisation of the Ordnance Corps. Tibby told him about her grandsons, back with their mother, and the various children she had fostered since Willie had been there last. On the Thursday, he visited his Gramma Fowlie in the Cottage Hospital in Ellon, where she had been taken some weeks before with a broken leg. He could see that there was more wrong with her than that, however, and he felt a stab of regret for not visiting her more often. When he went home, he asked his mother if she knew anything, and was distraught when she admitted that his grandmother had emphysema on top of everything else.

"It's only a matter of time," Emily added, and then, seeing how upset that had made him, she went on, "She knows, and she's all prepared for it. Even something like that hasn't knocked the spirit out of her. She's chosen the hymns for her funeral already."

"Aye," Jake put in, tears in his eyes as well. "Naething that's ever happened afore ever put her aff her stotter, nae even when my brother Davey was killed."

"Aff her stotter" was not a phrase that Willie had heard before, but he didn't need to ask. His father's voice had shown his pride in the woman who had borne him, and the young man, too, felt a rush of

254

loving admiration for her — having brought up a family on very low wages, having lost her husband just after her two sons had set up homes of their own, having lost her elder son in the Great War. She had even helped out her daughters-in-law on many occasions, financially and by just being there. She had never complained and always shown a smile to whomever she was speaking to, whatever she had felt like in private. It was a compliment that wasn't paid to many people, but Gramma Fowlie deserved every word.

The following day being Friday, when Millie Meldrum came home for the weekend — Willie knew from her letters that she was still attending the University — he decided to wait until the Sunday before going to see her. She would likely be going back by the early evening bus and that would mean a forenoon or afternoon visit with little or no chance of temptation for him.

His mind made up, he went to see the Reverend Fyfe, who had just come home from sitting with a dying parishioner, and was thus much cheered by his visitor. Willie had told no one except his parents that he was on embarkation leave, but he found himself telling this man about it, this man who had the magic touch of consoling people in trouble or in mourning, or just feeling unable to go on with life. Not that the young man was at that stage, but he did feel quite apprehensive about the future.

Mr Fyfe then related some stories of the heroism he had seen during the First World War, in which he had served as a padre. "I had not long been ordained," he explained, "when I felt that I could do more good by offering my services to the Army, and, without being overly proud of myself, I think I helped many young lads to face the enemy, and also men a lot older than myself. I hope you do not think I am trying to scare you, because I am not. As far as I am led to believe, this war is nothing like the last. There is not the wholesale slaughter that there was then, although I am not trying to make light of it. There is also much danger, and I would be glad, William, if you will allow me to say a little prayer for your safety."

His heart full, Willie mumbled, "Thank you," and bowed his head. It was not a long prayer, just a plea for God to look kindly on all the young men and women in the forces, not forgetting those on other kinds of war work, and advising his visitor not to lose his faith, no matter what the circumstances.

Willie left the manse feeling cleansed, feeling that the guilt he had carried with him for such a long time had been — not exactly exonerated, but definitely made less unbearable. He carried on to Wester Burnton Farm, where Mrs McIntyre persuaded him to have a bit of dinner, the farmer himself sat and spoke to him for about an hour and promised to give him a lift home at half past five. He also had a chat with Lachie the Daftie, whom he thought was looking much older than the last time he had seen him, but his wits were as sharp as ever.

"It's Willie, isn't it? Willie that spilt the bleed an' had half the Aiberdeen bobbies lookin' for a body?"

Willie couldn't help grinning. "Aye, that's me. Fancy you remembering that. You were the one that solved the mystery."

The old man beamed with pride. "I can mind mair nor that. I can mind you findin' a real body . . ." His words trailed off, a vagueness came into his eyes, as if he had remembered that this was something he shouldn't be speaking about. "I'm sorry, Willie," he mumbled, in a moment. "I forgot."

"It's all right. I got over it long ago."

"They never got him, though?"

"They did get him but —"

"Will he get hung up by the neck till he's deid?"

"He killed himself. He got off lightly."

"I never gaed nae place, but I aye kept lookin'. He coulda been hidin' among the hay-ricks, or in the byre or the stable, or . . ." He stopped, shaking his head as if at his own stupidity. "D'you think I'm daft? They a' think I'm daft."

"I don't." Willie was speaking the truth. He did think that the poor man was not quite twelve pennies to the shilling, but he certainly wasn't daft. There was wisdom there of a kind.

At half past three, Mrs McIntyre came out with two enamel mugs of tea and two thick wedges of home-made cake. "When you're finished this," she said to Willie, "you'd best come inside. My milkmaid has to get the cattle in."

His eyes popping with pride, the old man puffed out his chest and patted it with his hand. "Me," he beamed. "Good milkmaid, aye?"

257

"Very good," she assured him.

When Willie took in the mugs, he said, "He doesn't look very well, I thought."

"He shouldna be workin', but what would become o' him? He'd land in the Poor's Hoose, that's what. I'm he'rt sorry for him, but he's a thrawn aul' blighter. I keep tellin' him he should tak' it easy, but he just winna stop. At least you've kept him aff his feet wi' sittin' speakin' wi' him. I tell't him I'd get a new milkmaid to help him, but he wouldna hear o' it. So we'll just need to let him keep goin' till he canna go on ony langer."

"You're a good woman, Mrs McIntyre," Willie told her earnestly.

"Awa' wi' you. I'm a daft aul' woman, that's what."

"Jake, we really should open it." Emily touched the yellow envelope lying on the kitchen table. "I know telegrams always bring bad news."

Her husband believed that, too, but was more intent on calming his wife's fears. "It canna be very bad news. We ken Willie's here. He canna ha'e been killed, that's certain sure."

"Oh, I know that, but it could be . . . Oh I don't know, just something bad."

When their son walked in, looking much fitter than he had done when he went out in the morning, Emily said, "There's a wire for you."

His parents were surprised that he wasn't upset. In fact, he did not seem at all perturbed. It was almost as if he were pleased by what he read. He looked up, smiling. "I've to report back by noon the day after

258

tomorrow, so I'll have to leave first thing in the morning. It'll take over a day to get back to Portsmouth. I was sure we wouldn't be posted for a while yet, but we're surely going earlier than they'd planned."

"Oh, no!" Emily burst out. "You're not due back yet. Let them know they've made a mistake."

Jake laid his hand over hers. "No, Em, he canna dae that. He has to dae what he's tell't."

"But . . ."

"Nae buts, lass. It's orders and he has to obey them. He'll be put on a charge if he doesna."

Emily had to accept this. After all, her husband had been in the Gordons himself, and knew what he was speaking about. "Well, we can take our supper in peace and you can get to your bed early, Willie, for you'll have to be up betimes in the morning. I've got most of your things washed and ready for you, if you give me the semmit and drawers you've got on, I'll . . ."

"I'm going out, Mam. I'll take my supper, but I've got things to do."

Jake's penetrating eyes warned her not to ask the questions he could tell she wanted to ask, so she rose to dish out the stew.

Willie took his bike out of the shed, checked the tyres and found them as solid as they should be. He wanted to get this duty over as quickly as possible, but his resolutions faded as he neared the schoolhouse. He had to tell the Meldrums that he was being sent overseas, and he would have to try to sort things out with the

259

headmaster. It was all very well to have a speech planned out, but he knew, from past experience, that events never turned out as they were expected, and having to do it tonight instead of Sunday had made him forget half of what he meant to say. He was, however, still determined to lay everything out in the open. The man would be more understanding if he knew he was being told the truth.

He was glad that Millie wouldn't have arrived home yet, and, positive that it would be either young Janet or Mrs Meldrum who would answer his knock, he was surprised when Millie herself opened the door. She said nothing, merely held the door open for him to enter, and he walked past her, feverishly searching for a way to deal with this unforeseen circumstance. His entrance caused some consternation in the dining room. One of Mrs Meldrum's hands flew to her mouth, the other to her heart, while her husband lumbered clumsily to his feet, looking shocked, but with an underlying hint of anger.

Willie addressed himself to the man. "I'm sorry to interrupt you at your meal, Mr Meldrum. It was you I came to see, but it was about Millie, so maybe I'd better speak to her in private first. With your permission, of course, sir?"

"What you want to say should be said in front of me, I think."

"No, Father," Millie put in. "Let us have some time to discuss it on our own. This is just between the two of us until we iron things out."

His wife's practically imperceptible nod made Herbert Meldrum sit down. "All right, William, but even if you can get Millie to understand why you have never come to see her for almost a year, you will need a more convincing explanation for me. As for you, young lady, home by nine, no later. You can surely do all the talking you want in two hours."

"Thank you, Mr Meldrum." Millie took her bicycle, too, in order to get a suitable distance away and still have time to talk at length. They did not go as far as Cooper's Burn, but found another secluded spot that fitted the bill. It was growing dark, but Willie spread his greatcoat on the grass and sat down a little way apart from her.

"Let me have my say first," he begged her. "It's really difficult for me and I want to get it all off my chest."

She said nothing, regarding him with an expression he couldn't quite place. It wasn't anger, as it may well have been, as she had every right for it to be, but curiosity, with a slight touch of apprehension. He began by trying to excuse the long period in which he had made no actual contact with her; the reason for his not coming home on leave for the last three times. "I didn't want to repeat what I did that last time. The more I thought about that, the more I realised that it would only be a matter of time before I . . . before something happened. I couldn't possibly have been with you for any length of time and kept my hands off you. Millie, I love you more than I could ever tell you; more than life itself, but I knew it wouldn't be fair to you if I took my pleasure without considering what it would do to your career."

"I don't give a damn about my . . ."

"No, my darling, don't say that. It does matter, if not to you, at least to your father. I don't want him to be disappointed in you as well as in me, and he wouldn't just have been disappointed if you'd left varsity, he'd have been devastated."

"I know, but it's *my* life, and I . . ."

"Please don't make things more difficult, Millie, dear. What I'm trying to tell you now, is that if you accept my absolute promise that I won't look at any other girl, and that I'll write to you as often as I can, will you believe that it's not because I don't want to see you, it's because I can't trust myself if I'm near you? I promise to marry you after the war if you still love me."

"Of course I'll still love you!" she cried. "I'll always love you, surely you can understand that? I won't care if you make me pregnant a dozen times before the war ends . . ."

"Millie, Millie." He shook his head hopelessly. "You're not being realistic. Your father would probably throw you out, throw us both out, and never have anything more to do with us."

"I don't care. As long as I have you, I'll be . . ."

"No, you think that now, but there would come a time when you resented me, even hated me for wrecking your family life."

"I wouldn't! I could never hate you; I'll love you till the day I die."

"And I'll love you till the day I die, but . . . oh, Millie, my darling girl . . ." With a rush of dismay, he remembered that he hadn't told her of his posting, and leaned across and took her hand in his. "Listen, my dearest, I should have told you this from the beginning. I've been recalled. We're being sent overseas."

"No, Willie, they can't do that to us. Not when we're back together again. Say you're joking."

"I wouldn't joke about something like that." He became aware that she was crying, quite softly but tearing at his heart.

"Oh, Lord!" he groaned, rolled over and took her in his arms, their kisses taking them into the realms of a paradise neither of them could deny, and all Willie's long-debated resolves scattered into the inky darkness.

It was almost impossible for the two young lovers to pull away and accept that they had to get back to the schoolhouse, otherwise what they had planned could never come to pass. Splashing their faces in the rippling burn, they hurriedly adjusted their clothing and lifted their bicycles. On the way, Willie further revealed where he had gone on the times he had not come home on leave to Burnton. "I've made some good pals since I've been in the Gordons, one who reminds me of Poopie Grant, actually. Pat Michie's a year older than I am, but he depends on me for everything; he's so shy he doesn't like standing up for himself, and I sort of fight his battles for him."

"Like you did for — Poopie?"

"Exactly, and when I said I didn't want to go home . . ." He hesitated for a moment and then continued. "You see, I knew I'd never be easy near you because I wanted you so much and the best thing was to stay away from anywhere I'd be likely to run into you. Anyway, I never told him why and he never asked, but he invited me home with him. He comes from Elgin, and his mother made me very welcome. Pat and I had some great times together there. He took me round his relatives and showed me some of the places he thought I'd be interested in. He told me all about his childhood, how he'd been bullied at school and . . ."

"So now you feel protective of him, too? But I believe you also had a bit of excitement?"

"Ah, well, yes. I suppose you know I saw Gordon Brodie?"

"I heard stories. You know how things like that get around. No doubt you had felt it would be too dull for you to come home after all that."

"No, Millie, it's no reflection on you, so try to understand. I do love you with all my heart and soul, but I must keep at a distance. I can't trust myself when I'm with you."

"I think I understand . . . but you'll write to me, won't you? I'll be better able to stand us being apart if I have your letters to read."

"Of course I'll write, and I swear to you, as soon as I get out of the army, I'll come home and marry you. That's the dream I've had all the time." He cast a quick questioning glance at her. "If you still want me, that'll be. You might find . . ."

"Willie, I'll never want anyone else. I'll be waiting for you, for as long as it takes."

Less than ten minutes later, they went in to face the questioning, the arguments. It was quite apparent from their manners that Mrs Meldrum had talked her husband into a more receptive frame of mind. Of course, they weren't very happy that Willie wouldn't come to see Millie until the war ended, although he would keep up a correspondence with her, but the news of his posting let them know that this was what he would have to do in any case.

Herbert, however, didn't intend giving them any more leeway, and insisted on seeing Willie out, while Margaret took her daughter upstairs. "Now, young man," the dominie said, "don't think you've got away with the way you've treated Millie. She was deeply hurt that you never came home on your last few furloughs."

"I'm sorry about that, Mr Meldrum. Desperately sorry, but I was trying to be honourable. I love her so much that I was afraid I'd . . ."

"That you would have raped her?" The voice was cold and accusing.

"No, sir, I would never have forced her, but she loves me as much as I love her, and it would have been inevitable."

The stern face relaxed. "You know, William, you remind me of myself when I was your age. I loved Margaret so much that I had to keep her at arm's length for over a year in case I lost my head and took advantage of her, and when I told her so on our wedding night, she said she had been disappointed that I hadn't." The grey eyes twinkled suddenly. "You did the honourable thing, and I'm quite impressed. Goodbye, lad, and God be with you."

Millie did not sleep easily that night. Last time, she had hoped that Willie had made her pregnant and she could expect him to marry her — which he would have done, being such a decent boy — but that hadn't happened and he had never come back to repeat the act until tonight. Now that he was to be sent overseas, she didn't wish for any complications that would put the cat slap bang in the middle of the pigeons, for her father would forbid her to see Willie ever again.

She did fall asleep a little before dawn, a restless sleep in which she saw herself trailing away from the schoolhouse carrying a shawled bundle, while her father stood at the door, his eyes filled with hate, or more probably with contempt. Where could she go? Who could she turn to? There was no one except . . . Auntie Sophie? Would she take mother and child in? If not, what would become of them?

It was a great relief to awaken to the chorus of birds in the sycamore trees at the foot of the garden. It was still only just after seven, she saw, and Willie would be on his way to Udny Station. They had been . . . she had been, so stupid, letting her feelings run away with her last night. If she had said no, Willie would have stopped. But she hadn't wanted to say no, and she had only herself to blame if the worst had happened.

Willie was halfway to Aberdeen to get another train to King's Cross when the consequences of his actions of the night before rose up to hit him in the gut. What a bloody fool he'd been. Surely to God he could have held himself back and not let things go that far? He was a damned weakling, that's what he was. A lecher. A rapist. But it hadn't been rape. Millie had been as carried away by passion as he was. If she'd asked him to stop, he'd have stopped. Or would he? Had he been past the point of no return? Yes, he had. By gum, he had. Recalling the episode, his libido rising as quickly as his apprehension, he wondered if Millie herself was worldly wise enough to know how to prevent conception or stop it continuing even after it had occurred. He'd heard from other young men how their girlfriends had tried drinking liquid paraffin or gin and various other methods before they succeeded — or, in most cases, hadn't succeeded. He'd even heard of girls having to go to some back-street abortionist to get rid of what had grown into a well-formed foetus.

For God's sake, he thought, don't let what I did make Millie have to go through all that. And there were her parents to consider. Her father would go off his head with anger; he'd want to kill the man concerned with his bare hands, and, of course, he'd know exactly who the man was — the ungrateful lout who had accepted his money and got his daughter up the spout by way of thanks. Some show of gratitude. Feeling thoroughly disgusted with himself, Willie alighted from the carriage at the Joint Station and, recognising others of his unit also waiting for a connection, he went to join them. Anything to get away from his own painful thoughts.

CHAPTER
TWENTY

Millie Meldrum was very upset at Willie for not writing. He was still in this country — as far as she knew, anyway — so he couldn't be kept so busy that he didn't have time to write. As the weeks passed, the upset turned to worry that he had found somebody else. Her Aunt Sophie did her best to soothe her ruffled feelings. "I'd think they'll be kept busy getting special training now, preparing them for going overseas."

"He did say it was embarkation leave, but they wouldn't have sent them away yet?"

"I don't know for sure, of course," Sophie hedged now, "but my guess is yes, they would, and you'd better prepare yourself. He's not away on holiday, enjoying himself every minute of the day. I'd think they get very little time off."

"Enough to look for another girlfriend."

"Stop feeling so sorry for yourself, girl. Willie Fowlie is head over heels in love with you — even I could see that when he was here. He wouldn't look at another girl."

"But he only came home once before, when his basic training was done."

"He wrote and told you why. He wants to see a bit more of this country. I mean, I can understand him wanting to take advantage of travelling at the army's expense."

"Can you?" Millie said sourly. "I can't. If it was me, I'd rather come home to see my girlfriend." She looked flustered at that. "You know what I mean."

"Yes, my dear, I do know what you mean, but boys are different from girls. They're not so romantic, for one thing, and they're quite happy being in male company all the time."

Her head jerking up, Millie said angrily, "Are you trying to tell me he's a pansy?"

"Oh, for heaven's sake, girl! Don't be so bloody silly!"

Recalling what had gone on the night that Willie had volunteered for the Gordons, Millie had to laugh. Of course he wasn't a pansy. What on earth was she thinking about?

Although hundreds of affluent tourists had enjoyed long sea voyages before the war, the passengers on the packed troopship travelling to Egypt via the Cape of Good Hope were not so enamoured of it. There was the constant dread of the drone of enemy aircraft approaching and consigning their temporary home to the depths of the North Atlantic, plus the even more-to-be-feared silent U-boats, creeping near enough to release one or more torpedoes.

Despite this, the servicemen were mostly in a cheerful mood — outwardly, at least. It was during the nights, trying to snatch a few winks of sleep in whatever part of the ship they had been assigned to, that their imaginations took over. If we're bombed and the ship goes down, what are we supposed to do? None of the convoys are allowed to stop to pick up survivors. They were not pleasant thoughts and it would be best to push them aside and look on the bright side. But . . . there didn't seem to be a bright side. It was like running the gauntlet — taking your life in your hands.

Willie Fowlie, just as apprehensive as any, had an incentive to keep his spirits up. He could see that Pat Michie was absolutely petrified, and was liable to do something stupid if the ship was hit. With this in mind, he bombarded his friend with questions about his childhood — questions that took the other man's mind off the present. Pat, of course, hadn't been a "nickum" like Willie, but he made his brief accounts fairly amusing.

When they finally disembarked, the relief was practically tangible, but they soon found that it was not much safer on land. The 1st and the 5th/7th Battalions of the Gordon Highlanders, who were already part of the 51st (Highland) Division, now became part of the British 8th Army, and were soon involved in the bitter fight against the Germans under their commander, Erwin Rommel. The troops they relieved were given local leave, but the new arrivals had little time to draw a breath, let alone write letters home. Fortunately they were issued with printed cards, with comments such as "I am well" or "Hope you are well" etc., to which they just had to tick whichever phrase was appropriate, sign

270

it and add the name and address of the intended recipient.

The ensuing period was hell upon earth for all troops taking part in the struggle to gain possession of El Alamein, the Allies and the Axis forces alike, with each side temporarily taking the city in turn. Whenever possible, Willie Fowlie kept half an eye on his friend, and was pleased to see that Pat seemed to have conquered his blind terror and was giving a fairly believable imitation of acceptance of their situation.

They had all been given training in desert warfare, which helped them to stand up to their environment, but the days seemed inordinately long while the nights — unless they were on duty — seemed inordinately short. The night-time patrols were fraught with danger, unexpectedly running into a pair, or more, in hodden grey, or being shot at by snipers on the lookout for "Tommies" such as they.

Prior to what became known as the Battle of El Alamein, they had been given five days' leave to spend locally. Some of their comrades passed the time in heavy drinking, some in the whorehouses that seemed to be there for their special benefit, some, like Willie and Pat, took advantage of the freedom to explore as much of the area as they could. They would probably be moved on when their task here was successfully finished and they would never get the chance again. They were expected to go back refreshed and ready for action, but it was a motley crew who returned — several with life-sapping hangovers, some with medical problems from indiscriminate womanising, some quite well rested, but all desperately wishing they hadn't had to come back.

It was some considerable time before Emily, and Millie, heard from Willie, and not a letter that would satisfy them as to his whereabouts and well-being; merely a communication pre-printed on a postcard, indicating that he was well and in good spirit, neither of which statements was believed by the woman or the girl. Even the address where he could be reached — his Service Number, followed by the letters BFPO, for British Forces Post Office — told them nothing.

It did ease Emily's mind just a little, but Millie had much more to worry about than Willie's health and whereabouts. She had missed her show twice, and was frantic with fear, of her father and of the unknown ordeal ahead of her. She had once hoped for pregnancy in order to get Willie to marry her, but with him fighting God knows where, what was she to do? She couldn't expect him to come tearing home to give the infant a legitimate name, not now.

After spending many hours debating on what would be her best plan, she decided that she must tell Willie. He deserved to know. He was the father. The only thing was, did he want to be a father? They had never discussed that, although her instinct told her that he would be delighted — if things were different. If there weren't a war on. If he was where he could get home in an hour or so to be with her at the crucial time.

One Sunday evening, in her Aunt Sophie's house, she said she had some work to finish and went into her bedroom.

My Darling Willie,

I have thought long and hard about writing this letter, but I feel you should know. We should both have realised it was possible, but we were too blinded with love. My dear, I am expecting a baby in about 7 months. I suppose this will be as big a surprise to you as it was to me, and to be honest, I don't know what to do. I haven't told my parents yet, not even Auntie Sophie, I'm too scared. I've even thought of trying to get rid of it, but I want to know how you feel about that first. It's rather a cowardly step to take, when all's said and done.

I don't mind waiting for you to marry me when the war is over, as long as I know you still want to, so if you will please write back as soon as you can, I'll let things take their course. I don't know how my mother would take the news, but I'm sure my father will hit the roof. I do think, however, that I could possibly talk Sophie round to let me have it here. You know how good-hearted she is. Anyway, don't worry, I promise to look after myself properly, and I'll do whatever you want as far as the baby is concerned. I think you'll know what I mean. Just let me know what you think.

Yours with all my love and kisses.
Millie. XXXXXXXXXX

Laying down her fountain pen, she leaned back with a sigh. That was all she could do until he answered, as long as he answered in time. If an abortion was called for, it would have to be done before a certain number of weeks had gone by; she didn't know how many.

Another month sped past without any word from Willie, and, so worried by the delay, Millie confessed to Sophie. The cheery smile was wiped off her aunt's face, to be replaced with deep concern. "You haven't been taking up with any other boys?" she asked.

Millie didn't have to ask what her aunt meant. "No, it's Willie's. I'm afraid we misbehaved last time he was home and I'm scared to tell Mum. You know how Dad is."

Sophie pulled a face. "Yes, my love, I know my own brother. A genuine, liberal man with a vile temper when he is roused. He is old-fashioned in his views, Victorian even, and I don't envy you your task, but you will definitely have to tell him. He may surprise you, for he loves you with a deep, abiding love."

Millie heaved a long sigh. "Which means he'll be disappointed in me, and end up hating me with a deep, abiding hate."

"No, my dear, I don't think so. He'll be hurt at first, disappointed that you have gone against his teachings, but he will come round. I'm sure of that."

"So you're advising me to go home on Friday and tell them?"

"Yes — but it just came to me, Millie. Does Willie know?"

274

"I did write to him, but he hasn't answered yet."

"He'll be in the midst of all this fighting that's going on — North Africa or the Middle East, or something. He won't have had time to write. Don't wait any longer, dear."

The lines on her aunt's cheery face stopped Millie from asking if she could have her baby at the Spital, and she decided to throw herself on Willie's mother's mercy. Surely she'd be glad to help her grandchild to be born, even if the maternal grandfather refused to have anything to do with it.

Emily felt herself to be in the deepest quandary ever. The rumours that Millie Meldrum was in the family way were spreading like wildfire, and even Beenie Middleton had said to her yesterday, "You maybe werena fancyin' bein' a granny yet, but I dinna think it'll be that lang." Worse still, she'd seen the girl herself last Saturday from a distance, and there was no doubt about it.

Damn Willie! She thought he'd settled down after he got serious about Millie, and especially now he was in the Gordons, but he'd still been up to his old capers; only this time it wasn't just himself he'd landed in a fix. Poor lassie. Her father would go mad at her, maybe throw her out, and where would she go? Jake would have to be told about it whatever happened, and he'd be as angry as Mr Meldrum — there was no getting away from that — but what could he do? Nothing, as far as his wife could see. He wasn't involved in disciplining his son now; that would be the Gordon Highlanders' job, or the War Office.

Whatever, Willie was in for a rude awakening. Dismissed from his regiment? Clapped in irons and locked away for years? She might never see him again. Did she want to see him again, anyway? He'd been the bane of her existence ever since he was born; a "wee nickum" when he was still a toddler, but a disobedient rebel when he got older. My God, if he managed to get home after this got out, she would . . .

Lost in searching for a fitting punishment for her wayward son, Emily was startled by a timid knock. Positive that it was Willie, thrown out of the army, she stamped to the door and threw it open, to be completely taken aback at the sight of the pregnant young girl. "Millie Meldrum." She could think of nothing else to say.

"Can I come in, please, Mrs Fowlie? I've something to tell you."

Emily stood back to let her pass, frantically trying to make up her mind what to do. Fortunately, the decision was taken out of her hands.

"I suppose you know?" Millie didn't waste time.

"Aye." But the woman couldn't help adding, "The whole of Burnton must know by this time."

"I wondered if Willie had written and told you?"

"I haven't heard from Willie for weeks, and that was just a stupid card. All he had to do was tick some boxes.

Millie's face fell. That's the same as I got. I did write when I was sure about . . . but he surely hasn't got that letter."

Emily's fluctuating emotions suddenly took up a proper stance. This poor girl was at her wits' end, that was quite clear. Like enough her mother and father had been furious when she told them, and she had come here for at least a little comfort. It hadn't been Millie's fault. It had definitely been Willie's fault, but surely to God he hadn't taken her against her will? He would never have done anything like that . . . would he? "Sit down, Millie. We'll have a cup of tea."

Although this was their first actual meeting, they talked for a long time, Millie first explaining how she was as much to blame for her condition as Willie was, which made Emily open her heart to her. Even though she was the daughter of a headmaster, she wasn't afraid to tell the truth, however badly it reflected on her.

"You see, Mrs Fowlie, I love him. I truly love him, from the first day I saw him, when we were still at my father's school. I don't think he felt the same about me until we were older, though, and then, of course, we ended up at University together, and lived with my Auntie Sophie before he volunteered."

"You'd been devastated when he did that, I suppose."

"I was at first, but when he told me about his friend being killed and why he had joined up, I could understand."

"Poopie," murmured Emily, her throat contracting at the memory of the little boy who had been constantly in her house. "I don't think Willie's got over that yet." So their conversation carried on, with Emily laying out her own feelings towards her son. "He was a great annoyance to me," she admitted after relaying several of the scrapes he had got into. "I could only see him as a bad boy, though Jake kept telling me most boys were the same. But I still can't excuse him. Look what he's done now. He was old enough to know what it could lead to."

"But I knew what it would lead to, as well," Millie admitted. "I wanted it to happen. I thought it would be the only way to get him to marry me."

Emily's imagination stalled at the thought of Willie being a married man. It just didn't bear thinking about, and as for him being a father . . . "Look, Millie," she murmured, after a few moments, "have you told your own parents yet?"

"I've the feeling that Dad'll throw me out, and I wanted to have somewhere up my sleeve where I could go. Please understand I'm not forcing you into anything. If you don't want to take me in, just say so."

The older woman's thoughts were now in such turmoil that she didn't know how she felt about it. "I'll have to ask Jake," she murmured, procastinating.

"Oh yes, of course. That's all right."

"But I think you should go home and tell your mother and father right now. It's not right to keep such a secret from them, and anyway, I'm sure your mother must know by now."

"You think so? She's never said anything to me, and she can't have told Dad otherwise he'd have been reading me the riot act. Auntie Sophie says he's as strict as any Victorian father."

"Even so, it's your duty to tell him."

278

"And face up to the consequences?"

"They maybe won't be as bad as you think."

They said goodbye at the door, and Emily went inside to go over what had been said. She knew how Millie must be feeling at telling her father, because she was terrified at the thought of telling Jake. He wouldn't think twice about leathering Willie when he came home, even at the age of twenty-two. And now she had time to think about it, if she got hold of him herself, she would give him a real hot backside. She couldn't give him the clip on the ear she used to give him; he was much taller now than she was.

As Emily had suspected, Millie found that Margaret Meldrum was already aware of her daughter's condition, so it was only Herbert's reaction that they waited for, fearful and trembling. Millie broached the subject as soon as he came in from school.

"Dad, I was scared to tell you before, but . . . I'm expecting a baby."

His face gave nothing away. "Couldn't you have let me sit down first?"

"I'm sorry, and I know it must be a shock, but I want to know . . ."

"It's not so much a shock as you may think, Millicent. I am not blind, and when my daughter's waistline thickens to such an extent that she has to wear one of her mother's old skirts . . ."

"Oh, Dad, I didn't think you'd notice."

Margaret seemed stunned. "I didn't notice that."

Millie looked expectantly at her father. "What are you going to say about it, then? Are you angry?"

"Of course I am angry. What will William Fowlie do next to undermine my family? Not only has he filled my daughter's belly, he has ruined your chances of getting on with your career, and he will not be here to support you when you give birth. He has never behaved in a really responsible manner. I could overlook his faults before, because of his outstanding brain, but this . . . this is deplorable."

"But Herbert . . ." Margaret began. Ignoring the slight interruption, he went on.

"He should have known better."

"I wanted to have his baby," Millie burst out. "I made him do it."

"Then you, too, were old enough to know better." He briefly pondered over his next move and then said, "Are you sure the child is his?"

Both women gasped at this, followed immediately by Millie spitting out, "That's a horrible thing to say. You're accusing me of taking up with someone else?"

"I did not say that."

"It's what you meant, though, and if that's what you think of me, I'd be as well leaving right now."

Her heaving bosom and flaring nostrils warned him that he had gone too far, but before he could make reparation, his wife soothed, "Calm down, the pair of you. There was no need for that, Herbert, and no need for you to think of leaving, Millie. Whatever your father thinks or says, this is your home, and this is where you will have your child."

"Thanks, Mum." The girl was so overcome with relief, swamping her so quickly after her hopes had been dashed, that she swung round and ran upstairs to her room. Husband and wife looked at each other; he still seething with anger and bitter disillusionment over his daughter's immoral behaviour, as he saw it; she disgusted at his handling of the situation.

"How could you, Herbert?" she spat out. "Your own daughter! Yes, I know she's done wrong, but it's done and nothing can undo it." She paused for a moment. "Or were you intending to order her to have a termination?"

He glared back at her. "It would be the best thing all round, would it not?"

"Best for who? Only you; not Millie, and certainly not me. I am longing to have a grandchild."

His scowl did not lessen, but Margaret could detect a frisson of doubt in his voice as he said, "In spite of the gossip and rumours such a thing will cause?"

"Gossip and rumours don't mean anything. As we used to say when we were children, 'Sticks and stones may break my bones, but names will never hurt me.' If they are miscalling us, they are leaving some other poor souls alone. In any case, you've never worried before about what people said about you. Or is your skin not thick enough nowadays to shrug it off?"

"Margaret," he sighed, "what am I going to do with you? Your only child is going to produce an illegitimate child in a few months, yet it does not seem to have bothered you at all."

"No, no, don't think that — not for one minute. It's just that, being a mother, a woman, I can tell fairly early when a girl is pregnant, so I have had some time to come to terms with it."

"You knew? And you didn't tell me?"

"I knew how you would react. Normally, you are a decent, easy-going, gentle man, but if anything riles you, you can be like a raging lion. We are not living in Victorian times, Herbert, and although I know there is still much stigma attached to an unmarried girl having a child, it is not as much of a disgrace as it used to be when we were young. And I can bet that in years to come — maybe fifty or even less — it will not be regarded as a disgrace at all. It will be as normal as . . ."

"Apple pie?" Their eyes locking, they burst out laughing, the tension of the previous few minutes making them see this as far more humorous than it actually was.

Both Emily and Millie were growing really worried. It was three months since Willie had gone overseas, and they still had no idea where he was. "Does it matter?" Jake asked his wife. "Wherever he is, he'll be in the thick of the fighting — the Middle East maybe, or the Far East. There hasna been ony troops got into Germany since Dunkirk."

Emily regarded him with a jaundiced eye. "Some comfort that is. He's in as much danger from the Arabs or the Japs as he'd be if he was in Germany."

Somewhat shamefacedly, Jake nodded. "Aye, I'm sorry, Em. I wasna thinkin'."

"He hasn't written a proper letter since he was recalled. Just that silly cards."

"They're meant to let the folk back hame ken they're a' richt."

"How could he be well enough, if all he can manage to do is put a tick here and there and sign his name? That doesn't tell anybody anything."

She voiced a different opinion when Millie Meldrum came to see her again, obviously pleading for reassurance. "He'll be kept busy wherever he is, maybe nowhere near the enemy at all. It'll be a different kind of countryside from Scotland, or even England, or Ireland or Wales, and they'll have to learn all about it."

Millie's sigh was not of conviction. "I suppose so. But it's just . . . He should have got my letter by this time, though, shouldn't he?"

"The letter telling him about the baby?"

"Yes, and you'd think he'd answer it as soon as he could. I want to know what he thinks. I have to know, Mrs Fowlie, or else I won't be able to plan what to do."

Afraid to ask what the girl thought were her options, Emily wisely said nothing, and Millie went on, "It's too late for an abortion."

"You weren't really thinking of doing that, were you?"

"Not really. My father wanted me to, at first, anyway, but Mum talked him round. No, what I meant was — who's going to look after it? I'll have to earn my living to provide for it — I'm not going to give Dad any reason to think he'll have to support us — so thank goodness I'll have my degree behind me."

"You're going to carry on studying, then?"

"I don't see why I shouldn't. Nobody's said anything, so far, and they must know — I'm as fat as one of Johnny McIntyre's pigs."

They both laughed, although Emily couldn't help but feel sorry for her, as well as harbouring deep resentment that her own son had been so careless, so headstrong, that he couldn't control his passions. Of course, he never considered other folk's feelings, always acting on impulse. But this was no childish prank. He was a grown man, not the wee nickum he had once been. He had definitely developed into the devil incarnate she had suspected him of being. Thank heaven Gramma Fowlie had died before this disgrace overtook the family.

There was an air of resentment among the Gordon Highlanders now. As one well-built lad from Nairn commented, "How the hell could they mislay sack loads o' mail? My God, a letter frae hame's what keeps us goin', so how do they expect us to knuckle down to their bloody rules when we dinna ken what's goin' on?"

A low murmur of agreement went round his listeners, then another voice said, "What if they've lost the mail that's supposed to go out? Our folkses'll think we've been killed, or something, an' they'll stop writing."

Willie turned to his friend. "It's months since I'd a letter from Millie. I hope she's OK." Although he was also anxious to know if his action on that last night had had any repercussions, he did not mention it.

284

May 1943 saw the most vicious part of the battle so far, and, because all radio links had been destroyed, Willie, having volunteered to replace a wounded despatch rider, was sent to Headquarters with an urgent request for reinforcements. Coming back, the urgency off him, his mind turned to thoughts of his girlfriend. He'd been bloody stupid to stay away from her. She couldn't possibly have understood his reasons and must despise him by now. Well, he would write to her as soon as he could and tell her how much he loved her, and that he still meant to keep the promise he had made to marry her after the war. Or if he was lucky enough to get home leave before that, he'd take the plunge then.

Spotting something lying in the middle of the road some yards ahead, he slowed down and came to a halt before he reached it. Recalling rumours of booby-traps set for unwary travellers, he approached the thing warily, to be shocked into haste when he realised that it was Pat Michie. How he had got there was a mystery, but he needed help, and who better to give it than his closest friend? He was kneeling down trying to find out the extent of his pal's injuries, when his ears picked up a faint rustle and his eyes caught a slight movement in the neighbouring bushes. Too late he realised the danger, but at least he'd had time to tell that Pat was still alive. Flopping over his friend to save him from further harm, he thanked God for being given this chance to make up for abandoning Poopie.

CHAPTER
TWENTY-ONE

If this May weather was any indication, Millie thought, it would be a scorching summer. She was so hot, even at 3a.m., that she had thrown down all her bedcovers and removed her voluminous nightdress. She had been lying for a few minutes like this before she noticed that she could see the movements of the child she was carrying; small ripples in her skin, but along with that there was also a horrible nagging pain in her back. It was still ten days until the birth was due — according to the doctor — but quite possibly it was going to be earlier.

In the lulls between the well-spaced-out pains, her mind turned to the other person who should be — was — involved. Why hadn't she heard from Willie for so long? Why hadn't he answered the letter about the baby they'd inadvertently made? He must know she'd be impatient to learn his reaction; had he been pleased, or angry, or just numb? Yet it wasn't something you could remain numb about. He'd have to decide. If he was angry, he'd likely tell her he was finished with her because he didn't want to be saddled with a child after the war as well as her, but if he was pleased, he'd be assuring her that he still loved her, that he could hardly wait until he was able to marry her and make the child legitimate.

The agony gripped her again, for only a few seconds, and she resumed her troubled thoughts. What she knew of Willie — and she knew him very intimately — led her to think he'd be delighted, that he'd sit down as soon as possible and write her a letter expressing his undying love. She did, of course, realise that in a war the mail for servicemen was not dependable, but even so he must have received the important letter at least within two months of it being sent. Which would have been around five months ago. It couldn't be possible that he hadn't had some spare moments in all that time? Could it?

After another few fraught spells, Millie managed to fall asleep, so exhausted and upset that she didn't surface again until nearly lunchtime. Her mother could recognise the signs of stress on her daughter's face, but jumped to the conclusion that her worry about her young man was the root cause.

"Did you get enough sleep, dear?" she asked. "I had a look in before and you looked out for the count, so I didn't waken you for breakfast."

"Thanks, Mum, but I'm fine now." Recalling various tales she had heard about the hours it took for a baby to come into the world, Millie had made up her mind not to let her mother know about the pains she'd had. They might have been false pains anyway, and she hadn't had one for a while. There was no need for alarm.

"Do you feel able to have a little walk in the garden after lunch?" Margaret Meldrum asked now. "It's a lovely day and the fresh air should do you good. And the little fellow you've got in there," she added, smilingly patting the girl's hugely swollen belly.

Millie nodded. "Just a wee while, then. I get so easily tired. Was there any mail today?"

"Nothing, but look on the bright side, lovie. No news is good news. Besides, the baby won't be long in coming now. Only a few more days, I'd say."

"I hope so." Millie had also heard from more than one source that sometimes a child could be as much as three weeks behind schedule, with the poor mother carrying perhaps nine or ten pounds of extra weight around with her. But that wouldn't happen to her, she was sure of it. The little fellow inside her — as her mother jokingly called it — was in a hurry to get out. He'd been limbering up last night, getting ready for the epic journey.

Jake hadn't slept much. Apart from being too hot, he was reliving his time in the trenches over twenty-five years ago; the mud, the stink, the rats, the dead bodies, left where they lay sometimes until they rotted. The more he told himself to stop being morbid, to stop being silly, the more his thoughts centred on his son. Not that Willie, or any of today's infantry, would be fighting in trenches in this war, but he was in action against the enemy, be they German, Italian, Japanese or whatever. He'd had this peculiar feeling since he came to bed, like nothing he'd had before, so insistent that it made him wonder if God was giving him a warning that his son was in danger?

He rose at his usual time in the morning, telling his wife not to get up, because he was well aware that she, too, had lain awake for most of the night. He was to be furring up the tatties today, the field nearest to the house, so he wouldn't need to carry a "dinner piece". He'd be able to come home for his dinner.

Emily heard her husband closing the outside door. He had told her not to get up yet, but what good would it do to lie in bed on a lovely day like this? She'd be as well up and moving about, and maybe getting a bit of fresh air in the afternoon by tending her small herb garden and pulling up the weeds. Having worried all night about not hearing from Willie for so long, she knew that Jake had also lain awake, but it was something other than letters that was bothering him. The few odd times he had drifted off, he'd been thrashing about and moaning. At one point, he'd even screamed out, "Christ, that's the buggers started already. Do they never sleep?"

She had realised then that he was dreaming about the war, his war, and wished that he could have told her more about what had happened to him then. He'd never said a word about it, and now it was eating at him, making him think that his son was facing the same hardships. But Willie wouldn't have been in a trench, and he wouldn't have been fighting hand to hand with whoever he had to fight. The modern army was up-to-date. There would be fewer casualties than last time because there was less danger.

She couldn't get over how worried she had become for Willie. All his life she had doted on her two daughters and resented having a boy-child, especially a boy-child who did everything in his power to upset her. Now, both her daughters were lost to her, and he was all she had left.

He hadn't improved as he got older, though. She'd thought he had, when he was at the University. She had occasionally pictured him settling down with Millie Meldrum and giving her grandchildren. Instead of sticking to the normal way, the natural way, of things, he had upped and volunteered for the Gordons, left his lady-friend pregnant and then, it seemed, dumped her, for the girl hadn't had any letters from him, either. There were times when, as his mother, she wondered if she could possibly have done anything to change him, but she knew there was nothing she could have done, and the way she felt now, she was quite glad he was exactly the way he was. Whatever he did or had done in the past had been done without taking time to consider whether or not it was the right thing to do. She had always thought that she didn't love him, had always felt quite guilty about it, and yet, she could see now, there must have been a spark of love for him deep down in her heart. How else could the agony she could feel rising for him now have got there?

But she shouldn't still be in bed. It was nearly eight o'clock and the postie would soon be here. You never knew, there just might be a letter from Willie.

*   *   *

There was consternation in the Tillyburnie Post Office. Four telegrams had come through one after the other, and Petey Lornie, knowing each of the addressees personally, was reduced to tears. "Look at this," he muttered to Louie Riddle, the postman. "Two laddies that bide next door to each other, and two brothers. They've all been killed, round about the same time, though none of them in the same place. It's a damn disgrace, that's what it is. Think on that three mothers. What'll they be feeling?"

"Richt enough," the other man nodded. "An' I'll tell you this. If I'd onything to dae wi' it, I'd shove a bomb up Hitler's backside and blast him to smithereens. If he was oot o' the road, the world could settle doon again."

"I doubt that, Louie. There's an awful lot of Nazis nowadays, so you'd need to get rid of the lot of them, not just Hitler. Now, your first call's usually at Wester Burnton, isn't it? Well, if you take this two wires, that'll let Tommy deliver the other two to Whinnybrae, so they'll all get them about the same time."

"Aye, that's only fair." Louie lifted the sack of ordinary mail to put inside his little red van, and took the two yellow envelopes into the front with him. Delivering telegrams wasn't really his job — he didn't fancy having to break sad news like that — but he could see Petey's point of view. Young Tommy would take quite a while on his bike to get from Wester Burnton to the address in Whinnybrae where two brothers had lived.

His first call was always to the McIntyres at the farmhouse, so he told the farmer that two of his workers' sons had been killed. Johnny was all for going straight away to tender his condolences, but his wife advised him to wait. "Let them come to terms with it first." He agreed that they should wait until the afternoon, or even the evening.

Louie's next stop was just before he reached the Fowlies' cottage, where he found Jake in the potato field and handed over the envelope with a murmured, "I'm awful sorry."

The other man had ripped the top off and was staring down at the strips of typed words as if he couldn't believe what they said. At last he lifted his head. "You ken, of course."

"Aye, Petey thought this two telegrams would be quicker if I took them, for Tommy has another two to deliver in Whinnybrae. The two laddies there were brothers, but they'd been killed in different places at different times." His grip on the English language suddenly deserted him. "It's a bloody shame, twa oot'n the same faimily."

"You said you'd two. Who's the ither ane for? Somebody else aboot here?"

Louie nodded his head sadly. "Dod Middleton."

"Oh, no! Nae Malcie, as weel?"

"Malcolm, that would be right. Now, d'you want me to come in wi' you to tell Emily?"

"No, no. Aff you go an' deliver the rest o' your bad news."

"It's nae me that made the bad news, Jake." The postman looked accusingly at him.

"No, I ken that. I'm sorry. It's just . . ." He dragged the cuff of his sleeve across his eyes. "I dinna ken what this is gan to dae till her, but she'll nae want onybody else there."

Emily had just washed and dressed when she heard Jake coming in. "It's not near dinnertime yet," she called, wondering if the clock had stopped before remembering that Jake had wound it up the night before. One look at her husband's face told her that something was wrong, and before she could even ask, he held out the small sheet of paper.

"Oh, Jake! It's a mistake. He can't have been killed. They mean missing, not killed. Tell me it's not true, Jake. It says in the Battle for El Alamein, and there's a letter to follow. They wouldn't need to send a letter if they're sure he's been killed. Oh, please God."

Tears streaming down his face, his own heart feeling as if it had been ripped to shreds, Jake put his arms round his wife, and patted her back gently while they tried to face their loss.

Meanwhile, Louie, unable to find Dod Middleton, had delivered the news to Beenie, waiting with her until she opened it and scanned the contents. "I'm he'rt sorry, Beenie," he said as she folded up the communication and slid it back inside the envelope.

"I ken't it would come," she observed, quite calmly. "I ken't fae the beginnin' it would end like this for him. Folk aye thocht he was just a waster, hardly ever

293

workin' at a proper job, but noo he's gi'en his life for his country, maybe they'll think different."

"Aye, I'm sure they will. Look, Beenie, I'll need to get on wi' my round. Do you want me to get some o' the bairns to look for your man? You need somebody here wi' you for company."

"A lot o' use Dod would be, but I wouldna mind if you went next door and asked Emily. She's aye been a real good freen' to me."

Louie's face blanched. "I'm sorry to ha'e to tell you, but their Willie's been killed, an' all. I left Jake to tell her. Is there nae somebody else?"

"I wouldna ask ony o' they young wives in the next three hooses. A' they think on's their lipstick an' their fags. Gan aboot in skirts up to their bums — an' they never bide lang enough in one place to get to ken folk."

"What aboot Tibby Grant? She lost her laddie a while ago, so she'll understand."

"Aye, Tibby's a' right, but I dinna want to upset her. It'd mak' her think on her Poopie."

"I think she'd be pleased to be asked."

Only minutes later, the two elderly women, both with undependable husbands and both having lost a son who was very dear to them, were consoling each other in such a manner as to remove most of the lingering heartache in one and ease the renewed heartache and resentment in the other.

Eventually, drained and ashen-faced, Tibby said, "You say Emily's lost her Willie, as weel. Maybe we should go ben an' . . ."

"Jake'll likely be there for her."

294

"Aye, her man's nae like oor twa, the useless pigs, but she'll be pleased to think us two's thinkin' aboot her. I ken some fowk say she pits on airs, thinks hersel' better than us, but she doesna, really. I couldna've wished for a better neighbour than her when my Poopie was ta'en. An' her Willie — some fowk said he was leadin' my laddie astray, but, I tell you this, Beenie, I aye had a real soft spot for him, an' the minute your Malcie tell't him aboot Poopie, he went an' volunteered. That showed how close he was to my loon."

"He did tell he felt real bad for nae bein' there to help Poopie."

"Aye, that's fit I mean. Nae mony laddies would've gi'en up their fine education like that."

Beenie considered this statement for a second, and then said, "Aye. You're richt, Tibby. We should gan an' let Emily ken we care."

After covering the large almost circular area that included Wester Burnton Farm and its workers, the Mains and all its workers, Louie now made for the Tillyburnie schoolhouse before ending his round at the Easter Burnton Farm spread. It was wearing on for twelve o'clock, over half an hour later than usual, so, being an extremely conscientious man, and aware that most of the women he had not yet called on were waiting for a letter from a son, a sweetheart, a husband, he did not make his normal stop on the way to eat his "dinner piece". Mrs Meldrum, the dominie's wife, opened the door to his energetic use of the large brass knocker and accepted the slim bundle of mail he handed over.

"Nothing for Millie, I see," she commented, sadly.

Louie had wondered if he should mention the reason for him being so late, and she had given him an ideal opening. "I ken I'm nae supposed to tell onybody this, but it's well kent your Millie was seein' Willie Fowlie, an' —"

Margaret Meldrum burst in before he could finish. "Please don't tell me something's happened to him. Her baby's due in another few days, and —"

"Willie's the father? Oh, God, Mrs Meldrum, I'm awful sorry. I'd two telegrams to deliver this mornin', that's why I'm late. Willie Fowlie an' Malcolm Middleton — baith killed."

"Oh, dear Lord! This'll finish Millie. He promised to wed her after the war, and now, what'll she do?"

It crossed the postman's mind that Millie Meldrum was in the fortunate position of having a reasonably well-to-do father to provide for her, not like dozens of other girls who had nobody to provide for the infants they would have to bring up alone. Bastards, that what folk would call the poor mites, but he couldn't say anything like that to this lady, a pillar of the church.

The lady in question regarded him now with eyes filled with tears. "I won't ask you in for your usual cup of tea, postie. You'll understand?"

"Aye, Mrs Meldrum, I understand perfectly, but mind and tell your Millie I'm he'rt sorry for her."

"Thank you. She'll be grateful to know that."

Watching the man walk down the garden path to his van, Margaret took out her handkerchief and dabbed her unshed tears. What she had to say to her daughter would be the worst news she could ever deliver, and she, herself, would have to be in full control of her emotions.

Being a Saturday, Herbert was still at home, and lifted his head from the morning paper as she went in. "Isn't Louie coming in for his tea, today?"

"He was late and was trying to make up time." She hated herself for procrastinating. It had to be told, and the sooner the better. "He said he'd to deliver two telegrams. Tell two mothers their sons have been killed."

"Which mothers?" Millie asked in alarm. "Do we know the sons?"

Margaret braced herself. "Malcolm Middleton . . . and William Fowlie," she ended in a rush.

"Mum! No! No! Not Willie? Not my Willie?" She shot to her feet and rushed into her mother's open arms, as if she could not see and was groping for someone to give her comfort.

It was a few seconds before the headmaster himself stood up, his utter helplessness showing clearly in his face. All he could do was to put an arm round both his women, and let his tears — for his daughter's sake as much as for the young man who had become as dear to him as a son — stream down unchecked.

It was Millie who broke away first. The pains had returned now, far worse than before, and she was absolutely certain that her labour had begun in earnest.

In spite of this, she was determined to go to Emily Fowlie, to join with her in what must be a sorrow as great as, if not greater than, she herself was feeling. It had also occurred to her that, if she kept quiet about the pains until she was in the Fowlies' house, Willie's mother might, by some miracle, know some way of making the birth easier, and ensure that the baby was safely delivered.

When she expressed her wish, her father, of course, was against it. "I don't think you should be away from home for any length of time. Your labour could start without warning and I wouldn't have time to take you from the Fowlies' house to the hospital."

"It would only take about ten minutes longer than from here."

"And that ten minutes could be crucial."

His wife laid her hand on his arm, as if to calm him. "I think you should let Millie make up her own mind about this, Herbert. We won't be staying long; just long enough to show Mrs Fowlie that we care; that we all loved her son, not only Millie."

Giving in to this, Herbert still insisted on taking the little case that was sitting ready. "It'll save us having to come back to the house for it," he explained.

Not one of the three had taken into account the way a farm community can rally round a member who is in trouble, and they were surprised, and a little disappointed, to be introduced to Mrs Middleton and Mrs Grant.

"Malcie's Mam and Poopie's Mam," Emily observed, taking it for granted that the new visitors knew about their sons, too.

With seven people there now, Beenie told Jake to get a chair from her house, but Tibby said, "You'll nae need it. I'll ha'e to get hame or that twa grandsons o' mine'll ha'e the place like a midden."

"I'll walk up with you," Millie said, lumbering out of her chair. "I could be doing with a wee breath of fresh air."

Seeing Mrs Meldrum's anxious look as her daughter went out, Emily said, "It's not far; just the other end of the six houses."

Tibby took the girl's arm as they walked. "You're a brave lass. When Poopie said Willie had got a girlfriend, I was pleased for him, but when I ken't you was the dominie's lassie, I thocht you wouldna be richt for him. I thocht you'd be la-di-da, spikkin' wi' a plum in your moo, but you're naethin' like that. I think you wis the right ane for him, an' it braks my he'rt that he's been ta'en an' you winna get the happiness you deserve. You never get ower lossin' the laddie you love. I'll never get ower Poopie an' it's near twa year noo."

"I was sorry to hear aboot your son, Mrs Grant. I never met him but Willie spoke about him a lot. He thought the world of him."

"They were like brithers, an' Willie was like anither son to me." Tibby hesitated for a moment. "I'm gan to say something, an' mebbe you'll think it's nane o' my business, but I ken you're near your time, an' I could see you grippin' your teeth every noo an' then in there, so I'd say your labour had started. Am I right?"

"I'm afraid you are, but I didn't want to let my father know. He's booked me into the maternity ward at the hospital in Whinnybrae, and I wanted to have it at home."

The older woman waited until the pain that crossed the girl's face had passed. "I think you're nae gan to ha'e time to get hame. They're comin' real quick, the pains?"

"Nearly right . . . aahh . . . after each other."

"Aye. It's time, but we'll see things is a' right. I'll come back wi' you, but first we'll collect Beenie's Gladstone bag for her. You'll be fine wi' her; she's ta'en near every bairn in the place into this world, including my Poopie an' your Willie."

And so, in less than fifteen minutes, Millie was ensconced in the "ben" room, in the bed that had been Willie's sisters', with the rubber sheet under her and Willie's mother and her own mother in the kitchen getting a plentiful supply of hot water ready in the pans, pails and two large baking bowls they set along the range's hob. Beenie, in her huge rubber apron, was directing operations. "Push noo, aye, there's a good lass. Tak' a deep breath, an' anither push. Aye, you're comin' on like a hoose on fire."

Perhaps her labour seemed, to Millie, to take hours and hours, but when the infant slid into Beenie's hands, she exclaimed, "Look at that, noo! As bonny a laddie as ever I saw, an' he jist took two hours."

Margaret was despatched to tell the good news to Jake and Herbert, who had been sent outside at the very start, and who had been walking up and down the track with their pipes in their mouths, but doing little actual smoking.

300

"Come in, Grandpas," she laughed, "it's a boy."

All those present now agreed wholeheartedly with Beenie. This child was the bonniest baby boy they had ever seen; head covered with quite a thick layer of dark hair, chubby cheeks, lovely little fingers and toes and a pair of lungs, as Jake observed at one point, "Like a pair of bellowses."

After all his resistance to the visit, it was Herbert who was reluctant to go home, and his wife had to drag him away from the grandson who was to be a large part of their lives from now on. Beenie Middleton had stipulated that she didn't advise Millie to get up for at least seven days, and to wait another few days before she went home, and the Fowlies were more than pleased to have their new "lodgers".

The Meldrums came every day after school was out, but not one of the grandparents had the temerity to ask Millie what she was going to call the child. It was not until the day Emily was packing up her things in readiness to go home, that the girl said, "I hope it's all right, Mrs Fowlie, but I want to call him William."

Emily went over to kiss her. "Thank you for that, lass, and will he be Willie as well?"

"If you don't mind, I think it would be best to make him Billy, and he'll just have the one Chistian name. I don't like seeing anybody with a string of middle names, and anyway, I wouldn't have been able to decide between Jacob and Herbert."

"It's probably best," Emily agreed. "We don't want the two of them falling out."

Ten days later, left on her own again, Emily missed having the work of feeding and clothing the infant, but it did give her time to look back. When she had first learned that Willie had left his girlfriend with a "bun in the oven" as they said nowadays, she had been really angry, considering it a misdemeanour to add to the others he had committed over the years. While Millie was here, however, she had spoken of how deeply they had loved each other and had described some of the things Willie had said about being scared to touch her because he wouldn't be able to stop going too far. It was an intimate confession, and she had been quite shocked at first. She could understand it now, though — although she had never had the same problem with Jake.

Almost two months went past before a package arrived by Special Delivery, a small envelope which Emily had to sign for, obviously containing more than one sheet of paper, and marked, "On His Majesty's Service". The penny dropped then, and although it was addressed to Mr Jacob Fowlie she took out a knife and slit it open. After reading it through several times, she laid it on the table with trembling fingers. She couldn't believe it! Recalling all the bad thoughts she'd had about her son over the years, she really couldn't credit this. She spread out the communication now, and read it again with a mother's eye. Wait till Jake saw it! Wait till all Wester Burnton heard about it, and they would, for she'd broadcast it far and wide, she was so proud.

302

It was almost an hour and a half before Jake came in, looking surprised to see Emily sitting at the table, but no dinner laid out for them. Then he spotted the letter, and like Emily, had to read it more than once to take it in. "Well I'll be jiggered!" he said at last. "Jist fancy that! Oor Willie gettin' a Commendation for Bravery in the Field!"

"And there's a letter with it," Emily pointed out. "From his Commanding Officer."

"Let me read it for masel', woman." But he was smiling, a smile of deep pleasure.

It was only when he learned how their son had actually saved the life of another Gordon Highlander by using his own body to shield him, that Jake saw the light.

"He's made up for nae savin' Poopie! That's why he did it. Oh, Emmy, it must've ta'en a lot o' courage to dae that when he ken't there wis snipers roon' aboot him."

He stretched across the table and took her hands in his. "I'm that prood o' him, lass, to think oor son gi'ed up his life to save somebody else."

"He knew what he was doing, Jake, and he'd have been glad to do it. Oh, I'm going to tell every living soul I meet from now on."

Jake squeezed her hand in warning. "Nay, Em, that would pit folkses' backs up. An' Beenie widna be pleased that her Malcie didna get recommended."

"Her Malcie would never have had the courage to . . ."

"Aye, me and you ken that, but does she? No, it's best to keep oor tongues atween oor teeth. We'll need to tell Millie, of course, she deserves to ken, but naebody else."

Silence fell, but not for long. "You know, Jake, when I learned he'd been killed, my first thought was I should have known he'd end up dead."

Her husband's mouth twisted. "We a' end up deid, Em."

"That's not funny."

"It wasna meant to be funny, lass, but I canna see what you're gettin' at."

"Have I got to spell it out for you? It was his own fault. All his life he jumped in without thinking of the consequences. He always liked to be different from other people." She knew she was being unreasonable, knew that her heart would never be whole again, but still couldn't come right out and admit that she loved her son, had always loved him, no matter how badly he had behaved.

"Dinna look at it like that, Emmy love." Jake slid his arms round her, hugging her tightly. "You havena time to think of consequences in a war. You've just got to pile in an' dae the first thing that comes into your mind, the obvious thing. Nine times oot o' ten, you'll be lucky an' get awa' wi' it, but the tenth time's bound to come. Look on it that road, lovie. Apart fae his fit bein' broken in three places, he got aff lightly wi' what he did when he was a laddie —" His own emotion halted him briefly, but then he murmured, "He's a hero, lass, nae matter how you look at it. Dinna forget

304

that. A bloody hero. An' I'm the proudest man in a' Christendom."

The ferocity of this last statement got through to his wife at last, but it was some time before she was able to express herself coherently. "Oh, Jake, I'm sorry. I know he's a hero, and I know he didn't mean to be bad before. It's just . . ." She stopped to search for the right words. "I'd been used to my two well-behaved girls for so long, you see, and when he came along . . . I'd never had anything to do with boys, and he was loud and rough, and I was never done patching his torn breeks and darning his socks, and . . . Oh, Jake, I did love him. I did. I did, and I'm ashamed of some of the things I said."

He patted her back, unheedful that her flowing tears were saturating the collar of his shirt, unmindful that they were both well into their fifties and would be mortified if anyone happened to come and catch them. "We can put a' that ahin' us, my lovie. We've got a grandson noo, a grandson to be prood o'; you've naething to be ashamed for. Willie was jist . . . Willie was jist Willie, and we'll never forget him, but we'll ha'e to get on wi' oor lives. But keep mindin' one thing, my dearie. I've loved you fae the first time I saw you, I've never stopped lovin' you an' I never will."

Giving her no time to reply, he twisted his head to kiss her, their tears mingling, their hearts beating almost in unison, as they hadn't done for many years. They jumped apart at the sound of a vehicle drawing up outside, and barely had time to wipe away the signs of their emotions before a tap came on their door. All

Jake could see from the window was the tail end of a motor he didn't recognise, and before he was halfway to the door, it opened and their caller walked in.

Jake stared, trying to place the elegant figure who was looking at him in exactly the same manner as . . .

"Becky! Dear Lord, it's Becky!" his wife screamed, nearly knocking him over in her haste to welcome the daughter she had thought was lost to her for ever.

CHAPTER
TWENTY-TWO

The meeting, bordering on the hysterical, could not possibly have lasted much longer without the two elderly people breaking down altogether. Coming on top of what they had gone through earlier, although an answer to their dreams, it was too much to bear. All three had wept together, had kissed and patted, had laughed as well as cried, and Jake had to mutter, eventually, "Oh, I'll need to sit doon. I dinna ken if I'm imaginin' this or if it's really happenin'."

"It's really happening, Pop," Becky grinned, then turned to her mother. "I could be doing with a cup of tea, Mom, I've been on the go since dawn."

"Yes, of course. You sit down and I'll make some." Emily shifted the kettle nearer the fire.

"Wait or I get a good look at you," Jake said, pulling the young woman round to where he could see her better. "You're lookin' weel, ony road."

Becky was indeed looking the picture of health. Slimmer than she had once been, yet not anywhere near skinny, she filled her obviously made-to-measure two-piece costume very nicely, rounded bosom, nipped in waist, neat derrière. Its colour matched her cornflower-blue eyes. Her flawless skin was lightly tanned, her cheeks and lips were made up to look in the same shade, not too pale, not in the least brash, as she had once been. Her dainty feet were encased in Cuban-heeled suede shoes in the same shade of darker blue as the handbag she had thrown on the old couch. Her hat, on the floor where it had been knocked by the vigorous greeting she had received, matched the other accessories.

"There's nae shortage o' money wi' you, I'm pleased to see," her father observed now, "and your Mam's been worried sick that you maybe hadna two maiks to rub thegither."

Sitting down, Becky said, "For the first few years I was there, I didn't have two ha'pennies to rub together, but then I met Buddy."

Emily looked round from setting out cups and saucers. "Buddy? Is that his real name?"

"It's what he answers to, but his real name is Charles Grover Goldstein, the Third."

"He's a Jew?" Jake's voice gave no sign of disapproval or otherwise.

"Yes, he's a Jew, and he's a really nice guy. His grandfather, the first Charles Grover Goldstein, came from Russia in the 1880s, and started a small business that grew and grew till he had factories right across the States."

"Making what?" Jake asked, purely to show interest, nothing else.

"You know something, Pop, I couldn't tell you. As long as we've gotten enough to let us live the good life, I don't give a damn what they make."

308

Inwardly amused at how Americanised she'd become, Jake wished that he had his old daughter back, before remembering that the old Becky had also had a hankering after the good life. That was the reason she'd left home in the first place. "So how did you meet this Buddy?" he asked now, for she couldn't have been mixing with those kinds of people.

"Oh, Pop, it was the funniest thing," she laughed. "I was pretty near down to my last cent at the time, and I'd had nothing to eat all day, but my lipstick was down to the bare metal and I had to get a new one. It was a case of a hamburger and a coffee, or a lipstick and a coffee with a bun of some kind, and I wouldn't have been seen dead without my lipstick, so I went in a diner for a coffee and a bagel."

"What's a bagel?" her mother asked as she filled the teacups — the best china tea-set because this was an extra-special guest.

"Oh, it's a Jewish bun. I didn't notice it was a Jew-run diner."

"And your Buddy whatever was in there, as well?" Emily wanted to know.

"Yeah. He told me I shouldn't be eating a dry bagel, and when I said I couldn't afford to have a filling, he bought me a proper meal."

"That was very kind of him, and you got to know him better?" Like all mothers, Emily wanted to learn about her daughter's friends.

"Not half. He seemed to be taken with me so I went out with him a few times, then he started wanting to see me every day."

Jake was eyeing her contemplatively. "An' you were happy to let him spend money on you? Did you like him as much as he seemed to like you?"

"Well no, not really. I did like him a little bit, but that was all. Still, I'd been working as a salesgirl in a Woolworth's store and had got the sack for being late a few times, so I was glad this guy was buying my meals. Then he asked me to move in with him, but I drew the line at that, so I said no."

"I'm glad you still had some sense," Jake said now, although recalling her marriage to Jackie Burns, he realised that she had always been out for what she could get.

"Then he asked me if I would do him the honour of becoming his wife and I said yes. So you are speaking to Mrs Charles Grover Goldstein the Third."

Emily gave a smiling approval of this. "He sounds a real nice man."

"He is, Mom, and he lets me have everything I ask for — no quibbles about the cost."

"You landed on your feet, right enough."

But Jake wasn't so easily hoodwinked; something didn't sound right. "Aye, maybe, but we'll ha'e the truth now, Becky, if you please. I'm mebbe jist a common fairm labourer, but I'm nae daft."

"What d'you mean, Pop? That *is* what happened."

"No, lass. It's what you wish had happened." He looked earnestly into her eyes. "Isn't it, now? We're nae gan to judge you, so dinna be feared."

Her face drained of all colour except for two triangular spots of rouge on her cheeks, the young woman dropped her eyes and began slowly. "Yes, Dad, you're right."

And so began the saga of the first few months of searching for employment, spending the precious money her ex-father-in-law had given her to last until she got on her feet, but it lasted only weeks at the rate Becky was spending it. This, naturally, was followed by weeks of scrimping on food, on make-up and eventually on a place to sleep.

"You see," she explained. "It's not like Britain. Hardly anybody in New York has a maid and that's all I knew anything about."

Emily was appalled. "But there would be places you can rent at a fairly cheap rate? There must have been other people in the same boat as you."

Becky nodded sadly. "There were some that could afford a few cents a night for a bed, but there were the down-and-outs, like me, worse off still, that couldn't even afford that."

"So you had to sleep rough? Oh, my poor lass."

"It was the only thing I could do, Mom, and it was there I met the person who was the means of setting me on my feet again."

"You mean the man who married you?" Her mother looked rather brighter now.

"Nobody ever wanted to marry me. It was Helga Andersen, a German refugee. She'd been on her uppers for a long time till somebody told her the quickest way to make money was to ..." Pausing, Becky's face turned a deep scarlet and then she gripped her mouth as if she had taken a bite of some horrible-tasting substance and ended in a rush, desperate to get it out, "She said I should sell the only thing I had to sell — my body."

She glanced at her father, who had gasped with shock. "It was the only thing I could do, Dad, and Helga took me back to her apartment, let me have a bath, lent me some make-up and a lovely dress to wear. After that she took me out for a meal before she took me to her patch — that's what she called it — and showed me how to deal with the men in cars who stopped to speak."

"Oh, Becky," Emily said reprovingly, "you knew that was wrong. Why did you do it?"

"It was either that or throwing myself off the Brooklyn Bridge, and it wasn't so bad, really it wasn't. Most of my clients were decent men whose wives refused them their rights, and only two or three caused any trouble. They were all willing to pay well for the service I gave them and I did meet a man called Charles Grover Goldstein the Third who was known to his friends as Buddy, and he was very kind to me, but he didn't ask me to marry him. However, I soon managed to save enough to repay Helga and we shared the rent — and the other expenses — between us. It took me another year to put past enough to buy a place of my own in a better area, and so I was able to charge more."

Jake shook his head in disapproval, but said nothing, while Emily used sarcasm to show how she was feeling. "So what made you give up your money-spinning and come home?"

"I knew it couldn't last for ever," the young woman admitted. "When your looks go, the men stop bothering with you. Helga's on the downward slope now, but she wouldn't hear of me helping her. It was her that suggested I should come home. And that's when I realised how much I'd missed you all." She stopped suddenly, looking ashamed. "I've been so busy talking about my troubles, I forgot to ask. How's Connie? I bet she's got three or four kids by this time."

Jake stepped in first. "It's good you've remembered at last, but it's not good news, I'm afraid. Your sister's dead, Becky."

"Oh, my God! How did she die? In childbirth?"

"Not exactly, though she did die giving birth."

"That doesn't make sense. Dad, don't do this to me. Don't keep me in suspense."

He gave it to her with no frills. "Gordie Brodie murdered her. Her and their infant son."

"No!" she screamed. "Mam, tell me it's not true. Please."

"It *is* true," Emily said quietly. "Just a few months after you went to America, and I couldn't tell you because you never gave me an address to write to."

Silence fell now, an awkward, accusing, threatening silence, into which in a few seconds Jake said, very deliberately, as though wanting to shock his daughter even more, "And that's not all. Your young brother was killed at El Alamein, and you can surely imagine how your mother was feeling when we were told that. She believed she had no children left; two killed by another's hand, but one responsible for her own demise."

The very fact that he had said all this in perfect English was enough to make the girl realise how deeply he, too, had been affected. Jumping up, she ran to him, sitting on his knee when he held his arms out to her, and sobbing loudly into his shoulder, as if she were still a little girl. "I'm sorry, Dad, I didn't want you to know how bad things were with me, and even when I was OK again, I couldn't let you know. You'd have wondered why I didn't speak about my first few years in New York, and I'd sworn to myself I'd never let you know about that."

Father and daughter watched silently as Emily rose to make another pot of tea, saying as she rinsed out their cups, "Then I'll heat up the pot of broth Millie made last night."

"Millie?" Becky asked. "Who's she? Had Willie got married?"

Thus another saga was begun, of Herbert Meldrum's generosity, of Willie's entry to the University, of his reason for volunteering for the Gordon Highlanders. Becky had listened silently throughout, but now she said, "So Poopie was killed, too?"

"And Malcie Middleton," Jake said. "You mind on him?"

"I mind on him fine. Oh, Mam, Dad, it's terrible to think all that bad things happening, and there was I thinking I was the only person in the world bad things happened to. I've been really selfish, just thinking about myself, and I never thought you'd be worrying about me."

Shifting the newly refilled teapot farther back from the fire, Emily lifted the large black soup pot on to the swey above the heat. "Look, lass, I think we'd better put a full stop to all the bad things, eh? We can begin to look on the bright side now. We got word this morning that Willie has got an award for bravery — mentioned in Despatches, would you believe — so that's some good news. Not the first, though. I should have told you, Millie Meldrum gave birth in this very house to Willie's son, our grandson."

Clapping her hands in delight, though her cheeks were still damp from her tears, Becky exclaimed, "That *is* good news, both bits. Is Millie living here?"

"No, no, she was just visiting with her mother and father, but her labour had started before they came. She hadn't told them — I don't think she wanted to go to the hospital her father had booked for her, so she was quite glad to let Beenie Middleton do the needful. She was here anyway, with Tibby Grant. The dominie just took mother and son home not long before you arrived; just before we got that letter about Willie's award."

"So Millie won't know about that?" Becky was quicker on the uptake than her parents.

"No, of course. I'll need to tell the postie the morn. He delivers here before he goes to the schoolhouse, so he can tell them. It was him that told them about Willie." Emily still hadn't come to terms with her son's death, but she said it as calmly as she could. Having her younger daughter back again did help.

The following day brought several visitors, expected and unexpected. Louie the postman was first, of course, taken in to see Becky again, then Beenie Middleton, who had seen her arriving from her next-door window and had run along to tell Tibby Grant, arranging that they would visit the Fowlies the next day. Both were very curious to hear what she had got up to in America. Not that they were told much; more or less a rehash of Becky's first version, with Helga Andersen substituted for Charles Grover Goldstein the Third.

It was during his lunchbreak that Herbert Meldrum brought Millie and her tiny son, congratulating Emily and Jake on the return of their daughter before driving away with the promise that he would call for Millie after school.

Beenie and Tibby, already doting on the wee mite, made a great fuss of him, firing Becky with much of their enthusiasm. She had to admit that he was the most beautiful baby boy she had ever laid eyes on; not that she had ever had much time for infants.

Several teapots — and the rest of the soup pot — later, the two elderly ladies left in order to attend to feeding their own families, or, in Tibby's case, her fostered family. The three Fowlies relaxed now. Visitors were all right up to a point, but, "Enough's enough," as Jake put it, stretching his socked feet out to the fire,

316

"but five adults an' a wee bairnie's mair than enough at ae time."

They did have peace to eat the oatcakes — huge quarters of the large circles Emily browned on one side on the girdle on the fire and turned and set up on the trivet in front of the fire to brown on the other side — and crowdie cheese she laid out, and her girdle scones spread with home-made strawberry jam. "This is better than any of the fancy things I was eating over there," Becky commented, licking her lips. "You could make a fortune in New York, Mum, if you opened a restaurant."

"The Yanks'll ha'e to forego that pleasure," Jake observed drily. "She's mine."

After their hastily devised meal, Becky insisted on helping to clear up, and Jake decided to take a wee stroll down the track. "I'll be killin' two birds wi' ae stane," he explained as he took his old pipe and the little tin of shredded Bogie Roll off the mantelpiece.

"I've never liked him smelling up the kitchen with that pipe of his," Emily remarked, as she handed the washed plates to her daughter, "but he doesn't usually pay any heed to me."

Knowing that he was giving them a chance to talk more confidentially, and waiting for the questions to begin, Becky just smiled, but had to wait until they were seated on the sofa by the fire before the inquisition actually came.

"Now, lass, is there anything you haven't told me yet?"

"About what?"

"About your time in America."

"I've told you everything, Mam, and I'm deeply ashamed of some of it, but that's all that happened, honestly. I thought you and Dad would go mad at me and turn me away."

"I suppose that's why you spun that story about a rich husband, but I'm glad you came clean after all. I can't say I was happy about it, but I've no idea what happens in a city like New York. I suppose that kind of thing goes on a lot."

Becky sighed. "That kind of thing goes on in every big city, Mam, but that's not to say it's right. I knew I was doing wrong, but it was the only way I could support myself. Anyway, it's all over now, and I'm home to stay. I've given up my apartment, sold all my things and just took what I wanted with me. I'm going to make a new start here, Mam, and it seems to me, I came at the right time."

"You did, lass, you did. I was at my lowest ebb, I can tell you, but today's been the turning point. We got word about the award this forenoon, and that eased my pain a wee bit after seeing his mother taking my grandson off, and then you arrived. Oh, Becky, you've no idea how glad I was to see you. At least I've got one of my daughters back. What are you planning on doing now?"

"I haven't made any plans yet. I think I'll have a wee break first, but I won't have to be too long in starting to look for a job of some kind. I don't fancy going into service again, but there's nothing much else I can do. Shopwork, maybe, or a receptionist in a hotel or for a doctor or somebody like that. I can't type or do shorthand, so I'm no use for an office, and there's nothing else I can think of. Anyway, I'd like to know more about what happened to Connie — that's if you feel up to speaking about it."

Until Jake returned, therefore, Emily went over everything that she knew about the tragedy, eventually bringing in the fact that it had been Willie who had spotted Gordon Brodie, and where and how he did. This, of course, also led to discussing Willie's death and its aftermath for her.

"I don't know if you ever noticed," she said, a little hesitantly with her face still wet with tears, "I never loved him like I loved you and Connie."

"I know you were harder on him than you were on us, but I didn't think anything of it, for we were good girls and he was always misbehaving."

"Aye, but you see, I never thought it was just bad behaviour. I thought he was spawn of the devil. Gramma Fowlie used to say was just a nickum, and I thought ... well the Devil's sometimes called Old Nick, so I thought Nickum meant little Devil, and some of the things he did would make you think they were work of the Devil, and ... oh, Becky, I'm deeply ashamed of myself, for it turned out he was a hero, not a devil."

The tears came flooding again, and her daughter placed an arm round her. "Don't upset yourself, Mam. I don't suppose he ever noticed you loved Connie and me more, and you were never too hard on him. He did need to be punished for what he did, you know."

319

"Well, he's been properly punished now," her mother sobbed.

"Some folk would look at it differently, though. God has taken him up to heaven, that's how they would see it — as a blessing, not a punishment, and he had maybe done what he did for Poopie's sake. Who knows? Atoning for not being there for him."

"A blessing? Oh, Becky, you've made me see sense at last. That must be it, and it definitely must have been for Poopie."

"There you are, then. So stop blaming yourself, and be proud of him."

CHAPTER
TWENTY-THREE

1944

With time marching on now, Emily did not have time to feel depressed. Indeed, she had really no need to feel depressed; hadn't she her grandson to love and her newly returned daughter? At first, she had been fairly worried about Becky, who had failed to find a job during her first month at home, and had decided to try for something in Aberdeen. It was her sixth attempt before she had the successful interview — as a salesgirl in Boots the Chemist in Union Street — and couldn't believe her luck.

"They said I had a lovely complexion," she boasted, when she bounced in on air. "I'm to be put on the make-up counter, and I'm on a month's probation."

"You'll pass," her father said, grinning like he'd won the pools. "You've aye been a bonny lass, and you've a fine figure now, and all."

"Jake, what a thing to say to your own daughter!" Emily said, indignantly.

"Nothing wrang in that. She *has* got a fine figure, and that's what they need."

"There's just one thing, though," Becky said now. "With the pay I'll get, it's going to be a struggle to pay bus fares every day and pay for my keep as well."

Jake said nothing to this. He had no illusions about his daughter, and knew she was capable of milking them dry, if she felt like it. Emily, however, trusted her implicitly. "Ah, you don't need to pay for your keep. If you're away all day, you won't need anything at dinnertime, just your supper at suppertime."

"Are you sure?" Becky was the picture of innocence, but Jake still had doubts.

The matter was settled in a way that none of them had anticipated, not even Becky. By this time, Millie Meldrum, MA, had taken up a post in the Central School and was still lodging with her aunt in the Spital. There had been a bit of a struggle to decide who was to look after her son, but eventually the two grandmothers settled on sharing him. Every alternate Sunday afternoon, therefore, Herbert drove her and the baby to the Fowlies, and took them back the next week. It was an ideal solution for everyone concerned, except Sophie Chalmers, who was slightly miffed at being left out, but was talked into seeing that taking the infant to Aberdeen would be one too many change for him and also rather too much for her.

Thus it was that, when the Meldrum family arrived on the Sunday after Becky's good news, it was Millie who exclaimed, "But there's no need to worry about lodgings, Becky. You can come to my Auntie Sophie. She's got a spare room and she'll be delighted to have Willie's sister. She was very fond of him, you know."

Becky was more than delighted when she arrived at the Spital to be told that Sophie wouldn't take anything for her board, and started her new job in high spirits. Because it was something she did know a great deal about, she was quite at home on the cosmetics counter, and could charm even the most difficult of elderly females into purchasing expensive brands. She was, therefore, kept on as a permanent member of the staff.

Everything went smoothly now, and Emily accepted Margaret Meldrum's invitation to join them for Christmas dinner. Jake hadn't been all that happy about having to be on his best behaviour for so long, and was worried in case he made a fool of himself over which item of cutlery to use, but Becky managed to get round him, as she usually did.

Herbert Meldrum collected them, and Margaret apologised for not having the ingredients she would have liked to make the kind of Christmas dinner she had been used to making before the war, but there was nothing wrong with what she did produce, and it was six really satisfied — and quite merry — adults who sat round the fire in the evening. Billy was allowed to be a little later in going to bed, and was sitting happily on whoever's knee he happened to be on, chomping into an ivory animal meant to help his teeth to come through.

"He's very good," Becky smiled. "Some babies would be fractious with so many folk around them."

Millie giggled. "He's happiest when people are fussing over him. He loves company."

Emily's mind went back over the years. She had always made a fuss of her girls, and it had only been Gramma Fowlie who made more of Willie. Not wanting to spoil the atmosphere, however, she said nothing of this.

The good feeling, luckily, remained with them even after Herbert Meldrum drove them home at half past eight, and, completely exhausted, they had a last cup of tea and went to bed.

The normal daily and weekly routines were going well. Becky and Millie came home on the bus together every Friday evening and returned to the city every Sunday afternoon. They hadn't become close friends as may have been expected, because Millie was usually busy preparing her English lessons for the next day, while Becky had chummed up with Sally Cromar, one of her fellow assistants from Boots' beauty counter. They went to the cinema together sometimes, took walks if it was good weather, went into a tearoom or café for a coffee — a taste Becky had acquired in New York — and flirted with any boys who looked at them, although Becky was less exuberant than Sally. Her experiences with men were not something she wanted to repeat.

One night, however, as they sat in a small café just off Union Street, Sally said, "There's a man over there hasn't taken his eyes off you since he came in. Don't look round, he's coming over."

Becky froze, hoping that whoever he was had mistaken her for somebody else. She didn't want to get involved with anybody — not yet, anyway.

"Hello, Becky, I thought it was you."

Recognising the voice, she looked up in astonishment. "Jackie!"

"I'm called Jack these days. I heard you were home, but I wasn't sure if you'd want to see me."

Sensing an atmosphere now, Sally got to her feet. "Look, Beck, I'll leave you two to talk. I meant to go home early at any rate."

"It's OK, don't go," Becky began, but her ex-husband said, "Thanks, I'm very grateful, but we'll have to find a better place to talk, Becky. This is too public."

"I've lodgings in the Spital, if you want to see me home. I don't think my landlady will object."

He said nothing for some time as they walked along, and then, finally, "You didn't get married again?"

"No, did you?"

"No."

That was it, but Becky knew that it wouldn't stop there. He would want to know what she had been doing, and she couldn't tell him that. Or maybe she should. It would be best to be perfectly honest . . . but not at first.

When she let herself into the house, she told him to wait there for a minute, and went to ask for permission to take someone into her room. "A man friend?" Sophie asked, eyebrows raised in slight disapproval. She hadn't really taken to Becky, who was nothing like her brother.

"Yes, but he's my ex-husband and he only wants to talk. I left him in kind of a hurry, you see, and I think he wants to find out why I didn't tell him."

"And why didn't you?"

"It was his father who told me to leave, and . . . oh, it's a long story."

"Righto, then, as long as that's all there is to it." Yet the elderly woman still came out to take a look at the young man in question, before nodding amicably and retreating into her sitting room.

"You've obviously made a good impression on her," Becky smiled, somewhat nervously.

"I can do — on some women." The meaning was quite clear.

She sat down on the edge of her bed, but pointed to the only chair available, in case he thought of joining her. "Now, you wanted to talk?"

"I wanted to know why? You left me without a word, and I want to know what I did wrong?"

She inhaled deeply. "You did nothing wrong. Really, Jackie — Jack — it wasn't your fault, it was mine. I was a spoilt brat, always wanting my own way, and I loved living the good life — getting lots of new clothes, spending as much as I could and getting away with it."

"I was happy for you to have everything you wanted."

"I know, but I took advantage of you. I knew you wanted a family, and when I did fall, I didn't want to have to go through all the growing fat and the pain of giving birth, so . . . I had an abortion."

"What? I never knew that. I thought you had miscarried."

"Your father tumbled to it, though, and told me to get out, that I wasn't a proper wife for you." Pausing for

326

only a moment, she added, "And I wasn't, Jack. I wasn't."

"It was up to me to decide that," he murmured quietly.

"Yes, I can see that now." She looked at him earnestly. "Wouldn't you have felt the same?"

"No, I wouldn't. I loved you, Becky, still do, with all my heart, and I'd rather have you back than have a dozen kids."

"No you wouldn't. Not after you hear what I did in New York."

"I don't want to hear what you did in New York. I don't care."

"Please, Jack, I have to tell you. We can't have any kind of relationship unless you know."

Giving a vague nod, he settled back in the chair and let her go ahead. She left nothing out, not even excusing herself for the downward spiral in which she had been forced to travel, noticing that he dropped his eyes after she introduced the word "prostitute", but jerking his head up again when she called herself a "whore". "No, Becky," he protested, "I'll not let you say that about yourself. You were forced into it by circumstances, and nobody could blame you for that."

"Not many people would see it that way."

"Not many people love you like I do. Oh, Becky, can't you see I don't care what you did over there? It's what you did while you were still here that puzzled me, but now I know there was no other man involved, everything else is forgotten. I want you back, and if you don't want a family, that's fine by me."

"I couldn't do that to you," she protested.

"You could, and you will. Please, my darling, give us one more try. Marry me again, and we'll —"

"Live happily ever after?" She smiled sadly. "It won't happen, Jack. You'd soon come to resent me for not giving you children, and start remembering what I did." She regarded him thoughtfully for a moment or so, the clear-cut features, the neat wavy hair, and suddenly, as she looked into the dark brown eyes that were showing the full depth of his feelings for her, she felt a surge of affection for him; more than affection, she realised in some surprise. She had never felt this way before, about him or anyone else, and it was nice — very nice. Most enjoyable. But would it last?

Having obviously sensed a change in her, he asked, "Do you want to think about it, my dear?"

"I probably should, but you know me. I make up my mind quickly."

"And live to regret it sometimes, no doubt, so I'll leave you to consider everything properly, and then I'll ask you again. I'd rather wait a while and be sure of you than grab you now and chance losing you again some time later."

"All right, then, but you know something? I think I just grew up."

He grinned then, the same boyish grin she remembered, and after he had gone, she lay back on the eiderdown and recalled the way he had made love to her when she was his wife. The first few weeks had been a bit wild, but nothing like as bad as she'd had to put up with in New York, but after that Jackie had been

328

gentle, considerate, respectful even, and she knew for sure that they had a future together.

It was a week before she saw him again, ambling in some embarrassment up to the beauty counter in Boots. "Outside, at six tonight?" he asked, turning away relieved when she nodded.

CHAPTER
TWENTY-FOUR

October 1946

Emily Fowlie was really exhausted as she sat down on the Sunday afternoon after little Billy had been collected by his mother and other grandfather. As she remarked to Jake, "I'm really feeling my age these days. I'm turned fifty-seven, soon be sixty, and I'm just not fit to look after a boisterous three-year-old for a whole week at a time."

"Aye he's a bit of a handful, right enough, but I'd say his other gramma looks sixty-five at the least, an' you dinna look a day over forty."

"Get away with you, Jake Fowlie." But she was pleased, just the same.

On the following Sunday afternoon, when Billy was taken back for Emily's stint of having him, Margaret Meldrum turned up with her husband, because Millie hadn't come home that weekend.

"She's busy marking exam papers," Margaret explained to the other grandmother. But she waited until the two men had taken the little boy out for a walk, as they had taken to doing every week, before unburdening herself. "I'm feeling it a real strain looking after him now he's bigger. He's into everything, touching things he shouldn't be touching."

"You don't need to tell me," Emily smiled. "He's the same here, just like his father used to be."

"Of course, I've never had anything to do with boys before," Margaret excused herself, "but it's one thing after another. He's a right wee . . ."

"Nickum," Emily ended for her.

"How did you know that was what I was going to say?" Margaret was completely taken aback.

"That's what Jake's mother used to call Willie, but I thought he was the devil himself. I always did, and I'm ashamed of myself for it now."

"And so you should be. Your Willie turned out to be a true hero. I always knew he was the salt of the earth. So did Herbert, that's why he took such an interest in him. He'd have been the happiest man on earth if Willie had been our son-in-law."

Emily swallowed hard. She would never get over losing her son without ever having told him she loved him. "Ah well, it wasn't to be."

During that week, when little Billy came rushing in crying and covered in what she recognised as muck out of the midden, she hugged the chubby little body before stripping and scrubbing him, recalling sadly that she had been furious with Willie when he had done exactly the same.

Nothing of any real consequence happened for a few weeks, but about ten days before Christmas, when much preparation was going on in the schoolhouse kitchen, Margaret was busily tying up little gifts she had bought for various tradespeople and for her little maid,

Fanny, who had replaced Janet some time ago. Billy had been playing with the cat on the heathrug in front of the large fireguard that protected him from the fire, and as long as he was happy, and quiet, she wasn't really bothered about how he was amusing himself. He had asked her once what she was doing and she had answered him honestly, "I'm wrapping up Christmas presents."

Shortly after this, he had run out to fetch something, and when she saw him coming back with a towel, she thought nothing of it. It was only when the cat started yowling that she turned round to ask, impatiently, "What are you doing to that cat?"

"Kissmapezzie," he replied.

Understanding only the first syllable, she half-snapped, "Well, stop trying to kiss him and leave him alone."

There were a few minutes' silence, but when the yowling began again she rounded on him. "I told you to stop trying to kiss him. Can't you learn to do what you're told?"

The tears that sprang to his eyes made her pause in her task. "What's wrong, my lamb?"

"Kissmapezzie," he repeated, his piping voice wavering a little.

"Kissmapezzie?" she echoed, searching for the meaning, then, remembering that the cook she had employed some weeks ago seemed to understand his babblings, she opened the door to the kitchen and called for her.

332

"Aye, was you wantin' me?" The stout woman, a result of repeatedly tasting what she was cooking, came through at once, her hands white with the flour she was using.

"Yes, Mary. Can you understand what Billy's saying?" She turned to the woebegone figure on the rug. "Tell Cook what you're doing."

"Kissmapezzie," he said, looking hopefully at the other woman.

The cook looked back at her mistress. "Did you tell him what you were doin'?"

"Wrapping Christmas presents."

The two women gazed at each other, then, in a flash, the answer occurred to both of them, and at last, with a grin at her own stupidity, Margaret exclaimed, "Christmas present. Is that what you're saying? Are you trying to wrap the cat up as a Christmas present?"

He beamed at her happily, and she whipped him into her arms to kiss him. "Oh, my lovie, what a silly Grandma you've got."

"Sillagamma," he agreed, turning to continue his impossible task, but the cat had taken advantage of his inattention and made good his escape.

Billy continued his entry into sentence-making as the time went on, but never succeeded to any great extent. Emily, who could remember how fluent Willie had been at the same age, was a little worried about the boy's lack of progress, but Millie assured her that each child was different, and some took much longer to do things than others. "Some can speak early, some can walk

333

early. As long as they are making an attempt, it's nothing serious."

But something serious did happen — or to be truthful, something that could have had a tragic outcome but, fortunately, didn't. It started on another day when Margaret Meldrum was very busy and had asked Cook to look after Billy in the kitchen. Of course, she, too, was busy, and when the little boy managed to open the back door and went outside, she wasn't worried. The garden was entirely enclosed by a tall wooden fence, and the child was quite safe. The only damage he could do, she told herself, was to pull the leaves off a few plants, and that was all right as long as it kept him out of other mischief.

She didn't see the escapee lever himself under one of the struts of the fence and find himself on the path to freedom. This path divided the grounds of the house from the field some cows were grazing in, and Billy had always been interested in the cows, which he could see from the kitchen window as well as from the garden. As he toddled up to the gate, the cows, as all cows do, came towards him curiously, watching as he fumbled with the catch and coming out obediently as the gate swung open. Some went up the path, some went down the path, some stood uncertainly, not knowing what was expected of them. This was not their usual milking time, their liberator was not the usual tow-headed boy who led them to the byre.

For a few moments, Billy stood waiting for this small group to make up their minds, then he looked up the path at the five Freisians who were making their bulky way slowly towards the byre, and then, turning, he studied the four who were heading for the main road. Not that Billy knew where any of them were going. All that mattered to him was that he had freed them. Satisfied with himself, he went back to where he had himself escaped and finally to the kitchen, where Mary felt a little relieved that he had come to no harm in the garden.

It was about fifteen minutes later when Mararet Meldrum had to answer the door to a caller. "I was passing in my car," the man explained, looking quite flustered, she thought, "and I nearly knocked down one of your cows when I came round the corner. There's four of them on the road. They could cause a bad accident."

"My goodness, yes," she exclaimed, "but they're not our cows. This is the schoolhouse; it's Wester Burnton Farm that owns the cows. It's all right, though. I'll phone them and let them know. Thanks very much for telling us."

Johnny McIntyre was very grateful to be told, but completely at a loss to know how the beasts had got out, even warning the police to be on the lookout for some fool of a "townser" that thought it was funny to open farm gates and let animals out. Herbert Meldrum couldn't understand it either, when he came home at lunchtime and was told. "Did you not see anything from the kitchen?" he asked Mary.

"I was busy, Mr Meldrum," she said, a little guiltily, he thought.

"But Billy was with you all forenoon," Margaret pointed out. "He usually watches the cows from the window, doesn't he? He'd have told you if he'd seen anything different."

Billy himself came toddling through now, and the headmaster bent down to ask him, "Did you see anything over in the field this morning, Billy? Did anybody let the cows out?"

He smiled at the man beatifically. "Moocoosootapay." The three adults looked at each other hopelessly, then Mary said, "Wait a mintie. He's sayin' 'moo-cows'."

"He said 'moo-coos'," corrected Herbert.

"Well, that's me," she admitted. "I often say, 'Look at the moo-coos.' He likes to watch them."

"He is speaking about the cows, then. Right, Billy, what else did you say? Moo-coos what?"

"Moocoosootapay."

"Ootapay? What the devil . . .?"

Mary's hand flew up to her face. "Oh, that's likely me, an' all. I usually ask him if he wants oot to play, if he's standin' at the door."

With a twitch at the corner of his mouth, Herbert said, "So he's saying the cows were out to play? But, Billy, who let them out? Somebody must have opened the gate. Did you see?"

He patted his chest. "Billy."

It was some time before they solved the whole mystery — the sneaking under the fence, the opening of the latch. "By God, he's quick, this lad," his grandfather said proudly, "but we'll need to fix that fence so he can't get out again. Anything could have happened. There could have been some bad accidents, with the amount of cars that go on that road, not only the cows, either. Billy himself might have gone on to the road with them. It doesn't bear thinking about."

"I'm sorry, Mr Meldrum," Mary snivelled. "I didna ken he . . ."

"It's not your fault, Mary. Don't upset yourself. It's just this little . . ."

"Nickum," his wife cut in, before he could say anything stronger.

The last word, naturally, was Billy's. Looking at one after the other he pronounced carefully but forcefully, "Nickum!"

CHAPTER
TWENTY-FIVE

1947

When Emily was told of her grandson's latest escapade, she did not join in the Meldrums' laughter, but it was only when the visitors had gone and the mischievous little boy was safely tucked up asleep that she mentioned her thoughts to her husband.

"I can't get over how much Billy is getting to be like Willie. He's got the same eyes, dancing with devilment, the same cheeky grin that melts folks' hearts."

"But not yours?" Jake put it as a question, sure that he knew the answer, but he was wrong.

"Yes, mine as well," she said, sounding as if she were sorry rather than pleased.

"There's nothing wrong in that. He's a taking way aboot him. It's like father, like son."

"That's what's bothering me, Jake. Can't you see? He's going the same way as Willie. He'll be the same when he goes to school, he'll be clever, he'll deserve higher education, there'll be a war and he'll be killed — just like his father."

Jake showed shock at her pessimism. "My God, Em, you're fairly lookin' on the black side."

"It's obvious, isn't it? He'll grow up a lovable rogue, as they say, and he'll end up like most of them — killed through their own stupidity. No," she corrected herself, hastily. "Killed because of their own thoughtlessness. They don't consider the consequences before they do anything."

"Emmy, my lovie, you're tired. You're nae really fit to be lookin' after a wee laddie — a wee nickum," he added, trying in vain to make her laugh, because it had become a standing joke. "I'll tell Herbert next Sunday this'll be oor last week."

"No, no. I'm all right. It's just . . . oh I don't know what it is. Just a queer feeling I have, now and again, that something's going to happen — change. Don't ask, for I don't understand it myself."

Several more days passed, during which Emily prepared herself for a shock of some kind, but when nothing had happened by the following Sunday, other than Billy emptying the contents of her flour bin onto the kitchen floor when she had run out to take in the washing because the rain had come on. Unfortunately, the rain had been absolutely torrential, and her dripping feet and the water running off the long oilskin coat of Jake's that she had put on made a thin paste form on the congoleum, so that it became as slippery as ice. Negotiating it as carefully as she could she still skidded and almost fell, and the delighted little boy tried to slide on it, getting himself in a right mess in the process by constantly tumbling down, on purpose.

She was thus more tired than usual by the time Sunday came round, and was looking forward to her "free" week. At the usual time on the Sunday afternoon, Herbert Meldrum's car drew up outside the

339

gate, but it was Millie who came in to collect her son. "Dad's busy with some reorganisation he's thinking of doing at the school," she explained, "and I think he's beginning to trust me not to bash his car. It's over a year since I passed my test and this is actually the very first time he's let me touch it."

"I've heard some men think mair o' their cars than their bairns," Jake laughed, "but me? I'm content to be on Shanks's mare. Nae that I could afford a car, in ony case."

"How are you two, this week?" she asked now. "No problems with this little monkey?"

Emily shot a quick glance at her husband, who ignored the message. "Weel, lass, I'm nae that bad, but Emily's real tired. We was wonderin' . . ."

"Oh, don't tell me you want to stop having Billy?" Her eyes were filled with tears. "Mum hasn't been well at all this week, and the doctor says it's her heart. He told her she'd better let the child's other grandmother take over for a while, but . . ."

Her worry for her mother was so obvious that Emily's heart went out to her. She loved this girl, who could have been their daughter-in-law and was indeed just like a daughter to them. "No, it's all right, Millie. I've just been a bit down this week, that's all, but I'll be fine. Just leave him here."

"Are you sure, though? I don't want you cracking up as well. I know he's a proper handful."

"We'll be fine," Emily assured her.

"We can do your washing for you — I'm sure that would help. Dad bought Mum a new washing machine.

340

The old one was hard work, you know, with having to use the handle to make the agitator work, and the gas ring underneath took quite a long time to heat the water. Plus she had to fill it and empty it with a pail, but this new one's got a hose to fix to the tap, and one to take the water down the drain. Better still, since it's plugged into the electricity, that's what works the agitator, the water heats in no time. Marvellous. So don't you carry on slaving. I'll change your bed sheets and things, and let me have all your dirty clothes. I can come every Sunday morning, and take back the laundered things the next week. That should save you some work, mm?"

Overcome by this offer, Emily said weakly, "I couldn't let you do that."

"Why not? Just think of what you've done for me. Please, Emily, it'll let me think I'm not taking advantage of you."

"But you don't manage to come home every weekend, so . . ."

"I'll make sure I do come home. Anyway, Dad's speaking about getting Mum a woman in to help with the housework, and do the laundry and all the heavier work. It'll all work out perfectly."

She started by changing the sheets in the box bed in the kitchen, then went through to the other room to change those on her son's single bed, saying as she went through the door, "You can look out whatever else there is to wash."

Husband and wife regarded each other as if in shock, but at last Jake grinned. "By gum! She's doesna waste time, does she? Oor Willie would've been a lucky man gettin' a wife like that." He regretted the words the minute they were out, for his wife's eyes had clouded over.

"We can't let her do this, Jake. It would be like us taking advantage of her."

"She'll nae think that, never fret. She's young an' fit, an' willin'. If this is the change you've been worryin' aboot, it's the best thing that coulda happened. Except for Margaret Meldrum's he'rt, of course."

Billy didn't seem to mind staying with his "Gamma an' Ganda Fowlie", and nodded happily when his mother told him, "Grandma and Granda Meldrum will come to see you as often as they can."

It had all been arranged so quickly that Emily lay in bed that night wondering if she had been dreaming. This was certainly a change, but not what she had worried about. Still, she assured herself, as her mother-in-law used to say, "Never look a gift horse in the mouth." The washing machine would take a load of work off her shoulders, and give her more time to enjoy her grandson, wee Nickum though he certainly was. In any case, he'd be going to school in little more than a year.

Almost three weeks later, when she heard the car drawing up at the door, Emily thought at first that it would be Herbert Meldrum bringing back the laundry early for some reason, but it wasn't his car she saw when she lifted the net curtain to make sure. It was the Tillyburnie taxi, and a tall, gaunt young man was coming out. He gestured to the driver to wait until he made sure he had come to the right place, she thought — and then strode over and knocked on the door. She opened it warily.

"Mrs Jacob Fowlie?" he asked.

She liked the look of him, pleasant manner, very pale complexion, but he likely worked inside an office somewhere. If he hadn't looked so respectable, she would have thought he was just out of prison or some kind of confinement, but he wasn't that kind at all. "Yes?"

He turned and signed to the driver, who moved away at once. "You don't know me, Mrs Fowlie, but you may have heard of me. My name is Pat Michie . . ."

Her hand on her heart, Emily plumped down on the nearest chair. "Pat Michie? Willie's pal?"

"That's right. Oh, I hope I haven't upset you?"

Her eyes had filled with tears, but she brushed them away. "No, no. I'm surprised, that's all."

"I came to tell you — I don't suppose you know anything about how he . . . died?" Her negative head-shake made him carry on. "He saved my life, you see. In fact, he saved a whole lot of lives."

Motioning to him to sit down too, it didn't even enter her head to offer him a cup of tea, her usual method of welcoming a visitor. Her entire being was concentrated on hearing what she had longed to find out for some years now. It came pouring out, the awful truth of the tragedy that this young man had lived through; the guilt that still haunted him.

It had started with the withdrawal of the troops who had thought they had wrested El Alamein from the enemy; the reorganisation of the men; the realisation of one Commanding Officer that they needed help desperately; the request for a volunteer to replace the Despatch riders who had been killed in the fierce battle.

Although Emily knew at once who had volunteered, she said nothing, unwilling to break into a narrative which she knew was the truth, not some gilded tale the War Office had issued to cover up some dire mistake.

"So Willie roared off on the old motor bike, and I could have kicked him for being so foolhardy. We all knew there were snipers lurking in the scrub just beyond where we were encamped, for they had killed quite a few of our lads, and I just hoped he'd be extra careful."

"Careful wasn't Willie's style." Knowing her son's failings, she couldn't help saying it. "And extra careful was something he'd never have recognised."

Acknowledging this with a faint nod, Pat continued, anxious to explain how he had come into the picture. "A few of us were sent out to search for the radio equipment that had been dropped as we were retreating, and I happened to pick the area where the snipers were hiding — or maybe there was only one, I don't know. Whatever, I hadn't been there more than ten minutes when I went down with several bullets in my side. I lost consciousness, and they must have thought I was dead, for nobody came to finish me off. Willie must have come back some time after that, saw me lying in the road and tumbled to what had happened. I had come round by then, but I'm not really sure of this. I think he'd heard a movement and realised we were both in danger. Anyway, he flopped over me to save me, and took the volley himself." Pat looked up now, the sweat standing out on his brow as he recalled the scene.

"I'm sorry, Mrs Fowlie, I maybe shouldn't have told you, but I wanted you to know how brave he was. And it'll maybe comfort you to know something else. Just before he died, he looked straight into my eyes and said, 'This is for you, Poopie.' Do you understand that?"

Emily could not have described, supposing she had been offered a fortune for doing so, how she felt at that moment. It was as if God himself had looked down on her and assured her that her son had absolved himself of all the imagined blame he had carried on his shoulders for years. "Yes, I understand it. Do you?"

"Aye, he told me all about Poopie, so I know he blamed himself."

"And you think he went to meet his Maker easier because he'd atoned for neglecting Poopie?"

"I'm sure of it. What's more, because he delivered the message that we needed reinforcements, he saved a lot more lives."

They sat in silence for some minutes, each remembering the dead soldier in their own way — Pat as a close friend and comrade, Emily as the "wee nickum" who had been the bane of her life for most of his, and their emotions were too raw to speak about.

At last, with a start, the woman pulled herself together, remembered her manners, and offered her visitor a cup of tea. Their tongues seemed to be released with the refreshment, and the conversation centred now on current issues — what Pat intended to do with his life, how he would feel free to look for work, to make a career of some kind, and the time slipped past unnoticed. It was only when the kitchen clock struck twelve that Emily shot to her feet. "Oh my, Jake'll be in and there's no dinner ready."

Pat also stood up. "I'd better get out of your way, then."

"You can't go yet. You'll have to wait and meet Willie's father."

Jake, of course, the rough countryman that he was, took Pat's version of events much more calmly than his wife, outwardly at least, but perhaps much more affected than he seemed. Having only half an hour's break, he didn't tarry long, bolting the thick cheese sandwiches his wife rustled up, and the other two were left alone once more.

It was only after he'd dried the dishes and helped to lay them past that Pat noticed the box of toys in the corner of the kitchen and looked at his hostess for an answer.

"They're my grandson's," she smiled. "We were sharing him for a few years, but his other grandma had heart trouble, so we'd to take him all the time except weekends when his mother came home. She's a teacher in Aberdeen, and she's home on holiday just now, so she's got him till the schools start again."

346

Looking puzzled, Pat said, "Did your younger daughter come home from America? Is he her little boy?"

"No, no — well Becky did come back and she works in the town, as well, but it's Willie's little boy. Billy, he's called, and he's just as mischievous as his father was."

"And his mother? Is it Millie, by any chance? Willie spoke a lot about her."

"Yes, Millie it is, and she's a really nice girl. She got our Becky lodgings in her aunt's house in Aberdeen."

"I would like to see Millie, Mrs Fowlie. Could you let me have her address?"

"Her father's the dominie, so it's the schoolhouse, but you're not fit enough to walk that far."

"I could phone for a taxi."

"Oh, laddie, there's no phones round here, but I tell you what. If you stay the night, you could get a lift from the grocer's van in the morning. He's here about ten, and we're the last of his calls hereabouts, and I'm sure he goes to the Meldrums' on his way to the Mains."

"You don't mind me staying overnight?"

It turned out to be an ideal arrangement. It gave Jake an opportunity to ask as many questions as he wanted about the Battle of El Alamein, the dreary months Pat had spent in various hospitals for well over a year in Cairo being patched up, but not quite ready for battle. It was fortunate that the war had come to an end and this young man was no longer needed, yet he had been treated in various hospitals for well over a year before he was discharged with the warning "to take his time about looking for a job". Emily, already acquainted

347

with all the facts, was content to sit and listen, her heart sore for the son who should also have been present but had been too intent on clearing his conscience to consider anyone's feelings but his own.

Immediately this thought crossed her mind, she was ashamed. That wasn't the way of it. Willie's intention had been to save Pat, and in doing so Poopie had come to his mind. It was good. He had actually killed two birds with one stone — although that wasn't a proper way of expressing it. He was a hero, twice over — that was nearer the mark, for the salvo that ended his life had given a warning to all the soldiers in the area. Not only that, his journey had resulted also in bringing extra troops who swung the battle in their favour.

Millie Meldrum was shocked at first, yet delighted that the young man had wanted to tell her what had happened to Willie, and like Emily, she had to sit down. Younger, however, and much more resilient, she could withstand the assault on her emotions without breaking down, and could nod her satisfaction at his answers to her relevant questions. They had gone over the whole saga once and were probing a little deeper, when Billy bounced in.

"Me and Ganda feeded the ducks," he said, his speech having much improved since his mother had spent some of her holiday time trying to train him. She was by no means satisfied with his grammar, but enough was enough at one time.

Herbert waited only long enough to be introduced and to be told the young man's reason for being there,

348

before he went upstairs to see his wife, who had been in bed for some weeks now and was indeed showing some signs of getting over the trouble she had had.

Billy now proceeded to make friends with the stranger. "My Daddy was a shoulder," he announced.

"I know," Pat smiled. "I was in the army with him."

"Was you a Goddon Highland as well?"

"I was that."

The bond forged, the little boy sidled up to the young man. "My Daddy was brave. Was you?"

Pat grinned now. "Not me, lad. I'm no hero."

When Herbert came back, he said Pat was to stay for lunch, and he was welcome to stay for as long as he wanted. "It'll do me good to have some male company for a while," he laughed. "I've been under petticoat government for far too long."

"I'll have lunch, but I must get home," Pat apologised. "Mum thinks I should spend more time with her."

"Well, she's quite right on that, but couldn't you spend an hour or two with me? We could go for a walk in the afternoon. I'd like to know more about . . . well, just more."

It was almost six o'clock, therefore, when Herbert deposited his new young friend outside his home in Elgin despite his objections that he didn't want to take advantage. "Nonsense, my boy. I consider it my duty, since you've been good enough to let my daughter know what happened. I think that was what she felt so badly about, that she had no idea of what had happened to Willie."

"I wasn't sure about coming," the young man admitted. "I was scared it might upset her too much. I know it upset Mrs Fowlie."

"But I'm sure she was glad you made the effort." He refused to go in to meet Mrs Michie, but issued an open invitation for Pat to visit the schoolhouse whenever he wanted. "And remember to let us know when you get a decent job. Don't take any old thing. Make sure it's worthwhile, and if you need someone to vouch for you, I'll be pleased to oblige."

"I'll do my best, Mr Meldrum, and thank you for everything."

Neither the Meldrums nor the Fowlies gave out any information on who their young visitor was or why he had called, so the curiosity aroused in the area was left unanswered, and rumours ran rife.

"It was a debt collector to the Fowlies."

"But nae the Meldrums as weel, surely? They canna be short o' cash."

Or — "It was a man lookin' for Becky Fowlie. She'd stolen money fae him. But dinna ask fit wye he went to the Meldrums, 'cos I dinna ken that."

Or — "He was a solicitor — the Meldrums are suein' the Fowlies for their Willie puttin' Millie in the puddin' club."

"But they canna prove it was Willie, can they?"

"The bobbies can prove onything these days, even if the criminal's been deid for years. Onywye, a'body ken't Willie was the father."

And so it went on, with Jake itching to let fly at them and Emily telling him it would only make things worse. "Let them say what they like. They can't hurt us."

Another unexpected visit from Becky gave Emily good cause to worry. Her daughter never did anything unusual without it having an underlying motive, but what could she want this time?

"Millie tells me her mother's going to start taking a turn in looking after Billy again?" the girl began.

"What's Billy got to do with it?"

"Look, Mam, I'll come clean. I've been seeing a lot of Jack Burns, and he wants us to get wed again, and he says he won't care if I don't want a family. But, I know he does, so I want to —"

"You want to spend time with Billy to see how you feel. Is that it?"

"That's it — to a T. D'you think I'm off my head?"

"I know you're off your head, but it's nothing to do with me. You're old enough to make up your own mind. I'll give you one day — will that do?"

"I think so. I hope so."

Becky took over the boy the next forenoon; washed him, dressed him, made sure he had plenty to eat, played games with him, and after supper, put him to bed. "I'll just manage the last bus," she said, flinging her coat over her shoulders and making for the door. "I'm going to say yes."

She was gone before Emily could quiz her.

Jack Burns courted Becky properly, attentive and thoughtful, for the next four weeks before arranging for them to be married in the Registry Office in Bridge Street. Sophie organised a celebratory meal for the wedding party — the bride and groom, Millie as bridesmaid and one of Jack's colleagues from the firm of accountants as best man, and both sets of parents. It was a really joyous occasion and as an extra surprise, Sophie had also asked the Meldrums, who brought the youngest guest of the lot. Little Billy's presence dispelled any awkwardness that may have been between Tom and Flora Burns and their reinstated daughter-in-law, and the whole affair seemed to wipe the slate entirely clean.

In her heart, of course, Rebecca Burns realised that it would only remain clean for as long as she played fair with her reunited husband — which she was determined to do, in any case. Life returned to normal for the rest of the wedding guests, but when the bridal couple returned from their honeymoon in Pitlochry, they set up house in a rented, furnished bungalow in the Ashgrove district of Aberdeen.

Emily was in for another shock in a few months, not so drastic, nor so upsetting, but still enough to make her worry about it. Becky hadn't been home once since her marriage, nor had she written except for the odd scribbled note to say she was well, so it set the tongues wagging again to see her turn up late one Saturday evening.

Having had no warning, her mother jumped to the most obvious solution. "I suppose you're expecting?"

"Oh, great," her daughter snapped. "No 'Hello, Becky, how are you?' As it so happens, you're right. I am expecting, and I'm not all that happy about it."

Irritated, Emily sighed. "I thought you said you wouldn't mind, and Jackie really wants a family, doesn't he?"

"He doesn't like being called Jackie now, Mum. Can't you try to remember? Anyway, it's all right for him. It's not him that has to grow fat and horrible and suffer all the pain."

"Look, Becky, I think you're forgetting something here. If you don't give him the child he wants — at least one — old Tom will likely throw you out again. Without any money this time. Then where would you be? Back on the streets. And you needn't expect any help from us. Your father and I are both ashamed of you, you know that?"

For some moments, the young woman sat silently, plainly turning things over in her mind, so her mother went on, "Are you not happy with him? Is he not treating you like you thought he would? I'd have sworn he was a true gentleman, loving and generous. You don't know when you're well off, that's your trouble. How far on are you?"

"Just two months. He doesn't know yet, but I suppose you're right. Even after the terrible things I did, he's been good to me. He's never thrown it in my face, he's been kindness itself. I'm so selfish, it's not real, but I promise I'll be a good wife to him from now

353

on — and a good mother to his children." Stopping suddenly, she gave a mischievous grin. "However many he manages to make."

Emily couldn't help laughing at that. "It maybe won't be as bad as you think, anyway. Some girls have no problem giving birth —"

"And some have! Guess what I'll be like?"

But her mother could see that she had resigned herself to the inevitable.

"By the way, Jack's going to pick me up when he finishes work. He should be here about six."

"You'll stay for some supper, then?"

"No, thanks. He's taking me for a meal before we go home. Oh, I nearly forgot. He's going to pay for driving lessons for me, and when I pass my test, he'll buy me a car of my own."

"My goodness! And you were thinking of jeopardising your fine life? I don't understand you."

"I don't understand myself, sometimes. I know I could never find a better man than Jack, and I will behave myself. You've made me see sense."

Becky's next visit was exactly four weeks later, bringing her re-married husband, Jack Burns, who pumped hands energetically with his reinstated parents-in-law.

"I'm truly happy," he whispered to Emily, while Jake was laughing with Becky. "I know everything she did, and I must admit, it gave me quite a shock, but I got over it. She *has* changed, and I'm sure we'll make a go of it this time."

354

"I hope so," Emily said, very much doubting her daughter's sincerity in anything. Becky had always been self-centred, and she would soon begin to tire of this marriage, second time round. Of course, having their own house in King's Gate now — a fairly well-to-do area of Aberdeen — where she could more or less act the lady, might be all she needed to satisfy her, and if she had a couple of kiddies, that would take her mind off herself.

The following weekend brought a rather unwelcome surprise, although, as Emily told herself later, she should have been prepared for it. Pat Michie, who had got a job in Aberdeen a while back, looked quite uncomfortable as she let him in, and sat nervously on the edge of a chair for a few moments before he said, "I suppose you're wondering why I'm here?"

"You're welcome any time," she assured him, even if she was desperate to know.

"I don't know if Becky has told you . . ."

"I hardly ever see Becky."

"Well, in that case, I don't suppose you do know. I've been going out with Millie for weeks now."

"Going out? As friends, or more than that?"

"More than that. I love her, Mrs Fowlie, and I'd like to ask her to marry me, but only if you've no objections."

"It's got nothing to do with me." But her heartbeats had slowed down, a pain had started in her chest.

"It has everything to do with you. Can you bear the thought of Millie loving somebody else? Or of me being a father to your son's child? Do you see what I mean? I haven't said anything to her yet, and I never will if it's going to upset you."

She could find no words to answer him. Of course she was upset, but . . . had she any right to be upset? That was the crux of the matter. Millie was a free agent. She had certainly loved Willie with all her heart, but she was free now to love whoever she wanted. If she wanted this man, why shouldn't they marry? And as for Billy? Well, he did really need a father.

"I'm sorry," Pat said gently. "I can see your answer in your eyes, and I promise I won't mention this to Millie. I'll apply for a transfer to our Head Office in London, and make a definite break."

He stood up to leave, but Emily pulled at his sleeve. "No, Pat, let me explain how I feel."

The young man sat down again, a pulse beating at his cheek, and she wished that she had been able to decide quicker, and not given him the impression that she was against Millie marrying. "It's me who should be sorry," she began. "I couldn't think straight, but I can see now that this is the best thing that could happen. Poor Millie needs someone to love her, the same as wee Billy needs a man in his life, and I think you'll be a good father, Pat, I really do."

He took hold of her hand now. "Oh, thank you, Mrs Fowlie. That's the nicest thing you could have said to me. And I do love Millie, I love them both, with all my heart. I'll look after them, and we'll come and see you as often as we can." Then he gave a nervous laugh.

"Here am I making plans already, and I haven't even told her I love her."

"She'll know that, Pat. A woman always knows when a man loves her."

"But what if she turns me down?"

"She'd be a damn fool."

They both laughed at that, and Pat stood up again. "I can't wait, now. I'm going straight to the schoolhouse to ask her. May I ask you to wish me luck?"

"You won't need my wishes, I'm sure, but I do wish you success."

Pat Michie had been gone for little more than an hour and a half when Millie Meldrum turned up, and Emily could tell the girl was different as soon as she walked in, on edge, slightly uncomfortable, but not in the least guilty. When Billy came running in from the backyard, she made the usual fuss of him, though he was not quite so fond of being kissed as he used to be, then let him run outside again to play with the new tricycle Herbert had given him for his fifth birthday.

Emily had a little longer to wait to find out what was what, although she had a good idea. Millie took over making the pot of tea, filled the kettle and plugged it in. "You must be delighted with having electricity now," she smiled. "Having bonny, new shining kettle and pans instead of them being caked in soot."

"Aye," Emily nodded, "it's much cleaner, but I miss the old way, and Jake says he preferred the oil lamps to the electric light. He's scared to use a switch in case he gets electrocuted."

"That's silly, it's safe enough, and you waited a long time for it."

"Well, it wasn't Johnny McIntyre's fault. He was going to have it done in 1940 — that was what he'd planned — but the war started before that and all repairs, modernisation, even building, was stopped. It was a big upheaval of course, once they got started. We were all glad to see the end of it, and now there's word he's having lavatories put in."

"Just lavatories? Not bathrooms?"

"Bathrooms, I mean. Jake says he doesn't fancy having to go to the lavvy to take a bath, he likes having it in front of the fire, but you know him. It'll take him a while to get used to it."

The kettle giving a piercing shrill, Millie jumped up to mash the tea, and poured milk into the two cups sitting daintily in their saucers, as Emily always had them.

When she was seated again, the young woman looked somewhat apprehensively at the other. "I've something to tell you and I don't know if you'll be pleased or not."

Having had time to be resigned to what seemed certain to happen, Emily smiled. "I'm sure I'll be pleased, whatever you tell me."

"I've been going out with Pat Michie."

Determined to plead ignorance, the older woman repeated what she had said to Pat. "You mean . . . just going out, or going steady?" In her mind, there was a vast difference.

358

"It started with just going out, for company, really, for we were both kind of lonely. Becky had her Jack, and I had nobody. Nobody tangible, anyway. I felt life was galloping past me without me getting anything out of it."

Emily had believed, before Pat told her his side of the story, that Millie, of all people, would always remember Willie, would never try to replace him, but it seemed that it wasn't so. "And?"

"We could sense it happening, Emily, and we fought against it because it wasn't fair to you. Pat even insisted on us stopping seeing each other and it's been pure purgatory."

It took the older woman quite an effort to say, "But you've your own lives to lead. You shouldn't be worrying about me." Was she the only person left who would remember her son?

"I'll always worry about you, Emily, dear." Millie's eyes had filled with tears. "And if it's going to make you unhappy, Pat says he'll find another job in London, or somewhere, and we'll never see each other again."

The thought of such a genuine young man, a man who had been so close to Willie for years, a man that Willie had given his life to save, giving up true love for her sake, made Emily feel bitterly ashamed. She'd had her life, had a man who loved her, still had a daughter who, although she maybe didn't show her mother much love, did think of her now and then.

"You must think I'm awful," the girl went on, "but it's not a case of off with one love and on with another. I've told Pat that I'll always love Willie — I could never forget him, Emily — but I said I loved him in a different way. Maybe a more adult way. Willie and I were just teenagers, in the first throes of love, and that to me is the most important kind of love. I love Pat as a woman loves a man, and not only that, I know he loves Billy. He has asked me to marry him, but I said I couldn't say yes without telling you. If you don't think it's a good idea, I'll —"

Emily took pity on her now. "Pat's been here already today, asking what I felt about it, and I wished him luck. You both deserve all the happiness you can get after what you've been through, so marry him, my dear, with my blessing."

Jumping up, Millie hugged her tightly. "Oh, thank you, Emily, dear, thank you from the bottom of my heart. And you won't lose Billy, you know, because we'll be coming to Burnton every second weekend to see my parents, and we'll always give you a call too. You're still his grandmother, whatever else happens. We'll be going to Elgin on the in-between weeks, of course, to see Pat's mother.

Emily's mind took a gigantic leap forward. "Billy's going to be a lucky laddie. He's going to have three Grammas."

"You wouldn't mind?"

"As long as I'm still one, I don't mind at all."

Waiting by herself for her husband to come in for his supper, Emily couldn't help thinking how this marriage would affect her. She would have Millie, a young woman she had loved for some time now, as a

360

daughter-in-law, and Pat, who she was rapidly learning to love, as a son-in-law, or as near as dammit. And she would always have her memories of a little boy with mischievous eyes, a little boy she couldn't find it in her heart to love properly, a boy who had turned out in the end to be a hero. She would never forget her son, who had left behind his son, for her to love.

Another Wee Nickum.